D0384682

The Last Blue

The
Last
Blue

ISLA MORLEY

PEGASUS BOOKS
NEW YORK LONDON

THE LAST BLUE

Pegasus Books Ltd.
148 W 37th Street, 13th Floor
New York, NY 10018

Copyright © 2020 by Isla Morley

First Pegasus Books cloth edition May 2020

Interior design by Maria Fernandez

All rights reserved. No part of this book may be reproduced in whole or in part
without written permission from the publisher, except by reviewers who may
quote brief excerpts in connection with a review in a newspaper, magazine, or
electronic publication; nor may any part of this book be reproduced, stored in a
retrieval system, or transmitted in any form or by any means electronic, mechanical,
photocopying, recording, or other, without written permission from the publisher.

Library of Congress Cataloging-in-Publication Data is available.

ISBN: 978-1-64313-418-5

10 9 8 7 6 5 4 3 2 1

Printed in the United States of America
Distributed by Simon & Schuster
www.pegasusbooks.us

In memory of my dad,
David

SEPTEMBER
1972

Thirty-five years ago, Havens would have opened his eyes and thought of the day ahead as lacking. The surprise of old age is how comfortable a person can be with an empty day, how companionable it can be. If anything, Havens wants the day to empty itself even more, allow for memories to pay a visit, and should he decide to spend his time doing nothing more than sitting in his recliner and missing her, what's to stop him?

Havens is neither by nature nor by habit an early riser, and it is only out of a sense of duty to an imperious old pigeon that he gets up rather than turn over and doze a little longer. When he stretches his arms overhead and arches his back, his joints creak in protest. He looks in the mirror at a face that seems both familiar and startlingly foreign. Old age is a menace; there is no abating it. Every day it claims more territory. Forgoing shaving, he splashes water on his face and puts on exactly what he wore yesterday—a pair of saggy jeans, his red flannel shirt, a coffee-stained gray pullover, and sneakers mended at the toe with packaging tape—and humming tunelessly, wanders through the quiet house. He glances out the living room window at the pasture, pillowy with fog. The day, too, seems to be getting a late start. Havens would prefer to drink a cup of coffee before facing the pigeon, but the chirps coming from the enclosed back porch are insistent, so he leaves the coffee to boil on the stove and goes out to take his instruction.

"What are you in such a flap about?" He notices the bird has worked loose the bandaging on his wing and the joint is exposed again at the break. "You've picked yourself raw, silly." He removes the top of Lord Byron's cage and slides the window open so the pigeon can enjoy the brisk air. Fluffed up, the bird hops onto the window sill, gives in to instinct, and plummets. Eight months convalescing, and still the bird refuses to accept his decrepitude. Havens respects this in any being, feathered or otherwise.

He rushes outside to retrieve the bird, before applying ointment, bandaging the wound, and getting his hands pecked at in return.

"Quit it, would you. Violence is never the answer."

The bird knows Havens is a pushover. He tips over the seed tray as if to say, *Slop*.

Havens checks on the other patients, a noisy mockingbird almost feathered enough to fly and a rambunctious blue jay that cuckooed itself by flying into the kitchen window yesterday. Before heading to the barn, he puts down a dish of food for the black cat he has refused to name lest it get any ideas, and out of spite, the cat refuses to find himself more suitable accommodations and continues to deposit lizard parts on the back step.

The mule, Molly, is indifferent to him, interested only in the fresh hay he puts out for her. She eats enough for a herd. "You've let yourself go, you know," he says.

Of all the animals in his care, Gimp is the only one ever pleased to see him, and the three-legged goat is as agreeable a creature as ever there was. Havens pets him and opens the stall door so he can burn off his energy in the turnout and watches as the billy takes a stab at bucking and topples over instead.

It's while Havens is filling the water bucket that he hears the rumble of a car coming down his driveway. He's not expecting anyone, and those who know him know better than to show up unannounced. Unless something is wrong. You'd think the mechanism to stand guard would have become a little rusty over time, but no, he's braced.

He steps out of the barn and squints down the dirt driveway. Is it a rental? Nobody from these parts has a clean, new car, certainly no Ford Fairlane. Tourist, maybe.

Before the vehicle comes to a stop, Havens stands in such a way as to make his position clear, and still, a lanky man in his late twenties, maybe thirty, unfolds himself from the driver's seat.

"The craft center is another four miles down the road. There'll be a sign on the right." Havens flaps his hand to shoo him off in case he gets the idea that a reply is in order. Scrawny fella. Perhaps one of those religious types. Maybe he's deaf, Havens worries, because the guy continues to approach him.

"Good morning, sir. Is this Plot 45? There wasn't a sign." He has a soft way of speaking that Havens instantly decides is the result of over-mothering. Even though his hair is too long, his shirt is tucked in, and he's wearing proper shoes, not those leather sandals everyone traipses around in these days. He's not entirely objectionable-looking, but still, he has made Havens unsure of himself. To cover this, Havens raises his voice.

"Best be on your way now."

The interloper has more pluck than his appearance lets on. He takes another step forward, and says, "Are you Mr. Clayton Havens?"

Either the guy is peddling something, or he's one of those pencilnecks from the Clearcreek Mining Company with another pathetic offer to buy his land. "Whatever you are selling, I don't want it, so you hustle your hindquarters back down my driveway and find someone else to pester."

There is no change in the stranger's demeanor. If anything, he appears pleased with himself. Damned if he doesn't stand his ground and open his rattrap again. "I'm not selling anything, Mr. Havens. I'm here to ask you a few questions about some people you may have known a long time ago, a family by the name of Buford, I believe?"

There is only one life-form lower than a prospector, and that's a reporter. Havens has lost his knack. "Don't you Mr. Havens me. Now, I told you once already to leave."

"I was hoping you would be able to tell me where I could reach them. I was told you—"

Without waiting for him to finish, Havens spins around and treks to the barn. It's been ages since some outfit up north has sent a hack out here trying to sniff out a story on her. Always they speak like this, persistent-like, "when" instead of "if," acting like they're here to do you some big favor. Years ago, one of them pretended to want to know about Havens's work as a documentarian for the FSA and his later shift in focus to nature photography, appealing to his ego—"A blunt style uncommon for that period," he'd said of Havens's photographic style, as if Havens had invented it—but whatever angle they pitch him, they all want to get at her.

"Is there someone else I might talk to?" the kid yells. "I could come back later if this isn't a convenient time . . ."

Havens goes into the tack room and snatches the Winchester from the gun rack, then marches out of the barn toward the intruder. "I have nothing to say to you, not now, not later, not ever." He pets the muzzle.

Now the kid gets the idea. He backs up all the way to his vehicle, bleating about having been given the wrong information. "I'm very sorry for troubling you."

Havens keeps the rifle aimed at the rear window of the rental until it has made its way down the driveway and back to the street. Take a left, he wills. Don't you go driving into Chance.

Only a city boy would put on his blinker and look both ways on a road that never sees traffic. "Goddammit." The stranger hangs a right.

Havens hurries to his pickup and cusses when he sees the keys aren't in the ignition. It takes him a good fifteen minutes rummaging around in the house before he tracks them down and gets back to the old clunker, which sputters and objects to his impatience by backfiring. So much for flooring it into town.

Not much of anything remains of Chance anymore. There's the post office and Checkers, the sorry excuse for a food joint that sells dry hotdogs and something that resembles ice cream. It's a sad fact that Havens eats there a couple times a week. For teeth-pulling, religion, or proper policing, a person has to go twelve miles to Smoke Hole. Fortunately, Havens has need of none of these. What used to be the beauty shop is now something of a cross between a pawn shop and a tattoo parlor, and word has it that some of the finest narcotics in all Kentucky are cooked in the back room, but Havens doesn't trust anything he hears. Still circulating are stories about his being afflicted by seasonal madness, not that he's ever been inclined to correct them.

Every business enterprise in town is closed today and there's no sign of the Fairlane, and Havens is feeling downright lucky until his truck swings onto Second Street and he sees Flavil's red pickup parked in front of his general store, a blinking red OPEN sign in its window.

Rakestraw's is not the hardware and feed store it used to be, though its prices are still inflated, and it remains the congregating spot for those who elect to get their local news straight from the loose lips of its nosy proprietor, which is why Havens comes in here only when he absolutely has to.

Flavil Rakestraw is stocking his shelves. He's a bulky guy with a helmet of hair meant to cover hearing aids, which don't work, and Havens has to walk all the way up to him and tap him on the shoulder. At an almost unbearable decibel, Flavil says, "So, that fella flushed you out."

He goes on about how polite the guy was for a Northerner, how he expressed an appreciation for the history of the area, that he bought a carton of chocolate milk, and Havens has to all but shout to make Flavil stop pretending nothing is wrong.

"Goddamn, Flavil, we both know he didn't come on a grocery run."

Flavil resumes pricing the cans of Crisco. "Like I said, he was real neighborly, and some people would do well to take a lesson in being neighborly instead of just yelling at a man for no reason."

In a measured tone, Havens tries again. "Are you going to tell me why you sent him my way?"

"I treated him just like I did the others before, just like you said to." Flavil moves behind the counter and makes a zipping motion with his hand across his lips. "I had no intention of bringing your name into it, as God is my witness." Then he levels with Havens. "It's just that all the others have come wanting a picture, but this fella came with a picture. One you took back then." Havens doesn't have to ask. "Yup, she was in it," Rakestraw confirms.

Trying to calm himself, Havens considers the shelves of flour, sugar, and baking soda next to him. "Please," he says in a controlled manner, "would you not refer to her as 'she.'"

"Jubilee, I mean."

"And how did he come by one of my photographs?"

Rakestraw raises both his eyebrows and his shoulders. "He didn't say. But as soon as he showed me that picture, I knew he wasn't from some newspaper or magazine, because he didn't know who he was looking at or what he was looking at, not even their names. To him, there was nothing at all peculiar about her—Jubilee, I mean."

Havens schools himself not to take up the issue of what is and isn't peculiar. "What did you tell him?"

"Nothing, I swear. The Bufords of Spooklight Holler is all I said, and then he asked me where I could find them and that's when I told him you were the one to ask about that on account of it being your photograph. I laid it on thick how you don't take kindly to company." Flavil seems to be expecting thanks, and getting none, goes on. "I figured you wouldn't want him knocking on anyone else's door, and if you'd answer your telephone once in a while, you might find someone trying to give you a heads-up."

"I don't answer my telephone because I don't want to talk to anybody!" Havens fires back. "Least of all a reporter!" Havens makes for the door.

"He's not a reporter," Flavil protests, then changes course and yells, "There's no shame in talking about it."

Back in his truck, Havens swerves onto Main Street and drives through both four-ways without stopping. He makes a right at the end of town and winds through several of the residential streets, all of them empty. There's no sign of the white Ford Fairlane across the train tracks or along the bend where the trailer homes are parked. Whatever the guy wanted, he's cleared off.

Havens takes the circuitous way back home just to be sure, and eases up on the gas pedal as he makes each bend, rolling down his window to take in the musky smell from last night's rain. On either side of him are the hills, rising like limbs bent at the knees, the forest in repose. He can all but hear the land sighing. A quarter mile later the road straightens out again, the woods retreat, and the cemetery claims its turf. Being Decoration Day, every car in Chance is parked along the road, and though it's a little before eleven, the grounds are already bustling with activity—people of every age are clearing weeds, scrubbing tombstones, and dressing up each grave with flowers and festoons of every color. By the time the sun starts to dip behind the hills and the picnic blankets are laid out, each resting place will have been adorned, even those lost to time and memory, even those sons of bitches he was glad were six feet under.

Havens stops to let Bonny from the salon and her husband cross the street, each teeter-tottering beneath a stack of wreaths, and is about to return the woman's greeting when he spots the Fairlane in the parking lot. He swerves onto the gravel drive, pulling up behind the Fairlane and blocking it in. The new damn eyeglasses don't make a bit of difference from this distance—everyone's just blobs. Favoring his bad knee, he rushes through the entrance and scans for the stranger as he hurries along the stone footpath, bumping against poor blind Warren and knocking him off his pins, which sets off his dog and causes a round of Mrs. Dixon's finger-wagging. Zigzagging through the rows of graves is no easy feat either, and Havens has to avoid tripping over trowels, rakes, and flower garlands until finally he zeroes in on the old section of the cemetery, where the punk is talking to an elderly couple. "Hey you!" he yells in their direction.

The stranger stuffs the photograph in his jacket pocket and looks as if he's figuring his odds of outrunning a swarm of hornets, and instead makes the mistake of thinking he can bargain his way out. Havens drives him backward over one grave after another. "Get the hell out of here!"

The kid stumbles, then shakes free of Havens's grip. "What is wrong with you, old man?"

"What's wrong with you? Look around, do you see where you are? Don't you have any respect?" Havens knows he's making a scene and that he ought to pay attention to the figure entering his peripheral vision. "Nobody wants you to dig up the past! People want to be left alone!" He indicates the mounds of earth. "Do you think these people want their peace disturbed?"

The kid stops pleading his case when an ancient woman pushed in a wheelchair by an orderly extends a gnarled finger toward Havens as though it were a witching rod and screeches, "Murderer!"

Everyone in the cemetery freezes except Havens, who starts crab-walking, putting another row of tombstones between him and her.

"Murderer," she wails again, all but billowing smoke, and motions for the orderly to give pursuit as Havens rushes for the exit.

MAY

1937

HAVENS

❧

F rom the open train window, Havens looks out at a land of hills so remote it's hard to believe its location can be found on modern maps. Were it a living creature, it would be camouflaged, something resembling a dragon, only parts of which peek out from a shroud of its own steamy breath—an arched neck, a mile or two of exposed spine, a knobby tail dipping into the Shenandoah Valley. Beyond the sound of the train's chugging, the occasional chuff of steam, and the squeal of wheels rounding another bend, the land has a ferocious quiet to it, as if all sounds have been swallowed and only the gristle of silence spat out.

Springing up in cities across the Eastern seaboard is a sudden interest in this region, what everyone is now calling Appalachia. Much of it has to do with President Roosevelt's determination to raise the flag of regionalism on it, along with other miserable places like Oklahoma, the Texas Panhandle, and just about anywhere along the migration route to California, but the president also talked recently of connecting the producer and consumer not in the city but in outposts like the one Havens and his companion, Massey, are bound for. Under the auspices of portraying the great and diverse spirit of Americans everywhere, Havens and Massey, along with dozens of other journalists and photographers, have been dispatched by the president's do-good arm, otherwise known as the Farm Security Administration, to various outer reaches of the country. What the president needs, they have been instructed, are pictures and accounts of subjects who are on times hard enough to use a little government assistance but not hard enough as to be beyond all help. Put another way, their task is to help the president sell his New Deal to the public. Havens is not the only photographer that the FSA has kept from the breadlines, but gratitude hasn't been enough to quash his misgivings about this mission or to make him feel less like a propagandist than a photographer. Per his boss, Pomeroy, Havens is to capture the rugged, steadfast nature of hill people, whether they possess it or not, and to portray their hardship only in a way that will make the public sympathetic to their plight and ready to cast their votes accordingly.

Massey fishes out a book from his satchel and offers it to Havens. "*Towards Democracy*, Edward Carpenter."

Though Havens has had his fill of the political writings Massey regularly serves him, including Massey's own socialist jeremiads he pens for the *American Federationist*, he doesn't turn it down.

"Relax," says Massey. "It's not commie doctrine, it's poetry. The guy gives Wordsworth a run for his money, especially when it comes to Eros."

Havens opens the book at random and reads a few lines.

Carpenter, Massey tells him, was a philosopher and naturalist who bucked the Victorian mores of the day, quit his professor post, and moved to a farm, where he wrote his best work in a wooden pen stuck out in the middle of a pasture. "Euphoria in the midst of cow patties, right up your alley," Massey says.

Havens nods amicably until Massey brings up Havens's love life. "Things looked a bit strained between you and Betty at the station. Does she always fuss with you like that?"

"Betty's just Betty." Havens thinks now is as good a time as any to be preoccupied with the book.

"The way she was carrying on, straightening your tie, 'did you remember this, don't forget that.' I'm surprised she didn't hop on the train with you. Don't you feel she mothers you?"

Betty is seven years Havens's senior and she's never had children, so if she has some misplaced maternal instincts, what harm is there in it? "She just wants to help me."

"Help you what?"

"I don't know, not end up a bigger disappointment than I already am." Havens knows that look on Massey's face, so before his friend launches into a pep talk about the importance of believing in oneself, he ends the subject by saying, "Betty wants what's best for me, and there's nothing wrong with that."

"There is if that's why you marry her."

This train ride is going on much too long. "Who said anything about marriage?"

"Santos."

Havens sighs and lets his chin fall to his chest. He didn't tell Massey about the modest little ring he put on layaway at the pawn shop because he didn't want to defend or debate the conclusion that led to its purchase, which is that there comes a time when a man has to put aside thoughts of passion and consider what's practical. His brief failed marriage at twenty had been all about passion, and look how far that got him.

"I'm not telling you how to live your life," Massey continues, "I'm just saying, don't sell yourself short. As with art, so, too, with the heart." Massey gets out his notebook, pulls the pencil from behind his ear, gives it a lick, and starts writing.

"You went to see Santos again?" Havens knows Massey doesn't have anything left to pawn.

"He gives me a fair deal."

"Don't tell me you cashed in your father's officer's watch."

"Man's gotta eat, doesn't he?"

Havens watches his friend fill one page after another, never once pausing. Neither Massey's passion nor his output has diminished since they met at the *Cincinnati Enquirer* eight years ago. Covering the labor beat, Massey was a star who had already risen to the fifth floor by the time Havens hired on as an assistant photographer assigned to operations in the basement, and their introduction came about on April 1, 1929, after Havens's photograph of Louis Marx and his yo-yo made the front page, bumping Massey's report of the Loray Mill strike to below the fold. First, Massey gave the editor an earful about how 1,800 women sticking it to the Establishment, strike-breakers, and even the National Guard deserved more attention than a toy maker, and then he sought out Havens in the cafeteria, only to pump his hand and call it a fair fight. "Your Marx beat Karl Marx, but just this once."

So began a friendship that soon extended beyond the walls of the paper. They dined with Massey's band of pent-up activists and boozy poets, were hustled out of their wages playing pool, and hung out in Havens's darkroom, where Massey would show interest even in the photographs that ended up on the cutting-room floor. "You can't expect those jackasses upstairs to know what art is," Massey is still fond of telling Havens all these years later. After the stock market crash, the paper had to let people go, but Massey fought for Havens to be kept on the payroll, and out of loyalty, two years later Havens followed Massey to the start-up rag across town that was more sympathetic to the unions. Last year, that paper finally went belly-up, just a month after Havens was awarded the Pulitzer for his picture *Orphan Boy*. Like an over-burdened foster parent, the FSA took both Havens and Massey in, though Massey still moonlights for several dailies and Havens still takes pictures that end up never seeing the light of day.

Havens turns his attention to the book, but the rhythmic rocking of the cabin soon induces slumber.

※

It's mid-afternoon when Massey nudges Havens awake. "You're drooling."

Havens has a crick in his neck. He packs the book in his bag and takes half of the sandwich Massey offers him.

"I've decided we aren't going with the folklore angle."

Havens doesn't like the sound of this.

Massey continues, "We're going to show the devastation caused by the coal industry and the threat of industrialization on an agrarian way of life."

"Pomeroy said we've got to stick with the format this time—no tangents, no causes, no editorializing."

"What does that windbag know about field work? We keep turning in material and where does it go? Archives, that's where." Massey leans toward Havens. "The FSA is sucking us dry. I've not written anything I'm particularly proud of and you haven't shot anything that makes you light up, so I'm saying let's get back in the trenches, portray things how they really are, and when we're done, we'll shop our stuff around."

If Havens is expected to stand up and salute, he's not going to—not this time. "I need this job."

Massey folds his arms and wedges his hands in his armpits. "Well, I'm not doing one-dimensional profiles of banjo players and wood carvers so we can all mythologize the mountain man."

"Do both, then. Give Pomeroy what he wants, and shop your masterpiece around, and if the lords at *The New York Times* give you entrance to their court, then you can flip Pomeroy the bird. Just not before."

"Mr. Compromise."

Havens shrugs. "I've been called worse."

"The thing about compromise is how innocuous it sounds. So reasonable."

Havens rolls his eyes. Here we go.

"But it's not reasonable. Half-measure, that's what it really amounts to. And nobody likes stuff that's half-measure." The train whistle signals their approach into Chance. "Look out there." With the fevered expression of a prospector, Massey gestures at the densely wooded hills as though there were gold nuggets waiting to be plucked from them. "Somewhere in those hills is a story that I'm going to write the hell out of, and if you know what's good for you, you'll stop playing it safe and shoot what makes your blood flow. Get out there and take the best pictures of your career. That's our only chance to get off the public dime and get back into prime editorial real estate where what we produce actually matters."

Havens stares out the opposite window, where the view is much different—a small shoddy station with a platform barely longer than a diving board. Hardly a launching pad to this bright new future Massey has in mind.

They step off the train and pass through the shabby wood and brick station onto Main Street, Chance, Massey striding with confidence, Havens with the leaden gait of a man walking to a duel with an unreliable pistol. He hoists his camera bag on his shoulder and seesaws along with his tripod in one hand and his duffel bag in the other.

"What's that smell?" Massey turns up his noise at the fetid odor in the air, scanning for the culprit.

"That would be the smell of nature," answers Havens.

"Too much nature."

Two-story brick buildings straddle a couple of dusty street blocks with signs advertising nothing out of the ordinary—Steeple-Busch Shoes, Howell Furniture, Rakestraw Hardware & Feed, Ethel's Diner, Spurlock Drugs. About a dozen cars are parked along the wide, paved street.

"Well, howdo, Chance." Massey adopts a wide stance and puts his fists on his hips. A woman in a full-length dress from a fashion many years past skips in alarm when Massey tips his hat.

According to the last census report, Chance is home to fewer than three hundred people, even though it is equipped for ten times as many. Like many other towns in eastern Kentucky, it got its start shortly after the Civil War, when corporations swarmed in like termites to claim the hardwoods, but it was the demand for coal that brought the real boom. Thrusting its way through the mountains, the railway took coal on its way out and deposited laborers on its way back in, and soon there was a town like Chance around every bend. Many of the hills have since had their insides carved out and prosperity has taken off for other parts, leaving towns like this to slump into a state more pitiful than the one that preceded it.

Massey fixes on a point of interest. "Before we go set up base camp, how about a quick turn at the gin mill?"

As they start across the street, they are startled by honking noises. A man raps the center of the hubcap he's holding like a steering wheel, and makes more honking noises as he passes, then continues running in the lane without paying any attention to the Ford about to overtake him. Slowing, the driver of the vehicle pulls up alongside the running man, and yells out the window, "Get your black ass back up on the sidewalk, Chappy, unless you want me to run over it!" But the man with the hubcap only tips his hat and keeps running, making the sound of an engine shifting through the gears.

The establishment they enter is not much more than a bar counter weighted on each end by an old-timer, its fulcrum a stony barkeep. Packed tightly in front of the dartboard at the far end are three young restless-looking men, none of whom respond to Massey's cheerful greeting, but by the time Havens comes back from the john, Massey is buying them a round of drinks.

"Everyone calls me Tick," says the stouter of the bunch, quick to shake Havens's hand. He has a pale face, dark smears under his eyes, and the same uneven haircut as his friends, brushed forward over his forehead.

Massey nods toward the scrawny kid returning with the darts, whose manner of walking brings to mind hinges working themselves loose. "This young fella is Faro Suggins, the sheriff's nephew."

Faro squints at Havens and plants himself next to the third guy, who stares at Havens with the eyes of someone who works the gallows.

"And Ronny Gault here is the mayor's son." Massey seems pleased, as if Ronny's an acquisition, while Ronny makes it clear he shares none of this enthusiasm by downing the rest of his beer instead of shaking Havens's hand.

Havens has heard of hill people being tight-lipped and suspicious of outsiders, but liquor and Massey's interest soon make these three eager to talk. Massey unpacks the recording machine and asks if they mind going on record, and after a brief hesitation quickly dispelled by a demonstration of how the device works, they go back to talking as if it weren't there. None of them are employed or have any prospects for gaining employment, unless they want to relocate to Smoke Hole, the coal town twelve miles away. Faro and Tick cite relatives with black lung and say they can think of better ways to die.

Ronny says, "I don't see no point in going to work when every other week you're told to go on strike."

If this touches a nerve with Massey, he doesn't let on. "Do you think the mining companies are doing enough to ensure the safety of their employees?"

"I ain't got a fancy education like city boys, but I'm smart enough to know those union bosses aren't in it for the little guy, not as long as they're taking their cut. Besides, all the workers will be sent packing as soon as they figure out how to make a machine that cuts out the coal."

Faro elbows Havens. "You get Ronny liquored up and he'll talk you drunk, hung-over, and sober again."

"Well, stories are what we've come for, boys," says Massey.

Tick turns to Faro. "In that case, you ought to tell them about that bear that tackled you and damn near changed you into a woman. Not that it would take much."

Havens has little interest in barroom banter, but just as he is about to excuse himself and go outside to photograph the building, Ronny addresses Massey with a scornful tone. "What's the matter with your friend here? He don't drink, he don't talk, he just stands there staring."

"He's a photographer," Massey answers, as if this should explain everything. In an attempt to mollify the mayor's son, he orders another round of drinks. "Say, how about Havens here takes your picture?" He shoots Havens a private look as if to say, *Buck up.*

Skinning a cat would be a more pleasant task, but Havens reluctantly unpacks his Graflex. It becomes apparent that the men have never seen a camera before. Massey tells them that this is a landmark year for picture-taking, that Kodachrome has just been invented, and that full-color images are about to change everything from art to news reporting. From his wallet, Massey pulls a card, unfolds it, and hands it to Faro, who whistles at the color photo of a naked woman with parted red lips and long black hair brushed from one shoulder to expose a heavy pale breast.

"That's color photography, fellas. That's the future," Massey says.

"Well, ain't that a pretty future."

The men now regard Havens with respect, having assumed he is to be credited for the shot, which he is. Not quite the lowest point in his career, the photo is a reminder of how desperate a man can be for rent money, and whatever Havens regrets about the months he spent posing and photographing naked women also desperate for rent money is nothing compared to his regret for letting Massey have that dumb picture.

Now the men are only too happy to pose in front of the camera. While Havens takes a reading with the light meter, they throw their arms over one another's shoulders and complain about how slim the pickings are in Chance.

"The only one who's got any looks is Sarah Tuttle, but Ronny's courting her," says Faro.

When Massey asks what kinds of trouble young men can get into when they're not hunting tail, Tick flicks his cigarette ash and says, "There's blue coon hunting."

Havens thinks the fault is in his hearing until he sees Ronny's face redden. "Shut your trap!" he snaps.

"I didn't mean nothing by it, just—"

"I said shut the hell up, Tick!"

Involuntarily, Havens presses the shutter.

"What's blue coon hunting?" Massey asks, but Ronny and Faro jostle Tick outside before he has a chance to respond.

Havens turns to the barkeep. "What's blue coon hunting?"

Even before the question is asked in full, the man slides him the tab and replies, "Couldn't rightly say."

Headed for their lodging, Havens and Massey puzzle over what Tick might've meant.

"Were they trying to prank us, like snipe hunting?"

"Maybe it's code for poaching," Havens suggests, trying to think what species in this part of the country might be protected by the federal government.

"Maybe it's got nothing to do with game hunting at all. Maybe it refers to an activity of an illegal nature."

"Moonshining, you mean?"

"Or gunrunning, but whatever it is, they were quick to backtrack."

21

Curiosity is the swell on which every photographer rides, but for Havens, the tide has been ebbing a long time, so it is with more than a little relief that he finds himself now intrigued. "I guess we should find out," he tells Massey, who raises his eyebrows. "Just maybe we'll find that story of yours."

"Well, look at you."

HAVENS

‰

Massey has a leftover football injury that at opportune times becomes a limp and an easy way that gets him more action than any other man Havens knows, but when he is nosing around a story there is a famished way about him that makes women fix him hot dinners and men pour him the last of their good whiskey. It's this Massey who now takes off his hat in a sweeping introduction to the woman who opens the door to her boarding house, hands the woman his calling card, and announces his name as though it were the byline at the end of a published essay: "Ulys P. Massey, and this is my associate, Mr. Clayton Havens."

There is no hint of softness on the matron's whiskered face. "FSA, huh?"

Massey explains that they've come to do a report on Appalachia. Leaning toward her and lowering his voice, he adds, "We aren't telling folks the president sent us, so if we could just keep that between us."

Never has this well-used tactic fallen as flat as it does now. "This here's Chance, mister, so unless the president wants to know all about crop rot and coal mines, best you look for Appalachia in some other town." The woman starts to close the door.

"We're happy to pay double the going rate," Havens pipes up.

The door opens again.

"And my colleague here will do a beautiful photographic portrait of you for free," Massey tacks on.

Havens hopes his face is doing a decent impression of enthusiasm at the prospect when she offers them passage into the house.

"Name's Sylvia Fullhart." After taking their money, she leads them up a scuffed, squeaky staircase and along a hallway, where the wallpaper is beginning to peel and the smell of mold is most concentrated, before throwing open a door to a musty room under a sloping ceiling. Two narrow cots are separated by a washstand, and a single small window faces a back-yard of slag and a stand of imposing trees.

"Dinner's at five." She looks at Havens. "I'll sit for my picture after that."

Most of what Havens unpacks is photographic paraphernalia. He has been given a ton of black-and-white cartridges for this assignment but only two rolls of color film, of which he will make judicious use. He loads the Contax with standard black-and-white ISO 120 while Massey picks up Havens's portfolio.

"Don't waste your time looking at those," Havens tells him.

Massey thumbs through the latest black-and-whites—switchboard operators at the Union Terminal at Cincinnati Bell, the Saturday night goings-on at the Cosmopolitan, teenagers lined up in front of the Bijou Theatre—then singles out a picture of two dancehall inspectors, their stern faces a contrast to the revelry in front of them. "Okay, not heart-stopping, but pretty darn funny."

"What if I don't have what it takes anymore?" What if he's never had what it takes?

"You can't expect every picture to be a Pulitzer winner."

Havens used to be considered an unexceptional photographer—even his mother didn't keep the issues in which his photographs were published—but *Orphan Boy* changed everything. Overnight, he became reputed. People credited him for distilling the public's plight in what became known as the Face of the Depression, and those same people keep expecting him to produce more of that ilk, not what Pomeroy refers to as his "fussily composed pictures of weedy fields." Somehow, having made a name for himself, Havens now drags it around everywhere like a cadaver.

Massey puts the portfolio down, insisting, "It's a slump, that's all. Happens to the best of us."

"It's more than a slump." Each night in his dreams Havens develops grainy images of uninhabitable landscapes he has never visited and formless people without faces, and every morning he wakes up to see his camera zoomed in on him from the top of the bureau as though he has some explaining to do. "I don't feel anything when I take pictures anymore," he confesses.

"When that happens to me with an article, the subject matter's the issue. You've got to take pictures of what interests you."

"And what if I don't know what interests me?"

"Then get back into your element." Massey makes it sound so easy. "Pomeroy was going to send Stanley out here with me, but I told him you needed to do this. So here you go, your great outdoors you love so much." Massey yanks open the window and leans out. "It does go on and on, doesn't it?" He slams the window shut.

"And if I don't succeed here?"

Clapping Havens's forearms as though beating dust from cushions, Massey says, "Then we'll go to some other wilderness. Hell, we'll go to Antarctica if we have to. But first you have to get ol' ray of sunshine downstairs to smile for the birdy."

Three other boarders are sitting at small card tables in the front room when Massey and Havens go downstairs. Like a benevolent landowner out visiting his tenants, Massey has a chat with each of them while Havens slides into a chair at the far end of the room, hoping he won't be conscripted into taking pictures of anyone else.

After a less than inspired dinner of brisket, potatoes, and runny cherry pie, Sylvia Fullhart shoos the boarders back to their rooms and asks Havens if he prefers her to sit or stand. Massey is the one to arrange her in the wingback chair beside the dark fireplace.

As much as Massey's work is characterized by volume, a process that churns out page after page, Havens's is a study in economy. Rather than shoot a subject multiple times from many different angles and in varying lighting conditions, he prefers to observe a subject over a long period of time before pressing the shutter. This has always been his method, right from the age of fourteen, when his father spent two dollars and bought him his first camera, a cardboard Kodak Brownie Number 2, as a way to give a sickly kid something to do on his good days. That's when Havens would venture out to the backyard on pale skinny legs and use the lens to examine some beetle carcass or duck feather or half-buried bottle top. Scrutiny, however, works less well with human subjects. People don't want Havens waiting for some change in their expression or shift in posture to reveal something about their inner landscape—what he has come to think of as their tell. They want a portrait that flatters them.

While Havens observes Sylvia Fullhart through his 135mm viewfinder, deciding whether to do a simple head-and-shoulders or a full-length shot with more setting, she begins to run off the names and pedigrees of everyone in town. "But you'd be wise to obtain the blessing of Urnamy Gault first before trying to talk to folks. Get on the mayor's good side and you'll have everyone telling you their woebegones, but mind, that business about being on assignment for the president won't work on him either."

As is now customary, Havens sees nothing through the viewfinder that interests him and the light from the floor lamp seems to cleave Sylvia Fullhart's body in two. "The conditions are not ideal. I suggest we do this in the morning when we can take advantage of natural light."

"Just take the picture!" Massey and Sylvia Fullhart say in unison.

As though his shirtsleeves were made of cast iron, he lifts his Contax and attaches it to the tripod while Massey keeps throwing him a thumbs-up.

As soon as she hears the click of the shutter, the woman says, "I think I'd prefer a standing one."

Massey arranges her arms.

"Be sure to talk to Reverend Tuttle. He can tell you the history of Chance going back to 1830. Anything about the Chesapeake and Ohio you want to know, he'll tell you, and everything about the mines, too. He's the most learned of any of us."

"Would he happen to know anything about blue coon hunting?"

She gapes at Massey, one hand on her knee, the other on her hip, in a most unnatural pose. "You can't come right out with a question like that!"

Havens notices the woman's tell—a patch of eczema on her neck suddenly inflamed.

As though he's picked up the spoor of some animal, Massey presses her. "It's got nothing to do with raccoons, does it?"

Sylvia's eyes flick from Massey to the camera. She motions for Havens to stop pointing it at her. "Best you leave that business aside."

She won't be coaxed into saying more on the subject, and the men return to their room. Massey tells Havens that he tried researching race relations in eastern Kentucky, and what little he'd gleaned was from the whites' perspective only, which is to say, things aren't as bad as they are farther south. "But get this—the coal companies around here ran huge ad campaigns in the South recruiting Negro laborers and offering to pay black miners the same as white miners, and pretty soon the workforce was about half black and half white. On the surface that strikes a person as reasonable, doesn't it?"

Havens guesses where Massey is going. "But the white miners don't want to have anything to do with the black miners."

"Bingo," Massey says. "Which means working conditions that make hell look inviting. Except there's no way white miners are going to join ranks with black miners because they're too busy worrying Negro men are taking their jobs. Therefore, a weak union and a fat corporation patting itself on the back."

"So, if it's a racial reference, why the 'blue'?"

Massey shrugs and starts making notes, and Havens stretches out on his bed and wonders what they are getting themselves into.

❦

Reverend Arlen Tuttle is a frowning man with a tight-lipped way about him, which gives the impression that every word Massey utters will be stored and used against him one day. He holds his lapels and waits for

Massey to get through apologizing for interrupting his preparations for the Sunday service and explaining about the good work being done by the FSA before saying, "You paid a visit to the drinking establishment, I hear."

"The only way to depict a town with any accuracy is to visit as many places and speak to as many people as we can."

"If you want an accurate depiction of our town, you would do better talking to my parishioners than entertaining the likes of Ronny Gault."

A young woman with heavily applied makeup and a head full of ringlets rushes down the aisle. "Sorry I'm late, Pa."

"Where have you been?"

"Nowhere."

He gives her his handkerchief and tells her to wipe off her lipstick.

She gathers the pile of song sheets from the altar and tosses a few on each bench while Massey asks the preacher about the church's views on the coal industry and the labor movement.

"In the Lord's house, there are no picket lines or any other means used to divide people. In the waters of baptism, we are all one."

Finishing her task, his daughter begins trimming the altar candles, and Havens drifts over and introduces himself.

"Sarah," she responds.

"We met your boyfriend yesterday—Ronny Gault."

"Ronny's not my boyfriend, and you'd do well not to believe anything he tells you." She writes hymn numbers on the chalkboard.

"Does that apply to blue coon hunting?"

At the question, Sarah Tuttle behaves like someone who's hypothermic. She wraps her arms across herself and through clenched teeth says, "Ronny ought to be locked up for talking that way!"

Havens would question her further, but something has caught his attention on the shelf built into the back of the pulpit. "Is that a gun?"

"That's a snake repellent," says Reverend Tuttle, who removes the revolver. "A Smith and Wesson thirty-eight." He shows where a snake is carved in the mahogany handle. "A couple years back, one of Pastor Wrightley's parishioners came in here with a rattler in each hand, ready to set us straight on how worship ought to be conducted, and one of them got loose and delivered a fatal strike to Mrs. O'Dell's ankle."

Having a man of God in front of his pulpit with a handgun is too good an opportunity to pass up. "Do you mind if I take your picture?" Havens asks, and to his surprise, Reverend Tuttle agrees, striking a pose more befitting a bounty hunter than a man ordained to save souls.

Churchgoers with a slightly malnourished way about them start filing in and taking their places, and a man who is a good many dinners past fitting into his three-piece wool suit ambles to the front to join Massey, Havens, and Reverend Tuttle. "These the ones asking all the questions?" Reeking of cigars, he peers out from under the brim of his homburg with small blue eyes that give the impression cigar smoke is still rising up into them, and pulls his chin toward his neck as if to stifle a belch. "Name's Urnamy Gault, but you fellas can call me Mayor." He doesn't introduce the brittle-looking woman behind him who has a child on her hip, four in tow, and one on the way, though she appears to be a good deal past childbearing age.

Massey is in the process of stating their business when the mayor cuts him off. "You boys saved?"

Massey doesn't skip a beat. "I went to Methodist camp meetings in my youth."

"I'll take that as a no," Urnamy Gault says. "Never met a Northerner who was saved, have you, Reverend? Well, you boys couldn't have picked a better time to worship with us than Baptism Sunday."

Massey tries to make an ally of the mayor, following him to his pew; Reverend Tuttle takes a seat in the chair beside the pulpit and Havens slips outside, passing Sarah Tuttle, chewing her nails and eyeing him from the corner. He strolls the grounds to take in more of the surroundings. Along the slopes of the hunching hills are clusters of cabins, each with a rough field of corn, wheat, or tobacco, while the main river bullies its way through the valley below. Pastures give way to woodlands, which rise up to form an endless parade of mountains, the effect of which makes it hard to believe that elsewhere in the nation ships are leaving port, skyscrapers are being erected, and automobiles are rolling off factory lines.

After a while, he returns to the church and positions his tripod and camera thirty feet from the building. He has in mind a straight-forward picture, one depicting the only well-maintained, if unadorned, structure in the area, standing resolute as if to keep at bay the primitive forces of both man and nature. For scenics, he prefers to shoot with his Graflex Speed Graphic rather than the smaller and more convenient Contax. He sets the f-stop at F6 and the shutter speed at 1/125 and assesses the church first through the prism range finder and then through the lens used to correct for parallax error. Just as he is about to press the shutter, the doors spring open and a phalanx of congregants files out behind Reverend Tuttle, who holds his Bible as if it were a lantern.

Breaking ranks, Massey runs up to Havens. "Everyone's going down to the river to get baptized. Come on, this is going to be something else."

Havens closes up his Graflex, unscrews it from the tripod, and hurries to catch up to Massey, who has merged again with the crowd, now singing and clapping and marching along a narrow spit of dirt into the forest. They thread around mulberry trees and yews and oaks, and their song is no longer swept away by the hillside breeze but swells beneath the humid leafy canopy and takes on an adhesive quality. After skidding down a treacherous embankment and clamoring over boulders, the congregation bunches at a stream. Sarah stands beside her father, and, at his cue, begins to sing "His Eye Is on the Sparrow" loud enough to be heard on the other side of the forest. Massey jostles Havens through the throng for a position closer to the action. With her hands resting on the back of her hips and her eyes locked ahead, Sarah Tuttle's voice slides up to a note and holds it a long time in a high lonesome vibrato at the end of the phrase "I sing because I'm free." Havens has never heard anything like it.

Reverend Tuttle strolls into the water, makes an appeal to the heavens and an invitation to those assembled, and gestures to Sarah to start fitting white robes on those who come forward.

Amidst "hallelujahs" and "amens," the mayor is first to be yanked underwater. One after another, people make their way into the shallows, dressed as though for bed or surgery, each with a somnolent expression, and it does seem that some transformation takes place in the process of submersion, because each one returns to shore bright-eyed and smiling and a little shy, readying for an embrace as though having returned from a long trip.

Havens sets up his tripod and notices Massey pull loose his tie and kick off his shoes.

"What are you doing?"

Massey peels off his socks. "I'm going in."

"You can't do that." Havens tries apprehending him, but Massey elbows his way to the front of the crowd and presents himself in front of a deacon, lifting his arms in the air for a robe. Shooting pictures is pointless now, so Havens retreats to a boulder, where, a moment later, he feels a tap on his shoulder.

Sarah Tuttle looks grave. "Can I talk to you?" She faces the baptism, indicating for Havens to do the same, and gives the impression of clapping along with the congregation as she speaks to Havens under her breath. "What else did Ronny tell you? Did he say he was planning something?"

"You mean, blue coon—"

She cuts him off by raising her hand. "Don't call them that."

So they are people. "Was Ronny referring to Negroes?"

She shakes her head. "You work for President Roosevelt?" Sarah asks.

Havens clarifies, "We report to a department that collects information about people so that other government agencies can help those people. For example, if a town needs better schools or new roads—"

"You seem like a nice man. Are you?"

Havens hesitates. "Yes?"

Bedraggled and grinning, Massey has waded to the shore and is shaking hands with people.

"So, if I told you innocent people get hurt in this town and nobody does anything about it, could you help? Or your department?"

"Does this have to do with what Ronny and his friends said?"

Havens follows Sarah's gaze—Gault is talking to Massey. "Forget I said anything," she says, slipping away.

"Gault's just invited us to lunch," Massey reports, returning to Havens. He tips his head to one side and thumps his ear.

"I'm surprised he fell for it."

Massey rakes his fingers through his wet hair. "Do you think I just pulled a stunt to get in with folks?"

"So what, you're a convert?"

"Remember that time we went out to cover the mill workers' strike, the one that turned into a riot?"

"You threw a rock at a policeman, as I recall."

"I picked up a sign." Massey rolls his eyes. "The point is, going into the water felt like that. Don't you ever want to give yourself to something larger than just yourself? Be part of some bigger transaction, whatever it is?"

Havens changes the subject. "The preacher's daughter wants our help."

"With what?"

"'Blue coons' refers to people, but I don't think Negroes, and my guess is the mayor's son is involved in some kind of feud with them." Havens explains that Sarah's afraid for them, whoever they are, but that she clammed up as soon as she saw Gault approach Massey.

"Just when I was saying I didn't want to write about stereotypes, and I get the Hatfields and the McCoys."

"I think we must be very careful who we ask what," Havens says, watching Sarah Tuttle dart through the trees.

HAVENS

❧

avens and Massey take their seats on either side of Urnamy
Gault's dining table, along with four scrubbed boys, the
older of which has the infant on his lap. Likening baptism
to spring cleaning, Gault is advising Massey to get dunked in the waters
of salvation once a year. The mayor doesn't so much talk as proclaim,
and Havens and Massey have already been subjected to his opinions
on everything from national politics to local economics, and how big
corporations lure from small towns young able-bodied men who fall for
hopes of an easier life rather than taking up the honest one waiting in
their own backyard.

During Gault's protracted blessing, Havens helps Estil Gault carry
dishes to the table. She is a small-boned woman who appears to hold her
breath much of the time, as though she ought not to take more than
her share of anything, least of all air. When she is asked by her husband
as to their son's whereabouts, each word she speaks comes out pinched.
"Gone to call on Sarah Tuttle, I expect."

Gault scoffs and explains that Sarah Tuttle is giving Ronny the
runaround.

Havens returns to the kitchen for another dish, and finds Estil doubled over with pain. Pressing her hand against her belly, she eases into the chair Havens hurries to retrieve for her.

Havens pours her a glass of water. "Shall I call your husband?"

"It'll pass."

Havens is still deciding how long he should let it go before sounding the alarm when Ronny comes in through the back door and rushes to his mother's side. "Mama, you're ill."

"I'm fine." She scoots to the edge of the chair and raises her hand so he can help her stand.

"The doctor told you no more, and that was two babies ago, and now here's another one on the way."

Havens fills the pitcher with water while Estil tells her son not to fret.

"What's taking you so long, Estil?" Gault calls.

"You go on and start without me," she hollers back, stifling a moan.

Ronny's face darkens. "Why can't he lay off?"

"Please don't go in there and make an issue of it again."

As Havens is leaving the kitchen, Ronny is bending so his mother can hug him. "You're all I've got, Mama. I can't have anything happen to you."

Instead of greeting his son when he comes in from the kitchen, Gault keeps his eyes on his plate. "You arrive late and expect to eat at my table without washing up?"

"I'm not eating," Ronny grumbles.

"Your mother's gone to the trouble of cooking a meal that I went to the trouble of paying for that the Good Lord went to the trouble of providing, and it's too much trouble for you to eat it?"

Estil Gault gives her son a beseeching look, so he slumps into the empty chair, clipping the ear of the boy beside him before picking up his fork and stabbing at the food his mother puts in front of him.

"Your mother says I'm to loan you money for an engagement ring, but I wonder what kind of courtship it is if a suitor can't be bothered to escort his girl to church, especially when her daddy's the preacher and it's Baptism Sunday."

"Young people do things different than how we did them, Urnamy," Estil Gault inserts.

"I don't need your money," Ronny fires back.

Gault puts down his fork, daubs his mouth with his napkin, and takes a long sip of water. He turns to Massey. "Would you call it a particular kind of pride that makes a boy turn down a man's charity even though he's got no employment prospects, or would you call it just plain old mule-headedness?"

"Urnamy, please," says his wife.

"We Kentuckians are a proud people—that's one thing you boys can write in that report of yours."

Uncharacteristically quiet until now, Massey says suddenly, "Actually, I was hoping you could tell me what you know about blue coon hunting."

Gault does not break eye contact with Massey, not even with his wife gasping. "Now, I don't know where you would hear a thing like that, but I'll say this, if you've come here to depict us as ignorant snake-handlers, moonshiners, and superstitious hillbillies who've got nothing better to do than be at daggers with one another, you'd best get on the next train."

Havens glares at Massey, who must piss pure vinegar because he says, "Actually, it was Ronny and his pals who raised the subject."

"I said no such thing!" Ronny bellows, rising to his feet so fast his chair tips backward.

"We've been given to understand that coons don't refer to colored folk," Massey presses on. "So who are we talking about here?"

Estil Gault snaps at Massey, "The devil himself, that's who!"

Rising, the mayor demands an immediate end to the subject by saying, "Take the children upstairs, Estil." But she is fired up on the subject and turns to her husband.

"Why don't you tell them how the devil about burned down this town? Why don't you tell them how they make it miserable for everyone else?" She faces Massey, the only one still seated, still, in fact, eating. "Unless you want your life to become a living hell, you best steer clear of Spooklight Holler."

"Shut up about Blues! I'm sick of hearing about them!" Ronny thunders out of the room, with his mother in close pursuit.

Havens picks up his camera equipment and signals Massey to keep his mouth shut. "We are sorry for raising a subject that has caused Mrs. Gault such distress."

The mayor escorts them to the front door. "I don't know what all Ronny and Faro told you or what you've heard from anyone else, but I'll have you keep in mind that those folk quarantined themselves. Nobody forced them up that holler. My wife's prone to excitability, but she's right—best keep clear of that lot."

Havens shakes hands with him. "We sure will."

"Appreciate the warning," adds Massey.

As they cross the street, Havens checks over his shoulder—Estil Gault and Ronny are watching them from the upstairs window.

"Who the hell is quarantined these days except lepers?"

A block down Main Street, Havens waves over a kid on a bicycle and fishes out a quarter from his pocket. "Can you show us the way to Spooklight Holler?"

The kid shakes his head, so Havens offers another coin. Still the kid refuses, so Havens peels a dollar from his billfold. "Come on now, that's enough to replace those worn tires."

The kid snatches the money and pedals to the end of the street.

As soon as they catch up to him, he pedals a bit farther. The next time they catch up to him, Massey asks, "The people up the holler, are they sick?"

The boy shakes his head.

"Are you afraid of them?" Havens asks.

Again, he shakes his head, but half a mile later, he pulls off to the side of the dirt road and points to a path that leads into the woods, then pedals like crazy back to town.

❦

Havens hears the sound again. Some kind of birdcall, perhaps. He's already identified several species—mockingbirds, cardinals, chickadees, towhee, and two summer residents come early, the Kentucky warbler and yellow warbler. Massey has grown impatient with him for stopping every few minutes. "You're not on assignment for Audubon, for god's sake."

He and Massey have clocked several miles. As instructed by a tenant farmer, they followed the dirt path until it came to a stand of cottonwoods, and just as they'd been told, another footpath lay beyond, but less than two hundred yards into the holler, the path curved to the right and became unnavigable. When they had to crash through dense underbrush, Havens, sweaty, itchy, and irritable, suggested they might have strayed from the path, but now he isn't even sure they are in the right holler. Proposing they turn back only makes Massey more insistent on soldiering through the tangle.

Havens's sleeve rips on a thorny branch and he feels a gash open up on his forearm. Small bushy twigs keep reaching into his hair and roots knot instantly at his feet to form tripwires. Much of this environment is unfamiliar to him. The trees seem unnaturally tall, and apart from bluebells, bloodroot, and pink lady's-slipper, he's never seen the other flowering shrubs. Even the spiky odor in the air is foreign to him. Vines drape down from tree branches like nooses.

When they began their hike, the air was cool, but now it is thick and cloying. They've been at it more than two hours, and the stream that gave them fresh hope ten minutes ago seems to have given them the slip. He can't imagine anyone living up here, and yet they push on, Massey as if he is tracking some lost tribe, and Havens tussling with branches that seem to want to dispossess him of his camera.

Massey suddenly points to the ground, claiming to have found the path, but it seems too narrow to be anything but an animal trail. Havens tries not to think what kind of animal. He is about to insist they turn back when he hears the noise again. It is closer this time, but too brief and too indistinct for him to identify.

"Do you hear that?" Massey asks, cocking his head.

Rounding a collection of boulders, they come up alongside the stream again. Massey takes this as a good sign. "See, I told you we weren't lost."

Havens wets his handkerchief and applies it to the back of his neck, and then hears the sound again. Not a birdcall; rather, the unmistakable melody of human song.

Massey gestures upstream, where their view is obscured by trees. He puts a finger to his lips before flapping his hand in the direction they are to proceed, and they keep to the edge of the stream, where the spongy moss absorbs the sound of their footsteps. Distracted by the call of a whip-poor-will, Havens does not see the branch that Massey bent out of his way come flying back, and it strikes Havens on the side of the head, causing him to gasp. Massey swings around and fires him a stern look as though Havens has just driven off their prey. He sets a brisk pace while Havens stumbles and trips and does a poor job of keeping up. As they duck beneath low branches, the melody drifts toward them like a tease. Havens has to stop to free his tripod from another errant creeper, and Massey, having seen something, beckons him to hurry.

Havens pulls up next to him and peeks through the gap in the brush. Beside the stream, a young woman is struggling to wedge her heel into her shoe while using a glistening rock as ballast. Obscuring her face is a sheet of wet dark-red hair, and even though she is deep in the shadow, what Havens sees stuns him. It can't be. His body freezes the way a lesser animal's might do in the presence of a predator. Rigor mortis notwithstanding, his senses do not yield: her skin color is an unambiguous blue.

Havens thinks they should make themselves known with a greeting, and yet he keeps silent. He watches the water drip from the ends of her hair, allows his eyes to follow her exposed lithe arms to the curvature of her hips, where her damp dress clings to her. She twists her hair over one shoulder to wring out the water, and he wills her to move into the sunlight. It feels like a violation of her, this watching, but still Havens fails to do the decent thing. At the intersection of shadow and curve and color is his bewitching, and there arises in him an intense desire both to approach her and to turn back and forget he ever saw her.

Massey is jabbing him in the ribs, mouthing something. Havens has no idea what is required of him. He goes back to watching her. She's petite, slight, sylphlike, and she is about to step into the light. He wants to see her face. Massey hits him on the arm, frowns fiercely, and makes the sign for him to take a photograph. Havens raises the Contax. Step into the sunlight, he urges her silently. Step and turn. Let me see you.

A bundle is wedged in the fork of a nearby tree, and this is where she heads, where the shadow of the forest is pulled back like a curtain and the sunlight reveals her blue skin, silky and as luminescent as the speculum of a mallard. She turns just enough that he can make out her pensive expression. Her mouth is large for so delicate a face, and her full lips are the color of midnight during a full moon. Havens might as well be socked in the gut. Something inside him is turning. Some loosening is taking place, something that makes him aware that till now he has been a constricted man, a man with limbs and gut and mind screwed too tightly in place. This great unwinding is stripping the threads of all those bolts that hold him together, so magnificent a sight is she.

"Take it!" Massey hisses in his ear.

JUBILEE

❦

Sunday morning. Every once in a while when the breeze is light and comes from just the right direction you can hear the church bells. Soon folks will be making their way to Reverend Tuttle's church, and though that's just one more place where the Bufords aren't welcome, Pa still expects each of his offspring to stay on speaking terms with the Lord and spend a while in the Word, which is why Jubilee is sitting at the kitchen table with the family Bible. She opens the cover and gets stuck where she usually does, on the first page. Birth records, marriage registers, and death notices are for those who live in town, but for the Bufords of Spooklight Holler, this page and memory serve as the only archives, neither of which is too reliable. Some of the names written here have partial dates, a few no dates at all, and about a dozen names are marked with little ink dots to indicate Blue. Jubilee runs her finger across her paternal grandmother's name, Opal, the first to have been born blue. It's to her that Jubilee most often directs her prayers—petitions, mostly, that always begin with "Help." Of all the dotted names, none but Jubilee and her brother, Levi, remain. They are the last of the Blues. *Help keep us safe*, she prays once again. *Watch over Levi. Mend Thomas's wing that he might fly soon. Send a companion for little Willow-May that she might not be so lonesome.* After she whispers her amen, she tacks on, *Spare one for me, too.* Then, thinking better of it, she prays, *Never mind.*

Mama comes in through the back door and tells her the bath is ready. Sunday is also bathing day. As the oldest, Levi is entitled to bathe first, but since he's off someplace again, she has the rare treat of clean hot water. Mama busies Jubilee's little sister, Willow-May, with kneading dough, which means Jubilee has the wash hut to herself, another indulgence. She slips off her nightgown, pulls her auburn hair from its pins, and tests the water before getting in. The heat darkens her skin by several shades. Her blue skin—peel it off and fold it up, and it would be no bigger than a pillowcase, hardly enough to warrant the big fuss it causes.

She is washing her hair when she hears Chappy honking outside and yelling for her to come.

"I'm busy right now," she yells back. Chappy's kin came to these mountains from the Deep South as freed people to work on the railroads seventy-some years ago. A few work in the mine at Smoke Hole now, and some, like Chappy's grandma, are sharecroppers, and when Blues were run up this holler, they were the first to lend a hand. Jubilee and Chappy have been friends since they were babies. Chappy's grandma says the Lord made it so they'd be friends on account of their trials, meaning her blue skin and his different way of comprehending, but she knows they'd be friends, trials or no trials.

Chappy keeps pestering her. "Come out, Juby, hurry!"

There'll be no end to this till she agrees, so she climbs out, towels off, and puts on her clothes.

"You done yet, Juby?"

"Hold your horses!"

"But I came by car," he says. When she opens the door, Chappy has his hub cap steering wheel raised in front of him and is wound up about something. "You've got to come on a ride with me right now, Juby!"

Though folks in town say he's simple because he'll never learn to write his name, Chappy is always the first to notice something out of the ordinary, trouble especially.

"What's wrong?"

"Two newcomers in town."

"Revenuers?" she asks, in which case she ought to get word to Socall, whose still produces stump liquor strong enough to take a stain out of a shirt. It wouldn't be the first time a jealous rival ratted her out.

Chappy shakes his head. "No. These'uns are going around asking for stories."

Every so often a Northerner will happen into town wanting something nobody here thought to give—the last one went holler to holler asking everyone to sing him songs, and the one before that bought up dulcimers and fiddles even though he professed not to be able to play a lick. Jubilee doesn't see why newcomers are causing Chappy to fret so until he says, "They've already heard about Blues."

This gets her attention.

"You wanna get a good look at them so you know who to watch out for?" Chappy reports that one of the men is out on Folgers Hill. Although that's where the church is, there are plenty of places where she can keep from being seen, so she hurries back to the house for her veil, telling Mama that she's going out with Chappy. Chappy doesn't even bother to check over his shoulder for oncoming traffic the way he usually does, but has them take off down the path at full speed.

"Who is it that told them?"

Chappy makes a lot of engine sounds so he doesn't have to say.

"Was it Ronny?"

Chappy keeps his eyes fixed ahead. "I don't know why he's always so mean to you and Levi."

A mind poisoned against Blue can be passed to offspring every bit as easily as a crooked nose or a keenness with numbers, and Ronny got himself a double dose. Even before Urnamy was elected mayor, Ronny took it upon himself to police everyone he considered lower, Bufords especially. Pa's said a thousand times for Levi to ignore Ronny's provocations, but Levi doesn't always listen to sense, so whenever Ronny and his cohorts pay a visit to Spooklight Holler, afterward the Gaults will find damage to their

property. Pa's crops are tampered with; the Gaults' automobile's tires are
slashed. Pa's fence gets torn down; the Gaults' store windows get smashed.
As with the way of grudge-keeping, things build up, and it wasn't that long
ago that the Gaults' shed got torched and people ran around with buckets
in fear that the whole town was going to burn to the ground. Though it
couldn't be proved, everyone knew it was Levi. So did Pa. Levi was too old
for a licking by that stage, but Pa made him swear to stay clear of Ronny,
a pledge Levi, so far, has kept.

Avoiding the wide-open spaces, she and Chappy find a bush to hide
behind, and watch the man on the grassy rise. He's very tall and not what
you hear of city-dwellers, all spruced—his shirt is untucked, his pant cuffs
drag in the dirt, and his hair is a messy wave that falls in his eyes. Some
miners are better kept.

"What's he got with him?" Chappy asks.

Jubilee explains what little she knows of cameras, but Chappy can't seem
to grasp the notion of a contraption that can make pictures of a person's
likeness. The man looks skyward, shielding his eyes, as a red-tailed hawk
glides on a high draft, late in returning from its southerly home. With his
head tipped almost all the way back, the man stumbles over clods of dirt
and uneven ground out to the middle of the field so he can track the hawk's
path till it disappears from sight over the tree line, and then the tree that
lightning struck years ago catches his attention. There's nothing to see but
a rack of scorched limbs, and yet the man hurries to set up his contraption
twenty yards from it.

"He wants to make a picture of that?" Chappy asks.

After a while, Chappy says he has to go, and she tells him not to worry
about seeing her home, that she'll make her own way presently. She watches
the newcomer, though there is not much to see beyond a man enchanted
by a tree no one else would give a second glance. Except for her, folks in
these parts study nature only for the purposes of its utility. The afternoon
sun slips behind a dark cloud and the man considers the sky again and
then moves his camera a few paces to the left before bending to put his eye
against it. He straightens up, runs his fingers through his hair, and seems

so pleased with his find that she has the urge to go out to him and tell him that she, too, has always considered that very same tree a beauty. As if finding common ground with a Right-colored was a thing a Blue could do.

She wonders what Ronny might have told him about Blues. Nothing but filth, likely, and there are others sitting in that church dressed up in their Sunday best, goodness leaking out of them like tree sap, who won't have one nice thing to say on the matter either. Some call her and Levi the Tainted, forgetting Blues and their kin once lived alongside Right-colored back when there wasn't much to these parts except a general store and farmlands. The epidemic of 1899 put an end to that when someone went around proposing that the reason a third of the town had succumbed but not one of the dozen or so Blues was because Blues had made those folk sick, not influenza. Up cropped all manner of superstitions, and suddenly Blues were forced up the holler and told to keep to themselves.

Jubilee doesn't hear the footsteps till it is too late.

A big hand clamps across her nose and mouth. "Why ain't you covered?"

Her veil is balled up and shoved in her pocket, and as she reaches for it, he yanks it from her and throws it to the ground.

"What are you doing here? You fixing to put a hex on that man?"

She knows the voice. Knows his smell, too—like damp chicken feathers. To look at Ronny Gault's face is to wonder if he's run into a swarm of bees. Welts for lips and swollen eyes, skin that has the sheen of boils. She tries pulling away but the more she wrestles, the fiercer he grips, so she goes limp and lets him drive her by her neck back into the woods.

When she was eight and Levi fifteen, their cow went missing and no one doubted it was Ronny's doing. A week later Sheriff Suggins and Reverend Tuttle stood at their front door saying the special collection taken that morning to buy the church a new roof had been stolen, a large sum thanks to the generous contribution made by Mayor Gault.

Rather than proclaim his innocence, Levi challenged the men. "If you think I did it, why bother to ask questions? Why not just take me to jail?"

Jubilee doesn't know how it is with brothers and sisters in other families, but she and Levi are so close that if he was to be cut, she'd bleed, too, and if Levi was about to go off to prison, she was ready to commit a crime to go along with him. "Ronny Gault stole the money," she blurted, the biggest lie she ever told. "I saw him climb out the church window with a bag under his arm."

Instead of being locked away for telling a fib, she was marched to Mayor Gault's house where, near dumb with fear, she had to give her account again, which even to her own ears sounded dreamed up. As Sheriff Suggins made a fruitless search of the house, Ronny looked at her and drew his finger across his neck, then later that night threw a torch through the Buford living room window as a reminder that Jubilee's false witness had only made things worse.

Now Ronny pins her against a tree. "How many times do you lot have to be told to stay away?"

"You don't own everywhere, Ronny."

"Always did have a big mouth, didn't you? A big mouth with a lying forked tongue. Suppose I was to cut it out so you couldn't tell any more of your lies?"

Ronny brings out a switchblade, and she turns her head and pretends she's seen a sharp edge this close hundreds of times. "You leave one mark on me, and my brother will come for you."

This sets Ronny off. In one swift motion, the blade slices through her hair. He holds up the lock. "You tell your brother to come for me and save me a trip up the holler." He pushes her away. "Go back to your hole now." Staggering through the trees, she hears him yell about Blues being gone once and for all.

She claws through a tangle of underbrush and finds a hidden spot to sit awhile and gather herself. Ronny out here in the woods can only mean that he's set up his traps again. He's not the only one to hunt raccoons, especially since their pelts fetch so much money these days, but his leghold traps are cruel, the poor victims suffering often for days on end because he can't be bothered to check frequently, and most of the time he's too lazy to skin and cure what he catches but instead lops off the tails and leaves the rest, babies even. There's no such thing as teaching Ronny Gault a lesson, but Jubilee will not rest until she's searched the surroundings and triggered all the traps she can find, about half a dozen. On her way to the path that leads to her aviary, she comes across a large spread of pokeweed, and stops to harvest as much as she can bundle in her veil, careful to take leaves only from the young plants less than a foot high. Later, she'll boil it three times to get out the poison, and they'll have enough poke sallet to eat for three or four days in a row. Pleased with her find, she heads to the meadow, where she keeps her birds in the small shed her father built years ago. There she sets out seed and fresh water for each one, and though convention says not to handle convalescing birds if they're to return to the wild, she dotes on them and sings to them and confesses that she wishes at times that they'll never leave her.

It's late in the afternoon when she leaves the aviary and decides to visit the creek before returning home, and as she comes to the place where the creek widens into a basin, she spies Levi and Sarah Tuttle perched on a log together, Levi leaning over his flat-top guitar to neck with her. Just as startled as Jubilee, Sarah jumps to her feet. She's wearing a dress altogether too tight and too short, and either she's flushed from their activities or she's colored her cheeks too red.

Instead of approaching them, Jubilee aims to go around, but Levi rushes to her with an explanation. She walks faster.

He catches up and grabs her elbow. "Hold up, now."

"I can't believe you!" Pa is always saying for her and Levi to keep to their own business and not give those in town any more justification for hating them, and still Levi finds ways to defy orders. As much as Levi retaliates, he also instigates, and Sarah Tuttle is more than one step too far.

"We don't have to make a big deal out of this, okay?" If it weren't for his blue skin, Levi would likely have all the girls in town after him, the way he can slow down his talking and deepen his voice and make those dimples appear without even smiling, but his charm is lost now on Jubilee.

"What if someone else saw the two of you?"

He dismisses her worries by saying something they both know to be untrue: "No one comes up this way."

"How long has this been going on?"

"Nothing's going on. She and I make up songs together."

"Songs." Jubilee purses her lips.

"No, really. She sent a letter to her uncle, who works for a radio station in Lexington, and he's written back saying he'll help her make a recording and get it on the radio. She's going to sing my songs. My songs on the radio! You should hear her sing, Juby. Come get acquainted with her. I'm sure she'll sing something for you if you ask."

Sarah is now halfway up the bank as though she's of a mind to flee. If she had been with who everyone says is her boyfriend instead of with Levi, Ronny wouldn't have found Jubilee, and Levi wouldn't be putting himself in danger. "She's Ronny's girl, Levi. If he finds out, what do you think he's going to do? Sit back and watch? He'll come after you, and maybe me, maybe even all of us."

Levi hears only one part. "She's not Ronny's girl." He turns the color of gunpowder, and Jubilee decides against telling him about her encounter with Ronny.

"Does she even care about what could happen to you? Or is she just a vain girl who wants to rebel against her preacher daddy by courting the person least suited to her?"

"Lower your voice." Levi puts a little more distance between them and Sarah. "You don't know the first thing about her."

"I know she's bad news, that's all I need to know," Jubilee snaps back.

"I'm heading back," Sarah calls, which makes Levi go after her. With this girl, he visibly softens. He talks quietly into her hair, brushes those fussy curls from her shoulders, and offers his cheek for a goodbye kiss. As he watches her walk away, he fetches his guitar and strums a tune, and she starts singing, waving the music sheets above her head in farewell.

"I know you think this is me trying to take revenge on Ronny, but it isn't," Levi says when he catches up to Jubilee. "She really is something special."

Levi is somehow afforded privileges in the Buford family that no one else gets—that's just Levi, Mama says whenever the kitchen table gets turned over or a mug goes flying into the fireplace—but there's something altered about him now. He has the manner of a pardoned man.

"You have your reasons for being with her, but what are her reasons for being with you? Don't you wonder about that?"

"Is it so hard to imagine she wants to be with me because she has feelings for me?"

Nobody understands better than Jubilee this longing for love, but how can this business with Sarah do anything but bring harm to Levi? "You need to put an end to it."

"So you would have me give her up, the one thing that makes me happy?"

"If you don't quit her, I'll tell Pa."

"What do you know about anything?" Levi stomps off along the path, and Jubilee goes down to the water's edge, puts her bundle in a tree, takes off her socks and shoes, and soaks her feet. The water is warmer than usual. She wades out to her knees, then decides there's no harm in having a quick dip, so she returns to the shore, slips out of her dress, and goes in where the water reaches her thighs. She lays back. Her hair fans out around her. By the time she rises from the water, she's ready to smooth things over with Levi.

Dressed but for her shoes, she hears whispering, and her first thought is that Ronny's come for her. She spins around and two faces are spying on her from the bramble, one as though he's just come upon a bear, the other like the sun's blinded him. As soon as he lifts the camera to his face, she realizes he's the man from Folgers Hill.

HAVENS

Alerted to their presence, the blue woman flashes them a look from non-reflective eyes, eyes that seem to swallow light and offer nothing in return, before flinging herself away in fright, the tendrils of her wet hair flying out behind her. Skirt hoisted, she crosses the creek, splashing and kicking up stones in haste, and on the opposite embankment, she checks their progress before taking off. She runs like someone who knows how to outrun dogs.

Massey and Havens chase after her, stumbling through the water and losing their balance on the slippery rocks.

"Wait!" Massey shouts to her. "Come back!"

Havens has not recovered his voice. He hasn't yet recovered any other thought but one: what an extraordinary woman.

There is no song in the crease of the hills anymore, no breeze to carry the notes of an innocent tune, only the sounds of snapping branches, slapping footsteps, and labored breath—the sounds of men giving chase. The pursued makes no sound. She flies over boulders and crosses the stream again. They are no match for her. They follow her over a fallen tree until she darts into the overgrowth and vanishes.

"Come back! We just want to talk to you!" Massey calls.

Havens and Massey are out of breath. Neither of them has any clue in which direction they are to go. Bushes and ferns surround them, they are far from the stream, and Havens remembers there being a steep incline to the east, but now the grade is level. He isn't sure which way will lead them down the holler or deeper into it. They are lost, and they have lost her.

Massey is huffing and sweating, bent over with his hands on his knees. He lifts his head. "Have you ever seen anything like it?"

Havens can't find the words.

Massey straightens up, mops his forehead with the back of his hand, and shakes his head. "Blue. She was blue!"

"We frightened her." He can't get out of his mind her startled expression.

Massey casts about. "How many pictures did you take?"

Havens suggests they find their way back to the path, head back to town, and try again in the morning.

"Wait, you took her picture, right?"

"I—there wasn't any time to—"

"Jesus, Havens, the goddamn picture of a lifetime and you missed it?"

Havens imagines her imprinted on a strip of film—her innocence, her perfect form, her coloring. Even in the simple act of putting on her shoe, she was a portrait, an enigma, and he doesn't need Massey to remind him of the incalculable loss of not having captured that.

"I had to wait until she was out of the shade and properly lighted," he explains. "Even with color film, her skin tone would have come out looking like lead."

Massey goes from being irked to despondent. "We have to find her."

Dusk falls while they are discussing their next move. Massey insists they proceed around a stack of boulders, convinced he has heard leaves rustling, and Havens counters by mentioning that evening is fast approaching and the light is useless for photographing now anyway. "And we do not want to get caught in the woods at night. Let's take another stab at this tomorrow."

"Five more minutes," Massey insists.

Havens pushes past Massey, climbs over the large boulder, and stubs his foot on a sharp rock. He cries out. Thinking he might have broken a toe, he wills another step, but the pain becomes fiercer still and shoots from his toe to his ankle to his thigh. He feels faint. He looks down at his foot, but it seems very far away. Rising up from the cold ground is a disheartening numbness. This can't be the rock's doing. He wants to alert Massey but when he tries to talk he can't quite make his mouth work right. Instead of being anchored by the surroundings, he begins to see swirling patterns.

Massey yells at him not to move. "You've been bit by a snake! Right behind you. Don't move!"

A terrible tightness has taken hold of Havens's left leg while other parts inside him go slack. He feels his mouth unlatch. His thoughts flutter as though from an overturned drawer. Is someone shouting? He is trying to hold on to a recollection, something he's just seen but cannot now draw a bead on. He can't remember what has brought him to such a dark place, darker than night. His eyes are open and yet he cannot see anything. He begins to fall. Leaves are falling on him or are they papers? They are photographs, each one blank. All the photographs he has not yet taken are falling on him, burying him. He scans them, desperate for the image. He can't remember what the image was that he'd wanted to capture.

And there it is, coming out of the dark. A face. An exquisite, blue face. A vision.

He is so pleased.

Until there is nothing.

JUBILEE

S
he doesn't even run her fastest and still they fall behind. To better hear their intentions, she stops and hides behind a huckleberry bush. The friend does all the talking, saying, Go this way, go that, nothing about why they'd want a picture of her. Screaming and yelling for help comes next, then she hears, *Snake*.

She sprints out of the woods.

Pa's heard her calls because he dashes to meet her at the bottom of the field and Levi is not far behind with a shotgun. She tells Pa a right-colored man's been snake-bit and gives the whereabouts. Two of them. "But new-comers," she adds, so Pa doesn't have to worry about dogs and guns.

"Get word to Jeremiah Wrightley and tell him to meet us at home," Pa orders. "Then stay with your mother."

She does as he says, except for the last part.

By the time she catches up with Pa and Levi again, they are headed out of the woods with the two strangers, the one with the camera not long for this world. His face is twisted and sweaty. Pa's tied a tourniquet around his leg to stop the poison from traveling, and keeps saying, "You'll be fine, mister, you'll be okay," which means Pa thinks the opposite.

"It's my fault, Pa." She knows he has his hands full with a dying man, but she has to start taking the blame. She's never going to come away right from this moment if he succumbs.

Pa shushes her.

"But I shouldn't have led them that way." With Right-coloreds chasing, there are three ways to run through the holler—one where the poison ivy grows thick, one along the path that drops off on one side and it's easy for a man to lose his footing, and one into adder territory. She hadn't been thinking of any of these ways to shake free of them, but she could've easily led them to the start of the holler before disappearing, if she hadn't been thinking so much of the picture-taker's face, how it seemed as though he could take in the all of her in one go and not be sick.

"They were after you?" asks Levi.

Carrying his friend's equipment, the talkative one falls quiet and gives her that please-don't-tell look.

"They were lost. I think they wanted directions." She hasn't told more lies in her whole life.

Pa says for her to go up ahead and tell Mama what to expect. Instead, she falls behind the men and begs God to stop time and stall the venom. They are not halfway up the field when the man goes limp.

Mama steps aside so the men can enter the house, then gives Jubilee a shaking hard enough to rattle her ribs loose. "I'm about worn-out with worry. Why were you out there so long?" Mama's love always shows most in her crossness.

Jubilee kisses her grandmother hello and the three of them huddle at the doorway of Mama's bedroom, scarcely able to comprehend the scene before them—two strangers, one lying on the bed and another pressing Jeremiah Wrightley about his medical qualifications. A snake-handling, din-making man of no logic might be one way to sum up Jeremiah Wrightley, but there isn't anyone who knows more than he about snakes and their venom, and Pa tells the man that.

Only a person from a city would bring up the subject of a hospital. "We need to get him to a doctor. Do you have a telephone?"

While Pa explains about country ways, Mama asks if Jubilee knows where they come from and what they were doing up Spooklight Holler anyway.

She could answer that the man had directed his camera at her, but if she is to tell the whole truth, doesn't she also have to say Levi had been with Sarah Tuttle, and Ronny Gault had held a knife at her throat? Shouldn't she warn that trouble is about to follow like fire on a trail of gunpowder? But what if she's wrong? Sometimes the wrong thing a person assumes is all it takes to light the fuse, so she tells Mama she doesn't know anything.

Even ailing so, the one called Havens is a sight to behold. Sweat has stuck his hair down flat, and she has the urge to clear it from his eyes. His large smooth hands are clenched at his sides.

Jeremiah Wrightley spots her and asks, "You get a look at what got him?"

She shakes her head.

"Copperhead's my guess." To the other outsider, Jeremiah explains, "If this bite was going to turn real bad on your friend here, it would have swelled up a whole lot worse by now. It'll hurt like blazes and he's probably going to use that bucket a few more times, but give it a few days and he'll be on his feet again." He hands Pa one of the bottles from his tackle box, and gives instructions about mixing doses.

Jubilee follows Mama and Grandma down the breezeway.

"What if he succumbs?"

"He won't," Mama answers, even though it's early yet, with a long night ahead, and they all know the wee hours are when even the strongest can slip away.

Back on the porch, they notice Socall rounding the side of her house with her lantern in one hand and a shotgun in the other. Like Chappy's relations and most of the tenant farmers in the bottomland, Socall's what's known in town as a Blue-sympathizer, but she might as well be kin. She used to be the town's granny woman until she assisted with Levi's birth, and then the calls for her to deliver babies dropped off. She and Mama became best friends after that, and when the time came, Socall helped bring Jubilee into the world, and then a few years later, her little sister, Willow-May.

"You're to stay with Socall tonight," Mama says.

"But why? They've seen me already."

"We don't know the first thing about them—what they're doing up this holler, for instance—so give your pa time to assess what's best."

"They could've just been out for a walk."

"Nobody comes up Spooklight Holler for a walk," says Socall by way of a greeting.

Everything about Socall is big. She has big lips and a wide mouth, big cheeks, and hair that stands up big and bushy if she doesn't tie it down with a scarf—Socall's scarves are the size of tablecloths. The biggest thing about her is her heart. She's ten years older than Mama, and used to go by another name until she tired of her long-gone husband calling her a so-called wife and a so-called cook, and named herself Socall as a way to show him who was boss.

While Mama goes inside to gather a few things, Socall moves to the window for a peek inside, and Jubilee squeezes in beside her. Accommodating these strangers, the bedroom seems to have shrunk—their whole house, in fact, as if it will not be able to return to its original form even if the men were to leave this instant.

"Heavy on the manners, isn't he?" she says of the talkative one, who is shaking Jeremiah Wrightley's hand, then Pa's.

"There's nothing wrong with being mannerly."

"Folks were being mannerly all the while driving nails into the son of God." Socall takes the bundle of clothes from Mama and heads Jubilee down the porch and toward the path that leads to her house not quite a mile away, listing everything she knows about men and ending on a guilty verdict. "Most men are nothing but trouble, but those two are right-colored, Northerners, and city men—that's three counts against them."

Backed by a steep hill and walled in on both sides by woods, Socall's place is about as hidden as a place can be. Socall has a thing for color—the window shutters are pale blue and her front door a slap-you-right-awake yellow. One season she'll paint her front steps a welcoming color and the next season a stay-away red. Pa told her once she'd made her point on the issue of color, which she didn't take kindly to. "No point in arguing with a fence post," is what she said, something she tells Pa about every other week when they come to yet another issue on which they can't agree. Inside, her house is not dreary or sparse like the Bufords', and has enough furniture for five families, though she lives alone.

Socall heats up coffee, then pulls out a kitchen chair for Jubilee and lifts her hair. "What happened here?"

Jubilee doesn't know why her body will always go on answering for her even after she tells it not to.

Like a stench has come up suddenly in her nose, Socall says, "Please tell me it was not that coward," letting loose a string of cuss words and thundering on about the no-good likes of Ronny Gault and his father, the pitiful excuse of a mayor. Half the town she names.

"Not all people are like that, surely. Some must be decent," Jubilee insists.

"Some are decent and some just act decent; the trick is to figure which is which." Socall fetches a hairbrush and a pair of scissors and tidies up the butchered part. "Your hair always reminds me of a red fox's tail."

Jubilee is debating whether to tell her about the men having taken her picture when Levi lets himself in.

"Why are you two so jumpy? You expecting trouble?"

"And see how we are not wrong," Socall replies.

Levi hands Jubilee a small wooden box. Something shuffles inside.

Through the slats, she sees two wide eyes and a beak about the size of a pinky fingernail—a baby owl. "Hi, little guy!"

"I guess flying lessons didn't go too well." Levi is always going on about what a waste of time it is interfering with nature instead of letting it take its course, but half of her patients come from him. This one is meant as a peace offering.

They both make hooting noises at the baby owl. Socall hands Jubilee her Bible and tells her to tear out what she needs for nesting material. Few pages remain. Genesis and the other Books of the Law were used for lighting fires during the winter that wouldn't quit, the Prophets were shredded for the chicken coop, and much of the Gospels plug the holes in the walls to stop the drafts from chilling a person to the bone, which Socall claims is what the Good Lord intended all along.

Levi slings his guitar from his back, puts his foot up on a kitchen stool, and strums a lullaby until the owl nests down, then pours himself a cup of coffee, humming as he raids the cookie jar.

"You're sprightly given that there are two strange men in your house."

Socall's right. Ordinarily, Levi would be sullen and suspicious. "They'll be turned out tomorrow, so why fuss over it?" he says.

Jubilee can't believe this is her brother talking; neither can Socall, who goes nose to nose with him to determine if he's sauced. "If it ain't shine, it must be love."

Levi glances at Jubilee, who's quick to shake her head to indicate that she hasn't ratted on him.

"And who might the lucky lady be?" How Socall knows things is one of life's great mysteries.

"When do I have time for girls?" Not meeting Socall's eyes is a dead giveaway.

Socall adds a generous portion of what she calls Nature's Flavoring to her coffee. "I once loved a man I wasn't supposed to." She downs half her drink, then breathes out fumes and philosophy both. "There are but three things over which a poor soul has no control: his birth, his death, and who he'll love, and anyone who tells you an orderly tale about love has surely never encountered the real thing."

"There's love, and there's also just someone catching your fancy," Jubilee argues.

"A man can surely tell the difference himself," Levi counters.

Socall finishes her drink. "Here's how you tell the difference. You put on your best face for those you fancy, but you present your flawed self, warts and all, for your true love."

"And a true love is someone who'll do whatever they can to keep you safe."

"Oh honey, no," Socall corrects Jubilee. "There's no such thing as being safe when it comes to love. Give your heart away and there's no predicting what'll happen."

Levi acts as though he's won an argument, and Jubilee's of a mind to speak Sarah Tuttle's name out loud to put an end to such reckless talk, but Socall senses to change the subject. "What's that tune you were humming? Is that a new song you're working on?"

"As a matter of fact . . ." Levi picks up his guitar, flat-picks the intro—a merry rhythm suited for banjo—and sings in the cadence of old-time balladeers:

> *Gaily comes a damsel pretty tonight*
> *Fair as any has ever breathed*
> *Among a starry grove she 'lights*
> *My little lark sings for me.*

> *What can a boy give a maid so fair*
> *I have but a tune and a rhyme*
> *No fortune but your heart, cries she*
> *A love in three-four time.*

> *No pardon beyond the trees shall lie*
> *Lest soon I bid her adieu*
> *Only heaven can hear the harmony*
> *Of the lark and the boy so blue.*

"Well, don't quit there," Socall says when Levi rests his guitar against the chair. "Is he going to bid her adieu or not?"

"I haven't got that part figured out yet."

"How about he leads the lovely maid to my house next week for the frolic and asks her to dance?"

"Whereupon he steps all over her dainty feet and she calls the whole thing off," Levi replies.

"No, she won't, because he'll know how to dance once I'm through teaching him." Socall puts a record on her gramophone, which sets Levi off on a jig around the house to prove he's beyond instruction. Socall grabs his hand and holds it up as an arch for her to pass under, and after a few dizzying turns, she staggers in Jubilee's direction. "We're going to get you all learned up, too, so you don't sit in a corner like last time."

"Nobody's going to ask me to dance."

"What makes you so sure? I heard Wrightley's oldest has been making inquiries after you."

Jubilee groans. Wyatt Wrightley has the temperament of an empty pail.

"Up! Come on." Socall shimmies in front of her, grabs her wrist, and pulls her into a twirl.

There's no satisfying Socall with a half-hearted scuffle, so she sways her hips a little.

"Now you're getting the hang of it." Socall could have made the Lord himself come down off his cross to dance with her.

Snapping his fingers, Levi takes the coat rack for a partner and zips from one end of the room to the other, and Socall chooses her dance mate, a big bag of flour that she nuzzles and two-steps around the table. Jubilee fetches the box with the baby owl. Dancing in Socall's front room must be what heaven is like—just plain forgetting a person's worries.

HAVENS

❦

H e's awake." The woman beside Havens is applying a damp
cloth to his forehead. Her short, rust-colored hair is streaked
with gray, her cheeks are sunken, and her blue eyes are ringed
with wrinkles, and she's wearing an unbelted print dress that has all the
color strained out of it. "He's awake," she says again, keeping her gaze
fixed on Havens in such a way as to make it clear he is to respond, except
he can't think to whom she might be referring.

"He is?" he replies.

She raises the volume of her voice. "He's talking now."

Havens tries to figure out who she might be. Why is he lying in a bedroom with walls made from rough-hewn timber, and not his own, and why
can't he tell if it is early morning or late afternoon when he looks out the
window near the foot of his bed? In the corner are a small table on which
his camera bag rests and a hardback chair that looks as if it is about to collapse from the weight of his jacket. A narrow wardrobe takes up most of
the wall to his right, and hanging from a nail is the room's only adornment,
a small oval mirror.

A tree stump has fewer lines than the face of the slender man who
addresses Havens with a strange accent. "You gave us quite a scare."

Havens has the peculiar feeling that he is onstage, in a period play perhaps, which would explain the rudimentary set, the old-fashioned costumes, the stilted way these characters deliver their lines.

"Would you care to take some broth?" The woman holds a ceramic bowl in front of him.

He can't answer because a pain is gripping his left leg, ankle to groin, with such intensity that he becomes dizzy and nauseated, and he rolls to his side, where the woman meets him with a bucket. After heaving, he settles against the pillow, and the woman puts the cloth back on his forehead before hurrying from the room.

The man takes her place. "You don't remember being snake-bit, mister?"

It takes drawing back the covers and seeing his bandaged foot and swollen purple toes to make sense of this. Havens cannot recall being injured, only giving chase through the tangled woods after a strange woman who struck him first as having been elemental in that setting, regal almost, until forced to flee and, just like that, vanished, making her somehow ethereal.

The woman returns with a bitter drink, insisting it's a cure, so he does as he's told and finishes it.

"My wife here doesn't care too much for Wrightley, and I'll grant he's on the unconventional side, but on the issue of snake bites and their curing nobody knows better. He's been bit a dozen times."

"More venom than blood running in his veins," the woman says.

Havens tries not to groan even though his leg feels as if it's been caught in baling wire.

"Tomorrow we will see about you putting some weight on that foot, but for now you stay put." He directs Havens's attention to the chamber pot beside the bed. "You holler when you need help."

Massey walks in as the couple is leaving. He lays his hand on Havens's shoulder. "Welcome back, buddy."

"How long have I been out?"

"Almost twenty-four hours. It's Monday." Massey closes the door, fetches the chair, and sits beside him. "I'm so sorry. It's my fault. This wouldn't have happened if we'd done as you said and turned back."

"Hey, I'm not a gonner."

"It looked iffy there for a while."

"Where are we? Who are these people? I think this is their bed." Havens pushes aside the covers and tries to move his legs, but intense pain shoots from his toe to his hip, and black spots mar his vision.

"You stay where you are, sport." Massey tells them they're in the home of Del and Estil Buford, then, lowering his voice, adds, "You're not going to believe this."

Havens tries to shift into a more upright position.

"This is where she lives; those are her parents. What kind of dumb luck is that?"

Havens feels a flutter in his stomach. "You've seen her again? Have you talked to her?" Havens must apologize to her for spying on her and chasing her. What must she think of them? What must her parents think?

"They've stashed her at someone else's house."

"They know what we were up to and they are still letting us stay here?"

"They don't know. She covered for us. She said we were trying to ask for directions." Massey whispers about a brother who is also blue. "You should see him, he's like some throwback to another era. I tried talking to him, but the guy acted like he'd just as soon scalp me, and he cleared off, too."

This only makes Havens more certain that they should be on their way without delay. What if these people are not as friendly as they are making out to be?

"Neither of them appears the least bit sick. I'm telling you, Havens, we've come upon something extraordinary."

"The FSA isn't going to be interested in this."

Massey is thinking along the same lines. "No, but *Time* will be."

"If we pitched it right, maybe even *National Geographic*."

Massey agrees. "It's got to be more than, 'Hey folks, here are some blue people.'"

But there's a bigger problem than angle. "I don't see how I am going to get a picture," says Havens. "Even if she turns up, it's not like I can ask her to sit for a portrait."

"Maybe you're going to have to settle for a couple of fleeting shots. I'm going to snoop around and see if I can find where she's hiding out, and you work on getting mobile."

Massey moves his chair to the table, lights the oil lamp, and begins scribbling in his notebook.

A fleeting shot. Massey makes it sound so simple. Advances in technology have led to most of his colleagues using the single-lens reflex camera to produce quick shots, easy converts who now talk up spontaneity as though it were a necessary component of any good shot. Not so for Havens. Part of it is that the stand camera best suits his style of deliberate and exacting attention to description, but also he remains committed to the idea that the economy it takes to produce a single image can say more about a subject than a series of cheap snapshots. The other way to put it is that Havens isn't any good at introducing spontaneity into his work because he lacks the requisite instinct for it, and unless his subjects are cemented on foundations or seated on chairs, he can't be sure what they are likely to do. If he didn't have the reaction time of a blindfolded man in a boxing ring, he would've taken that picture of the woman at the stream when he had the opportunity. Instead, here he lies.

While Massey writes, Havens imagines what backdrops might suit her best. Even against a plain white sheet, would she not make the most magnificent picture?

⁓

Havens wakes up to Massey yanking on his arm. "Quick! She's outside."

Havens doesn't need to ask who.

Though the room is dark, the window displays a sky layered in violet and pink bands.

Massey hoists him to the edge of the bed. "Hurry!"

Putting his foot in a pot of boiling water might be less painful than standing. The dizziness makes him sway, but Massey wedges his shoulder in Havens's armpit and all but drags him to the window, where the view is of a gentle grade cleared of timber and planted with sorghum already thigh-high. To the east is a rippled hillside over which the retreating darkness seems reluctant to relinquish its hold, and above, a sky entertaining rumors of morning.

Massey gestures to the right. At first, Havens can't see anything but a dim outline of a henhouse about eighty yards away, but gradually a silhouette distinguishes itself from the murk and glides toward the house. The woman from the creek.

"I'm going out to talk to her."

"No, don't. You'll scare her off." Havens wants the day to make haste now, wants the sun to quit dallying on the other side of the hill and display her. "Hand me my camera."

Massey props Havens against the chair and thrusts his Contax at him before slipping out of the room. Havens adjusts the aperture for low light and looks out the window, but she is gone again. Always disappearing. He watches the strange land become stranger still, aware that something has been disturbed in him. He recalls attending a presentation once by a famous ornithologist in which the man spoke of the *rara aves*, that rare, elusive creature every birder and explorer hopes to see. A man can't walk ten feet in the world without tripping over duplications and counterfeits, and in any medium the same ideas are repeated in the same worn patterns. Generations of photographers have gone to their deathbeds without ever encountering firsthand an example of originality, and here she is. His *rara aves*. Capturing her on film is sure to bring substantial enough payment to keep the ship afloat a few months more, but the kind of picture he has in mind would do much more than that. It could revive in him a purpose, even restore the very principle that first made him take up photography—that making images is born of a desire to share with others, to connect on some intimate level with another person; to be known, in other words.

Her sudden appearance in front of the window startles him, but if she is as surprised as he is, she does not show it. In the dawn light there is nothing of spectacle about her, only iridescent grace. A shimmering blue-gray, she might as well be formed from mother-of-pearl. Her long auburn hair is tied back with a scarf and her features are a study in precision, and although the light prevents him from knowing the exact color of her eyes, they keep him from moving. Her face is a perfect rendering of two-point perspective—the width of her forehead, the angles of her cheekbones, and the tapering outline of her face have made her eyes the two vanishing points on a beckoning horizon and her mouth the bewitching focus. Even her slight overbite is dazzling. It surely cannot be with the same fascination with which he views her that she continues to inspect him, parting her lips as if she might have something to say, then thinking better of it. He ought to stop staring and yet he cannot. She might as well be a myth, sprung up from the fields, raised by the elements, able to command the beasts.

His heart is thumping. He realizes he has stopped breathing, and cannot seem to start up the mechanism again. Make art—that's what he must do.

As soon as he raises his camera, her expression of curiosity turns to crossness. She makes a stop sign with her hand and dashes off. Havens cranes his head to track where she might have gone and sees nothing.

He is still using his camera as a scope when Massey rushes into the room.

"I saw her come past this way; did you get a picture?"

Havens lowers his camera, letting it hang at his side like a partially severed hand. He doesn't bother to answer.

JUBILEE

❧

You're not supposed to be here," scolds Willow-May when Jubilee creeps inside the house. This morning, her sister's dressed in Pa's Sunday suit, britches and suspenders and shirt, but she is wearing someone else's hat—one of the men's. Jubilee pulls it off her head and throws it on the table and puts her finger to her lips, glancing through the breezeway toward Mama's room. Pa and Levi have gone to trade with some of the other farmers, the newcomer she needs most to watch out for is in the barn, where the lamp is burning in the window, and Mama's getting an early start on laundry, gauging from the wood smoke near the wash shed.

"He's asked after you," Willow-May says in a loud voice.

Again, Jubilee indicates for her to whisper. Knowing her sister is a seasoned eavesdropper, she whispers, "He did? To who?"

"To Mr. Massey. He hasn't asked a single thing about the snake, though. I'd want to know about the snake, wouldn't you? I wonder how long it was."

Her sister's likely to go on and on, so Jubilee shushes her and puts on a stern face that shows she means business, then creeps along the breezeway to the doorway and peeks inside.

The Bufords have a squashed aspect to their faces, but his is long and narrow with creases on each cheek. The rest of him is stretched, too, and his feet stick over the end of the bed. Her feet are dirty and rough and might as well be hooves, but his unaffected foot is pale, as if it's never been without a shoe. What kind of place does he come from that he has to keep his feet covered? Some scalding place, has to be.

It's his hands that catch her attention again. She's never seen a man whose hands weren't calloused or gnarled or missing part of a finger, but his don't even have a spot of dirt on them. No ring, either.

But why is she dallying? She spots the camera on the chair in the far corner. Right-coloreds steal what you wouldn't think could be taken from a person—a man's pride, a mother's urge for more childbearing, a maid's virtue—now these men have stolen her likeness. It's only right that she steal it back. She makes her way across the room, appraising the rest of him as she goes. Apart from the effects of the venom, he has no sickness on him—no scabs or sore places or scars. He's barely even whiskered. If an angel fell to earth this is what it might look like. Thief, she reminds herself, not angel. And yet one who also stops what he's doing to follow the flight path of a hawk and who finds beauty in a tree nature has rebuked. She takes another step toward the camera and checks his face, then another step, and another. She knows the character of every last board in this house, which ones give you away and which ones can keep a secret, and her last step is as silent as all the others, silent enough to hear his breathing change. She swings her head his way just as his eyes open. They are the color of scrubbed floors.

"It's you," he says.

Why does he greet her so cheerfully, as if they've already been introduced?

"Please, don't go," he calls as she bolts for the door.

She sprints through the front room and flies out the kitchen door only to slam straight into the unyielding form of Mr. Massey, who insists on helping her to her feet even though she pulls away and asks him please to stop. She's never heard a Right-colored apologize before, and instead of how you'd think it would sound, stingy-like, Mr. Massey takes more blame than there is to take. She excuses herself, but he puts his hand on her arm, and that's how she realizes his apology is meant to serve some other purpose.

"Can I talk to you for a minute?" he asks, presenting his teeth for inspection.

Fixing her attention on his hand makes him release it.

"May I at least know who I have the pleasure of addressing?"

If Mama catches her here, she'll have sharp words for her, but Socall will also catch an earful for not paying closer attention, and Jubilee might never get another chance at that camera, so instead of answering, she hurries toward the path that leads back to Socall's.

He falls in beside her. "I just wanted to thank you. If it hadn't been for your quick response, I'm not sure Havens would still be with us. Boy, are you fast—you had me beat, and I used to be my school's cross-country champ."

Imagine, speed the feature that most distinguishes her. She maintains her silence and wonders if he's a bit like the Farnsby boy, who can't tell a green tomato from a ripe one.

"Won't you at least tell me your name? That can't hurt, surely."

To be rid of him, she gives it, which only encourages him.

"Jubilee. What a beautiful name. The fiftieth wedding anniversary."

Her name is no big parade and banners waving. It comes from the mandate in Leviticus that after every six years must come a Sabbath year, and after the seventh Sabbath must come the Jubilee Year. Supposedly, all things are to be made right then—debts forgiven, prisoners freed, and land going back to who first owned it. Some days Jubilee sounds like justice served, but some days like Blues will have to eat up more hell. "It's just a name. It doesn't mean anything," she tells the newcomer.

"How old are you, Jubilee?"

"Twenty-three."

He nods like this has taken some great doing on her part. "Is your last name Buford or are you spoken for, Jubilee?"

She wishes he'd quit saying her name like that. She steps up her pace.

"You don't have to go back to your hiding place for our sake, if that's where you're headed. I know what some in town say about you, but I assure you, we hold none of those opinions. In fact, I think you are remarkable." He goes on calling her this and that, making out like she is snow in July.

"I'm just blue, mister. That's all."

"Yes, blue," he says, as though he has just now put his finger on it. "Forgive my impertinence, but may I ask if you are ill—because you don't seem ill to me. I'm curious if there is a name for your condition. Your brother has it, too, doesn't he? But not your little sister. Has it been this way since birth or did it develop later?"

She tires of Mr. Massey's questions. "Some say it's catching."

That stops him in his tracks. Mr. Massey shoves his hands in his pockets, takes a step back, but then runs after her with a wagging finger. "I do believe you are teasing me, Miss Buford."

"I have to go."

Mr. Massey keeps up his questions until he sees Levi and Pa riding toward them.

Bringing Lass to a halt, they climb down from the wagon, Levi stepping so close to Mr. Massey that the brim of his hat bangs up against Mr. Massey's forehead. "Had your fill of looking yet?"

Mr. Massey doesn't seem the least bit put off. "I fully appreciate that you're wary of me. I would be, too, in your position."

Levi scowls. "What would you know about my position?"

Pa cautions Levi, and asks after the one still in bed, but Levi doesn't give the man a chance to answer. "We don't need reporters sticking their noses in our affairs." This is what always gives people the wrong idea about Levi, like all there is to him is the hottest part of the flame.

Putting a bit of space between him and Levi, Mr. Massey takes out his notebook and flips to a page. "There are those in town who have some pretty strange notions about you and your family, and I thought you might care to comment, maybe give your side of the story."

Levi confronts Pa. "See, I told you. You ought to have sent them back to town already." Levi snatches the notebook, leafs through the pages, and reads what's written. *"I don't rightly know how blue is spread."* He ducks out of Mr. Massey's reach to read more. *"You can't be touching the same things or sitting on the same chairs, I do know that."*

"I assure you, those are not my opinions at all," Mr. Massey pleads. "If you read further, you'll see they are attributed to Mrs.—"

"'One place you'll never see a Blue is the doctor's 'cause they don't want folks to know they don't bleed.'"

Pa insists Levi give the man back his book, but Levi keeps at it, and Mr. Massey clasps his hands behind his back and drops his head.

"You heard Pa. Give it back," says Jubilee.

"Here's one about you," Levi tells her. *"'The girl used to be the kind of Blue a person could tolerate until she started frequenting the graveyard. Blues aren't satisfied worrying the living, see, they've got to worry the dead too.'"* What Levi comes to next makes him fling the book to the ground. "We aren't interested in being one of your stories!"

She picks up the notebook and hands it to Mr. Massey, but not before seeing the offending words underlined. *Claims of inbreeding.*

"It's true, people have spoken to us," Mr. Massey responds. "And I'll admit, curiosity got the better of us. A journalist lives by his instincts, and mine were telling me that there was one heck of a story up here, so yes, we came to investigate, but I respect your right to privacy and I won't pen one word without your consent, sir."

Before Pa can say what his wishes are, Mr. Massey speaks of writing about the Ohio Valley flood last year and before that the Union Stock Yards fire in Chicago. "I know folks don't necessarily want their hard times blabbed all over the front page, but we're not hacks," he insists. "I've spent years covering the unfair treatment of laborers, and Havens has taken photographs that brought federal attention and funding to starving inner-city children. He even won the Pulitzer."

Levi mock-claps after Mr. Massey gets done explaining that stories can bring about change for the better. Mr. Massey can surely hear what Levi says when he pulls Pa aside. "Folks in town get wind of us talking to these outsiders and they're going to send a posse up here."

"The man was struck by a snake, son. He can't even walk."

"I can give them a ride to the gas station, and one of Wrightley's boys can take them the rest of the way."

Pa puts up his hand. "I won't have them in town keep me from my Christian duty. We are going to give these men our charity until Mr. Havens is recovered enough to walk himself off my porch."

"Charity? Name one instance when charity did us any good." Levi's right. In town there is charity toward the middle child of Hester and Phyllis Granger, who grew one leg faster than the other, and Philip Burns, who has to be tethered to his twin sister lest he wander off into the hills and never come back, and even a few slaves who passed through these parts on their way up North are said to have received charity, but charity has its limits and Blues are on its other side.

Pa returns to Mr. Massey with one condition. "There'll be no story or pictures."

Mr. Massey agrees without hesitation. Looking at Jubilee, he tells Pa, "Surely there's no point in your children having to hide now. I cannot take advantage of your kindness if it comes at their expense, sir."

Levi says, "You can't take a Right-colored at his word, Pa," but Pa gets up on the wagon and holds his hand out to Jubilee. Down the line, Levi could very well turn out to be right and they might all come to view this moment as a terrible lapse in judgment, but for once, it feels good not to have to hide, to get up on that wagon bench and sit up proud beside Pa while a Right-colored looks on.

HAVENS

Havens struggles out of bed, does a poor job of making himself presentable, and gathers his belongings, certain that he and Massey soon will be carted off the premises. The young woman knows of his and Massey's intent or she would not have attempted to gain possession of his camera, and by now Buford and the other family members must know, too. His hopes of some kind of redeeming portrait were far-fetched to begin with, but unless he adopts the methods of a sniper and sets his aim on her from some tree branch or from behind some bush, even a fleeting shot is unlikely. Equally worrisome is what she must think of him.

He hobbles from the room into a narrow breezeway that joins the sleeping quarters to the communal rooms of the house, and is afforded his first breath of fresh air in two days, along with a bit more of the view of the outdoors. The old woman is on the porch, along with the youngest Buford child, who sits among her books with a chalkboard on her lap, while Gladden Buford tends a flower bed below them. Rather than call to her, he hops through the next doorway into a living area, which smells of wood smoke, lard, and sweat, and where sunlight forms seams between the wallboards. For a crude dwelling in which everything is grained—the rough-hewn walls, the floor, the furniture—there is a sense of order. Taken up mostly by a dining table, the main room leads to a kitchen from a bygone era, accommodating an iron stove, a churn, pots hanging from nails on the walls, and two-by-four shelving on which meal bins and cans of preserves are stacked. There arises in him a desire to photograph the scene, but he cannot risk being caught with his camera, so he settles himself on a chair. The first thing that strikes him as odd is that the window shutters are attached on the inside of the house and have planks for barring them. Peculiar, too, is the front door, which is twice as thick as the walls and reinforced with sheet metal. He searches for clues for these fortifications and finds them just to the right of the door latch—three small bullet holes. Havens feels uneasy.

He is trying to situate his foot to alleviate the throbbing when Massey, Buford, his daughter, and a blue-skinned man he takes to be her brother enter the house, each with varying degrees of interest in his being up. Havens guesses that the presence of Buford's blue children is the reason for Massey's beaming, Massey, who now offers to pluck the nose of the young child, Willow-May, as she rushes to his side.

Buford makes introductions, but it takes some prompting for Levi Buford to shake hands with Havens, while the young woman, Jubilee, does her duty with no display of personal feelings one way or the other.

"Pleased to make your acquaintance, Mr. Havens," she says.

If a statue came to life it would have no less of an effect on him. Havens takes her hand, registers her firm grip, and requests she drop the mister part. Her eyes—green with flecks of hazel—confirm his first assessment, vanishing points. He forces himself not to dwell on her lips, stained as though from blueberries.

"I promised Buford the film from your camera," Massey informs him.

Looking first at Jubilee, then at her father, Havens swears, "But I didn't take any pictures."

"Just so there isn't any doubt." Massey fetches the Contax, even though Buford says he takes a man at his word.

Havens winds the film to the end and removes the canister, then offers it to Buford. While this still leaves Havens with eight black-and-white film packs, he's down now to only one roll of color film. For his part, Massey rips several sheets from his notepad and offers them to Jubilee, who reacts as though she's being a handed a posy of poison ivy, so he shreds the pages himself and slaps the fragments on the table.

These gestures seem to earn no small tally of Buford's trust. Addressing Massey, he says, "I wonder if you would be interested in a tour of my land."

"I want to come, too, Pa," says Willow-May, gazing up at Massey.

Buford orders his eldest daughter to change the dressing on Havens's foot and fix him a plate of food. "I should think you'd want to go easy today," he tells Havens.

"We'll trade notes later," Massey whispers in Havens's ear before following Buford and Levi out the back door.

Too busy attending the lyrical tone of her voice, Havens misses the first part of what Jubilee says and catches only the apology for nearly getting him killed.

"Killed? No, you saved my life. I'm the one who must apologize."

Jubilee brings a fresh dressing, a basin of water, and a small wooden crate, and indicates for Havens to prop up his foot.

"You don't have to do that. I can do it."

She ignores him and unwraps the bandage.

He cannot stop staring at her. It takes him much too long to break the silence. "It must have been frightening to have two strange men chasing after you." She keeps at her task. "I am very sorry for the distress we caused you, but we meant you no harm." Havens wonders how he can even have the gall to say this last part, as though there exists only one kind of harm.

Her tone gives away nothing. "Blues are used to being chased and we don't scare near as easy as you think."

Havens is alarmed by everything in that sentence. "You call yourselves Blues?"

She shrugs. "We call you chasing-types Right-coloreds."

Remembering what Ronny Gault said about blue coon hunting, he wants to ask her exactly what she means by chasing so she can tell him that those bullet holes and her condition don't have anything to do with each other. A dozen things he wants to know, but he asks, "Why are you being so kind to us?"

Now she looks up. "You think we aren't capable of being decent like other people?"

"No, I didn't mean it like that. He fumbles his apology. "You're very kind. Very decent."

She inspects his bare foot, which is scabbed at the site of the puncture and discolored and swollen more than twice its normal size. Embarrassed by the smell, he tells her again that he will take over the task, but she daubs the wound with a wet rag. "Mr. Massey told us you're from Cincinnati. What's it like?"

"A typical city, I guess." It occurs to him that she may not have any idea what he means by this. "A lot of tall buildings, crowded, busy, not terribly exciting."

She wraps a fresh bandage around the gauze. "I bet a person never gets lonesome in a city."

"On the contrary." He wants to tell her about being invisible and ordinary, that whatever uniqueness is not bred out of a man is trained out of him. "Where I live, a man can fall down in the middle of the street and people will step right over him."

"Would you step over someone?"

"No."

"Has anyone ever stepped over you?"

"Well, no." And just that easily, she lets him know his struggles don't come anywhere close to hers.

Jubilee returns the basin to the kitchen, assists him back to the room, and puts his camera on the table beside him. "Mr. Massey says you make your living with this."

"Not a lavish living, but yes." He doesn't want her to leave. "But I also take pictures for my own benefit. Sometimes I see something that interests me and I use my camera to try to understand it more."

She walks to the door, turns around, and says, "I don't want you to aim your camera at me again."

⁂

"It's not enough that this family is treated like lepers when clearly they're not contagious, they also have to contend with vandals." Having returned from his walk with Buford, Massey describes the scene of Buford's sorghum field to Havens. "About a third of his crop has been hacked to pieces, and the stalks weren't even three feet high. I was ready to march down to the sheriff, but Buford just lit his pipe and kept looking at his crop like he was way past getting angry about it."

"Does he know who did it?"

"He didn't name names, but I got the sense he knew."

Havens reports on the bullet holes, the reinforced front door, and Jubilee's remark about having been chased before.

"Bigots," says Massey. "Except they're not motivated by socioeconomic status or race. It's bigotry based on medical factors." Massey wags his finger. "That's going to be my angle."

Up until this very moment, Havens has held the position that a journalist is never to serve the subject he documents but rather the public, and beyond the public, he is to serve the greater good—the democracy afforded by a free and inquisitive press. Now he isn't so sure. "What if we endanger this family by proceeding with this story? What if it gets printed and they wind up getting hurt?"

Massey counts off his fingers. "One, there is no 'if' about getting the story into print. Two, whenever journalists don't report stories because they want to protect their subjects, they collude with the perpetrators of injustice, and three, we have a shot at helping this family by flipping the beast over and revealing its underbelly, which means there's a good chance the cowards will back off."

"Yes, but can we be sure it won't make things worse for them? You print a story, and the bigots decide they've been unfairly portrayed—who do you think they're going to retaliate against?"

Massey scoots his chair closer to the bed and lowers his voice even more. "I'm not contradicting you, but we're here. We're exposed to this story. There isn't a perfect choice, but as professionals we are obligated to tell it."

Havens isn't ready to concede. "You told Buford we would drop it."

"He's no different from any other reluctant source. Once I get him to trust me, I'll make the case for the story, and if he still drags his feet, I'll offer him anonymity."

"And if that doesn't work?"

"Come on, name one occasion when a source turned me down."

"That editor at Hearst who wouldn't go on record about being ordered to downplay the economic crisis."

"Okay, but that guy was a jerk."

"How about the boxer who was bribed to throw the fight against Primo Carnera, but backpedaled before your article went to print?"

"All right, all right."

"I'm just saying it would be easier if these people hadn't saved my life."

"Hey, a dead photographer is only slightly less useful than a morally conflicted one."

"Plus Buford's daughter ordered me not to point my camera anywhere at her."

"Of course she did; she doesn't trust you. You've got to let her get to know you. Open up, talk to her, be yourself."

"Oh, God." Havens stares at his friend.

"Right, good point. Pretend you're me, then." Hearing his name called, Massey turns around and waves at Willow-May.

"You said you'd come and see my chickens."

Massey rises. To Havens, he says, "When she brings you food, talk to her. It's not that hard."

Jubilee knocks before she enters, then sets a glass of water on the bedside table and hands Havens a plate of cornbread. "Do you need something for the pain?"

The sensation is of being scalded toe to knee. "I'm fine."

She lingers while he scrambles for something to say. "I looked for you earlier. Your mother said you went to your aviary. You keep birds?"

"Injured ones only. I mend what can be mended, and turn them loose when they're ready to make their own way. Sometimes I tend bigger critters."

From experience, he knows the chance of rehabilitating any injured wild creature is low, but birds in particular, and he's lost count of the baby birds he tried to hand rear only to bury them in his backyard. Somehow, it's easy for him to picture her in such a setting. "Do you have any training?"

"Learning the hard way."

He expresses interest in other animals she's rescued, and she lists foxes, jackrabbits, 'possums. "I saved a young bobcat once. Pa said I made him too tame to be much good out there on his own, but I see his footprints once in a while."

"I tried to tame a frog once."

She doesn't permit herself to smile. "I'm not partial to frogs."

"Well, if you were a kid spending another summer sick in bed while other boys were at the swimming hole, a frog would make a fine friend."

"Frogs won't eat what you give them; they're stubborn about catching their own food."

"As I discovered too late." Havens gestures to the chair. "Won't you sit down?"

She doesn't move. "What ailed you?"

The few times he's discussed his childhood illnesses with anyone he's ended up being pitied. "It wasn't just one thing."

"How long were you sick?"

Havens spent what should've been the best part of his youth in bed watching the shadows creep across the walls, the tree outside drop its leaves, and icicles form prison bars across his window. He shrugs. "A while."

"Did you have to go to a hospital?"

"A couple of times," he answers, subtracting four visits.

"I don't care for doctors."

"A miserable lot," he agrees. "Next time I'm sick, I'm going to insist on a veterinarian. Those guys pat their patients' heads and scratch their chins and tell them what good boys they are."

This time she does smile.

Before she leaves, she says, "Don't tell my sister the frog story or you'll have a family of them hopping around in here."

"Perhaps I won't need a frog for company," he suggests.

After dinner, they hear music coming from the porch, and Massey assists Havens down the breezeway to where the Bufords are assembled—Buford playing a dulcimer and Levi a guitar. Jubilee, her mother, and her grandmother are singing, and Willow-May is twirling from one end of the porch to the other. Though not fully dark, two oil lamps bathe the front of the house in golden light, setting the family as though in amber, ornaments of another era.

"Pull up a bench," Buford says.

"Where I come from, everyone listens to the radio at night, but this is much better," Massey comments. "What was that song you were playing? It sounds Irish."

"Levi made up that song himself," Gladden beams at her son.

"You're a songwriter?"

Levi shrugs off any admiration. "You can't walk a mile in these parts without bumping into a songwriter."

His mother protests. "Most folks sing what their grandsires sang and their grandsires before that, but Levi's songs are all from his own head."

"Would you play us another one?" asks Havens.

"Play my favorite, 'Gander Goes A-Courtin','" insists Willow-May.

"You're too old for nursery rhymes," Levi says, but the girl will have her way and launches into the verses complete with hand gestures, which she insists Massey learn.

"How about you fellas? We've got Grandma's old banjo inside, if you're inclined."

"I have enough trouble clapping my hands. Havens, though, whistles a mean tune."

All eyes swing in Havens's direction, and Buford asks for a tune, prompting Havens to admit he's not one for an audience.

"We're not your audience," says Buford. "We're your friends."

"Go on, Havens," Massey urges. "Don't be coy."

"All right, my mother's favorite," he relents. After whistling a couple of bars of "Red River Valley," Levi joins in on guitar, and Willow-May takes Massey's hand and swings it side to side. All the while Havens keeps Jubilee in the corner of his eye. After he's done, the Bufords applaud his meager offering. Feeling pleased with himself, he allows himself a discreet glance at Jubilee, who steps from the dimmest recess of the porch into the light.

JUBILEE

Mama blocks Jubilee's passage onto the porch, saying, "You're not bringing that bird in the house."

Jubilee's early trip to her aviary was meant to avoid exactly this. "It's to cheer up Mr. Havens. Please, Mama, I won't let him out of his cage, and I'll take him back this afternoon."

"If I see one dropping."

Jubilee rushes along the breezeway and taps on the bedroom door several times before she hears the invitation to enter.

Propping himself on one elbow, Mr. Havens rubs his eyes and grins. "What a pleasant way to wake up."

Jubilee holds out the cage. "This is Thomas. He's shy at first, but he'll warm to you soon enough, and he's much better company than a frog."

Mr. Havens pats his lap. "Put him right here." He peers through the slates. "A northern flicker, and a very fine specimen at that."

He knows birds. She unlatches the cage door so he can get a better look.

"Well, aren't you a dapper fellow." Mr. Havens acts like Christmas has come early. "Won't he fly off?"

"He could if he wanted to, but he won't. He's been ready to leave for weeks already, and I can't figure why he won't even try to fly."

"What happened to him?"

She explains the treatment for a broken blood feather. "But I think he's lost his nerve."

"You don't know if you've got the stuff anymore, is that it, buddy? Not sure you want to go back out there and risk your neck again? I know the feeling."

Jubilee clears a place on the desk for the cage. "I'll leave you two to get acquainted." There aren't any chores that can't wait, but she uses this as her excuse to leave instead of the real reason, which is she's already exceeded the limit of what to say to a stranger and can't think of anything else to add.

Mr. Havens thanks her, and says, "I hope you'll come back soon to check on us."

Out of sight, she lingers on the other side of the door, just barely able to make out what he says to Thomas.

"I bet I know why you haven't left. You've become just a little bit smitten with your nurse, haven't you?"

⁂

Out on the porch, Mama darns Pa's socks, Grandma dozes in the rocker beside her, and Jubilee finishes churning the butter. It's the fourth day since the men arrived and already their presence is beginning to have the feel of routine. Pa has taken a liking to them, especially to Mr. Massey, who is now out checking the traps with him, and if Mr. Massey didn't know anything about hunting and farming before, he's well on his way to becoming an expert. Mr. Havens spends less time in bed and more time in the front room or on the porch with Thomas, who has been given consent to stay another night. When he's not giving Thomas his attention, Mr. Havens watches everything she does, even the smallest chores. Don't people do chores in the city? Even now, he watches her through the living room window. Finishing her task, she takes the butter to the cellar and goes into the front room, where her sister has fetched his camera and is pestering him to show her how it works.

"Put that thing down, Willow-May!"

Her sister swings the camera at her instead. "I'm going to take your picture."

"Stop, I said!" Jubilee grabs it and shoves it at Mr. Havens and orders her sister outside. "Go scare up some ants for Thomas's dinner."

"Don't be cross with her," Mr. Havens says. "It's my fault for bringing out my photographs." He lifts a stack of pictures from the side table and says, "I thought you might be interested to see what it's like in a big city."

She takes up next to him and scans the first picture he hands her, a crowded station platform that must be a mile long, passengers leaning out of train windows, a man hoisting a trunk up the train's stairs. The next picture is of a streetcar crammed with so many people it's a wonder no one ends up on the pavement. Buildings five times as high as any tree, a bridge that crosses water surely too wide to be a river, and a row of men hunched in front of sewing machines—everything is so foreign.

"Is that a radio?" Two old people sit on either side of a big wooden box in a tidy carpeted living room.

"Yup." He points to the man turning the dial. "My father's tuned into Walter Winchell, and my mother is frowning because she doesn't like having her picture taken."

A camera nosing in on Jubilee's irregularity is enough to make a person squirm, but why would it bother a lady as nice-looking as Mr. Havens's mother, in her neat dress and those pretty pearl earrings? If Jubilee were right-colored and dressed this way, she could imagine sitting for a picture being a pleasant experience.

"I like her hair." Nobody around here wears her hair that short. It must save her a lot of bother. Jubilee would like to study his parents and their home for clues about Mr. Havens, but her focus is pulled suddenly to his nearness, to his breathing, and the awareness that he is watching her. She feels the heat in her cheeks. "Mr. Massey said you won a prize for one of your pictures."

"I didn't deserve it."

She shuffles through the other pictures. "Which of these is your favorite?" she asks.

He plain will not look at the pictures. "I haven't taken it yet."

Outside, someone hollers a greeting and Jubilee rushes to the door in time to see Uncle Eddie lumbering up the path, his lopsidedness making him look like a river bank about to collapse. His left foot is bandaged again on account of the gout, which means he will be in a worse temper than usual, and there's no telling how he'll act around their guests, but if he's liquored up, it'll take a tractor to pull him out of here should he get situated.

"Send him away, Mama. Say we're busy."

"You just stay out of his way and don't go provoking him." Mama's soft when it comes to Uncle Eddie because he was raised as her brother, though he's really the orphaned child of Ma's dead sister, Adeline. Even though he's kin, Uncle Eddie has it in for Blues. According to him, Blues are to blame for the town drying up, for the job he lost, the wife he can't find. When they lay out a coffin for him, he'll blame blue before getting in it.

He uses the porch rail to hoist himself up the steps, sweating and grunting from exertion. Meanness has stacked up unevenly on his face. The thick fleshy ridge that forms his brow casts a shadow over his eyes, which are already dark and hard as knots on a tree. One eye is always unnaturally wide as if it does all its looking through peepholes, the other squinting any time anyone says something kind. His cheeks hang low and are flamed now as though at some insult. Uncle Eddie doesn't come to visit; he comes to have his fire stoked.

Mama offers him her cheek but he doesn't kiss her nice, more like he's wiping his oily mouth on a rag. He ignores Grandma and leers at Jubilee when Mama's back is turned before swinging open the screen door and thrusting himself inside.

"Who the hell are you?" he asks Mr. Havens.

"This is Mr. Clayton Havens, and his companion, Mr. Massey, is out with Del." Mama hastens to add a brief account of how the men happen to be here.

Uncle Eddie ignores Mr. Havens's hand and fixes on his camera instead. "They said one's a picture-taker, so that must be you." Uncle Eddie doesn't give Mr. Havens a chance to speak. "Folks in town have been wondering about the sudden appearance then disappearance of two Yankees and here they are, consorting in my own sister's house and me not even knowing. My, my, my."

"Just until Mr. Havens here recovers from his snake bite, is all."

"Why're you so jumpy, Gladden?" Uncle Eddie slumps into Pa's chair and bids Willow-May to come sit on his lap even though she's two sizes too big for that. "Take our picture," he orders Mr. Havens.

"Yes, please, Mr. Havens, please." Willow-May is bouncing on Uncle Eddie's lap until he collars her to sit still.

"Mr. Buford and I have an agreement, I'm afraid."

"Yes, Del's had Mr. Havens promise not to take any pictures, Eddie."

Uncle Eddie says, "If I keeled over and died, Del wouldn't bat an eye, so why would he care if someone took a picture of me?" He flags Mama to his side. "Gladden's got to be in it, too." He glares at Mr. Havens. "You print your own pictures?"

Mr. Havens says it would require a small dark room and that his chemicals are still at Sylvia Fullhart's, but yes, he develops his own pictures.

"It's settled, then. You'll take our picture and print it and give it to Gladden so she can put it up on her mantle."

There is no talking Uncle Eddie out of it.

"Are you sure, Mrs. Buford?"

Mama faces Mr. Havens with a caved-in look while Uncle Eddie smarts. "'Course she's sure!"

Mr. Havens situates his camera and assesses the window light, then asks Mama to move a little forward and turn her face slightly to the left. It's a good while that he views them through his camera and fiddles with the knobs, and Uncle Eddie, stomach sucked in all this time, grows impatient and snaps, "Are you going to take the damn picture or not?"

As if to avoid buckshot, Mama flinches at the sound of the click and bolts to the kitchen, and Uncle Eddie pushes Willow-May off his lap, stands with his chest puffed out, and orders Mr. Havens to take one of him on his own, which turns into several pictures until Mr. Havens insists on taking his camera back to his room.

Uncle Eddie asks Jubilee why she hasn't yet poured him a drink. "Seems to me you could do with a lesson in manners." Uncle Eddie first checks to see no one is looking before thrusting his hips at her. "You've got a lot to learn about a lot of things."

"I'd prefer to stay ignorant."

A runaway once took up with Uncle Eddie, but when it was rumored that he was keeping her shackled, he took her to church and married her in front of everyone. Two days later she was gone. Ever since then, he's had his eye on Jubilee. To serve as his next servant, she reckons.

Mr. Havens returns, and Uncle Eddie asks Mama why Jubilee's not wearing her veil, with guests around. "Until you get used to it, it'll put you off your food," he tells Mr. Havens.

Giving the impression he's biting down real hard on something, Mr. Havens says, "I think I might get some fresh air, Mrs. Buford, if you'll excuse me."

Jubilee offers her assistance, then thinks better of it—many in town are afraid of being stained or coming away cursed or falling down dead at the touch of a Blue—but Mr. Havens quickly reaches for her hand and holds it as though it were a silk purse. His hand is warm and large and wraps all the way around hers. He chooses the rocking chair at the far end of the porch.

"I have a hard time believing that man in there could even be related to you."

"I don't pay him any attention. You shouldn't either."

"What kind of man talks to a lady that way!" Mr. Havens is riled up, and going on about respect, but she's fixed on that one word, "lady." No one's ever called her that before. "I hope you know that what he said in there is not anything like how I regard you."

She tries keeping her heart from beating any faster.

"I think you're beautiful."

It's folly to search someone's eyes to determine if he's telling the truth—it's the hands that give a person away, big sure gestures. When Mr. Havens delivers his compliment, his hands are relaxed and still, one wrist resting on the back of the other.

"And now, I've embarrassed you," he says. "I'm sorry."

"He never knew his own daddy, and I suppose that can make a person sour." She doesn't know why she's making excuses for Uncle Eddie. She explains the enmity that's gone on for years between Pa and Uncle Eddie on the issue of inheritance, Uncle Eddie insisting Ma's considerable dowry was the reason he was left with only the small parcel of land at the bottom of the holler and Pa insisting that even the most fertile land won't yield profits without labor.

Mr. Havens absorbs it all, and asks for more, this time how long Bufords have lived in the area.

"My great-grandparents moved here from Lexington." She tells about Everet Buford leaving Ireland to escape the potato famine and setting up a cabinet-making business in Lexington, and meeting Pearl, the childless war widow, and suddenly it's not just nerves that makes her talk so, but his being so interested in everything.

"What made them move all the way out here?"

"Their baby girl, Opal. She was the first one born blue." Out it pops.

"Her parents must have been so scared they were going to lose her."

"Everyone thought she would die that first day, but she didn't. Nothing the doctors did could fix it, and eventually they gave up and said for her to be moved to the mountains to see if clean air would cure it, and by then my great-grandparents had had their fill of prying eyes and wagging tongues. So, here's as far as you can get from anywhere."

"And Opal didn't die?" Mr. Havens guesses.

"No, and two years later, she had a little brother, Aubrey, who was right-colored, and then two other brothers came along after that, and both of them were blue." Jubilee gives Mr. Havens the short version of Everet's sending word of land-owning opportunities to his youngest brother, Langston, who arrived in the area with his two motherless children, and likewise Pearl's brother, Arthur Price, and his family, and that the three families lived and farmed and prospered in offspring, offspring who grew up and married and had children of their own. What she leaves out, though, is that one of the offspring is Mama, the grandchild of Arthur and May

Price, and another is Pa, the first and only right-colored of four sons born to Opal and, yes, Langston, her uncle. Mama won't speak of this and Pa professes a muddling in his mind as to how tightly kin is related, but follow one strand from Pa and it will be knotted with one from Mama, and further back, knotted with itself. That this is why blue babies were not altogether uncommon in the families is something she definitely won't tell.

"There used to be a whole bunch of relatives, but it's just us now. I think that's mostly why Mama puts up with Uncle Eddie."

Mr. Havens asks what happened to the others, but Jubilee spies Pa and Mr. Massey making their way to the house, and hurries out to caution Pa about Uncle Eddie. When Uncle Eddie visits, Pa always has a ditch that suddenly needs digging or a fence that needs mending, but instead of doing an about-turn now, Pa takes the stairs two at a time and rushes inside.

What Uncle Eddie and Pa discuss soon turns to raised voices.

"Unless you intend to have her live all her days with you, I'm the best offer she's ever going to get!" yells Uncle Eddie.

Mama's got her apron pressed to her lips and Pa's shaking his head as though he were a wet dog. A sick feeling comes over Jubilee. For Uncle Eddie, with his sorry deficiencies in character and estate, there's no one worse off than a Blue. He doesn't want her; he needs her to step on so he can keep himself from the mud. Jubilee looks around, dismayed to see from Mr. Havens's frowning face that he has heard all this, too.

Pa says he's not letting his daughter go off with anyone, least of all Uncle Eddie. "You can't even take care of your own livestock, much less a wife."

"You're a fine one to talk, letting your mongrels run loose."

"I don't know what you're talking about."

"Word gets out that your boy is fooling around with the preacher's daughter and that's going to bring a whole lot of trouble this way again. Seems to me a concerned father would want to keep his daughter out of harm's way."

Pa turns to Mama. "Do you know anything about this?" He sees Jubilee in the doorway, and asks her the same question.

"Where's your boy now, Delbert? You don't have any idea, do you?" Uncle Eddie jabbers on about having seen Levi and Sarah at the old Granger place, and Pa is still waiting for Jubilee to answer.

Rather than give up Levi, she declares, "I won't ever marry a man I don't love!"

Leaden, Pa tells Uncle Eddie he will take care of the matter.

"I don't know." Uncle Eddie drags out his words. "This predicament's put me in an awful bind, Delbert, me being Urnamy Gault's close business associate and all." It's true that Mayor Gault and Uncle Eddie ran in the same circles as boys, but "business associate" means only that whenever he's short on money, Uncle Eddie peddles the crappie he fishes out of Granger's pond to Gault. "If he finds out I knew my nephew was moving in on his son's sweetheart and didn't say anything to him, it'll jeopardize our business arrangements, and where will that leave me?"

"Levi will never see the girl again," Pa swears.

Uncle Eddie tests his bloated foot before heaving himself out of the chair. "Putting that Blue of yours on a leash is not likely to do the trick this time." Uncle Eddie hobbles toward the door. On his way out, he says, "But my offer for this one still stands."

Jubilee follows him down the steps. "Don't tell anyone about Levi. Please!"

He appraises her chest. "A man with his hands full at home doesn't have time to go out talking to folks, does he?"

⁂

When Levi returns from delivering Socall's shine, Pa doesn't wait for him to take off his coat before he starts demanding answers about Sarah, and how Levi owns up is by glaring at Jubilee. "You couldn't keep your mouth shut, could you?"

Pa talks over Jubilee. "Don't be blaming your sister for any of this. It's Eddie who saw the two of you—him and who-knows-who-else."

"Why do you even let Eddie step foot on our property?" Levi fumes. "You know he'll turn on us for a bottle of beer!"

"You make my point, son, but he'll have nothing to tell if there's nothing between you and the girl except for a happenstance encounter."

"And what if what's between me and Sarah is not happenstance?"

Pa and Mama exchange weary looks. Pa rubs his bloodshot eyes and stands at the window, where he has a view of his fields all torn up. In the same tone he used when he told Levi his dog had to be put out of its misery, Pa says, "Sarah's a ticket too dear for your pocket, son."

"Why? Because she's right-colored?"

"You've got to wonder about a girl that pretty who has her pick—"

Levi lifts his hand before Mama can finish her sentence. "I'm her pick, don't you get it? She picked me because she can be herself with me, because I don't judge her on her looks or how she ought to act on account of her last name."

"You promised your pa you'd never pair up with a Right-colored," Mama says.

"Which might as well mean pair up not at all!" Full of spit and fire, Levi turns to Pa. "Why does it always have to come down to color?"

"Son, you don't think there are some Negroes and whites in this state who wish they could be together who haven't asked the same thing?" You're not special, in other words, Pa's saying.

"Yes, but at least black folks have one another. Jubilee and I are alone. If Gault finds out about me and Sarah, let him. So what if they come after me? I'll be ready."

"And what makes you so sure they'll come for you and not also for Jubilee?" Pa's rebuke takes the stuffing out of Levi. "How do I keep your sister safe? Is Eddie right in proposing I have her move in with him?"

"I am not going to marry Eddie," Jubilee insists.

"Eddie's to stay the hell away from her," Levi says, but Pa's appeal is working. In a weaker voice, he says, "It should be nobody's concern but mine."

"What concerns you, concerns all of us, and we all know Gault's boy has been spoiling for another fight. Except this time, womenfolk are involved."

The silence is like a crowbar trying to pry loose every last portent.

Levi's shoulders sag. "Okay, I'll call it off."

"The sooner the better," Pa adds.

Mama rubs Levi's arm. "We know this must seem awful unfair, but in time you'll see—"

He shakes Mama off. "Just keep Eddie away from Jubilee."

Jubilee should feel glad—without Sarah, Levi will be safer—but there's something about him now that reminds her of the melancholy depicted in Mr. Havens's pictures of people, that somehow what's been taken from them can't ever be replaced.

HAVENS

⁂

All morning Havens has been sitting on the porch with the bird, first trying to give the impression he wasn't waiting for Jubilee and then doing his best to signal that he was. Still she has not made an appearance. Eddie's visit yesterday left everyone in a somber mood, Jubilee especially, and before it was yet fully dark, everyone had retired, Buford bedding down on the porch having rigged a system of trip-wires and tin cans filled with stones around the house's perimeter. Today Havens has overheard the family talking of raids as in the past, and right now they are inside agreeing that Jubilee is to stay close to home and that Levi's delivery of moonshine to Socall's customers this afternoon will be his last for a while. In an effort to reassure his wife, Buford is offering to ride down to Eddie's place to gauge his inclinations, which is raising a debate about the merits of letting sleeping dogs lie.

Something catches Havens's attention. About forty yards from the house, the grandmother is hurrying toward the woods, one hand clutching her suitcase and the other clamped to her head to keep her bonnet from flying off. Because he doesn't know her name, he calls out, "Grandma!" If anything, she accelerates. Climbing off the porch, Havens cups his hands around his mouth. "Come back, Grandma!"

Jubilee overtakes Havens at the water pump, and catches up to the old woman, puts her arm around her, and steers her back.

"Where was she going?" Havens accompanies them to the house.

"She's got her times mixed up again. She thinks it's back when Blues started disappearing, and she wants to go with the families who decided to leave the holler."

The old woman utters not one word, but tests Jubilee's grip every few steps and looks longingly over her shoulder at the retreating woods.

"They're gone, Grandma. You stay with us now."

"What do you mean, people disappearing?" Havens asks.

"Pa's eldest cousin, Sherman, was the first to disappear and no one ever found any sign of him, then one of the Ellis's sons was found drowned in the creek—that's Pa's cousin on his sister's side. And summer that same year, the Prices lost both their sons to the coal mine, an accident supposedly, but everyone knew different. They were Blues, is why."

"Wasn't there an investigation?"

"The law has never been quick to investigate what happens to families with Blues," she answers. "Everyone figured they were on their own, and the consensus was to leave the area."

"But not your father."

"Levi and I hadn't been born yet, so Pa didn't figure he and Mama needed to uproot, and then when Levi came along, it didn't seem on the scale as before. Besides, Pa had heard from some of his kin that they were no better off in Tennessee, some even worse. Better the devil you know, Pa maintains." She thanks Havens for his help and ushers her grandmother inside while Massey, having holed himself up in the barn to write, joins Havens on the porch.

"You hearing this?" he says, listening to the Bufords through the open window.

Havens nods.

"Is Gladden really serious?" Massey asks under his breath. "She wants to recruit some tenant farmers and a few Negroes to help them form some kind of defense?"

"If Ronny hears about Levi and Sarah, she's convinced a posse will come up here."

"Oh, I'd say it's a pretty safe bet Ronny will hear about it. That Eddie guy is a rat through and through."

Havens beckons Massey to sit close, then fills him in on the grandmother running for the hills, and Massey becomes charged by the explanation Jubilee gave, eager to corroborate her claims and drive home the premise of his article, that prejudice left unchecked always ends in foul play.

Havens interrupts. "I think there's a way to incentivize Eddie to keep his mouth shut."

Massey starts mumbling something about not meddling any more than they already have, but Havens cuts him off. "You explain to Eddie that you're writing a story that's going to make headlines, and we offer him the role of hero." Havens has given this a lot of thought. Given the effect his camera had on Eddie, he's convinced it will work. "Eddie's picture in a national magazine with a caption describing him as the one man who stood by a family persecuted by everyone else in the town—he'll lap it up."

"I don't know," Massey mutters.

"If he doesn't go for that, we make a not-so-subtle suggestion that he could end up being portrayed as the scumbag who sold out his own family."

Massey looks like a man being asked to split his inheritance five ways. "I think you're forgetting something. Buford's consent."

"You're going to talk to him anyway, so do it today." Havens is about to suggest they march inside right now for a consultation with the farmer, but Willow-May plods out of the house clutching her doll to her cheek. Except for the dress sewn from a flour sack, she could be a child from any neighborhood in Cincinnati. Customarily chatty, she is now pensive, and takes a seat on the top step without paying any attention to Havens and Massey.

Havens nudges Massey and nods toward the girl.

Massey gets the message, leaps over the porch railing, and calls out to her from the patch of soft grass in front of the house. "Do you by any chance know how to do a cartwheel?"

She doesn't answer so Massey performs a handstand, making his legs wobble before falling over onto his back.

She puts her knuckles against her lips to keep from smiling. "That's not a cartwheel."

Massey vaults to his feet, dusts off the seat of his pants, and scratches his temple. He does a forward roll, springs to attention, and gives a curt bow to his audience member, who is now standing on the lower step.

"That's not a cartwheel either."

"Yes, it is. A very good one, I might add."

"No. You have to go sideways."

Massey makes a show of pondering this before lying flat on his belly with his arms stretched out in front of him and rolling himself over and over, which succeeds in making her set her doll on the step and run to the grass and flip herself over arm to foot.

"How'd you do that?" Massey assumes the pose of a man who does not trust his eyes.

"Here, I'll teach you."

Massey mimics her every move, each time ending up in a contorted mess on the ground, which makes her laugh. When he sticks out his hand for her to help him up, she takes it only to find herself pulled into the grass beside him for a big tickle. Her roaring brings the rest of the Bufords to the porch.

Massey rises to his feet with the girl on his shoulders and pretends to teeter one way, then another.

"Look at me, everyone! Look at me!"

"Get down from there before you break the poor man's neck."

Willow-May ignores her mother and fixes her sights on Havens. "Take a picture of me! Take a picture!"

Massey carries Willow-May to the porch, but she grips his neck and orders him not to put her down. "Please, Mr. Havens, take a picture. The one you took yesterday isn't going to be good."

Gladden Buford informs her husband of Eddie's stunt yesterday.

"Papa, please let him."

"Havens can develop the pictures here and give them to you." Massey explains that it would just be a matter of fetching the developing supplies from the boarding house and using his cellar as a dark room. "Go on, Buford, say yes. Havens has been racking his brain on how to repay you, and this way, you'd have a beautiful portrait of your girl."

"No payment is necessary for what's the decent thing," Buford replies, but Willow-May keeps pleading, and the man eventually nods.

Bouncing and cheering from her perch, the girl orders Havens to fetch his camera.

He scans for Jubilee to see what she makes of this, and instead of paying any attention to the matter, she walks Thomas over to the bird bath.

"You have to sit still or you'll be a blur," he tells the girl. He doesn't take near as long as he usually does to shoot the picture.

"Another one!"

"One's plenty, Willow-May," says Gladden, but the child is accustomed to getting her way. She slides down Massey's arm and insists Havens take a picture of her and her doll.

"How many frames do you have left?" asks Massey.

"About half."

"There's no point in letting them go to waste." Massey turns to Buford. "What do you say, how about letting Havens take one of you and the missus?"

Buford's uncertainty is no match for Massey's charm. The farmer adjusts and readjusts his hat and stands where Massey instructs and squints into the glare with a serious expression while Gladden stifles a sigh, unties her apron, and pulls tendrils of hair from her face before reluctantly joining her husband's side. Havens takes three shots, then looks over at Jubilee, who is coaxing Thomas back into his cage. In a confiding manner, Massey leans to Buford and explains that black-and-white film will make no distinction when it comes to the skin tone of his other children and that perhaps they ought not to be left out. How can Buford object?

"Why not."

"Right, one with everyone!"

Levi will not be persuaded, and stalks off around the house, so Massey coerces Jubilee by carrying the bird cage. "You too, Grandma." Massey helps the old woman to the swing beside Gladden and situates her suitcase on her lap, then poses Willow-May, kneeling in front with the bird cage, and stations Buford and Jubilee at the back, where Jubilee immediately shifts so her father mostly blocks her. Massey is setting up something other than a nice family portrait—he's both winning Buford's trust of the camera and acclimating Jubilee for when she will be photographed later in color. Jubilee covers part of her face with her hand and averts her eyes.

How can Havens put her at ease? If he could somehow convince her that she belongs in the frame every bit as much as a white-tailed spotted deer in a still meadow. "Hands to your sides, everyone," he says instead. A split second before he takes the picture, Jubilee's gaze falls to her feet.

"Keep your eyes on the camera, and let's have a less serious one this time," Havens suggests. When he looks through the viewfinder, no one but the grinning Willow-May seems to know what he means, and Jubilee has disengaged entirely from the process. Again, she looks away just as he releases the shutter. He has one shot left. This time he counts aloud to three, but takes the picture on four when everyone has shrugged off their poses and Jubilee's eyes turn to the lens. Havens can't remember ever having shot so many photographs in so short a time, but with this last frame comes more than a small sense of accomplishment.

⚶

Buford has given Massey a ride to town to fetch the remainder of their personal items, and Massey has promised to return with Buford's consent. Before evening, they will pay Eddie a visit. Gladden, Willow-May, and the old woman are inside, leaving Havens and Jubilee and the bird alone on the porch. She's asked if she can look at more of his pictures, so he's given her a batch of black-and-whites and warned her that she's not going to like them. Poring over each one as she does gives him an excuse to study her. Everything registers in her face, even if momentarily—her curiosity, her

97

sympathy, and now a wrinkle in her brow at the portrait of welterweights at the Cincinnati fight club.

"We've never had our picture taken before," she says.

"I hope you aren't going to be disappointed with the results. People aren't exactly my strong suit. I once had a boss explain that the reason people look stiff in my photographs is because I make them uncomfortable, but it's ten times worse when I pose them."

"What is your strong suit?"

Explaining the technique for achieving high contrast garners a polite nod, so he says, "I used to think I was pretty good at nature photography. But that was a long time ago."

"Pictures of animals."

"And landscapes." He tells her about Charles Strasser, the tutor his father hired to help Havens keep up with his schoolwork, who was the first person to nurture his aptitude for nature photography. "I don't know how much of his own money he spent buying me film, probably everything my father paid him, but we'd go out on a trail in the countryside and he'd be so patient while I shot the same scene over and over, from different angles and as the light changed. Sometimes it was a meadow, sometimes a tree or a row of sunflowers. Nobody except Charles could appreciate what I was doing, but in the end we were both a little naïve to think people were going to buy pictures of trees and rock formations and slightly out-of-focus flower close-ups."

"I would buy one."

He has to keep from reaching for her hand and squeezing it. "The best thing about nature photography is you don't have to pose a mountain or a tree. You just have to wait, and it'll show you everything that's special about it."

She thumbs through more photos and stops at the picture of a dozen or so children in a one-room schoolhouse. Each looks whipped by life.

"Pretty glum, I know." He tries to take the photographs from her, but she pulls away from his reach.

"I like to look at them."

"Then that makes you the only one."

"When you see a picture of someone who's sad, maybe you don't feel so alone."

On this Havens has to set her straight. "All these pictures are of things as they seem, not as they are. People always say photographs don't lie, but they do. They omit, and omission is much more devious than an outright lie." He points to the schoolchildren. "Ten minutes after I shot that, those kids were running around in the playground, laughing their heads off."

"Then why not take that picture?"

"Because those who employ me have certain ideas and they want pictures that will confirm those ideas."

"Must be very one-sided ideas." As she sorts through the rest of the pack, she says, "Folks around here have one-sided ideas, too, and go around acting like their ideas are facts. If they had cameras, I'm sure they'd use them to get their proof."

"I'm glad they don't," he says. Their eyes meet, and he wishes he could promise her he won't be one of those people. "A photographer who is committed to the truth doesn't set out to document the first fact he comes across. For example, if I were to take a single photograph of a barren tree just to propose some irrefutable fact, everyone would agree that it was a dead tree, and not be any the wiser about it ever budding or blossoming or the hundred other magnificent things that characterize it."

"You'd have to spend a lot of time with the tree," she agrees. "You'd have to take many pictures of it, from many different positions, to depict it as it truly is."

Havens isn't sure they're talking about trees anymore. "You've just described my problem." And were he to submit a hundred pictures of the tree, there is always that editor who selects the barren one. "I'm not proud of any of these pictures." He takes them from her. "If I was any good at what I do, a viewer wouldn't feel more certain of the world looking at my pictures; he'd become aware of how little he knows of it. It would make him wonder." If a picture isn't a portal to wonder, it's as useless as a reflection on a rippled pond.

Neither of them blinks. Her eyes are apertures opened up all the way as if to assess his motives, his surely pinholes against her shine.

"Maybe you should go back to taking pictures of what you love," she suggests.

His attention is drawn to how perfectly framed she now is, resting on the porch rail, her shoulder leaning against the post. Backlit, she has assumed an attentive posture, and he's never had a more urgent impulse to shoot a picture. Never mind trees—behold essence.

"Mr. Havens?"

Against the glare of a white sky, she is dazzling, and so utterly unaware of it. If only he could reproduce her likeness without exaggerating her or distorting her, without her one uncommon feature overshadowing her kindness, her sensitivity, her intelligence.

She stands up, smooths her dress.

"Birds," he blurts. "I've also always loved taking pictures of birds."

She walks over to the flicker. "What about Thomas?" She crouches in front of the cage. "You wouldn't mind having your picture taken, would you, mister?"

What Havens most wants is to load a full roll of film and photograph her. Her, from every angle.

"Shall I fetch your camera?" she asks.

As Havens is setting up the shot, she says, "When your foot's a bit better, we can go to my aviary and you can see if you'd like to take pictures of my patients." She smiles. "Maybe tomorrow."

JUBILEE

Mr. Havens has told Mama he can no longer keep her from her own bed, insisting he bunk with Mr. Massey in the barn, and because it'll be a couple hours yet before Pa and Mr. Massey return from town, Jubilee has volunteered to move his things and make up a cot while he makes use of the wash shed. In his room, she lingers beside his bed. Her thoughts have turned to him all afternoon and she has found reasons to go to him. The poor man drinks every cup of coffee she brings him. No one, not even kin, has ever paid her the kind of attention he pays her, as if everything she says matters.

She removes his sheet and lays her hand on the pillow, still dented from where his head has lain. She picks up his white T-shirt from the floor, folds it, then brings it to her nose. The smell of pine being sanded smooth. At the table, she stacks his pictures, wondering about the lives of these people—who they love or used to love, or whether anyone stopped loving them and if that's what makes them all appear so sad. She tidies around the basin, touching where he has touched, and catches a glimpse of herself in the mirror on the wall. What would his camera make of her? What does he see when he looks at her? Does he see what she isn't, what's missing?

She pauses in front of the cupboard where his jacket hangs. She leans forward. It has a different smell than his shirt, more like an old book. Her fingers trail down the sleeves. She lifts the cuff of one sleeve and drapes it over her shoulder, then, checking the doorway, she dips her hands into his pockets and puts her forehead against the jacket's lapels. She pulls out a used train ticket, a spotted feather, and a white cotton handkerchief. She puts everything back but the handkerchief.

Once she finishes making up the cot in the barn, she places a sprig of lavender on his pillow and goes outside, where she spies him sitting on the log bench outside the wash shed, carving on a small piece of cedar from Pa's lumber pile.

"You know how to whittle?"

"I knit much better than I whittle." Mr. Havens slips the wood into his pocket, puts away his pocketknife, and makes room for her on the bench.

"Knit?" She misjudges and sits way too close, breathing in the smell of soap and shaving cream, much too aware of his shaggy wet hair making his collar damp. He explains about his father keeping him occupied during periods of bedrest with all manner of activities, but he's especially proud, it seems, of all he's knitted over the years. He's in the middle of offering to knit her a potholder when she interrupts.

"I was wondering if you might like to take some pictures now."

"Sure. Pictures of what?"

"Will your foot let you walk on it for ten minutes?"

Up he springs. "There's only one way to find out." Fetching his equipment, he asks her what she has in mind, but she tells him only to hurry, and leads him behind the barn to the upper trail, which is mostly just tall grass on both sides baking in the late afternoon's full sun. The hill prompts its shadow to follow them and below, Willow-May comes out of the house and searches the barn and calls for them, wanting to tag along. Jubilee turns to Mr. Havens with her finger on her lips, ducking and having him do the same until they reach the trees.

The forest is still damp from the shower that passed over in the early hours, the cool air smells salt-and-peppery and beneath the cottoned silence is the soft crinkling sound of beetles scurrying to their shelters, plants rolling up their leaves and cinching their petals together, tree limbs relaxing their hold on what's left of the day. Golden beams of light fall from the uppermost branches like drapes.

"Doesn't an old woman in a cottage live in here someplace, the one with an appetite for little children and strangers from Cincinnati? Shouldn't I be dropping breadcrumbs or something?"

Jubilee waits for him to catch up. Grinning, she says, "I'm the one you ought to be afraid of, haven't you heard?"

He laughs, and she crooks a witchy finger.

Instead of forking off to the newer path, which starts its drop into the ravine, she keeps to what's left of the original, much-narrower trail for another fifty or sixty yards, and stops in a clearing about twenty-five feet from the dead end, a granite boulder and the downed tree unlucky enough to have once been in its way. Both boulder and tree have long been fused together with moss.

"You can set up your camera now."

"What am I taking a picture of?" She points where he's to aim. "A rockslide?" he says.

She walks a little ways ahead, turns around, and drops into a crouch. "Aim here." He has to lower his stand almost all the way to the ground before kneeling to see through his camera, and when he raises his head, he seems thrown. "Are you sure?"

"Not me, silly." Returning to his side, she has him sit, then whispers, "It might be a while, but be ready. And try not to make sudden moves."

They both face forward. When his shoulder nudges her shoulder, she pretends not to notice. He turns to her as if to say something, and she leans sideways just enough so he can whisper in her ear, but he doesn't say anything, just holds in his breath. He swings his head forward. Not a minute later, he faces her again. Again, she tilts her head toward him.

"What?" she whispers.

"I—"

"Would you rather go?"

"It's very peaceful here," he whispers through her hair. Her ear tingles. She ignores the fact that his hand is right beside her knee, his fingertips grazing the edge of her skirt. If they can just keep looking straight ahead.

But he keeps turning to her.

Isn't this what he said he loved about his outings with his tutor all those years ago, waiting for the right moment to photograph something special? Why is he so restless? "What's wrong?" she whispers. The instant she matches his gaze, he grows still. He doesn't blink. He doesn't move a muscle, only his breathing changes, becomes more of an effort, like he's become a bit winded. Beneath that fresh-laundered white shirt, his chest rises and falls.

Up ahead, a movement pulls their attention from each other to the hollow underneath the log where a furry orange and brown face with two pointy ears peeks out. Slowly, Havens moves his hand to his camera, but as soon as he shifts his weight for a view through his lens, the fox kit pulls its black front paws back into its den. Of the litter, he is the most bold, but he's not sure what to make of Mr. Havens. Soon enough, though, he crawls out from the den, sniffs around for whether Jubilee's brought scraps again, and gives his sibling the all-clear by sitting down and scratching himself with his back paw. The second kit doesn't like to put up with his brother's one-upmanship very long, and ventures out to nip his brother's muzzle and provoke a tussle. Jubilee nudges Mr. Havens and points to the den's entrance, where the timid third littermate watches the antics of his siblings.

The foxes quickly become accustomed to the noise of Mr. Havens's camera, and he shoots whenever they pause from chasing each other and pouncing, bushy red tails flicking one way and another. For her part, she mostly watches Mr. Havens, who, it turns out, is not so immersed that he doesn't beam at her, eyes sparkling. Leaning to the right, he motions for her to move in front of him and look through the viewfinder, and to her delight, there she sees a pocketsize scene worthy of a book of folktales. Suddenly, his hand is around her wrist. In slow motion, he lifts her hand and situates her fingers on shutter, and just then both foxes look their way, and, together, Jubilee and Havens press the shutter.

She slides from his reach. She tries to act casual. If she appears to be watching the foxes, she is really trying not to pay any attention to his body. He's not bulky like a man who throws sacks of grain all day, neither is he wiry like some of those mangy layabouts who line up for Socall's shine, and she tells herself it's just the novelty of the city, that the hairs on her arms standing straight up have nothing to do with his heat. His arm brushes up against hers, and she thinks she's nodding at him, agreeing about foxes or picture-taking or whatever it is he's telling her, but she can't be sure.

"I've run out of film." Has he had to repeat himself?

They're to go home now. She stands, dusts off the leaves, and steps back to give him room to fold up his stand, and gets herself snarled in a bush. What's worse is not being able to free her own hair. Levi would sort out her embarrassment with one yank, but Mr. Havens unwinds each strand gently, apologizing for even the slightest tug.

"You have beautiful hair," he says of her bird's nest.

On the way back, Mr. Havens is lively, thanking her and asking her everything she knows about the family of foxes and whether they can return so he might have a chance to photograph the mother, and she decides that she's been imagining things, until his hand rests on the small of her back, letting her go first where the trail narrows. She points to a row of mushrooms growing like doorknobs at the foot of a tree so he won't keep staring at the back of her, and as soon as the path widens again, she hangs back and lets him walk ahead. Though he's limping worse, he won't let her carry his stand.

She catches herself stepping in every one of his footprints.

Coming out of the woods, they look down at the farm and see Levi has just returned. He puts the saddle away and turns Lass out in the pasture, before heading for the back door. Even from this distance he looks beat.

"It's not easy to give up someone you care about," says Mr. Havens.

A kindness to her brother is a kindness to her. "You've had to do that?"

He lets out a heavy sigh. "Once, a long time ago." He tells her about his tutor's daughter, Virginia, how she would often come for walks with them, until she turned seventeen and decided it was time to ask him on a date.

"Except for my cousins, I'd never been around girls, so I wasn't at all sure of myself, but she was full of confidence."

Before she has time to think better of it, the question is out. "Did you take pictures of her?"

He nods.

"I'm sure she was very pretty."

Again, he nods. "She had strong opinions and she could be moody, and at the time, I thought that made her interesting to photograph."

Jubilee regrets bringing up the subject. She resolves not to say another word.

"We were nineteen when we married, and neither of us knew what we were getting into," he says, stopping before the path winds down to the barn. "And then we discovered we weren't ever going to have children. A complication from mumps, it turns out; not exactly the news a husband wants to give his young wife when she's got her heart set on being a mother."

"That's why you aren't together anymore?"

He won't let himself look sad. "I hear she's happy. She's married to a history teacher, and they have three boys." They start down the path. A lightness returns to his tone when he says, "What about you? Have you broken any hearts?" and it seems only fair that she should volunteer a private matter.

"There was a boy once."

"Aha!"

She thought back to two summers ago, when Tick Hickman would meet her in the quiet glade with flowers in his hand; she'd longed so much to be loved it hardly mattered who it was that came, only that someone was willing to show affection, and Tick had none of the roughness or meanness of other town boys, not till the end, at any rate. "It wasn't anything like you hear in ballads, if that's what you're thinking."

"It never ends well for the lovers in ballads, does it?" he jests.

"Why does one of them always have to die?"

"Where's the ballad where she gets tired of his snoring and him leaving his stuff all over the place so she decides never to cook his favorite meal again, just Brussel sprouts and boiled eggs every night?"

Jubilee laughs. "And where's the ballad where he stops noticing her and makes up songs about his dog all day?"

Softly, he says, "He'd never stop noticing her."

They're at the barn door now and Mr. Havens rests his stand against the wall. Neither of them speaks. She raises her shoulders. "Well, I'll let you—"

"If you have any other special places, I'd love to see them."

"I could show you something in the morning. I don't know that you'd like to photograph it, though—it's pretty spooky."

He mock-shivers. "It's a date!" he says. "A deal." He reaches toward her and she feels like that shy little fox that knows only how to watch or retreat. "Hold still." She feels his fingers in her hair, then he hands her a twig and acts as if he can't see her going ten shades darker.

⁂

"Yoo-hoo!" Socall calls from the other side of the yard. She's come for dinner. Carrying a pie in one hand and a brown jug in the other, she meets Jubilee and Mr. Havens at the kitchen door. She hands Mr. Havens the pie. "How you doing, Snakebite?"

"Almost back to normal, thanks to Jubilee." Stammering, he's quick to add, "And Mrs. Buford. Everyone, actually. Everyone's been so kind."

"Is that right?" Socall raises an eyebrow at Jubilee and goes inside, where Mr. Massey and Pa are deep in conversation and Levi is letting Willow-May wrestle him.

Mama greets Socall by saying, "I told you not to bring any more liquor," to which Socall replies, "I'll quit bringing it the day you quit being such a sourpuss."

Socall pours Grandma a glass of shine, then looks down her nose at Mr. Massey. "Heard you've been making the rounds in town again."

Pa answers for Mr. Massey, boasting that his cellar is about to become a picture studio, and Socall acts like she's got seeds stuck between her teeth.

"Pictures of what? Don't tell me your ugly mug, Delbert."

While Pa and Socall trade banter, Mr. Havens pulls Mr. Massey to one side, and whatever exchanges between them leaves neither looking too pleased with the other, but soon Mama has us all gather at the table and Willow-May reminds everyone about Socall's frolic on Friday, an invitation that seems to perk up Mr. Havens. Mr. Massey, though, says, "I expect we'll be gone by then."

Nobody looks as sorry as Pa. "Why the hurry?"

Mr. Massey first glances at Mr. Havens before saying something about deadlines.

All through supper, Pa talks about the land, how it once produced hemp to make rope for sailing ships, but when steamboats came along, he decided to farm tobacco. Two glasses of Socall's shine and he lays out a full history of transporting produce on wagon trails first, then railway, then on the new highway built a few years back. Every time Jubilee checks, Mr. Havens's eyes are fixed on her.

Mr. Massey says highways have led country people, young especially, to urban areas. "Have you given any thought to moving?"

"Blues moving to a city is Pa's worst nightmare."

"No, not the worst." Pa's low tone is meant to caution Levi not to test his patience.

"Cities do offer a degree of protection you might not get from a town as remote as Chance," says Mr. Massey.

Levi scoffs. "In a city, I'd blend right in, wouldn't I?"

"I'm not saying you wouldn't draw attention," and here's where Mr. Massey pauses and takes stock of Mr. Havens, who's staring back with knit brows. "But nobody could hurt you or threaten you or prevent you from exercising your rights, at least not without running afoul of the law and getting himself hauled into court."

"It takes some nerve to lecture a man on his rights as if he don't already know them," Socall says. Pa motions for her to settle down, but she's on a roll. "There're two sets of law books in this country. One set for those with money and influence and the right color skin, and another for everyone else." She lifts her glass, a finger cocked at Mr. Massey. "Don't tell me it's different up north."

Mr. Massey wipes the corner of his mouth, weighing whether or not to take her on. "You're right. But when the blindfold slips from Lady Justice, is it enough to notice it, or does someone have to report it?"

"Oh lord, tell me you're not suggesting what I think you are." Socall turns to Pa. "The man is going to write about blue."

Pa is busy correcting her when Mr. Massey says, "There are terrible misconceptions about your family, sir, and I don't need to tell you how dangerous misconceptions can be."

Mama leaves the table because she doesn't like skin talk. Wild-running-at-the-mouth talk, she calls it. To her, talk about blue is never just talk, there's always something to follow it—fists sometimes, bruises, hurt for sure.

"You've likely heard that my son's the instigator, but the troubles go back to when my mother was young, and she never did put a foot wrong."

"Unless you count catching the eye of a Right-colored," counters Levi.

"Not just any Right-colored," Socall adds.

Pa explains that before Boyd Gault became mayor, long before he became Urnamy's father, he took a shining to Opal and set out a-courting her, until his own father caught wind of it. "Boyd's father was the one who'd decided blue would bring misfortune or sickness or death to anyone who got too familiar with it."

"What happened?" asks Mr. Massey.

Pa rakes his fingers down his cheek and pinches his lips together and then sighs the way a person does before giving in to a dare. It's a partial account, to be sure, but that Pa even tells some of the story doesn't seem natural. It's not the liquor; it's being friends again with Right-coloreds. It's Mr. Massey listening and nodding and acting like everyone's one-colored.

"All manner of pressures were brought to bear and that's when Blues were told not to mix with people from town."

"Don't tell me they cited laws prohibiting mixed marriages," Mr. Massey guesses correctly. "That's absurd."

"You have any idea what would happen to a Negro if he even entertained the idea of feeling affection for a white woman? He wouldn't make it to the courtroom, I'll tell you that much, and for Blues, it'd be no different."

"Dictating who a person can and cannot love is tyranny!" You'd think Mr. Massey's been the one given restrictions on who he can marry.

"So we give in to pressure, and live like cowards, which is worse than tyranny," Levi chimes in.

Pa turns to him. "Don't think I wasn't a young man full of starch once, but live long as I have, and you'll realize it takes less courage to get even than it does to get by."

"Intimidation, threats, acts of violence—these don't stop on their own." Mr. Massey says he has a proposal for Pa. "Let me do a story about the trials of your family, the history of the Bufords, along with the Prices and the Ellises, tracing the origins of blue. I'll research case histories of other families that were stigmatized for similar reasons, and consult with medical experts—"

"You think people around here are going to listen to you tell them how wonderful Blues are?" interrupts Socall.

"I'm not suggesting my article will end years of deep-seated prejudice overnight, but it will do two things—those who are the instigators will be put on notice, and those who've looked the other way or been on the fence or maybe even too afraid to speak up will have information and facts instead of superstition."

Socall turns to Mr. Havens. "Does your friend here live on the moon?"

"You're overlooking another possibility," says Pa. "It could make everything worse."

"Worse how exactly?" counters Levi.

Jubilee wants the arguing to stop. "Who else is going to your frolic, Socall?" Nobody minds her except Mr. Havens.

Mr. Massey suggests another reason for his article. "What if someone somewhere reads the story who knows how to help on the medical side of things, maybe knows of a treatment?"

"Oh lord, the man's talking about cures now." Socall pours herself more shine. "Would someone please enlighten him."

If Pa was starting to be swayed, he swings back the other way. "Don't think we haven't tried all kinds of cures. My poor mother was about sucked dry by leeches."

Why must there now be all this attention on what's wrong with blue? Jubilee leaves the table with her plate while Pa explains that one doctor ordered Blues to be scrubbed with salt, another for them to be washed with ammonia, and yet another that they be startled on a regular basis—as though by then they weren't already scared witless. Dipped, scraped, peeled, boiled, and peppered—that's what's been done to Blues, thanks to doctors.

"A lot has changed in the medical field in the last thirty years," Mr. Massey persists.

Few subjects are as tiresome to Jubilee as cures. She puts water on to boil for the dishes. When Mama was laboring with Levi, Socall had to call Dr. Eckles to get Levi turned around, but no sooner was he born than Dr. Eckles began paddling his bottom something fierce to get him to take his first breath and quit being so goshdarn blue until Socall told him that Levi was breathing just fine. "God have mercy, I've delivered a ghost" were the doctor's words. What kind of cure is there for a diagnosis like that? Because of that man's words, people acted like they had some kind of license—license to throw stones at Blues to see if they'd pass through, license to put their hands around their necks to see if Blues needed air like everyone else, license to force them to keep to themselves, to cover themselves so nobody else had to look at their color. Force them not to speak, not to touch anyone, and, above all, not to go getting any notions to love a person.

Pa's giving his theory about blue, likening it to sheep, that among white ones will occasionally come a black one, which leads to more discussion about how a story can change the destiny of blue. There are twice as many opinions than there are people at the table.

All of a sudden, Mr. Havens is beside her. Gently, he removes the dishrag from her hand, letting his fingers slip between hers. "Let me."

She takes a towel, and chances a look at him. He is smiling at nothing in particular.

"Something amuses you?"

"Just thinking about those foxes."

She passes him plates and twice their hands touch in the soapy water, once when she's sure his thumb hooked her little finger deliberately.

Softly, he hums. She looks at him.

"I'm working on a ballad," he says. He shows a great deal of interest in the soiled plate.

Heat's turned her nails dark gray, which means her cheeks must be a deep violet by now, her lips dark blue. Strong feelings can make her look ten-days dead, and letting him see her go from twilight to midnight is like having her skirt ride up and not smoothing it down. She ought to excuse herself. Instead, she hands him back a plate that's already been washed and points to where food is still stuck, and he scrubs it and gives it back for drying, and when he comes to the end of all the dishes, he puts the stack back in the water and washes them all over again. "I didn't do a proper job," he says, humming again.

When it comes time for pie, he is quick to help Mama clear the table, and he volunteers to serve, insisting Jubilee sit so he can bring her the first slice. Rather than take the only vacant chair on the other side of the table, he eats his pie standing beside her.

Levi tends the fire and Mama pulls Grandma's suitcase from her lap as soon as she falls asleep, handing it to Willow-May to unpack. Pa and Mr. Massey have put aside their discussion, and Socall is regaling them with funny stories about the husband she chased off.

"Are you married?" Willow-May asks Mr. Massey.

"Me? Gosh no, nobody will have me, but Havens here has a sweetheart. He's the man to ask about romance and things of that nature."

What lightness Jubilee felt only moments ago now has the quality of ash.

Mr. Havens acts deaf when Willow-May asks if his lady friend is pretty.

"She sure is," Mr. Massey answers for him. "Ask him to show you the picture in his wallet."

Willow-May pesters Mr. Havens until Jubilee snaps at her to quit, and that's when Mr. Massey says, "He's going to marry her," looking straight at Jubilee.

Pa is congratulating Mr. Havens and Socall is filling glasses with shine and Mama is asking if a date's been set, and Mr. Havens doesn't seem to know whether to keep glaring at Mr. Massey or shake Pa's hand or make a dash for the door. He glances at Jubilee and opens his mouth, but before he can say anything, she grabs a lantern and storms out the back door. She marches over to the barn. How could she have been so stupid! Why had she permitted herself to think of him in that way, allowing herself to believe he could've felt something for her? Had the cruelties of others taught her nothing? To him, she was a novelty, nothing more. She'd made a fool of herself! Charging into the barn, she locates Thomas's cage on the stool beside his cot and snatches it and thunders back outside. "Don't you get yourself in a flap!" she rebukes the startled bird, even though water and seed are flying through the slats, and when the bird keeps fluttering about, she flings open the cage and grabs the bird and says, "You want to fly so bad, just go! Go on, fly away, you stupid bird!" From her palm, Thomas looks up at the night sky. Never has it been so empty. Jubilee slumps to the ground with her back against the wash shed, darkens the lantern, and sets Thomas down beside her. "Don't you have somewhere else to be?"

Being alone is what she's good at, what she's meant for. Hurt is what happens when a person forgets that.

Thomas flutters up onto her lap. She makes her finger a perch.

HAVENS

S o impenetrable is the dark that Havens can see nothing beyond the two-foot circle of jaundiced light from his lantern. His head seems to graze the overcast sky, a vast caved basement ceiling with a blown lightbulb, and every footfall seems at risk of stepping off an edge or landing in a hole or a steel-jaw trap, but he must find Jubilee. What exactly he'll say he doesn't know. Perhaps he'll start by explaining about that awful photograph of Betty.

Five months Havens and Betty have been going steady, after having become acquainted through Massey. For a month or so, Betty had been Massey's gal, though she was in every conceivable way the opposite of his usual fare. Massey typically goes for musical or artistic types, foxy girls with erratic temperaments, and Betty, with a homespun way about her, is in the typing pool—a believer in checklists, five-year plans, and coupons. It irked Havens the way Massey would bring her to a soiree only to leave her sitting on a divan all evening, and one night he told her she could do better, not expecting she would find him to be a suitable substitute. Having always felt at a disadvantage with women, especially on those occasions that have involved disrobement, Havens felt comfortable with Betty, competent even. She recently outlined the terms by which she would permit

114

him to go all the way, and to his surprise, he'd already met them, though neither of them would chalk up the amorous enterprise as earth-shattering, he's sure. In learning of his assignment to Kentucky, she'd suggested Havens take her picture so he'd have something to put in his wallet, but he kept coming up with excuses—the lighting was wrong, the lens needed cleaning, he'd run out of film. If he could sleep with her, why could he not take her picture? Determined, he'd set up his Graflex, propped her on a stool, and was horrified to hear himself instruct her to say "cheese," before firing off three shots he knew were overexposed. He never even bothered to develop them. On the station platform, Betty gave him an unflattering photograph she had paid someone else to take. The least he could do was put it in his wallet.

Having circumvented the house, Havens searches the length of the backyard, calling softly through the doorways of the tool shed and wash shed, both of which might as well be black holes, and hearing only the high-pitched siren of a thousand insects warning of a night that has turned feral. Jubilee could be within arm's reach and he wouldn't be any the wiser.

Lighting a second lantern in the barn, Havens notices the flicker is gone. He does not want to get ready for bed. Instead, he waits in the doorway, imagining every sound signals her approach. Right up until the last moment, he hopes the advancing lantern belongs to her.

"I shouldn't have brought up your private life, I'm sorry," Massey says, breezing past Havens. "But it's probably good that it came out, don't you think? It would be a shame if Jubilee got the wrong idea."

"What wrong idea?"

Massey puts his lantern on the desk, unbuttons his collar, his cuffs, and surveys his notes. "Nice guy from a big city being so attentive—*here's your pie, let me wash your dishes*; it just seems to me that a girl who's been a target all her life might start to see you as some kind of savior."

"You can't talk about her like that; you don't know how she thinks. You don't know anything about her! And you're the one acting like everyone's savior!"

Massey swings around.

"What was that business about Levi moving to the city and pursuing a music career? How far-fetched was that?" Havens accuses. "Except nobody bought it, so best you get your head around the fact that we're going back with what Pomeroy asked for, and maybe you can write an article about needing to preserve the Appalachian culture, or whatever it is the publishing highbrows are likely to get excited about, but that's it."

"Whoa. All this because I brought up Betty?"

Havens rips the photograph from his wallet and shoves it at Massey. "Here. You're so concerned about her all of a sudden, you have it!"

"Ah, this is about Jubilee. That's what's eating you." Massey heaves a big sigh and suggests they're both getting too involved with the Bufords, him being especially fond of Willow-May, and that they have to keep their feelings out of the matter if they're to do right by them.

Havens is in no mood for a lecture. "Don't you get it? Buford's not going to agree to your story."

Meeting Havens's ire is Massey's infuriating self-assuredness. "I don't need him to. Levi will."

"Were we even sitting at the same table?"

"Sarah Tuttle's going to get him on board." Massey recounts having bumped into her outside the post office, where she solicited his help and gave a little more context about the banishment of the Bufords and the other families. "Want to know how young innocent Opal was kept from marrying Boyd Gault? By being forced to marry her uncle. Forced. Imagine being dragged out of your house in the middle of the night, marched to a meadow, and then roped to your next of kin by the mayor, for god's sake, while law enforcement looks the other way." Massey relays that anyone related to Opal, whether blue or not, was forbidden from having contact with townsfolk unless they were ready to suffer the consequences, and that even rumors of contact could lead to consequences. "According to Sarah, there were raids to see if everyone was sleeping in their assigned beds. Those three young men Jubilee told you about, who went missing—maybe it was just because they were blue or maybe it was because they were eligible bachelors who went fishing outside the family pond. So, where does that leave you today if you're blue? Either you marry your despicable Uncle Eddie or you disappear mysteriously, which is what Sarah's afraid will happen to Levi if no one intervenes."

Inbreeding and blue people—Havens can only imagine how the story will come across to Midwesterners, people like his mother. "You can't write about them intermarrying. It would humiliate them."

"If Jubilee and Levi are to have a third alternative, I don't see how I can't write about it." Massey spreads out on his cot. "It's not the exposure that causes damage to people's lives; it's the cover-up."

After a while, Havens says, "They'll have to watch out for more than just Ronny; everyone with a camera will come up here and hound these people."

"Maybe," Massey concedes. "On the other hand, more focus on the family from the outside means better protection for them."

Havens kills the light, gets under the sheet, then kicks it off again. Some creature too large to be a mouse scurries along the outside wall. After a long silence, he says, "If Levi agrees to the story, we don't need a picture of Jubilee."

Massey doesn't respond.

Havens knows he's awake. "Unless Jubilee consents, I'm not taking her photo, and that's all there is to it."

⚓

When Havens wakes up, Massey has left a note saying he's gone to Chance to send a telegram to the FSA to request an extension on their trip. Havens dresses with haste and hurries his morning ablutions before doing a reconnaissance for Jubilee, but encounters only Buford and Willow-May. The girl is steering a clutch of chicks into a crude enclosure of rocks and twigs in the front yard, and Buford in his customary overalls is on the porch smoking his pipe and reading what appears to be Massey's notes.

"Won't be long before you're running around on that foot," he says by way of a greeting.

Noting that the birdcage is gone, Havens remarks on the weather, which prompts a lengthy response from Buford about seasons and farming and the toll both can take. "A man may hold the deed to the land, but it's wrongheaded to ever think he owns it. Forty acres can whip you one year and reward you twenty-, sixty-, even a hundred-fold the next, and if you go through that cycle as many times as I have, you'll wonder if the land doesn't own you."

Buford references the conversation from the previous night. "You boys are concerned about us, and I know you mean well, but it's not as simple as packing up. My pa always used to say, you can't outrun trouble." He pinches his lips and draws them to one side as though suffering from a toothache and stares at his field. "It's true we don't have much. Some years we have less than what we were born with, but in my view, a city's where the poorest live. I went to Cleveland once. I seen able-bodied young fellas work in rabbit hutches, some knucklehead ordering them to work faster, and those were the lucky ones. The ones in the factories got nothing but one job, tightening a nut on a bolt. Now that's poor. That's a man yoked worse than my mule. Even if Levi was to hire on, he'd never survive something like that."

Havens says he's not a fan of big cities either. "But a lot of displaced farmers from Oklahoma are starting over again out West."

"You tell me where a man can go in this world and not find people hating other people. If skin ain't the reason, it'll be what God they pray to or what side of the river is best to build a house."

How can Havens argue that?

"Massey wants me to think on it more, but my mind's made up," Buford says. "You be sure he doesn't get any notions of taking matters into his own hands."

Ending the subject, Buford offers to help Havens set up the darkroom. He runs a cable from a gasoline generator on the back porch down the cellar stairs and attaches it to Havens's red lamp, saying he's glad to hear they will be staying on a while longer. "Sure's been good having another set of hands around here."

Havens pushes aside jars of canned goods to make space on the counter for three tubs—one for developer, another stop, and a third for fix.

"Didn't know pictures was laundry," says Buford, watching Havens string twine from one corner to the next, before zeroing in on the box of Kodachrome. Buford reads the label. "*Kodachrome daylight magazine.* Sounds like something you'd load in a pistol."

Havens panics and snatches the box before Buford reads the word "color" emblazoned on the other side. He tosses it into his camera bag.

Once everything is set up, Buford surveys the scene. "All this equipment must set a man back a penny or two." He asks the going rate for a camera, and Havens tells him. "I could buy me a hog and half a dozen shoats for that!"

"Maybe I should trade it all in; maybe I'll make a better goatherd than a photographer."

Buford pats his arm. "I bet you do just fine. But it is curious to me that with all this expense, they send you out here. What kind of pictures are they wanting, exactly?"

Havens explains that he's expected to return with a representation of everyday life for Eastern Kentuckians, at which point Buford thrusts out his hands, palms up, showing the grime as if it has rewritten his fortunes. "Dirt's our life." Buford's eyes suddenly light up. "I've got an idea for your picture. Grab that camera of yours."

Though his foot is still somewhat inflamed, it's functional enough to hustle after Buford, who looks like he's doing the two-step with the tripod. At the wash line, he stops to help his wife hang sheets. For two people who labor sunup to sundown, you'd think they would be nothing more than a summation of their functions, but even in this small task is affection. Filled with secrets and longings, they cast shadows more graceful than celestial beings.

Buford leads Havens past the vegetable garden to a slight rise where the vista is unobstructed. To the left is a swath of chartreuse, the modest field of young corn, and to the right is a stand of scrubby gray-green oaks, leaves shimmering in the cool morning breeze. Directly ahead, bathed in lemon light, is an infinitely repeating pattern of minty hills, each with a hidden valley cobwebbed with mist.

"Dirt will about break a man's back and it won't ever let you forget where you're ultimately headed, but it also feeds you and humbles you, and from just the right spot, it'll reward you with a glimpse of heaven."

Havens attaches the Contax to the tripod, aims it, and adjusts the focus, and when he turns around to invite Buford to look through the viewfinder, the man is headed for his field. Unlike portraiture, the natural landscape is never static, and it is easy to pass up one moment when it can be trumped by a moment of surpassing grandeur. Diffusing the light, a single cloud can pass in front of the sun and reverse the season, rewind an era even, and fool a man into thinking he's years ahead of Daniel Boone. A high-altitude, breakneck wind can race weather across the sky in such a way that decades seem fast-forwarded to some desolate future. He's thinking of Betty. Were he to marry her, she would tend him and help him and suffer him, and he would berate himself for not doing a better job of loving her. What's wrong with you? is the question he would ask himself every day. Friends would recommend a new car, his boss a vacation, the doctor a tonic. His wife would suggest a second honeymoon, and he would make love to her with the diligence of a mechanic under the hood of a car. What is the remedy for the man at the feast with no appetite? Through all the birthday celebrations and milestones will come flash floods of longing to be the man behind the facsimile.

Havens is repositioning his camera when a movement at the edge of the forest catches his eye. He pans to the right, focuses, and sees Jubilee stepping out of the woods. He waves at her, and she keeps walking. He abandons his equipment and races toward her, which only causes her to pick up the pace. "Jubilee," he calls, waving again. Trying to keep from putting his full weight on his foot, he ignores the pain until he stumbles.

She stops, and he raises his arm to signal he's fine, that she's to go on.

"Do you need help, Mr. Havens?" she asks as she approaches, even with him doing his level best not to look the part of an invalid. And the "mister" part amplified like that, a bad sign.

"Wasn't looking where I was going." He flashes her a sheepish grin. "I'm fine."

"I see Pa brought you to his favorite view."

"I'm sorry about last night. It should never have come up," he blurts.

This morning she is a vivid blue, the color of a robin's egg. Whether temperature or mood affect the changing tone of her skin he cannot tell, but she has no less of an impact on him than the time-bending background behind her.

"I didn't take her picture and I'm not going to marry her."

Jubilee shifts her weight from one foot to another and keeps her gaze on those hills. "You don't need to explain your private life to me."

He ought to leave it at that, but he wants her to look at him again. "I think we've just been keeping each other company, the way lonely people do. Until something better comes along." He feels relief for having said it, for exposing at least one of the less honorable parts of himself. He surely won't be leaving any false impression with her now.

After a pause, she turns toward the house. "Well, I'll let you get on with it."

"Actually, I thought I might take a break."

On the way to the house, he asks after Thomas and how her other birds are doing, which of them will soon fly off, whether the owlet has tested its wings again, and her answers become less dutiful. The conversation turns to migrating birds, and by the time they reach the porch steps, she's offered to take him on an outing after lunch.

He trips over his own feet to open the front door for her and follows her into the kitchen, where she rolls up her sleeves and lathers her hands with soap. She catches him staring. "Have you had breakfast?"

"How about I cook for you this time? Do you like omelets?" He selects eggs from the basket and cracks them in a bowl, and she fetches the ham and slices off two thick pieces. Even the smallest movements fascinate him—how her wrist turns and reveals an even softer shade of blue underneath, the way her hair falls over one shoulder, that she bites her lip when she concentrates.

She has to remind him about his skillet. "Your eggs."

After he dishes up, he pulls out a chair for her. She starts eating and he becomes fixated again. She breaks off a piece of bread and puts it in her mouth and dusts the crumbs from her lips. He forces himself not to watch. Abruptly, he snatches up his fork and takes a bite, then pulls a face. "They're burned!" He removes her plate. "Who's ever heard of someone who can't even cook eggs?"

Her smile is high beams, and he decides burned eggs aren't such a bad idea after all.

꙰

Avoiding the noonday sun, Havens rests on the porch, where the breeze provides just enough relief from the mugginess, but not his impatience. Once Jubilee finishes her chores, she comes to get him. Other than a few rest stops to give his foot a break, they spend the afternoon selecting locations and setting up the Graflex. She spends almost as much time behind the lens as he does, though she won't be persuaded to pull the trigger except on two occasions—once for a vine-covered chimney, the only remains of what once was a cabin and which she insisted looked like a hunched old man, and a second time at the spider tree, which he refused to photograph.

"It's creepy," he said.

"It's not creepy, it's beautiful," she insisted, peering through the view-finder aimed at the black gum tree, all its boughs enshrouded in webs, the work not of spiders after all, but thousands of webworms.

"It's not what it seems," she adds. "That's what I love about it."

Even when he's run out of film, they stop to admire and imagine different natural treasures—to her, the fist-sized spiny mushroom is a hedgehog; to him, the slope terraced with deadfall is the decayed rib cage of a giant. When they come across a patch of galax, he plucks one of the waxy heart-shaped leaves and presents it to her, and neither of them has to imagine.

JUBILEE

❧

he men come up from the cellar, Mr. Massey as if he's on springs. "Either you all are the most photogenic bunch of people ever to have faced a camera or else Havens here is at the top of his game again." He wipes the table with his handkerchief. "Go on, Havens, show them."

Mr. Havens catches Jubilee's eye before laying out his pictures. He's been down there most of the evening while everyone else, having been instructed not to disturb him as any bit of light would ruin his work, has been milling around the front room trying not to watch the trapdoor. Now there's a rush to see the end result. A collective sigh of approval rises from the assembled.

She's heard that some primitive people won't allow for their pictures to be taken, believing it to be a kind of thievery, and seeing these pictures, she's inclined now to disagree. Instead of stealing their likeness, Mr. Havens has returned to them accented versions of themselves. Grandma seems like she's come on a far journey, Willow-May sits as though she's riding on top of a hay wagon, and Mama like she knows nothing but to wait out the course of things both good and bad. Pa stares out from the frame, a proud man, his kin portrayed as he's always wished—not distinguishable by blue, but tied to time and nature same as any other family. And there she is—in gray tones, not a shade darker or lighter than anyone else. Instead of turned away as she'd intended, she is clutching the button on her blouse, pressing her lips to keep from smiling and aiming her eyes at the man in front of her with what was supposed to be her secret admiration of him.

"Juby, why'd you make that face?" Willow-May complains.

Jubilee reaches over her sister's shoulder and places the picture of Pa and Mama on top of the family portrait. "You should put this one in a frame, Mama."

"Didn't you marry yourself a handsome fella, Glad?" Pa squints at the picture from various distances and acts like he's being introduced to his long-lost twin, before giving Mama's behind a pat.

She flicks him with her dishtowel, which makes him assume the bearing of a man shot in the ribs. In slow motion, Pa falls to his knees and rolls onto his back.

"Gosh darn it, Delbert, I only just washed that shirt," Mama half-scolds.

Seldom is Pa silly.

Levi, too, casts aside some of his gloom and asks about the process of printing pictures, and Mr. Havens explains about film speed and light readings, inviting him any time to the cellar for a demonstration. Between them forms a place where there is no blue. When Mr. Havens catches her eye, there, too, is a place without blue.

Had Pa any experience in receiving gifts, he'd know to be gracious. Instead, he treats the pictures as a trade, offering Mr. Havens his horn pipe, one of his few prized possessions, which Mr. Havens is quick to decline.

"These pictures are my thanks to you for your hospitality."

"You've done Havens a huge favor," adds Mr. Massey. "It's been ages since he's produced anything near as good as these pictures."

"I guess I just needed the right inspiration." Only when everyone's attention goes back to the photographs does Mr. Havens look at her again.

She ought to do something other than hold a man's gaze so. She hardly knows herself.

"That being the case," suggests Pa, gathering up the pictures, "you ought to take more while you're here." He arranges them on the mantle, and everyone forms a circle of chairs in front of those pictures, as if any moment the figures will come to life and step down into their midst.

Mr. Havens cocks his head at her, and lays another batch of photographs on the table. Thomas on the porch rail, his weak wing stretched out like a lady's fan; the baby foxes capering about; Pa's view nothing short of a depiction of Zion. Mr. Havens has made a story of her world, one picture like the first page of a novel, another like the next-to-last page where the reader longs to know how it all ends.

"What do you think?"

She faces him with admiration. She wants him to photograph everything of her life, to see it as he sees it, to see how he feels about it. These pictures are different from the ones of the big bustling city—she's had no first-hand experience by which to compare reality with his portrayal of it, but these surroundings are as much a part of her inner landscape as they are part of Kentucky, and how he's depicted them is a window into how he feels about them. About her, even.

Pleased with her reaction, he says, "They're yours," but she shakes her head. "You must keep them." That way she can be a story he'll never forget.

❦

Having put aside his songwriting and guitar-playing, Levi keeps mostly to himself, busying himself in the toolshed and making repairs to the roof before winter arrives. Pa tends the crops when he's not making a farmer out of Mr. Massey, who divides his free time between writing in the barn and going into town. Jubilee, who is now always awake before sunrise, races through her morning chores so she can take Mr. Havens out into the woods. Each day he is able to walk a bit better, and their outings take them farther and farther afield. Though the men's stay is no longer a matter of Mr. Havens's injury, Pa wouldn't hear of them moving back to the boarding house and couldn't hide his disappointment when Mr. Massey announced that their departure was to be brought forward. Everyone chimed in when he suggested the weekend, so now he's promised to stay until after Socall's frolic, maybe even leaving as late as Tuesday next week. Futile as it may be, Jubilee has sought to delay their leaving in her own way, finding more subjects for Mr. Havens to photograph, which turn out mostly to be places where they sit and wait for the subjects to appear—nests, burrows, the branch where the baby possums sleep hanging from their tails. Twice she's taken him to her aviary, where he photographed each patient multiple times, as well as her hut from every angle and distance. Even objects you wouldn't think would warrant a picture, he photographed—her water pitcher, the bag of seed propped beside the barrel, the cowbell hanging in the doorway. When he's had his fill of pictures, there is never any hurry to return to the house. Instead, they follow the shade around the meadow, talking sometimes, and sometimes letting the birds do all the jabbering. One of their games is to compete to see who knows which call belongs to which bird. She lets him win on occasion. One time a certain frantic chirping had them both stumped. Mr. Havens said they were the dots and dashes, boasting that he knew Morse code, and when she asked him to prove it, he translated, "In this meadow sits the clever maiden who knows almost as much about birdcalls as the handsome man beside her." She'd punched his arm.

Today she's taking him to her favorite place, a hidden spot, and maybe there they'll wait for angels to appear.

On the last stretch of the trail, she takes his tripod and has him close his eyes. "No peeking."

He covers his eyes with one hand and holds out the other for her to take. "And now, ladies and gentleman," he says in a stage voice, "the fair maiden leads the poor trusting fellow down the garden path."

Getting him through the rocky crevice is tricky, and more than once she causes him to bump his head. "Sorry," she says. "Nearly there."

"It's not an apology if you giggle."

A few more steps, and they leave behind every sound. "You can open your eyes now."

He lets out a big breath at what he sees—woolly green granite walls on all sides and an amber pool where an altar would go. After a heavy rain or during the snowmelt, water will rush over the ladder of rocks and fallen branches, but now only silvery daylight trickles down. "This is my church." If any prayer ever had a chance of being heard, it would be here. *Can't he stay?*

While Mr. Havens sets up his camera, she frees herself of her shoes and flits to the edge of the water, where she peers at her reflection. There is nothing particularly distinctive about her color, certainly nothing that could put a person off—she's part pebble, part leaves, part speckled sunlight. Toeing her image turns her into ripples. For a moment, she fantasizes he's going to photograph her, but when she turns around, he is sitting on a boulder some distance from his camera, as if he and it have quarreled. "Is everything all right?" She can't read his peculiar expression.

"Fine."

"Come feel the water!"

He smiles, but he does not join her.

At its deepest, the water comes only as far as her shins. Her fingers sieve a rhododendron blossom and a couple of leaves from the surface, and she feels Mr. Havens's attention track her to the other side of the pond. She's never brought anyone here, not even Levi, and she wonders if this hasn't been a mistake, because Mr. Havens is now putting away his camera.

"I think I should go back," he says when she approaches him.

Fetching her shoes, she tries to cover her disappointment, and he says, "You don't have to leave. Why don't you stay and enjoy your time here?" Already he's picked up his belongings and is headed for the exit.

Everything she has wished in secret has made her as fragile as a clay figurine. Packing straw would be more useful to her than wishing he would stay and see the story of who she is. Moments later, she's alone, her hideaway little more than a pen. What's to enjoy anymore about being hidden? She picks up a handful of stones and shatters that foolish reflection.

❦

Mr. Massey is still not back from town, Levi and Pa are at Socall's helping her get the house ready for the frolic, and now that Mr. Havens is in the cellar making photographs again, she ventures from her room, where she retreated before supper last night and has spent the morning nursing a fictitious headache just to avoid him. Willow-May has hounded Mama and Grandma into a game of cards, and now insists Jubilee join in. Her sister's games have rules that change with every hand.

"As long as you don't cheat," Jubilee tells her.

"You're just sore because you never win" is her reply.

Mama reads the sheet of paper on which Grandma is supposed to be keeping score. "Looks like Grandma's winning this time."

Willow-May grabs the paper, does the sums in her head, pencils in new totals, and scolds Grandma, who grins and sneaks another card into her lap.

Mama is dealing another hand when there's a knock at the door. Theirs is a door that's been banged on, every once in a while kicked in, and one time shot at, but never has it been knocked on. They all look at one another.

"I'll get it," offers Willow-May, but Jubilee tells her to stay where she is.

When Jubilee opens it, she has to resist the instinct to slam it shut. Even high-colored, sweated-up, and hair all tangled, Sarah Tuttle is pretty, and she has chosen a Sunday dress for the occasion of disturbing the peace.

"Who is it, Jubilee?" Mama calls.

Reeking of cigarette smoke, Sarah says in that no-nonsense way of hers, the way of people who've been fussed over by others all their lives, that she needs to talk to Levi. No good afternoon or please excuse me.

"This is not a good time," Jubilee tells her.

Again, Mama asks who's come.

"He's not here." Jubilee attempts to close the door, but her visitor starts yelling for Levi, which brings her and Mama face-to-face.

"You shouldn't be here." Mama peers past her as if to see whether ranks have formed up behind her.

Either Sarah's been raised to have no manners or agitation's got the best of her. "I'm not leaving until I talk to him."

"You're not to see each other anymore, so whatever you have to say to him you can say to me and I'll decide if he needs to hear it."

Scowling, Sarah tells her, "We aren't all the same, you know. We aren't all ignorant and prejudiced and agreed on how your family ought to be treated, and you of all people ought not to judge someone before getting to know them."

Maybe years ago Mama could have been provoked by such a rebuke, but not anymore. "We don't want any trouble, so be on your way." She gives Sarah that look that says she will outwait God if need be.

"Well, trouble's coming whether you want it or not." Sarah stomps off down the path, and Mama goes back to her seat. Jubilee watches Sarah get a good long way before running after her. When she catches up, Sarah is smoking a cigarette and won't even look at her.

"It's not that he doesn't want to see you, it's that he's sworn not to."

"Leave me alone."

"Why can't you see it's better this way?"

Sarah swings around. "Better for who?"

"What good has it done acting like you two can be together? Instead of pretending you don't know circumstances would never allow it, why won't you let this make-believe come to an end, for your sake and Levi's?"

"Make-believe, huh?'" She takes another drag on her cigarette and considers the clouds before giving Jubilee a once-over. "Do you think I chose to fall in love with Levi Buford? Do you think that's how love works? That you assess all your options and pick the one who makes the most sense?" She tosses the cigarette to the ground and grinds it with her shoe. "People put a nickel in the plate on Sunday and think it buys them the right to order the preacher around and order his daughter around, too—sing this, wear that, visit this one, pray for that one, be better than every other girl, but don't act higher. Levi is the only person who's ever just let me be me, and I couldn't talk myself out of loving him even if I wanted to."

Compared to her firm words, Jubilee's come out jellied. "In time you'll forget how you feel now."

Sarah loses patience with her. "You just tell Levi I'll be waiting for him at the Granger place until he shows up. Tell him he's going to want to hear what I've got to say."

Jubilee is in the middle of explaining that the Granger place is where they were spotted by Uncle Eddie when Sarah takes off. The same determined steps that brought her up the holler take her back. How does love get to act that sure of itself?

HAVENS

❧

By the time Havens makes an appearance at the house, Massey has cornered Levi on the porch, an encounter Havens was hoping to have avoided. Massey had woken up Havens with a sheaf of papers in his hand, a rough draft of the article, which had kept him up most of the night. "All that's missing are the photographs," Massey bemoaned, trying to recruit Havens for a tag-team effort to secure Levi's consent. Consent was Massey's department, Havens reminded him.

Who knows how long Massey's been at it, but Levi does now seem less reluctant to have his picture taken than when Havens shot the family portrait last week.

"If for no other reason, you should tell your story for Sarah's sake," Massey implores Levi. "What other hope do the two of you have for a future together? A lesser person would've walked away and found someone else, but Sarah's a fighter, and she's betting on the come."

Levi rubs his forehead. "But what if my pa's right? What if your story is proof to the town that we poisoned your minds?"

"Their minds are already poisoned," Massey counters. "You're not going to score any points with them by not going on the record. Nobody's going to congratulate you."

Levi folds. "Okay."

"So, you'll let Havens here take your picture?"

"I want to read the story before it gets printed, and if there's anything I don't like—"

"Anything that doesn't sit right with you doesn't get published."

"And Pa ought to read it too."

"Deal!" Massey claps Levi's shoulders. "But let's hold off on telling your father until you've given your go-ahead on the final draft."

Havens sets up his camera while Massey fetches a chair, and Levi soon returns with combed hair, a fresh white shirt much too large for him and buttoned to the neck, and suspenders. Havens would prefer a shot with him beside the chestnut tree, but Massey positions the chair so the house looms in the background, the shotgun resting against the porch post, an obvious prop. Havens suggests he be photographed with his guitar, but he declines.

Once the tripod is positioned, Massey whispers for Havens to get in closer and hands him the Contax loaded with the color Kodachrome film, flapping his hand to signal that Levi has signed off on color.

Two minutes later, the ordeal is over, and Massey shakes Levi's hand like he's won a contest. Levi heads back into the house just as Willow-May charges around the side of the house with Jubilee in tow.

"Pictures!" the girl squeals.

Massey scoops her up, deposits her on the chair, and ruffles her hair. "Just one picture this time, sport."

Havens and Jubilee have not talked since their outing yesterday afternoon, and she avoids his glance. As soon as he takes a shot of the girl, she runs to Jubilee's side and uses her arm as though it were the water pump.

"Now one of Jubilee!"

Even as Havens is unscrewing the camera from the stand and explaining that no one should be forced to have her picture taken, Massey is ushering Jubilee to the chair, and the girl is protesting, "But she does want her picture taken!"

Massey claps his hands at Havens to hurry the proceedings along, speaking of the light not lasting, as if he's some expert on the matter.

Gone from Jubilee is the carefree manner from when they went into the woods together; now she picks at her nails.

"Don't be nervous, dear. It's not going to hurt one bit." Massey turns to his cohort. "Will it, sport?"

Willow-May offers Jubilee her doll. "Don't be such a scaredy-cat."

Havens squints through the viewfinder of the Contax, wishing Massey would quit telling Jubilee how pretty she is. It makes her uneasy. Havens straightens up. "There's a shadow . . ." He motions to her cheek.

Massey rushes to bring her chair a little closer, arranges her shoulders when she sits down again, and tells her not to think of it as posing. "Don't even look at the camera. Focus on something over Havens's shoulder and just pretend he doesn't exist. No lady has ever found that hard to do."

Havens adjusts the lens, and she is studying the doll on her lap and fidgeting worse than before. Massey notices this and confiscates the doll.

"Just relax," Massey tells her, which has the opposite effect. She tenses and shifts uneasily.

Havens runs his hand through his hair. "I think we should do this another time."

Massey asks Jubilee if he can show her how it's done. Exchanging places, he crosses his legs at the knees, throws one hand behind his head, and ogles the camera with puckered lips. This makes Willow-May giggle and Havens cringe. Jubilee doesn't know what to make of it.

"I'm just fooling with you. You are doing great."

Massey snaps his fingers at Havens.

Through the lens, he watches her tuck her dress around her knees, cross her ankles, fold her hands, and uncross her ankles. Eventually, she raises her eyes. He can't bear to see her this way, obliging.

"No, it's not going to work," he decides.

Her expression becomes grave.

"You haven't done anything wrong," Havens assures her.

"No, she hasn't," Massey hisses. "She's lovely. Take the picture!"

"No," says Havens. To Jubilee, he adds, "I'm sorry."

She springs to her feet, takes her sister's hand, and dashes back to the house, a very dark shade of blue.

Massey is agape. "What the hell was that?"

"It wasn't working. You saw her, she was uncomfortable."

"Well, what do you expect when you behave like that? What's the matter with you?" Massey slaps his arms against his sides in frustration. "She was right there, ready and willing."

Through gritted teeth, Havens corrects him. "Not willing! Forced."

"It's the picture we wanted."

"It's not the picture I wanted!" Havens balls his hands into fists. He has a mind to smash his camera against a rock. "I don't want some snapshot to slap alongside your article!"

Massey holds up his palms. "Whoa. I didn't know we were going for the *Mona Lisa* here."

"Not all of us are out to change the world. Some of us are just trying to create something special, something unique." Something that suits her.

Massey folds his arms, rocks back on his heels, and looks at his shoes.

"These people have been so gracious to us—Jubilee saved my life—and what do we do in return? We exploit them."

"Exploit them? We're featuring them in a story that's going help—"

"Please! Can we not even be honest with each other about what we're doing here?"

Havens packs away his equipment and stalks off in the direction of the woods.

❧

Havens clears the clump of blue gum trees, follows the path another quarter of a mile, and crosses a glimmering stream into the secluded meadow that backs up against another heavily timbered hill. He passes a broad canopied tree sprayed in tiny pink blossoms and humming with bees, and even before he reaches her little wooden shed, he can hear her singing. Like the first time he happened upon her, he feels he ought to call out some warning.

Again, he does not. Coming here uninvited is an intrusion on her privacy and part of him thinks to turn back, but the weaker part of him, the part that has come to dominate every thought and action, compels him forward.

Morning rays spill from the doorway. Wearing her pale yellow cotton dress and work boots, Jubilee is cleaning the cages of chickadees and finches, and before he can greet her, the northern flicker gives him away with a warning cheep.

She spins around, using her hand as an awning for her eyes. "Mr. Havens."

He can't think how people start conversations. "How are the patients today?"

"On the mend. But I don't think anyone wants to be photographed." She spies his camera bag, and he casts it aside hastily.

"I came to apologize. You shouldn't have been put on the spot—"

"Willow-May's the one for pictures," she interrupts, "not me."

He attempts to explain that she wasn't the problem, but again she cuts him off. "Yesterday you made it very clear why you won't shoot certain pictures."

She can only be referring to his refusal to photograph the spider tree. My God, he thinks, I've made her feel hideous. "Jubilee, no. That's not it at all!"

With her back to him, she resumes lining the cages with old newspaper.

"I do very much want to take your picture! Please believe me!" In his appeal, he describes the purpose of setting, how every detail must serve as context for the subject. "I looked through that lens, and it was all wrong. Nothing complemented you."

She pivots around. "Then what about at the pool? What was wrong with that setting?"

Havens drops his head, sighing. She's right. In that nave, he realized she belonged to the natural world and the natural world to her, and only a photograph that illustrated that relationship could do her any justice. Does he admit this to her? That with his epiphany came an almost irrepressible desire to photograph her in that moment, and that he knew if he captured her right then there wouldn't be anything he could not photograph, that he wouldn't be shackled anymore to his failures, his doubt, his lack? But however sublime, the moment would have been self-serving, almost predatory. To display her in that way would be to make her his *rara aves*, his conquest, his crowning achievement, and she has become much more to him than that.

Having grown tired of waiting for a rebuttal, she fills bowls with birdseed.

"I did very much want to take your picture yesterday, do want to."

She scoffs. "Because you feel sorry for me now. So I'll feel like a regular girl like the one in your wallet."

He snatches his camera from the bag and offers it to her like a surrendered weapon. "Take it."

She frowns.

He forces it in her hands and says, "Now throw it down. Please just break the damn thing."

This takes her off-guard. Shaking her head, she says, "I'm not going to break your camera."

"I want to capture the way I feel about you, not just how I see you. If you don't believe that, I don't want to keep it. Give it to me. I'll break it."

"No," she says, putting the strap over her head. Even so slight a smile bends the light.

"I'm a phony," he confesses. "All I ever do is stage the commonplace to appear extraordinary, and since I've met you and spent time with you, I want to be a better version of myself, or maybe return to an earlier version. Being with you has given me back a little faith in myself, and no regular girl could do that."

The breeze blows a strand of auburn hair across her violet lips, and reflexively, he reaches for it and tucks it behind her ear. He allows his fingers to graze her cheek.

The longer she looks at him, the further away she seems to get. Neither of them moves, and she seems to be looking at Havens from a distance greater than three feet. Suddenly she slips past his grasp and flits outside with his camera. He follows her, but she skips a few steps ahead. Turning toward him, she lifts the camera to her face and he waves his arm at her to stop. She takes two steps backward. He keeps telling her no, which makes her more adamant.

"Oh, go ahead then, take my picture, that's one way to break the damn thing."

She looks for the trigger, then puts the camera at eye level again. He puts his fists on his hips and thrusts out his chin.

He hears the click. "Right, it's broken. Can we throw it away now?"

"Another one."

"But I have only one pose."

"It's not a terrible one."

This time he offers his side profile and a ridiculous pose. Anything to have her smile.

When he faces her again, she has taken a step closer. She still has the camera up to her face, but she is not teasing him anymore. He drops his hands. He presents himself to her.

She lowers the camera an inch, looks at him over its rim.

He has the urge to unbutton his shirt, unhook his ribs, show her his heart.

The camera is at her waist now. Her examination of him peels away layers of guilt and shame, bleaches his bones. She takes another step nearer, and then another, and he can only stand and watch.

Between them now is a space wide enough only for weather to pass through, if wind or sunlight had the nerve. He can feel her breath, the heat of her body. Her fingers reach for his. Her touch is so slight. With her eyes locked on his, she opens his hand all the way. She grazes his palm with her fingertips, and he leans toward her. She presses the camera in his hand and folds his hand over it.

She whispers into his lips. "Take my picture."

Matching her shallow breath, he tells her quietly, "No."

"Take it."

The air is so still. Nothing moves around them. Static has built up between them from the great friction of things being pulled into stillness.

The air is charged, they are charged. Havens could stand this way forever. Her knee brushes up against his leg. By an ancient instinct and against his better judgment, he circles her waist with his arm. *What am I doing? Let go of her.* But his arm will not obey and his hand will not submit and his strength will not succumb to reason. He ropes her into his chest. His legs become posts. With her in his arms, he could support the weight of buildings. He will not be moved.

"If only I could loan everyone my eyes." This beautiful woman who restores creatures and strangers alike.

She twists from his grip. "Take my picture." She lays her hand on the side of her neck, looks at him, then starts to tilt away.

It is surely easier to lift a bridge off its foundations than raise the camera still loaded with color film, and yet he does. He looks through the view-finder and feels caught in a prism of blue light. He can no more assess her than he can assess the air after a thunderstorm, and her color now seems only to be a small part of this. Such unspoiled goodness will make a man want to pull rainbows from the sky and tie them around her neck.

Instead, he has to press the shutter.

How does he not fail her?

Hearing the click, she beams at him and turns.

He presses the shutter.

He presses the shutter.

He forsakes every good sense calling for him to stop.

He presses the shutter.

❦

Once he starts taking pictures of her, he cannot stop. They say Monet painted Camille every day, right up until the time she drew her last breath. Havens understands that compulsion. As soon as they return from the aviary, he hears that Massey has gone to interview sharecroppers in the neighboring holler, so he trades the Contax for the Graflex, grabs several cartridges of black-and-white film, and rushes to find

Jubilee again. She is sitting on the flat white rock near the corner of the house, her back to him, a sprig of lilac in her hair, talking to Willow-May. He sets up his camera in record speed. In photographing subjects, Havens has always been a patient man. Used to be. Now he can't wait two seconds before firing. He calls to her, and she wrinkles her nose at him before turning back to her sister. He releases the shutter again.

Not just one, but every photograph he has ever taken is a hoax compared to these. He doesn't have to develop them to know each is a keeper. He is impulsive, firing away, with every frame feeling himself change from witness to participant. Now only three feet away from her, he photographs the tilt of her head, her hand mid-gesture. Two feet away, he takes a close-up of her elbow, her splayed fingers, several shots of her hair falling out of its braid. He forgoes adjusting the f-stop or fiddling with the focus or making sure the horizon is straight. What he is photographing is not only her but her effect on him. Photographing her as she watches the sun drop down from the cloud bank like a rope of light onto the pasture feels like light is breaking through in him, too. When he takes a picture of her bending to unbuckle her shoes, he feels something inside him being unbuckled, and every time she faces him, it's as if she reaches through the lens, pries open the aperture, and leaves her fingerprints on his heart. Picture after picture, he is letting her touch him. What he is photographing is the process of her taking possession of his heart. Here she sits, a thief, laughing and tossing her hair, with his heart in her lap.

JUBILEE

✤

Having slept hardly at all, Jubilee forsakes her bed as soon as the first bird starts to sing, dresses quickly in the dark, grabs her shoes, and tiptoes barefoot out the back door in time to see the gibbous moon set behind the prow of the hill. She pauses beside the barn door, and hearing no signs of stirring, pads along the damp earth to the privy and then the wash shed.

Havens startles her when she comes out. "Good morning!"

"I was worried you'd still be sleeping."

"Nope, I've been waiting for you." Grinning, he holds up the basket of eggs and tells her he's made all the hens mad at him. She deposits the basket at the kitchen door, and they hurry to the start of the trail behind the barn, where he takes her hand and leads the way, and she acts as if this is the most natural thing in the world. Nobody would guess his foot was poisoned two and a half weeks ago the way he bounds along now. Halfway up the hill, she realizes he doesn't have a camera with him and offers to run back for it, and he says, "Just us this time."

At the crest, they find a flat rock that'll seat two, and he lays down his jacket for her. Shoulder to shoulder, they face the horizon, an orange sash sewn to the hem of a faded blue hoopskirt. Though this is what they agreed on last night, she doesn't want the sun to come up anymore. Put a padlock on it. Handcuff the hands of his watch, too.

"I don't want to go." He squeezes her fingers. "How am I supposed to leave this place and forget you, Jubilee Buford?"

"The same way I'm to stay and forget about you."

"You have an easy task, but mine is impossible."

She's tempted to tell him her nighttime thoughts, how she's going to be an old woman one day and the moths will have eaten away her memory so she won't perhaps remember the names of people she knows or how the birds used to eat from her hand, but this man will be safe from time because she will have tucked him beneath memory, stored him in that place where blood takes its orders to flow and lungs to fill and eyes to empty themselves of tears.

From the pocket of her apron, she pulls out his handkerchief, which she had planned to give him at the time of his departure. "I made you a present."

"Thomas! And he's flying," he exclaims at the little bird she embroidered on one corner, his grin tapering off, maybe at the prospect of his own beckoning skies.

"I'm not going to be home when it comes time to say goodbye," she announces. "It'll be easier that way."

After a long pause, he says, "We can let Socall's frolic be our farewell. That is, if you are going to permit me a dance?"

"If you don't mind having your feet trampled on."

A match head strikes the flinty horizon, its flare turning every late-sleeper into a raucous minstrel, and while they are serenaded by the creatures of hill and vale, that which cannot be wells between them.

Before they set back down the path, he asks her to close her eyes. He presses something in her palm. "I wish I had something precious to give you."

It's a birdcall whittled into the shape of a nesting bird and threaded with yarn.

"It's a bit piercing, I'm afraid." He slips it over her head. "Try it out."

She puts it to her lips and blows a high, lonely wishing-note meant to journey hundreds of miles north. "Will you hear that?" In the golden light, she faces him straight-on, all of her blue and unashamed. She presents herself as though she's never been a hunted thing, as though there's never been a time when a Right-colored didn't come for her at a clip. She stands as though she and he were formed by the same hands.

He lifts her wrist, studies her fingers, rubs his thumb across each of her midnight nails before pressing her palm against his chest. "Do you feel that?"

Swung about and set back down on one foot is what she feels. Running at full speed, shoes flying off, breathing so hard it burns. Pricked awake and dreaming both.

"I don't know what to do about it," he says.

They say to starve a fever.

"Fix it," he whispers.

She splays her fingers and drives the heel of her hand against his chest. She lets her forehead fall against his chest, breathes in his smell, and closes her eyes as his hands fold around her head. He strokes her hair. Eventually, she lifts her head and raps her knuckles against his chest, softly at first, then harder.

He puts her fist against his mouth. Her fingertips unfurl and touch his lips as if to read what is too soft for her to hear. He kisses her hushing fingers, and she rises on tiptoe so he can kiss her mouth. He isn't a greedy man. He kisses like a man eating the last peach of the season, pausing halfway, and then savoring the rest.

❦

Mama meets Jubilee at the back door. Jubilee knows she's late for her chores, but Mama doesn't wait for her to finish apologizing.

"Where've you been?"

One small hesitation, and Mama's on to her. "I told your pa it was a mistake to let you spend so much time with him. No chaperone, even."

"Nothing happened, Mama. We're friends." As if even friends isn't the biggest thing ever to have happened to her.

"A pair ought to be yoked evenly or it ends up with one always owing the other," she says. "Have you not heard me and your pa getting Levi to understand that?"

"Loving isn't two mules plowing, Mama."

Mama's cold assessment goes on too long. "Don't you go mistaking that man's attention for affection, Jubilee Buford." Mama says the word "affection" as though it were a rusty nail Jubilee's foot was about to come down on.

HAVENS

⁂

In the cellar, Havens has Jubilee stand beside him as he pours into three separate basins the developer, the short stop, and the fix, explaining each step. "Just as long as I get to say which ones of me get thrown away," she insists.

Though he is impatient for each image to appear, he works with diligence, carefully dipping and bathing the sheets before handing them to her to hang up to dry. In the red glow, they marvel at the landscape shots—the spindly trees gathered on each side of the brook, bending toward one another like relatives at a reunion; the premature moon rising above the piney spires; the one Jubilee insisted would be worth the wait, an elk buck emerging from the morning fog.

"These are so good!"

He's never taken better photographs. "It's your doing." Photographing with her has made him find his calling again. With haste, he develops another batch, eager for the portraits of Jubilee, and what he said before about photographs not being facts, he ought now to retract. Her surroundings seem to crane and bend just so they can be included in the frame with her. The mountains deserve credit for showing scale, for showing both how delicate and commanding a person she is. Trees dress themselves in sheen as an act of solidarity with her light, dewdrops reflect the sincerity in her eyes. The horizon, too, must be credited. A man could follow it all the way around and back to this same spot and not meet anyone as wondrous.

He studies each one. "Nothing I've ever done can compare with these."

That she doesn't have any reaction makes him worry, until she covers her smile with her hand.

Aim a beam of light at a prism and it will refract a rainbow, the short blue wavelength bending the most, but Havens's pictures reveal the reverse: Jubilee is a prism through which all colors enter and are fused and are emitted back into the world as a beam of bright white light. He gestures to the one where she is sticking her tongue out at him. "Now, there's a trouble-maker."

She retaliates by pointing to the photograph she took of him at her aviary. "You look so serious."

"Being a male model is serious."

She asks if she may keep it, and he asks her to choose any of the others, too, and while she considers her selection, he moves behind her. "I'm going to come back and visit you and give you another chance to take a better picture of me."

She turns her head to the side. "You are?"

"Soon," he says. "Before you change your mind about me." He gathers her braid in his hand. She doesn't move, doesn't tell him no, so he turns his wrist under it, then drapes it over his shoulder as he bends his head to her neck. She smells like damp freshly fallen leaves. He wants to do what any man since the beginning of time has wanted to do with the woman who has taken hold of his heart, but he also wants to pay tribute to her uniqueness. She is not any woman. For the life of him, though, he cannot think of one original gesture, and so he does what he cannot keep from doing. He hooks his finger into the neckline of her dress and pulls it slightly to one side, and as she shifts her weight to her heels, he kisses the curve where her neck and shoulder meet, where she holds herself together in such a taut line. There is a small shiver in her, and a deep riving in him. He moves his mouth back up to her neck, parting his lips so she can feel his breath, so he can taste her skin. He kisses the tip of her ear. Her arms drop loosely at her sides. He reaches down and finds her right hand. She splays her fingers, and he weaves his between them. "Don't forget what we have."

Above them is a knock on the trapdoor. "Havens, you down there?"

They startle apart. Jubilee dashes up the stairs past Massey, who rushes down, flapping a telegram. He waits for the trapdoor to swing shut, then announces, "We've got an offer! A cover story!" Only now does he survey the wash line of photographs. He whistles. "Oh my God, you've become obsessed with her."

Possessed is what Havens is. Dispossessed. No longer are all his vital parts under his control. They have a new owner—ask any toe, any artery, any nerve.

Havens snatches the telegram from Massey's hand. "*Look* magazine? They're not going to want a story about prejudice and social justice."

"*Look, Time, The New York Times, National Geographic*—they're all expressing serious interest!"

"*Look* will only want the shock value," Havens keeps insisting, still having trouble registering that Massey has even made contact with these publications.

"We want a guarantee on a cover, and *Look* was the first to offer one, which is our leverage with the others." Massey can't keep from being distracted by the photographs.

"But you were supposed to wait till we got back to Cincinnati. You weren't going to send telegrams. What if Buford gets wind of this?"

"Who's going to tell him?" Massey crosses his arms.

"It's a small town! People talk!"

"Well, things are heating up in town and I didn't think we could risk delaying getting the story out there." He holds up his palms as if to say, Guilty.

"You haven't given a copy of your article to Levi yet—what if he backs out? Or is this you going it alone again?"

"Who else is going to take the lead? Tell me? Because all I see is you out taking pictures"—he gestures at the line of photographs—"of gimp birds and bunny rabbits, so yes, I took the initiative!"

Havens lunges at him, driving him backward. "We're going to town right now and you're going to send a telegram saying the deal's off!"

"We can't call it off. They'll just send someone else up here to do the story, and they won't give it half the justice it deserves."

Havens feels winded. Each of those news agencies knows the Bufords' location now.

"Then we're going to come clean with Levi and Buford."

Massey drops his head. "It won't do any good." What he doesn't need to spell out is that Levi's consent is no longer a factor.

Havens gets Massey by the forearms and shakes him. "What the hell have you done!"

Ripping himself free, Massey insists Havens collect himself.

"My father grumbled day and night about how the railways treated him. He was passed over for promotion half a dozen times by guys way less qualified, he wasn't paid for overtime, and he was injured on the job more than once, but when the union came in and gave him the chance to improve his situation, did he take it? No. He didn't want to rock the boat. Christ, he crossed the picket line. A month later, he gets hurt so bad he can't ever work again, and does the company come to his aid? Fuck Benjamin Massey, they said."

"I'm not interested in one of your speeches!"

Sighing, Massey sits on the step and rubs the spot above his left eye. "What I'm saying is people seldom know what's in their best interest. They keep putting themselves in harm's way and somehow think they're playing it safe, until one day"—Massey punches his fist against his palm—"bam! Game over."

"Get up, we're going to find a way to fix this!" Havens grabs Massey's arm and starts yanking him up the stairs.

Massey wrestles free. "Don't pull the plug on this. Please. I need this story. I'm out on the street at the end of the month."

The news stuns Havens, and Massey slumps back down on the step. "Don't worry—they're not going to let go of a Pulitzer winner any time soon, but without this story, what do I do? Wind up working for a greeting card company? Or worse, like my old man?" Massey gives Havens an imploring look. "I didn't plan for this story to turn up, but it did. Maybe I could've gone about it better, but is it so terrible to think this story could save all of us?"

Havens grabs his Contax and unscrews the back, and while Massey is launching himself toward him, he removes the canister and reels out the color film until every frame is exposed.

⳹

By the time Havens gets upstairs, the house is empty. Everyone has left for Socall's frolic except Gladden, who is waiting for a pie to cool. She gives Havens directions, and he takes off. Without pictures, Massey has no story, but it's true that others will hunt Jubilee and Levi to see for themselves, and when they do, blue is all they'll see. Blue, as though that's all there is to them.

Jeremiah Wrightley has set himself at Socall's front door as the official greeter of the frolic, and though Havens makes it clear he's anxious to find Buford, the man insists Havens oblige him with an inspection of his foot. The man regards the puncture site and promptly rolls up his sleeve to show the scars where he was bitten worse, and introduces the two young men in gray trousers, gray shirts, and gray felt hats beside him. "These here are my begats, Wyatt and Ransom." The bulkier of the two has on a filthy neck brace. Something is being said about the occasion of that injury, but Havens excuses himself, casts about the living room, and ventures down the hallway, checking the other rooms, one in which two small children are sprawled on the bed like discarded coats.

When he returns to the porch, the one called Chappy has just arrived. He leans his hubcap against the porch rail and pumps Havens's hand and introduces his grandmother, his aunt, and two girl cousins. Havens wants only to find Buford, but Chappy's grandmother says, "Sit a while, fella, and keep an ol' lady company." She stakes out the rocking chair closest to the door and recounts how Chappy's father ran off and married a floozy and how his mother succumbed from a broken heart not a year later and how if it wasn't for the Lord's benevolence, Chappy would've starved.

"I said that man was trouble. Slicker than a pan of grease. A man like that had more vanity than a roomful of girls at a beauty pageant."

Havens spots Jubilee approaching the house with a covered basket, and the pistons in his chest start up again. She is wearing the short-sleeved white dress with a yellow ribbon around her waist and a white shawl, which has slipped off one shoulder. Her hair flows down her back. Watching her is to get the impression she is skipping just ahead of concern, gliding past dangers as though they do not exist. Her arms swing in wide, carefree loops and she lifts each foot high to clear the weeds. He half expects her to grab the hem of her skirt and pirouette the rest of the way.

She greets Chappy and smiles at Havens when he opens the screen door for her. He catches the scent of mint in her hair. He ought to find Buford first, but he follows her inside, where Levi and his guitar have set up with a fiddle player, a banjo player, and someone with a squeeze box. Jubilee whispers something in her brother's ear, and in response he strikes up a tune. What begins as a merry love song takes a sudden sad turn.

As morning breaks she takes her leave
A ribbon 'round a curl gives she
Nevermore to meet, they carve their names
In the budding sycamore tree.
I'll sing, sing, my voice shall ring
through the hills and the hollers too
I'll sing, sing, the true love song
of the lark and the boy so blue.

The next song is no less plaintive, and the dancing commences. Women, unsmiling, take the hands of men who behave more like harnessed mules about to drive across pitted land than dance partners. Havens watches Jubilee unpack her basket, greet Socall, and find a chair in the corner. Though she avoids looking at him, he knows she's waiting for him to make good on his promise. What harm can come from postponing bad news a few minutes longer?

Havens makes his way around the perimeter of the room and is just about to ask her to dance when the snake handler scoops her from her seat and delivers her into the arms of his son with the neck brace, who then trots her around the living room as though she were a filly needing to be broken in.

Havens can't bear it. He cuts in.

His hand closes around her delicate wrist. She pulls back her shoulders and lifts her chin. He holds her politely at first, the way men are taught to do with women who don't belong to them, and then he holds her as if they belong to each other. He lowers his hand from her shoulder to the small of her back and pulls her so close she has to step between his legs, and even closer, where she must surely feel the drumming going on in his chest. *Mine, if only for a song*, he thinks.

"This isn't goodbye," she whispers, curling her fingers around the creases in his shirt.

How can he give her the news when she is pressed against him, when nothing has ever felt this right? Maybe they are dancing or maybe the room is dancing around them. The walls seem to have sucked the other guests into the grain, and the floor has opened, and they are dancing on clouds.

He lowers his head and rests his chin against her brow. "I am such a muddied man, Jubilee, and here you are, a pure brook."

"I'm just a girl."

"No, not just a girl." He smooths the back of her hand with his thumb. "I'm sorry," he says. "So very sorry."

She searches his face, and when he does not say why he is sorry, her hand glides around to the back of his neck and her fingertips reach into his hair, and he moves his hand a fraction farther down the small of her back. Each of them steals a little more of the other, tries to fit into the space of the other, seal all the gaps.

So lost is he in the nearness of her that she has to repeat herself before he comprehends.

She is smiling. "I think Mr. Massey is taking our picture."

Havens follows her gaze and drops from her embrace. Slunk back in the corner of the kitchen, Massey lowers the Contax from his face, pivots, and cuts out the back door.

"Stay here," he tells her, then charges after Massey. "Have you no decency?" he shouts.

Massey glowers back. "You're the one who should be ashamed!" His attention turns to Jubilee, who has hurried to Havens's side. "Has he told you what he's doing here?"

Jubilee turns the color of slate.

"Please go wait inside," Havens asks her.

"Who's really taking advantage of her now, hm?" Massey accuses him. "I trusted you!" Yelling about taking matters into his own hands, he says, "I knew you'd screw something up, but guess what? I brought an extra roll of film, so I don't need your color pictures because I have my own!"

"What's he talking about?" asks Jubilee.

Massey lifts the camera at her.

Havens shouts for her to run, and she sprints across the yard and scurries between a gap in the bushes. Havens is racing after Massey when he hears her cry out. He turns around and tears through the bushes into a small glade, where he finds her in Eddie's clutches.

"You looking for something?" Even from three feet away, Eddie reeks of alcohol, and gauging from the jug in his hand, he has come to the still to avail himself of Socall's liquor.

"Let her go!"

"She's going to dance with me, aren't you, Blue?"

"Don't you call her that!"

Jubilee tries to free herself, but Eddie yanks her against himself. "Blues like it rough, ain't that right?" He sneers at Havens. "You go on now, and leave us—"

Havens punches him in the mouth.

Eddie stumbles and then regains his footing. Blood gushes from his nose. He smirks and calls her names, and Havens lunges at him and knocks him to the ground. Before Havens can go after Massey again, Eddie makes a grab for Havens's throat, which Havens counters by ramming the heel of his hand against Eddie's jaw. They tussle in the dirt until they are pried apart by Buford and Levi, and no sooner are they on their feet than Eddie gives Buford the slip and lands a hit squarely on Havens's chin. He feels his head about to crack, loses track of direction. He puts his hands out, but cannot right himself, and hits the dirt. Someone is coaching him into a standing position, telling him he's all right, everything's fine, when nothing is all right, nothing is fine, things are going from bad to worse with the worst yet to come. He scans for Jubilee and sees her on the other side of the still. He wipes his mouth of spit and blood. "Someone go after Massey and stop him." Buford tries getting Havens to catch his breath, but he yells again for someone to apprehend Massey. "He's got a picture of Jubilee!"

"What do you mean?" Levi asks.

"He's got a color photograph of Jubilee that he's going to sell to a news magazine! He's got to be stopped!"

When the shot rings out, Havens thinks a bullet has done the job. Everyone freezes, except Eddie, who stumbles a few paces to one side and then the other.

Buford, Levi, and Havens peer through the bushes. Riding up on horseback and calling for Levi to show himself are Ronny Gault and his flunky, Faro, both armed with rifles. Massey is nowhere in sight. Havens swivels around for Jubilee and finds her clutching her brother to keep him from going out to confront his enemy.

"Don't say I didn't warn you, Buford." Eddie couldn't be more smug.

Coming to a halt in front of the barn, Ronny announces, "Levi's got to come down to town and turn himself in."

Socall steps out her back door. "For what reason?"

"What he did to Sarah Tuttle is a crime. He turns himself in tonight maybe he can spare himself the rope." He addresses the bushes as though Levi is quail to be flushed out.

"Done what to her?" Buford shows himself.

Faro is eager to deliver the news. "She's in the way on account of your boy's forcing."

Havens indicates for Levi to retreat into the woods with Jubilee, but instead, Levi barges into the open and presents himself like a fixed target. "Sarah didn't claim she was forced."

"Only because you threatened to cut her throat." With a hardened face, Ronny adds, "You're going to hang this time, Levi Buford."

Levi approaches Ronny with his finger pointed at him. "If anyone's done any forcing, it's you. The sight of you makes her sick, so you leave her the hell alone."

Socall returns to the fray, this time with her shotgun. "You boys push off now." Taking aim when they refuse to move, she says, "I don't mind shooting either one of you. In fact, it'll give me great pleasure, and I don't have a problem going to the gallows for it, neither."

Ronny turns in his saddle to face her. "You want the sheriff to come up here and take care of this?"

She lets off a shot. "Now, I'm not going to waste the other one."

Ronny and Faro steer their spooked horses away from Socall's house, Ronny shouting over his shoulder, "Nothing's going to get you off this time, Blue!"

JUBILEE

❧

Havens sets out after Mr. Massey, and Socall insists everyone
go back indoors and resume their frolicking to give the
Bufords time to take in the news. Pa is bent over, his hands
on his knees.

"I won't ask you to feed another mouth, if that's what you're worried
about," Levi tries to assure him. "I'll figure out a plan."

As if he's been put in stocks, Pa raises his head. "Is that what you intend
to tell her father, that the plan is for his daughter to take up with a—"

"A what?" Levi is the color of a sky before a real bad storm. "A blue coon?
Say it, Pa. If it'll make you feel better."

Mama's turned into an old woman. "Levi, please."

Pa screws up his eyes and tilts his head as though he's listening for a
sound faint and far away.

"Sarah can clear this up," Jubilee offers. "She'll tell the truth that she
wasn't harmed or forced, and I'm sure—"

"Nobody's going to badger Sarah," insists Levi.

"There's only one course of action," Pa decides. "First thing tomorrow
we will head to town for a sit-down with Reverend Tuttle, and then we'll
stop in and have a word with Sheriff Suggins."

Havens is hurrying toward them, calling for Pa to hang back, but Pa scowls and turns his shoulders, making it plain he's long past attending to the needs of these men. To him, they've gone back to being outsiders. "Best you be on your way now," he tells Havens, who mops the sweat from his face, which is already swelling up where Uncle Eddie hit him.

Jubilee doesn't want to look at him. In his arms, she'd made wishes, even though she knew there was never going to be a pretty cabin on a sunny hillside where heaven and blue could live together. All she needed were the memories of their time together, right up to that Kentucky waltz, but even this has been taken from her. Now what's she left with?

Taking a deep breath, Havens explains that Massey is going forward with his story and a secret film that makes color pictures. What he says sounds equal parts fable and bluff. "A magazine has offered to print the picture on its cover." This news hits Pa worse than Sarah being with child.

Levi is first to reach the conclusion. "Everyone's going to learn of us and come up here."

Havens looks like he'd sooner chew six-inch nails than admit that Levi's right.

"Why would you boys do this? Why would you put us in such a predicament?" Pa's eyes look like they're meant to draw out pus.

"To profit off it," Levi answers.

But if it was about profit, Havens would not now be laying bare their plan. He talks as much to her as to Pa. "At first it was about getting a story, and I went along with it for my own selfish reasons, and then I wanted to believe we could do some good with it, but I should've spoken up earlier." Havens explains that he destroyed the color film that had Levi's picture on it, and wasn't aware till now that Massey had brought an extra cartridge. "If that story gets out, they're going to come up here like bounty hunters, and I don't want you to get hurt," he says, looking first at her, then at Levi and Pa and Mama. "Any of you."

"Well, it's too late for that," says Pa.

"There's no excuse for breaking your trust, and I can't tell you how deeply I regret our actions, but the most pressing thing right now is that we stop

Massey from boarding the next train. If we catch him, there's a chance we can talk him out of it, and that will buy you a week, maybe two, before a news outlet sends a team out here, which hopefully will give Jubilee and Levi time to find a hideout."

"I'll take Socall's mare and cut through the canyon," says Pa, issuing orders for Levi to give Havens a ride down the holler and for the women-folk to hurry home.

"I'm so sorry, Jubilee," Havens whispers. "So very sorry."

She doesn't have a chance to ask Havens what she most wants to know—has everything been a lie?

HAVENS

❧

Havens is barely seated when Levi shakes the reins for the horse to take off. He looks behind him. Buford is saddling a horse and his wife is ushering her daughters and the old woman toward the path. He wills Jubilee to looks his way, and by some miracle, she does, just briefly. That's enough for him.

Once they pass Socall's property, Levi steers the buggy across a muddy ditch and along the weedy path that leads into the woods. Not slowing for the turns, the buggy veers left and right, at times on two wheels. Trees whizz by. Unless he keeps his head ducked, he's likely to be scalped by overhanging branches. The horse gallops along a path so narrow it can hardly be described as a path at all, and still Levi snaps the reins against the horse's neck, the smell of its sweat coming at Havens like a blast from a heating vent, the buggy bouncing to such a degree it's a wonder the wheels don't come loose. Even when they reach that part of the path that nudges a wall of granite rock on one side and falls away to a shadow on the other side, they do not slow. Down the gravel hill they fly, Havens doing his utmost to remain seated and Levi talking of having ought to have cottoned on sooner. "That business about him helping me find work, that was all baloney, wasn't it?" Havens notices the drop-off just inches from the wheels and imagines his funeral—a small crowd at the graveside, very little eulogizing, his mother weeping more to attract condolences, and the mourners eating cake afterward and saying what a shame he didn't publish any more photographs after *Orphan Boy*.

The tight gorge spills out into a meadow. In the distance are three wooden cabins, each separated by a field of disheveled-looking tobacco, and a small herd of listless cattle grazing nearby. Havens asks, "Aren't we almost there?"

Levi doesn't answer.

"I think I'll get off now."

Because Levi ignores him and keeps going, Havens reaches over and pulls on the reins and brings the buggy to an abrupt stop. "You don't want to get caught up in something down here. Better to go back and take care of your sister."

"And leave everything up to you?"

"I don't see that you have much choice." Dismounting, Havens says, "You have every right to hate me, but I want to assure you that I'm going to do everything I can to protect your sister."

Levi says the word of a right-colored man means little to him. "My sister's the one to see good in people, and she better be right about you." Levi gestures to a dense patch of underbrush. "Railway tracks are just on the other side. Follow them about a quarter of a mile, and you'll come to the station."

Havens hurries, hoping he's not going to be too late. Maybe Buford has arrived at the station by now and has confronted Massey. After days of being almost pain-free, his foot starts acting up, but he forces himself not to slow down, and still it takes far too long to reach the station. He hobbles across the train tracks, hoists himself onto the platform, and scans the area. There is no sign of Massey or Buford, but near the end of the platform is a bearded man in black pants, a black double-breasted jacket, and a black cap that identifies him as the stationmaster. Havens rushes up to him.

Partway through Havens's physical description of Massey, the man interrupts him and in a drawl asks, "You one of them up at Buford's?"

Havens confirms he is. "My partner had a camera with him; you wouldn't have missed him."

The man assesses Havens from head to foot. "You the one recuperating from a snake bite?"

"I just need to know if he has been here and if he boarded a train. Please, it's very important."

"I expect Buford has persuaded you that he and his lot are the injured party in all of this."

Havens does a poor job of hiding his impatience. "I'm a photographer, sir. It's my duty not to be persuaded."

"Is that right?" The stationmaster takes out his fob watch and sucks his front teeth.

Massey would have had to buy a ticket. Havens dashes to the ticket window just as a woman comes out of the office and locks the door.

"This here's the snake-bit one, Verily," the station master says.

The woman with the funnel-shaped body is much too eager to identify herself as Sherriff Suggins's sister, before adding, "Your friend was wise to leave town, what with trouble coming."

Havens cusses under his breath. "When's the next train?"

"Four-twenty tomorrow, and it'll be the only one on account of it being a Saturday."

Massey will waste no time in getting his story to an outlet, and this is going to put too much of a delay between them. Havens makes for the depot's exit. He needs to come up with another plan. He'll confer with Buford, maybe he'll have an idea. Maybe someone would be willing to give him a ride or loan him a vehicle.

Verily Suggins trots up beside him. "Some folks had a lot of sympathy for Del and Gladden when they moved back into town and tried to take up like normal folks, but I always said it would skip a generation and come out worse in their offspring, and now look what that Levi Buford's done—taken his devil-doings out on poor Sarah Tuttle. And to think it was Sarah's mother who showed that family the most sympathy." Verily Suggins lifts her handkerchief to her mouth. "They's coldblooded, them Blues."

"You obviously don't know the first thing about them!" Havens pulls away from her clutches and takes off down Main Street, hoping to catch sight of Buford. Perhaps he has gone to see the sheriff. Limping, Havens makes a beeline for the local lock-up, but when he sees the post office across the street, he changes course. Had Massey promised *Look* the exclusive, or did he go with one of the others? If he can find out, he can send a telegram that'll put them off the story, at least until he can lay out his case in person.

It's just gone five o'clock and the door is locked. Havens peers inside. Behind the counter is the postmaster. Havens bangs on the door and waves his hands, and still it takes the old man ages to cover the short distance to the door. He is tall and slight with a face that's narrow, bearded, and uneven, and he's wearing a gray suit that looks like it belongs on a corpse. If he is surprised to have a stranger barge into his office with demands, he doesn't show it. In the halting drawl of someone who's lived through a stroke, he confirms that Massey has paid the post office several visits over the last few days, the most recent of which occurred an hour ago.

"I know he sent a telegram—I just need to know where it was sent. It's very important."

The postmaster is noncommittal.

"Look, I know I'm putting you in a bit of a bind; I'm just asking for this one exception to the rule. We are partners, Mr. Massey and I; we are working on the same assignment." Producing the FSA calling card has no effect.

"Don't seem like partners to me."

Havens decides to level with the old man, revealing Massey's plan to print personal pictures of a family in Chance without their consent. "All I'm trying to do is keep innocent people from getting hurt."

"I never did have anything against Buford and his kin," the postmaster replies, each word labored. "Twenty-five years ago, the town assigned me the task of informing Buford that he and his family weren't welcome here. At the time, I thought I was doing the right thing. I thought I was going to keep innocent people from getting hurt. Turns out I was wrong. Keeping those folks away from the rest of us has been a stain on this town."

Havens is buoyed. "Yes, so we can both help them now." Hoping to cue the man on the matter of expediency, he consults his watch.

"It's got so the young people don't remember those families ever being here in Chance, being one of us." The postmaster hooks his thumbs in his waistcoat. "And it's the youngsters who get riled up. Having an enemy can give a young man a purpose, twisted though it may be."

"If you could just tell me where the telegram was sent."

The man recounts the second time he was dispatched to the Bufords. "Doc Eckles vowed he wouldn't deliver another Buford baby, blue or otherwise, and I was supposed to make Buford see the folly in having a family." The postmaster pauses a long time, before continuing. "A man has an intention to do well by his neighbor, and yet somehow he finds himself aiding a terrible wrong."

"Was it sent to New York, perhaps?"

Despondent, the postmaster reiterates that the law prohibits him from disclosing the information Havens needs, all while sorting through a stack of papers from a wire basket. "Now, if you will excuse me a moment, I need to attend to a matter in the back."

Havens looks down and spots the telegram the postmaster has separated from the others. Written in Massey's hand, it is addressed to the offices of *Look* Magazine, Des Moines, Iowa. Bastard!

HOLD COVER FOR BLUE GIRL. EN ROUTE WITH FULL-COLOR PICS.

Parasites with cameras and notepads will be headed this way, eager to depict beastly things about her, and no matter what Massey writes, she will be considered a curiosity, certainly not a woman with fears and dreams like everyone else. At her expense, readers will snatch up magazines and entertain themselves, using her as a measure against their own deficiencies, as a consolation for their incredible fortune of being ordinary.

He checks the time. Des Moines is an hour behind—someone will still be at the editorial desk. He calls to the back office. "Excuse me, sir? I need to send a telegram right away."

The postmaster already has a blank form in his hand.

Without hesitation, Havens writes: BLUE GIRL PHOTO A HOAX! DO NOT PRINT. ON MY WAY WITH EVIDENCE.

The accusation alone of printing a falsehood can bring any reputable publication to a close, and a new one still trying to get established and competing for advertising dollars surely won't go near it. The old man is tapping away on the telegraph and Havens is weighing everything he is giving up for this win when someone bangs on the door. Chappy's face is pressed against the glass, panic glazing his eyes.

"It's Jubilee! She's been taken!"

JUBILEE

O n their way back from Socall's house, Jubilee is antsy about getting home and not at all keen when Mama has them go by way
of the burying place first. Whenever Mama's worries threaten
to get the best of her, she pays Grandpa a visit, even though he's been six
feet under for fifteen years. Not since someone tried to dig up Opal and
make off with her bones have Blues gotten buried with the rest of the
departed. Instead, they are buried without a grave marker, near some or
other tree and far enough from the creek that the floods won't come and
wash any remains away.

Grandma forgets most things but not where Grandpa lies. She lumbers
over to his grave and sets down her suitcase before helping Willow-May
gather wildflowers, while Mama crouches and talks to Grandpa as if he's
supposed to scoot over and make room for her.

On the matter of the future, even when it's within smiting distance,
Jubilee's at a loss. For Blues, the future has always been a rope with all
the slack let out, a line you can hardly pull yourself along on, except now
it's snapped taut and it's not a matter of proceeding to the other end but
rather about what's on the other end coming for her. "We ought to get
home, Mama."

Mama rises and shakes the dirt from her skirt, and with a frosty stare, says, "Don't think you're blameless in all of this."

Smarting, Jubilee responds with Sarah's words. "You don't get to choose who you love."

"You'll choose to do as the rest of us and forget you ever met him!"

A quiet grows up between mother and daughter thick and prickly as a patch of stinging nettles, and Mama heads off as though she's dragging a gravestone behind her.

Forget him, Mama said. Even after what's been done, never.

❧

It's less than an hour till dark and neither Levi nor Pa has returned home. Mama has changed out of her nice dress and is still scrubbing clean floors, asking Jubilee again why she thinks Levi is taking so long. Run off with Sarah, is her guess, but saying so would only make Mama fret worse. Instead, she goes out to the barn. From the pallet she strips his sheet and presses it to her face. How is she to bear this? Before he came, blue skin was the heaviest burden to carry, but his being gone weighs more. She takes the birdcall from around her neck and blows, softly at first, and then hard.

Chappy comes by to see how they're doing, and to give Willow-May a break from Mama's worst conclusions, Jubilee grabs a couple of mason jars and suggests the three of them go catch fireflies. In the twilight, they wander to the bottom of the field, where the gathering clouds are thick and low, and the air smells of rain. Color has faded from everything except Willow-May, who is so pretty in her cornflower blue print dress and red skull cap. Her sister is waving her jar in the air, wading deeper into the tall grass.

"That's far enough," Jubilee calls out to her.

"But I don't see any."

The damp breeze that's been darting around their ankles suddenly springs up into the trees, startling the leaves, and just like that, Jubilee knows something's wrong. The sound of a sharp whistle blown between two fingers confirms it, that found-them whistle. She swings in the direction

164

of the sound and sees two men charging out of the thicket. She tears through the grass toward Willow-May, yelling for her to come, and neither of them seems to move any closer to each other, neither of them nearly as fast as Ronny and Faro chasing them.

"Run, Willow-May! Chappy!"

She almost reaches her little sister when someone barrels into her from behind. Willow-May screams and Jubilee lifts her head off the ground in time to see Faro scoop up her sister and head for the dark woods. Ronny yanks Jubilee up by the arm, shouting at her to get up, and she stumbles to her feet and kicks at him, though it does little good.

"Chappy! Chappy!" she screams as Ronny drags her into the woods. She keeps yelling for Chappy, and Willow-May keeps yelling for her, and as soon as they make it to the trees, Ronny lets go of her arm, and she takes this as a good sign until he raises the barrel of his rifle and aims it at the field where Chappy is speeding after them, siren blaring.

"No!" She knocks the barrel as Ronny lets off another shot, the explosion about bursting her ears.

"Go for help, Chappy!" she cries.

"And they said blue coons was hard to hunt," Faro mocks.

Dragging her deeper into the woods, Ronny tells her to quit bucking. Faro is just ahead with Willow-May in his arms and she's screaming something terrible, trying to wriggle free. She knocks off the miner's hat he's wearing. He struggles to keep his hold on her while trying to put it back on, and bends her arm the wrong way, making her yelp.

"You're hurting her! Let her go!" Jubilee screams, wrestling and thrashing against Ronny. She remembers the birdcall, raises it to her lips, and blows as hard as she can, but Ronny rips it from her neck and throws it aside.

Willow-May keeps fighting Faro, who looks as though he's about to drop her sister on her head. His face is a mad mix of malice and glee.

"Let her go!" Jubilee shouts. "She's done nothing to you!"

Ronny yells for Faro to keep up, but they fall even farther behind.

"She's biting me!" Faro squeals, and Ronny gives the order to cut her loose.

"Run, Willow-May!" Jubilee says, but instead of fleeing to safety, her little sister runs toward her. "No, go home!"

"Juby!"

Ronny aims the rifle at her, ordering her to clear out, and Jubilee springs at him and shouts for Willow-May to go home. After she takes off, there's just a widening silence. When Willow-May gets back, either Mama will have to pursue them or she'll have to go find Pa, but either way it'll be too late.

They run her through the woods. When she makes her legs go heavy, they drag her through the trees and slide her down a steep, gravel bank. There's no stopping or slowing them, so she quits resisting. Better they get it over with. She runs loosely alongside them as though she were a mule tethered to a galloping horse, and they run until the men tire, then they walk, Faro with his miner's hat lamp assuming the lead.

They walk a good deal farther, until they get to a clearing. Faro's lamp lights a rock overhang and several tarps covering the entrance of what must be a shallow cave. She catches a glimpse of raccoon tails nailed to a wooden post at the entrance. The beam from Faro's headlamp swerves to a nearby tree, and he says, "You hung yourself yet, Blue?"

Levi is bound by his wrists and tied to a branch above his head.

"Levi!"

Her brother won't look at her.

Faro gets right up in Levi's face. "Think you can wipe yourself clean on one of our kind and get away with it?"

Levi seems to stare right through him.

As a soft mist settles on them, Faro shines the light so Ronny can tie Jubilee's wrists together with a rope. The way he sizes her up makes her feel like a rickety old bridge, one not up to bearing the weight of what he has in mind, but Mama always says to stand up tall and proud, so she does her best to keep her knees from giving way.

"We've given your brother a chance to account for his filthy ways, but he won't, so we thought we'd bring him something to persuade him," Ronny says.

Faro jabs Levi with a stick, and Levi tries kicking him, but loses his balance.

"You're the ones who are filthy!"

Ronny lines up his face with Levi's. "Own to what you did to Sarah, and you can pay a lighter penalty, or be stubborn about it and bring more grief on yourself and your sister."

"Tell them what they want to hear," she begs Levi.

Instead, her brother spits at Ronny. "I won't say what isn't true."

Ronny's mouth turns crooked. "You made Sarah a whore, say it!"

"And you wanted to plant a blue devil in her!" adds Faro.

Jubilee appeals to her brother, "Please, Levi, just say it."

"Listen to this, a blue coon making sense."

Levi sneers at Ronny. "You hate blue so much, you ought to hate half your own self."

"Levi, hush!" Jubilee starts bargaining with Ronny. "Let us go, and we'll never bother anyone again. You won't ever see us again."

But Levi blurts out, "You haven't figured out yet that Urnamy Gault's not your daddy?"

Even the crickets grow quiet. "Did he just call your mama a whore?" Faro asks.

"Eddie's not blue, but he's kin to blue." Levi goes on despite Jubilee's rebuke. "So that makes you, Ronny Gault, a—"

"You're lying!" Ronny lunges at Levi, who strikes back with bunched hands and chops bitter air instead.

It takes this long for Faro to cotton on. "Wait, so is he saying Eddie Price is your real pa?"

While Ronny is shouting that all Blues do is lie, Levi challenges him, "Don't take my word for it. Go ask your mama."

Ronny kicks him, and he spins and stumbles and half-hangs himself in the process, and then Ronny gives the order for the rope to be let loose from the tree. The two tackle Levi. Like some other person has risen up out of the ground and is doing the yelling is how Jubilee screams for help.

After they've bloodied Levi and bound his ankles, they come for her.

"Leave her!" Levi groans, trying to free himself.

Angels turn away, ghosts head back to their graves.

Her clothes are peeled off and cast away from her like skin, while Levi keeps offering himself like some lamb. "Take it out on me, you cowards! Finish what you started!" What he does not say, though, is one word about Sarah.

The darkness becomes a rag mopping up Jubilee's cries.

They do not force themselves on her. Instead, they yank her by her hair and lead her to the tree where Levi swings madly at Ronny again and punches her by mistake. Her jaw splits in pain and she falls to her knees. She puts out both hands to settle the ground but it goes on wobbling like an overturned plate.

When she comes to, it's hard to focus on anything but this terrible pain, like her head's caught in a trapper's snare, and to ease the throbbing, she tries lifting her hand to her forehead, only to find it's been bound to something.

"They're disgusting," Faro says.

"Worse than hogs," agrees Ronny.

"Guess they can't fight their own nature."

"You lie here and think about what you've started." Ronny walks into the darkness. Faro's miner's lamp flickers and then blinks off.

She cannot cover herself or move without dragging the weight of a tree.

"We've got to get to my pants. My knife's in the pocket." Levi is somewhere close, so close, and she tries freeing her arms to turn and locate him, and she feels his hot breath on her shoulder. It's not the tree she's trying to rid herself of, but him. They have been tied together like mating dogs.

Levi tries lifting one of his legs, then an arm. "Come on, move with me." He tries propelling them both forward. They struggle and shift their bodies, and fall one way and then another, and move one inch farther away from their target twenty feet ahead.

"Pretend you're someplace else," he says eventually, and they lie as still as shelves of wood.

It's drizzling now. "Why didn't you just tell him what he wanted to hear?"

"I won't own to what I didn't do and I won't tar Sarah's reputation."

Why can't he see this isn't just about Sarah anymore? "If Ronny finds out who his real pa is, you think he's going to be nicer to us?"

"It can't make things any worse."

"He's got his mama's honor to defend now, don't you see?"

"Don't cry, Juby; I'm going to fix this."

It starts to pour.

HAVENS

⚜

Buford, Wrightley and his sons, Chappy and a few of his relatives, and Havens constitute the search party, and if paltry numbers aren't bad enough, they have to contend with the avalanche of darkness with nothing but frayed lamplight. Two hours into their search it starts to rain, and the downpour forces them to seek shelter till dawn. Havens can't bear to think of Jubilee out in this weather, and as each hour passes, it becomes harder to hold to the hope that she is somewhere dry and in the custody of her brother.

At first light, Havens pairs up again with Chappy, who does not slow down except when Havens stumbles or lags, both of which occur with frustrating regularity. The ground has turned to slop and the wind has a bite to it, but the rain is a manageable drizzle.

"Juby!" Chappy calls, over and over.

Havens cups his hands around his mouth and cries out in all directions, "Jubilee!"

What they hear in return is the patter of rain. On they trudge, alternating their calls into the mute forest, Havens trusting that Chappy knows enough not to get them lost.

"Hear that?" Chappy points to an area of the woods below them.

"Jubilee?" They slide down an embankment and race between spindly blackened trees in the direction of a faint cry, and come upon what looks like a hobo's camp. Havens has to command himself not to show his distress at the sight of Jubilee and Levi. He and Chappy tear off their jackets and throw them over the naked pair, the cold having turned them a deep shade of steel blue. Havens drops to his knees in front of Jubilee and pushes her hair out of her face.

"It's all right. It's all right, Jubilee," he reassures her, though nothing could be further from the truth.

Chappy unties Levi while Havens frees Jubilee with fumbling fingers. He notices that the rope tying her waist to her ankles has left deep grooves in her skin. A metallic taste builds up in his mouth, the taste for revenge. He sits her up. Her lips are ink-colored, and beneath her eyes are dark purple shadows. From head to toe, she is nothing but a bruise. She does not answer when he asks whether she is hurt or whether she can walk or if there were others besides Ronny and Faro. He scours his mind for something to say that will at least make her look at him, but all he can think of is what he doesn't know to be entirely true: "You're safe now."

Levi unties the knots at his feet, leaving Chappy to wring his hands, and rock back and forth. When he starts making his siren noise, Levi snaps at him to be quiet. "They could be on their way back!"

Havens hands Jubilee her muddy dress, careful to keep his eyes averted, and then guides her cold wet arms into his jacket. Terrible images come to his mind. He tries to dispel them so as not to be overcome, so he can be of some use to her. Never before has he felt capable of killing someone.

Having struggled into his pants and yanked on his boots, Levi staggers toward the trees.

"Where are you going?" Jubilee begs with a hoarse voice. "Levi!"

It pains Havens to think how she must have screamed for help. He tries to steady her, cupping her elbow, but she flinches and pulls away.

"Leave me and go stop my brother."

Near crippled from the pain in his foot, Havens follows after Levi only to recognize the futility a minute later. He returns to Jubilee. "Let's get you home."

"Go after him, please."

"He's gone."

Havens retrieves the hubcap from the mud, wipes it as best he can, and returns it to Chappy, who no longer seems to know what to do with it. Havens circles his arm around Jubilee's shoulders. "It's over now."

Shuddering against him, she joins hands with Chappy, saying, "No, it's not over."

The first house they come to is Socall's and the woman flings open the door and crushes Jubilee in a fierce embrace. Though he's tired and in shock, Chappy sets off to the Bufords to take word of Jubilee's safety.

"Levi's gone and stirred up a hornet's nest with the issue of Ronny's siring," Jubilee tells Socall.

"Oh lord."

"And now he's taken off somewhere. We must find him and bring him back home."

"He's likely gone to check on Sarah. I'll take you home, then ride down to the Tuttles'," says Socall.

"He might have gone to look for her at the Granger place."

Socall assures Jubilee she'll stop by there, too. "Don't you worry now; Levi knows to keep his head down."

Havens nods his agreement, even though the look on Levi's face as he took off into the woods suggested quite the opposite, and if Levi's state of mind in any way resembles Havens', personal safety is the last of his concerns.

Socall steers Jubilee to the bedroom to change and Havens collapses in the nearest chair, easing off his shoes and unwinding the bandage. He tugs off two blackened toenails. As soon as Socall returns, he relays what little he knows, and she stares out the window at the brooding sky clearing in places. "Gladden filled me in about the business with the photographs." He waits for her to yell at him, but instead she offers him a drink, says, "I'm not saying there's pardoning what you've done, but most everyone I know fails to see past her color. You know how special she is."

"I should've put a stop to it sooner."

They turn when they hear the bedroom door squeak. Standing in the doorway wearing a dress several sizes too big for her, her hair making a wet patch on her shoulder, Jubilee looks like a patient not quite recovered from a life-saving surgery. Her slight and brave attempt at a smile can only be for their benefit.

"Stand here by the stove, get yourself warmed up, and then we'll head off," Socall instructs. She hands Jubilee a drink and rubs her back. "They're going to pay for what they've done."

Jubilee's chin trembles, but she does not cry. "They didn't—they didn't touch me in that way."

Havens can't hide his relief.

Slowly her skin fades from navy to a soft gray-blue. As chaste as a morning sky, she turns to Havens. "Were you able to stop Mr. Massey?"

Havens's tongue is a thick piece of rubber. He shakes his head. "But I don't want you to worry about the picture anymore because I've come up with a solution."

"What's that?" Socall asks.

"I'm going to tell everyone it's a hoax."

"Who's going to believe that when your friend has proof that it isn't?" Socall contests.

"They won't believe the picture is true because I have my own proof." For the first time, Havens is about to speak the truth about *Orphan Boy*. "Proof of another hoax." He explains how a ploy that was meant to keep him from losing his job resulted in an image that struck a nerve with the public and, much to his surprise and dismay, became a symbol for all the hardships the nation had suffered. As one critic stated, in no other picture was the despair of the times more starkly portrayed.

"I offered the boy's mother twelve dollars, and staged the whole thing." What he has kept secret he now tells in full, one despicable detail after another—how the boy's mother didn't understand at first what Havens wanted, that she'd brought her boy out to the alley behind the tenement building in clean clothes, polished shoes, and combed hair, with his school reader tucked under his arm. To convince the mother to have the boy wear his scruffiest clothes and to go barefoot, Havens made up a story about it being a costume of sorts, that the portrait was a kind of audition. Oliver Twist, he said, and how eager the boy was to get the part, rubbing dirt on his face and arms, mussing his hair, putting on his saddest face. Havens posed him sitting with his back against a chain-link fence, and handed him a prop, an opened can of beans. Scoop some out with your fingers, Havens instructed. He hadn't planned on the dog. That bony stray that came begging was pure luck, and as the boy fed it the beans Havens pressed the shutter. That was the shot.

"The boy's mother wouldn't take the money in the end. She said if I could just take one picture of her little boy in his clean clothes and give it to her, that was payment enough. I told her I'd be back the next day to deliver it, but of course I didn't go back. I still have the picture, and that is my proof." He'll also provide the boy's address so the press can verify his statement with the mother.

Havens feels scoured. Expecting to find condemnation in Jubilee's eyes, he sees only that same attentiveness on which he has come to rely. "It's not going to matter what Massey says, even if he claims he took the picture himself—though I doubt he'll push the issue. No one's going to touch it."

At last Jubilee speaks. "You'll lose your job."

"It won't be that bad." It'll end his career. It may well mean an end to employment of any kind—after all, who will want to hire a cheat? What matters most to him is that this time tomorrow the pictures of Jubilee will be tossed in the trash.

Jubilee is pressing for some other way, and Socall tells her the best thing anyone can do for a guilty man is to give him a chance to work it off. "Let him do this for you." Grabbing her hat and shotgun, she outlines her plan to get Jubilee home and give Havens a ride to the station. "Best say your goodbyes now while I hitch the wagon."

How Havens longs to envelop Jubilee, to hold her, to never let her go.

Jubilee moves to the window and Havens stands behind her, noticing how the trauma has cinched her shoulders. He wants to draw his finger along the back of her goose-fleshed arm. He wants to run his hands along her shoulders, under her arms, and down her sides. He wants to kiss each bruise. Between them is a thin layer of heat and even this is a hindrance, even the particles between them are restrictive.

Taking a deep breath, as if she were about to step under a waterfall, she leans back against him.

"Jubilee, I'm so sorry." He wraps his arms around her, buries his face in her hair.

"I wish you didn't have to go," she whispers.

They watch as Socall brings the wagon around, and he tightens his hold on her, sways her.

Socall whistles for them to come.

Jubilee looks at Havens's watch. "You've got four hours yet to wait." She tells him about an abandoned shack behind the graveyard. "I could wait with you."

"You can't go out again. You need to stay with your family."

She turns around to face him. "I need to be with you. Just for a little bit longer."

"You've just—"

She presses her fingers against his mouth. "If we were certain we had years ahead of us, then I could say goodbye now, but what if we have only these next few hours?"

He wants to pledge years, but she says, "Promise me you'll meet me there."

Any reasonable man would insist she begin forgetting about him right away, but he has long since stopped being a reasonable man. He is lost in her. Gone. Far, far gone. Though he could deny himself, he can deny her nothing. "I promise."

JUBILEE

Pa, Jeremiah Wrightley, and Chappy arrive home nearly three hours after Socall and Havens set out for town, and all this time Mama has had one hand on Jubilee and the other on Willow-May, as if a great wind could tear through the house and blow her two daughters away. They all meet in a huddle on the porch steps, Pa looking as though he's lost his entire crop to pests, and Mama like she is going to have to feed her children scraps of leather. Once Pa gets done holding Jubilee and assessing her and questioning her, she reports that Ronny is likely now inquiring about his real father, which makes Pa even more pale and sick-looking. Mama lets the last of the light go out of her eyes and Pa stares out at the land that has taught him not everything blooms and ripens with ease—hardly anything, in fact.

Jeremiah Wrightley says, "Well, that's not going to go over too well with Urnamy."

"Estil will surely deny it and maybe that'll be enough," Pa says.

To give her father some hope, Jubilee mentions Havens's amended plan to undo Mr. Massey's intentions.

"The worst mistake I made was letting those men in my house."

Doesn't he know it's no small thing to tell the world your lie? "He's going to lose his livelihood over it, Pa."

"I don't ever want to hear you speak of them again," he commands.

Before the men set off again to search for Levi, Chappy tells her his cousin Edgar has closed his gas station for the day and rounded up friends and kin to scour the hills, reminding her that Edgar was a buffalo soldier in the 92nd Infantry. "Ain't nobody can hide too long before Edgar's going to find where," Chappy says.

Apart from Chappy's grandmother, Jubilee doesn't know his other relatives too well. Much like what she and her family have learned to do, much like anyone on the receiving end of hateful treatment would do, they pretty much keep to themselves, and that they are now aiding in the effort to find Levi makes her wonder if the Right-coloreds in town won't ever really get their way, that Negroes and Blues and whoever else they deem lower won't "mind their place."

She, Mama, and Willow-May join Grandma inside. It's less than an hour till that train comes and Mama is insisting that Jubilee now eat what's in front of her. After scoffing down a couple of hasty bites, she dashes to the sink with her plate still half full, announcing a quick visit to her aviary to tend to her birds.

"You're not going anywhere after what's just happened. You're staying right where you are."

"They haven't been fed for two days, Mama."

"They can get by."

But Jubilee grabs her veil and promises to be back in less than an hour. She rushes outside, figuring which route will get her to Havens the quickest. Keeping low, she scurries across Spooklight Meadow and scans all directions before racing across the corner of Jeremiah Wrightley's land. For a good long way, the bushes and trees offer cover, but she has to contend with the open stretch along the old miner's road. At a flat-out run, it will take her only ten minutes to get to the turn-off to the graveyard and the next screen of trees, or she can backtrack to the creek and go around Granger's pond, which will mean she won't get to the shack in time. She puts on her veil and starts running.

As soon as she hears the engine, she bolts for what used to be the filling station, tears through the back entrance, where the door hangs by cobwebs rather than hinges, and startles a flock of crows whose wings stir the dust into air thick as fleece. She crawls under the jumble of wood that used to be the counter and listens to the vehicle get louder and louder until it seems as though it'll drive straight through the building. Nothing sounds like dread more than a car skidding to a stop. Go, please go. The driver kills the engine. She strains for voices, for footsteps, any clue of an approach, and after several long minutes, she hears, "Ssh."

Don't breathe. Don't move. How long does it take for dust to settle?

The porch creaks. Footfall with no drag between steps—they are careful to pick up their feet. A pause in front of the broken window. A whisper. Scurrying along the side of the building. Then an unnatural hush.

All at once the back door and front screen door fly open, and boots thunder over to her.

"I guess you Blues just don't learn, do you?" Ronny tosses aside the lumber and grabs her veil. "Get up!"

Beside him, Faro says, "You coming to town to take us on, like your brother, or to rat on us?"

"That son of a bitch was stupid enough to think he could come to our town and tell everyone I'm the bastard son of Eddie Price."

"Levi's not going to do that," she protests.

"No, he ain't." There's a darkness to Faro's agreement.

"Where is he?" No amount of begging persuades them to say, so she pleads for her release. "Please let me go. A friend is expecting me."

"Blues don't have friends," says Faro.

Ronny's frowning face suddenly clears. "Hold up, you mean the news-paper man?" Ronny and Faro trade glances.

"She's going to have that Northerner print lies about you and your mama in his newspaper," Faro proclaims.

Denying it does no good. "We can both go to him," she suggests. "He'll tell you he isn't going to print anything about you."

"Don't think you can barter with me! We're not equal!" Ronny grabs her by her hair, pulls her outside, and forces her up on the bed of a pickup. Tick is behind the wheel, and Jubilee petitions his help, but he doesn't mind her. What he does do is hit the gas when Ronny yells for him to.

"We got rid of one, and now it's time to get rid of the other," Ronny says, as the pickup lurches forward.

"What do you mean? Have you done something to my brother? Have you hurt him?"

Ronny yells at Tick to drive faster.

"Where is Levi? Please tell me!" It has to be a bluff. They're just trying to scare her. Levi has to be with Sarah someplace.

"Born a coward, lived a coward, and died a coward." If only Ronny wasn't so matter-of-fact.

She wants to say, "You're lying," but her jaw is locked in place, and a quick freeze takes over her body. She searches his face, then his hands, sees his knuckles are raw and bloodied. Elsewhere are signs of a battle—grazes on his elbows, a rip in his pants, that he favors one side of his ribs with a muddied arm. Her ears fill with the sound of cracking ice. Her eyes become iced-over pools. She can't picture Levi, not how they say.

The truck has barely come to a stop when Ronny hauls her off the pickup bed onto the gravel. It takes a moment to figure out that she is on the north end of town. Ronny and Faro drag her toward the train tracks, and she can't understand what they are saying. She can't feel her feet or her hands.

"Guess that makes you the last of the blue coons," Faro says, just as the train's whistle sounds. He is saying something else, but she is now preoccupied with the boots he's wearing—old and oiled, belonging to someone who knows how to care for leather because there's no going into town to buy a new pair when no one will sell to a Blue.

It takes all her effort to make herself heard. "Those are my brother's boots."

"No, they ain't," says Faro.

Ronny pulls a bunch of change out of his pocket. "Next thing, she's going to accuse us of stealing his money."

Socall's money that Levi collected from delivering her shine to the tenant farmers yesterday! Her heart seizes up.

Everyone looks down the track as the train rounds the bend, its wheels squealing, and Faro and Ronny tighten their grip on her arms. The train rushes toward them, its whistle blasting.

"On the count of three!" Ronny says.

She starts bucking as the rumble gets louder. "Tick, please! Help me!" She can't hear anything now on account of the roar, can't see anything but Levi lying somewhere, color running out of him. The train's getting closer, air blasting at them from the tracks, and she wrenches and pulls as the two men start to swing her.

"One—two—"

The train is about upon them—

"Three!"

HAVENS

❧

While Havens waits for Jubilee, he perfects his plan, estimating the time it will take to fetch the damning photographs and get to the offices of *Look*. It will work. It has to work.

In the musty tumbledown hut beside the cemetery he paces up and down, reassuring himself that she's on her way, that she'll arrive any moment, but the more time that passes, the more restless he becomes. He legs it out to the road to see if she is coming and, disappointed, hurries back to the cabin to resume pacing and waiting and worrying. He consults his watch again. Just over half an hour before the train comes. Leave now, and he can make it and be at the magazine's front door by the end of the following day, or keep his promise to wait for her. He goes outside for another reconnaissance. What's keeping her? From his position on the slight rise above the town, he can see part of the station. It won't be long before a whistle will signal the train's approach. It was for selfish reasons that he agreed to meet her here.

She's on her way. She'll be here any minute. But what if she should arrive moments after he leaves—won't she be disappointed he didn't keep his promise? She'd asked of him only one thing.

Damn watch! Why does it speed up?

Of course she's not coming. How could she come? After the night she's had, she can't still be awake. She's collapsed on her bed. The Bufords have insisted she rest. Levi has returned and the family is trying to piece itself together.

She's not coming, and it's for none of these reasons—it's because she's reconsidered. She doesn't want to see him again.

He scans the hills one last time, then picks a handful of flowering weeds beside the cabin door and arranges them in the shape of a heart on the floor. Then he bolts.

Every creeper, rock, and bush impedes his race to the station, and in crossing the creek, now full and running fast, he loses his footing. By the time he reaches the platform, he is soaked, muddied, and bone-tired. With the last of his cash, he buys a first-class ticket and is the first to board when the train comes to a stop, and he heads to the front row of the first car, shrugs out of his soggy coat, and slides into the seat beside the window. How he wishes he could have held her one last time, had a final moment, however fleeting, to speak of his heart, to say goodbye. Perhaps it's better this way.

The conductor stops beside him, punches his ticket, and tells him to change trains in Lexington. "There's a dining car just for first-class passengers, but there's usually a card game going on in the one in coach, if you care to socialize."

Havens can't imagine being in anyone's company but hers.

He scrunches up his jacket and wedges it against the window as a pillow, then shuts his eyes. Left behind in Buford's cellar are all his black-and-whites of her. Those depictions, lovely as they may be, couldn't ever serve as a substitute for the tangible anyway.

JUBILEE

Together with Ronny and Faro, Jubilee is thrust backward, tumbling to the ground against her captors as Tick launches himself on them.

The train flies by.

Faro keeps her from scuttling into the bushes by grabbing her ankle. "You ain't getting off that easy!"

Ronny and Tick are arguing over what's to be done about her now, Tick yelling that she doesn't need to die. "It's not right, Ronny!"

"You got a better idea how to get rid of her?"

They squabble out of earshot, and she can't see why they bother. The pounding in her ears makes her deaf, and nothing about her works the way it should. If it did, feet would stand, legs would walk, eyes would see straight. She gets only as far as her knees. She believes one part of her ordeal has come to an end when Tick helps her upright and speaks with a soft voice, making her promise not to breathe a word of what's happened to anyone.

"I'll never tell."

"Especially not to any newspaperman."

She must be doing something that satisfies him because he returns to Ronny and Faro, and has them empty out their pockets. Once he's collected all the coins, Tick crosses the tracks and jumps up on the station platform.

Ronny says, "You got lucky today, Blue."

Levi is dead and she's to feel lucky?

When Tick motions to them from across the tracks, they hurry to meet him behind the last car, Ronny limping from some injury. Holding a ticket, Tick says, "Louisville far enough away, Ronny?"

Ronny is saying things and Faro is saying things and all she sees are mouths opening and closing, faces swimming closer and further away until Ronny yanks the veil over her head. He orders Faro to take off his boots and hand over his socks.

"My brother's boots," she mumbles.

Ronny shoves the dirty sweaty socks at her. "Put them on, Blue!"

She doesn't know what he means.

Ronny stuffs her fists into them. Stumps now. She starts to cry and is told to shut up—as if crying's something she can control—and Tick explains how this is for her own good, that she's to cooperate, or Ronny won't be stopped next time. The last few people on the platform are boarding, and she eyes the station's entrance, desperate for Havens to step through it. This is the train he means to take so why isn't he here? Surely, he can't still be waiting for her. Why did she make him promise to wait?

Ronny keeps her hidden till the last passenger boards, and then drags her to the back steps of the car and shoves her, climbing up behind her, saying he'll stick her with his knife if she so much as bleats.

It's Levi's pocketknife, the one Pa gave him all those years ago. "My brother's knife." Seems all she can do for Levi now is name what belongs to him, what belongs to him no more.

Ronny adjusts her veil and pushes her into a seat at the back of the car. Only three other passengers are present, two men tucked behind newspapers and a woman who refuses to look their way. On the platform outside, Faro and Tick are speaking to the stationmaster, who walks right past the train window facing dead ahead and blows his whistle. She keeps scanning for Havens. He'll come. He'll rush through those doors and run straight for this car and leap onto the stairs and take her in his arms. He will comfort her and take her by the hand and tell the sheriff about Levi. The train jerks forward. She presses her stumps against the window. Not yet. Give him one more minute. Another jolt, and slowly the train begins to move. She gets up—she can't stay here.

Ronny shows her the knife, so she begs. "I have to go home. I have to tell my parents. Please. I'll never bother you again."

He snorts.

She barters and promises, pulling on his shirt with her stumps.

He hits them away. "Now, listen close. If you come back here, you'll end up like your brother. If you run your mouth about this to anyone, same deal."

The train picks up speed, the wheels clack faster and faster. It's not too late. If Havens arrives now and breaks into a sprint, he can still board. She flinches when the train's whistle sounds. In a few seconds, they'll be going fast enough that nothing will catch them.

Ronny shoots out of his seat and staggers to the back of the compartment. She follows him. He opens the door, turns around and shoves her so hard she falls backward. From the aisle floor, she watches him launch himself into the air. She rises, rushes to the doorway, and steadies herself with the rails. Trees and bushes are a blur. Jump, she tells herself—broken, twisted, or dead, it'll be better than this. The wind whips her veil against her face. She lifts the hem of her dress and bends her knees, and a cold hand clamps around her elbow.

"Everything all right, miss?"

She is wheeled around by the man in the black uniform, who says for her to take her seat right away. He waits for her do as she's told. She slumps into her seat, looks out the window. Smoke blows past. The steep hillside is covered with laurel. The man is still standing beside her and he's repeating something which makes no sense.

"I need to punch your ticket."

"I don't—I—"

He reaches for her wrist, where the ticket is sticking out of the top of Faro's sock. Can't he see something is wrong? Lift your veil, show him. But won't he then ask questions, demand answers? Won't he call for the police at the next stop and insist she name names?

"Louisville. You're looking at ten and a half hours, more if there are delays. Best you get comfortable." He punches a hole in the card and hands it to her.

Levi is somewhere. Pa is still out looking for him. Mama is at home sitting in front of plates of cold food. Havens is keeping his promise. And here she is. When will anyone think to look for her? How long before anyone realizes she's gone? And what use will it be when they do? Everyone dear to her is lost. Instead of feeling empty, inside her swells and bloats like a rotting carcass. She could surely attract flies. She doesn't cry. She gags and gags.

Keeping upright takes every effort. A terrible thickness surrounds her. People push past her, fill the seats, empty the seats. She sits on her stumps, makes herself small, makes herself a thing that doesn't matter. The last Blue.

SEPTEMBER
1972

Having sped back home from the cemetery checking his rearview mirror the entire way to make sure the upstart out-of-towner wasn't following him, Havens now parks his truck beside his work shed and sits with his hands clamped around the steering wheel. He lets out a big breath. How much worse could things have gone? Instead of chasing off the stranger or getting any clearer picture as to his true intentions, he'd run smackdab into that old crone and her unrelenting grudge. Thirty-five years the grudge has suckled on her, and now it is so monstrous the woman seems little more than its host. There can't be anything else keeping her alive. Nevertheless, it seems Havens might have chosen to wait for the stranger to return to his rental car rather than charge through the graveyard, disturbing the respectful activities of Decoration Day. If the dead had been resting peacefully before, they sure as heck were wide awake now, and that young man, whoever he is, is likely getting a blow-by-blow of what some distorted versions call the Spooklight Killing Spree.

Eventually, Havens gets out, picks up a stick long enough for poking the undergrowth for snakes, and makes his way up the incline behind the house on rubbery legs, the deadfall crunching under his feet while broad branches of poplar and maple trees reach from overhead as if to scoop him up. Almost immediately, his head starts to clear. Though the woods can kill a grown man a hundred different ways, few things can calm him the way they can, and all it takes is a few feet along the footpath to feel nestled in nature's bosom.

Swatting to keep the deer flies from biting, he passes where the nettles are chest high and covered in clusters of tiny white blossoms, taking extra precaution not to rub up against them, and steps over a clump of fresh-sprung cohosh to climb up the ladder to the treehouse he built years ago. He ducks beneath the crossbeam and steps onto the platform on which the filtered light makes yellow swirls. Reclaimed barn boards form three of the walls, but instead of the north-facing wall, he nailed a railing so he could look out at the expansive view of timber and blue hills, now shawled in wispy clouds. Havens leans on the railing, lifts his face to the breeze, and scans for that place, a particular dip in the ridgeline, the marker for where she used to live. How he wishes she had been here this morning, even though he knows she would not have approved of the way he'd handled things. She'd have known what to do.

A low rumbling disturbs his thoughts. Months can go by without anyone paying a call, and now two intrusions on the same day and it's not even lunchtime. He climbs down from the treehouse and takes a shortcut through the stand of sassafras saplings and tromps through the sour grass. In his haste to step over a few errant logs by the woodpile, he loses his balance and bumps the gardening bench, sending the birdcage that needs mending crashing to the floor, but he still manages to get to the top of his driveway in time to see that white Ford Fairlane come to a stop about halfway to the house, where the left fork splits off to the barn. From his vantage point, the driver will be able to see Havens clearly, but because the sun is hitting the windshield directly, Havens cannot see him. Instead of proceeding the rest of the way up the driveway, the car idles. Havens adopts a wide stance and waits. Perhaps the kid has brought someone with him this time, maybe someone from the cemetery, and the two of them are debating what to do. For all Havens knows, that witch is in the passenger seat shouting instructions, her wheelchair ready to pop up out of the trunk, chase him down, and run him over. It wouldn't be the first time she rolled up here breathing hot revenge. Whenever a reporter shows up, Havens knows she's been working the phone lines, and if she can't bait the true-crime writers, she dials up that other breed of bloodsuckers, the ones who like to write about Bigfoot sightings and lake monsters and the Virgin's face appearing on pancake griddles.

Though he doesn't have the stamina for another face-off, he trudges down to the car, bends down to look in the driver's window, and seeing no passengers, motions for the kid to get out of the vehicle.

"You afraid I'm going to shoot you?" Havens makes a show of his empty hands.

The kid does as he's told.

"You are persistent, I'll give you that," Havens says.

"Nobody will talk to me."

And here Havens considered himself a man who'd lost the ability to be surprised by people. He slides his hands in his pockets, more than a little pleased to be having the upper hand, and says, "Well, there are other ways to get your story—the county library in Smoke Hole has newspapers going back that far."

"I keep trying to tell everyone I'm not here to do a story. I'm here about the people in this picture and what they—"

Havens thinks it's high time he took a look at that picture. "Tell you what—how about I trade you that picture for my confession?"

"This is my mother's picture; I'm not giving it to you!"

"Well, then, let's start with why your mother put you up to this."

"My mother didn't put me up to anything! My mother is dead!" The kid is fired up now, and Havens struggles to reorient his thinking.

"Do I know your mother?"

The kid glares at him and gives the name, Hannah Ashe, which doesn't ring a bell, and then explains about her having died two weeks ago. "The first time I saw this picture was the day she was buried, and all I know is that the people in it must have meant something to her, but it seems like there's some kind of law against finding out what that was."

Havens raises his palms and pulses them at the kid—the same gesture he uses when his mule gets a wild hair and kicks at her stall door. "Why don't we slow down, okay, son."

"My mother was a very private woman," the kid continues. "She didn't like to talk about the past, and then she dies, and suddenly I start learning about things she kept to herself. You think you know your mother. Maybe she's not as strong as other mothers, maybe she's more nervous than anybody you know, but she's cooked for you and sang to you and walloped you for cheating on a test in fifth grade, and you think you know her." As if to amend any wrong impression that might be forming in Havens's mind, he points his finger in the air and takes an emphatic tone. "She was a good mother, a really good mother."

Parched and lightheaded, Havens needs to sit someplace cool so he can think. "I'm sure she was."

"My whole life has changed since she died. Nothing's the same. Nothing." The kid presses his lips together to keep them from quivering and swings his head side to side. He could not appear more miserable.

"Why don't you come up to the house for a minute, catch your breath? It's been quite a morning." The truth is Havens feels bad for having treated a young man mourning the death of his mother so poorly.

Stepping as though to avoid booby-traps, the kid starts following Havens.

"How about we start over, and get properly acquainted. You know my name already."

"Rory Ashe," the kid offers.

Havens extends his hand, and after some reluctance, the kid shakes it briefly. Keeping his voice low and his words slow as if negotiating with a hostage taker, he asks, "And where's home for you, Rory?"

"Lexington."

Havens doesn't know anyone from that city. He leads Rory around to the back of the house and invites him into the enclosed porch, and the kid parks himself on the edge of the rocking chair beside the birdcage, where he starts cheeping at the pigeon.

"Watch out for that one," Havens cautions. "He's got a temper."

Rory remarks about the bird's bandage, and Havens tells him that he is the least cooperative patient he's ever tended, nothing at all like the blue jay and the mockingbird. Havens explains why they're in his care.

"So this is some kind of bird Red Cross?"

Havens smiles. "That about sums it up." He tells the kid the place is sometimes wall-to-wall cages.

"That old lady at the cemetery called you the devil."

"Well, I guess even the devil likes company." Havens hands Rory the jar of sunflower seeds and indicates for him to fill up Lord Byron's dish.

"Actually, you're a lot less scary than my boss."

"Whatever you do, don't let word get out. I have a reputation to protect." He's warming to the kid. "Mind if I take a look at that picture now?"

Rory reaches into his jacket pocket and hands Havens the photograph. "There aren't any names written on the back, only *Chance, Kentucky*, which is how I knew to come here."

Barely glancing at it, Havens touches it against his chest. The family portrait, in black and white. He reaches over to the side table for his reading glasses and gives the image his full attention. Jubilee is in the back row facing the camera, although not directly and not exactly smiling. Here she is, this beauty—utterly without guile—her eyes the start or end of a tunnel, he could never tell which and still cannot, but how they undo him still. He peers at her face for a long time—young as she is, he can see her wisdom. So graceful is she in this picture that a person would never guess at her burden. He removes his glasses, hands back the picture, and lets his eyes come to rest on the ground as if his strength has drained from him and pooled at his feet.

"Do you remember taking it?" asks Rory.

"As if it were yesterday." He also remembers developing it down in Del Buford's cellar, how he felt duplicitous and excited and then proud to present it as a gift. For a short time, it sat on the mantel in their living room, and now thirty-some years later it has wound up in this man's possession.

"Something terrible happened to them, didn't it? That's why you chased me away and why nobody wants to talk to me."

Jubilee would know what to say about this picture. She'd tell the story perfectly. For Havens, though, there are half a dozen different ways to tell it depending on who's doing the listening—a sheriff, a judge, a priest—and each version would be riddled with omissions and half-truths, but what is he supposed to tell this young man?

Whatever idea has just sprung into Rory's mind has made his eyes grow wide. Lowering his voice, he asks, "What that old lady called you in the cemetery . . . was she referring to what happened to these people—" Rory hesitates. "It wasn't you who—you didn't—I mean, you weren't the man who—?"

"Whoa, whoa!" Havens waves his hands. "Kid, you've got to line up your crosshairs before you go firing off rounds like that."

Havens waves off the kid's apology and goes into the kitchen. Rinsing a couple of mugs, he looks out the window to see the noonday sun turning the earlier gloom into a cloud-scalloped sky. When he returns to the sunroom, Lord Byron is perched on Rory's hand—not just perched, but preening, too.

"How long did it take you to train this bird?"

Havens puts down the cups, rolls up his cuff, and shows the peck marks on his hand from early this morning. "Does this look like the doings of a tame bird?"

The pigeon refuses to be returned to his cage and instead climbs up Rory's shirt to his shoulder. "I'll be damned." Havens suggests Rory assert his authority unless he wants to get covered in bird shit.

"That's okay, I like animals." Looking a lot less forlorn, Rory takes a sip. "The shopkeeper in town told me you were a world-class photographer. He said you were as famous as Ansel Adams."

"Right, which accounts for my lavish lifestyle." Havens gestures around the room full of mismatched furniture, houseplants in cracked pots, and throw rugs with threads balled up where the cat scratches its claws. He asks Rory how he makes a living.

"I work in a record shop, but I play in a band on weekends—that's my real job."

Rory has to explain what a synthesizer is, and even then Havens is still a bit fuzzy. He decides not to ask what "psychedelic" means.

With renewed purpose, Rory returns to the matter of the photograph. "Is it true they were blue? That's what the man at the store told me."

Havens knew it. He takes a deep breath. "You know what my favorite thing is about black-and-white photography? You don't get distracted by this or that color, because if blue is all you're looking for, it's all you're going to see. You're going to miss what makes someone similar to you and different from you, and you miss what makes someone memorable."

Havens checks his watch, figuring how to hurry this along. "Let's talk about your mother for a minute." Havens names each person in the picture, starting with Del Buford and ending with Willow-May. "Did your mother ever mention any of those names?"

Rory shakes his head.

"Did she ever live in this area or have friends or relatives who lived here?"

"Not that I know of." Rory takes a stab at finding the connection. "How about the Bufords—did they ever live somewhere else besides here? Maybe Lexington?" Rory explains that his father's job as an engineer moved them around to a number of places. "Maybe my mother met them through her charity work . . ." He mentions a couple of places, including Johnson City, where he attended elementary school, and then he says, "How about Louisville? We lived there for a year when I was really little." Rory leans toward Havens, his head tilted to one side. "Louisville? Is that it? They moved to Louisville?"

Havens has stopped listening to his visitor. They say a smell can take you back in time, but sounds—that haunting train whistle, those clacking wheels racing along tracks—they take you to what seems foreordained.

"Are you okay, Mr. Havens? Can I get you something?"

Rory returns with a glass of water and the dishcloth dripping wet.

The thing they never explain about trains is that no matter the destination, you cannot board and disembark the same person.

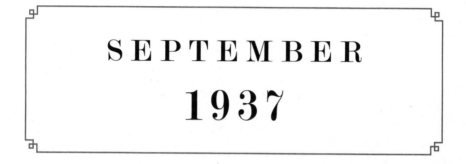

SEPTEMBER
1937

JUBILEE

T he train rounds the last bend before pulling into Chance, the clacking wheels slowing on the approach to the station while the beat of her heart ratchets up to full-speed. Jubilee takes a few deep breaths, tells herself that everything is going to be fine, better than fine. How different life is going to be for her now, for Mama and Pa and all of them.

Four months she's been away and so much has changed for her, right down to being a passenger on a train. Leaving, she'd been at the very back of the third-class car, an outcast riding on someone else's ticket, and returning, she is in a first-class sleeper, paid for from her own purse. Even before the train comes to a full stop, she is up on her feet, suitcase in hand, adjusting her little satin hat. She was the last one to board the train four months ago. This time, she is the first off.

What she sees doesn't line up with her memory, not exactly. The scale is wrong, for one thing. The station has shrunk. Gummy legs carry her along the platform to the front door, where she hesitates and looks out onto a much-shortened Main Street and the stunted version of town sitting cowed by the hills. The air feels right, though. She takes a deep breath, tightens her grip on her suitcase and steps onto the sidewalk, almost colliding with

Verily Suggins, Faro's aunt. Jubilee has spent the entire train ride figuring how best to conduct herself on her return, picturing and preparing for any number of reactions from the townsfolk. None of this helps when the moment presents. She comes to a dead halt, uses her suitcase as a fort between her and the woman, and waits for Verily to point her finger and say, What are you doing here? Nothing would make Jubilee feel more at home than a scare, but polite as you like, the woman instead says, "Pardon me, miss," and all but curtseys around her.

After this test, Jubilee chooses the sunny side of the street. She still can't get over what it feels like to have no veil and no gloves. A man walks her way. He tips his hat as he passes her. Another man walks by, and then a woman, and Jubilee studies their faces, their shoulders, their stride, but nothing changes when they see her. A group of young people come toward her at a clip, only to file past her as though she were a lamppost. She becomes a bit giddy. The simple joy of walking. Will she ever get used to it?

She pauses in front of Rakestraw's store to read the signs. CHEW COPENHAGEN, IT'S A PLEASURE. NEW LARGE POTATOES 6lbs/23c. APPLES DELICIOUS 4lb/25c. ORANGES/TANGERINES 1c.

Mr. Rakestraw comes out with a bucket of apples and sets them on the wooden shelf. "Enjoying the cooler weather?"

He shines an apple and offers it to her. Refusing her coin, he remarks on her suitcase. "We don't often get visitors to Chance. You the new schoolteacher?"

"No."

"Visiting kin?"

"Thank you for the apple," she replies.

"You take care now, miss."

She can feel him watching her and decides to cross the street again, careful not to go the speed at which Blues usually move from place to place. Her return deserves a slower pace, a sure foot.

It has rained recently, and everything is turned to mirrors—the puddles in the street, the chrome bumpers on the parked cars, even the air has a gleam to it. Steering around those gathered in front of Caldon Enterprise,

Jubilee catches a glimpse of the news posted in its window: PRINCE GRILLS ROOSEVELT, ITALIANS URGED TO OUST MUSSOLINI. A little girl in a blue dress is out on the sidewalk with a jump rope, her father standing to the side so she can skip back and forth. She comes Jubilee's way, pigtails flying behind her, tongue hooked at the corner of her mouth, and instinct is like a hand yanking the scruff of Jubilee's collar. Though she swerves to one side, turning her face away, the child keeps leaping through her loops, saying, "Excuse me, thank you." Half a block later in front of the town hall, it is the same way. Five boys are playing with stick guns, and not one thinks to raise one at her. It's the most peculiar feeling—wanting someone to notice her.

And then she spies Chappy in his usual parking spot at the end of the block outside the post office, reading that same newspaper page. She steps up her pace.

"Hi, Chappy!"

He looks up. Chappy's grin takes up most of his face and he waves his arm as though she's clear across town and not right in front of him. You'd think he was barefoot on hot rocks. "Juby!"

She puts her suitcase down so they can do their old crosswise-handshake-and-elbow-knot greeting.

"You're different!" He touches her cheek as though to check if Jell-O has set.

"I cut my hair, too."

His inspection goes on a while. "And those ain't your clothes."

She sways her pleated skirt. "They used to belong to a very pretty lady. She gave them to me."

He points at her shoes. "Them's yours."

She laughs. "I've got a fancy pair in my suitcase, but I can't hardly walk in them."

Chappy grows shy all of a sudden, looking at her from the corner of his eye. "Don't worry, Juby—you're still fine-looking."

"Hey." She swats his arm. "I'm still me." Which is only partway true. It'll take her a while yet to figure what size portion of her has changed and what has a ways yet to change. "You still you?"

He frowns at what he reckons is a silly question, so she asks a better one. "Have you been working on your car lately?"

"She's got new brakes, and I gave her a tune-up last week." He asks where she's been.

She'd arrived in Louisville and departed from Louisville, and there doesn't seem much point in listing the in-between places where she only ever spent a week or two so she just says, "Louisville."

He slaps the newspaper against his thigh. "Louisville! They've got all kinds of automobiles out there."

Jubilee doesn't tell him about the day she stumbled out of Union Station onto Preston Street, where a hundred cars raced one way and another hundred the other, making the city such a screeching place that she fell into a crouch and covered her ears with her hands and stayed that way till someone threw a coin at her feet. "Your set of wheels is better than all of those by far," she says.

Chappy touches her forearm with the backs of his fingers. "Say, I bet you'll be needing a ride home."

"I sure am."

He wiggles his cap, and says, "Good thing I got her all gassed up this morning." He picks up his hub cap in one hand and her suitcase in the other, and nods at the fresh air beside him. "Hop in front."

As they start down the road, Chappy says, "You've been gone a long time."

It might as well have been years, but now that she's back, four months has a fleeting feel.

The pickup truck that races up beside them is Ronny's, but only Faro is inside. He leans out the window and whistles a catcall, mistaking Jubilee for a newcomer. Her knees lock up and she turns her face the other way, and hides behind airs. Faro jabbers something to Chappy, but her ears are stuffed again with Ronny's threat that she never return, and her eyes become pulpy at the memory of Levi. She needs to get home. She needs to lie down in Mama's embrace.

"Mind if I floor it, Juby?" Chappy asks as soon as the pickup has sped off, and the two of them sprint out of town, racing past the old filling station, where Ronny and Faro found her, and around the bend that leads to coal miners' houses. At a hard run, she and Chappy pass Willy and his two sisters on their cart.

Chappy waves furiously and yells out, "Juby's come home!"

"Jubilee?" Willy whoas his mule to a standstill.

She waves and keeps running. "Maybe we don't tell folks just yet."

"Sure thing, Juby."

They speed past the tenant farmer's place, those same three scraggly children still hanging on the gate, and tear along the dirt path that rounds the millpond, where the Wrightley brothers are fishing for crappie. The boys do a double-take as Chappy and Jubilee whisk around the bend.

They slow a little on the uphill and a little more when they cut across the graveyard, and by the time they reach Spooklight Holler, she's tuckered out. Chappy says the flat tire will give her time to rest and points to a nearby log to serve as a bench. She watches as he takes out the wrench from his back pocket, gets on his haunches, and starts twisting air.

"Have you seen my folks lately?"

With his back to her, he says, "You'll find your pa a little on the changed side." He brings up the time his grandma learned her son, Leroy, wasn't coming back from the war. "He's got that look about him."

"And my mama?"

Chappy purses his lips.

Every morning that she was away, Jubilee would startle awake with a plea for Levi's safety on her lips, and she'd remember where she was and how she came to be there and had to go through his dying all over again, cup after cup of maggots, until daybreak would seep through the cracks of the trailer and her breath would no longer come in fits and starts, and the weight on her chest would lift enough that she could get up and go to that tent. If this was what grief did to her, she can't imagine its toll on Mama.

After all these weeks, the air finally sounds right again, thick with bird chatter and insects nattering away and trees shifting as though to find a more comfortable position.

"Say, you ever heard from that mister who got bit by the viper?"

Just the mention of him, and she can feel Havens's touch on her cheek, hear his voice promising to wait for her at the shack. "No, why would I?"

Chappy wipes his hands with the oil rag, stands, and kicks the invisible tire. "He sure was taken with you. I ain't never seen a man as struck by a lady, not even when Otis come for my sister."

"Maybe he was just struck by blue."

"You always had a special way about you, blue or no blue, and he was one who could tell that."

He mops his forehead and looks off to the east, where the mountains form a heaven-high hedge between her and Havens.

"When we were out looking for you and Levi that morning, he said you were the most caring person he ever met and how you didn't deserve nothing but the best kind of treatment. The rain sent everyone for cover, but he wanted to keep going. He about wore himself out. Then the sun comes up and he sits on a big old rock and starts to cry, and says how everything is his fault. I never seen a happier man than when we come upon you, Juby."

She picks up her suitcase and takes her place beside Chappy. "Do you mind if we don't talk about that again, Chappy, and I'd really rather not talk about him, either."

"Sure, Juby." He picks up his hub cap and makes engine sounds, and they take off again.

Not twenty yards later, Chappy says, "Like I said, he was real taken with you."

"Chappy, please."

They fall into an easy silence that lasts a minute. "He was first-rate."

"Chappy!"

"Sorry." He glances at her and shrugs, then makes so many honking noises he scares a flock of blackbirds from the dogwood tree.

Way down past the end of his field, where the land leaves off being level and turns into a slope, stands a crooked old man with his hand shielding his eyes as though he's awaiting the arrival of someone whose delay has gone on too long, as if he's trained his eyes for disturbances caused even by insects and tuned his ears all the way to Tennessee.

Jubilee waves her arm.

Nothing.

Chappy cups his mouth and hollers into the wind, "Jubilee's—come—home," but she doesn't know what of it reaches Pa intact, because he keeps standing like he's expecting the three Magi, not the two of them. She hitches her skirt and climbs the hill, and suddenly Pa's caught on and comes barreling hatless toward her. Five feet in front of her, though, his feet act like they've hit a patch of ice. His hands clasp his head as if it's got tangled in a thorn bush. He opens his mouth, but no words come out, just one big sob.

She knows from treating wounded animals to step carefully. "Hi, Pa."

Pa reaches for her hands and cries and falls to his knees, and when she bends down with him, he sits in the dirt with his knees bent, pulling her into his shoulder. "My girl, my girl." They rock awhile.

"How can it be?" he keeps saying. Eventually, Pa looks sideways at her. "I thought you were—" He rocks her some more. "Where have you been all this time?"

"Louisville, mostly." She wonders if everything she says is going to take a good deal of rocking for the meaning to sink in.

He smiles through his tears. "You found a doctor?"

"A doctor found me."

The long walk up to the house gives her time to explain some about her coloring. She keeps insisting it's a treatment, but Pa keeps repeating everything she says, substituting with the word "cure," though cure it is not. She tells him what Dr. Fordsworth told her boss. "I'm a patient receiving medical attention, Pa." She takes out the bottle and hands it to Pa, who unscrews the lid and treats the small blue pills the way he does scat when he's hunting game, emptying a few in his hand so he can smell them and roll them between his fingers.

"I'll be gold-darned," he says, as if they were Jack's magic beans.

JUBILEE

ama's room smells like food starting to spoil. Daylight makes
its way past the shutters only as far as the foot of the bed, as
if it knows better than to venture any farther.

It's a rolled-up blanket on the bed that Jubilee addresses. "Hello, Mama."
The shape stirs.

"Gladden, look who's come," says Pa, himself not yet fully recovered
from the thunderbolt of her return. With the same shaking hands that
held her, Pa now reaches for Mama. He seems to be making a bed more
than getting a person upright, and as simple as his task is, it takes him a
long time to make even a little progress. It scares Jubilee that her mother
has to be dealt with in this manner.

"Up you get. There you go."

A small frail woman who looks like a distant relative of Mama's sits on
the edge of the bed and stares at the floor.

Jubilee approaches the bed, her feet coming to rest right below Mama's
gaze, and looks down on the top of Mama's head. Her scalp is showing.
Jubilee digs her nails into her hands to stop herself from crying out. "Hello,
Mama," she tries again.

Pa keeps talking real loud in her ear. "See, it's Jubilee."

"Mama?" She is desperate for her mother to see her. "It's me. I've come home."

Like pipe cleaners, Mama's skinny arms wind around Jubilee's knees. She draws her closer without making any sound and presses her head against Jubilee's legs, those scrawny arms somehow keeping Jubilee from falling to pieces. She doesn't talk and she doesn't lift her head. All she's seen of Jubilee are shoes, brown nylons and the hem of her costly hand-me-down, and this is enough for her.

Pa all but yells, "Jubilee's got a surprise for you, Gladden. Take a look."

Mama's arms loosen a little and she lifts her eyes. So she doesn't get a crick in her neck on top of everything else, Jubilee gets on her haunches.

Mama sucks in a breath so big it's a wonder there's any air left in the room for anyone. The creek might as well be flowing with molasses the way Mama stares at her, as if the field is sprung up with maypoles instead of corn, a veined membrane instead of a sky.

"It's fixed, Mama." Well, one part. Others are broken past fixing.

Mama pushes the hair from Jubilee's forehead, cups her face with bony hands, and peers at her with a brow so creased, Jubilee half-expects to be asked who she is. Mama's eyes dart to Jubilee's hands—pale pink nails, fingertips the color of Mama's after she's brought them out of a basin of warm water. Mama's gaze travels along Jubilee's wrists, pale as a sheet of paper, up her arms, and back again to her face, and she knows what Mama sees: the whole of Jubilee drained of blue and filled with the nectar of peaches.

Mama consults Jubilee's palms, where fortunes have changed just like that. No longer are they crossed with black lines, but embroidered with tiny pink stitches. Jubilee understands now why people call them lifelines. Mama turns Jubilee's hands this way and that, as though they are gloves she might like to try on.

"A doctor in Louisville found a cure for her, Gladden."

Mama doesn't mind Pa. She just keeps her eyes on Jubilee.

"Do you like it, Mama?"

Hinges rusted shut is how she comes to think of Mama's mouth. Why won't she say anything? All Jubilee gets is this searching look, as though Mama's trapped inside a glass bottle.

"Pa, can she hear us?"

Mama strokes Jubilee's hand, then puts her cheek against it.

"Her hearing's fine," he hollers. "Isn't that so, Glad?" Turning to Jubilee, he drops his voice. "She doesn't talk hardly at all anymore since you and your brother—" Pa doesn't end the sentence. "Isn't this something, Gladden? Jubilee coming home, and then cured on top of that? Isn't she just a picture?"

Mama smooths Jubilee's hair before pressing her fingers against Jubilee's cheeks.

"Think you might want to come sit out in the front room with us? Jubilee's got such a story, and I haven't heard the half of it. I made her wait to tell it so you could hear, too." Pa's words trail away as Mama glances at her pillow. Her hands slip away like reeds in a stream.

"Okay, then, we'll let you have a little lie-down," Pa says. "I'm going to rustle up something for Jubilee to eat and we'll come get you and see if you won't have a bite."

Pa covers her with the blanket and turns her back into a bedroll, and when they step out of the room, Jubilee turns around, and two gleaming eyes blink at her.

Grandma is sitting by the fireplace with her suitcase on her lap, and she scowls at Jubilee as she did when Jubilee first walked through the front door. Grandma doesn't know her at all.

"This here's Jubilee, Ma." But Pa still can't convince her.

Jubilee follows him to the kitchen, where he appears to have forgotten where everything is kept, so she brings him the mixing bowl, and points him to the flour bin, and after every step, he stops to admire her again. Color has won him over.

Jubilee gets out the whisk and hands him an egg.

"Shall I fix it, Pa?"

"No, no, you sit." He starts mixing up batter for the biscuits, looking at her again and again. "You're glowing. Like there's a lamp on inside you."

At this rate, they will never eat. Jubilee starts frying up the bacon. "So you said Willow-May is with Socall?"

"This house has been no place for a child." He explains that Mama, Grandma, and Willow-May moved in with Socall during the weeks he spent looking for Jubilee, and when Socall brought them all back, Willow-May refused to stay, and now comes to visit every other day or so. Pa talks of being gone for days at a time, long enough for Mama to have gotten the idea that Pa was dead somewhere, too. "I searched every bend and crease of those hills for you, and never once did I imagine you'd be so far away or I'd have gone there, too." Pa is trying not to cry. "I'm sorry I didn't find you, my girl."

"No, Pa. I'm sorry for not getting word to you." She pats his back. Each day she was away, she'd aimed to finish her letter home, at least to let Mama and Pa know she was alive, but two or three lines in and she'd decide again that her being dead would hurt them less than knowing she was in that place. How exactly she spent her days is something she's resolved never to tell, certainly not Pa.

"What matters is that you're home now," he says, composing himself. "And tomorrow I'll send for Willow-May."

On the subject of Mama's condition, all he has to say is "Something with her wiring," as if she's an electric circuit instead of the flesh-and-blood mama who needs to get up and tell Jubilee color is going to make everything right.

Pa cups her shoulder. "Don't you worry none. Now that you're home, she'll be back to her old self before you can say Jack Robinson." He says this at full volume, declarative-like, as if all it is going to take for them to be who they once were is loud sure-speaking.

Jubilee sets the table and when she comes to Levi's place, she can't bear not putting anything out for him, so she goes down to the cellar and fetches a candle that's never been burned, making it a point not to dwell on that line of twine where pictures of her once were pinned, and when she goes upstairs she checks the mantel, just in case the family portraits are still there. They aren't.

Mama won't be coaxed from her bed and Grandma has forgone her meal to repack her suitcase, so only Jubilee and Pa and her conjured brother gather for dinner. Barely pecking at his food, Pa says for her to start her story wherever she wants.

To get Ronny out of the way, she begins with being thrown on the train, and because this causes Pa to get up and pace and grow more agitated with each lap, she shrinks the middle part of her story to include only the kindness of strangers on her arrival in Louisville, the kinship she found among a few souls similarly unfortunate and the charity of those who paid her to do menial tasks.

"You found work?"

She considers whether it is more palatable to Pa if she says she'd lived the whole time the way she'd first started out, as a tramp, or to tell at least a portion of the truth. Even a short delay in answering causes Pa to fret, so she says, "I hired on at the Kentucky State Fair."

Instantly, Pa's face shows relief. "Did you work with the livestock? Because I know they take real good care of the animals at those big fairs. They got veterinarians on hand day and night, don't they?"

It would be easy to go along with this, but she doesn't want to start off her right-colored life on the wrong foot, so she says, "I know you want to know more, Pa, but it was a mostly hard time that needs to fade some, and talking about it keeps it fresh."

"That's why your mama can't talk about Levi yet."

So that Pa won't be tormented thinking it was hell from beginning to end, she gets to the part she knows he'll like best. "The fair's where I met the doctor." Stooped as though he'd spent his life turning over rocks to see what was under them, Dr. Fordsworth showed up one hot humid afternoon without warning, his arrival the result of a flier one of his students had shown him, and, after admitting being skeptical given the kind of operation she was a part of, he peered at her face, neck, and arms as if there weren't a person inside her skin. Once his looking was satisfied, he behaved like a boy being given a candy apple.

"Dr. Fordsworth is a famous doctor of the blood at the University of Louisville," she tells Pa. "He knows more about blood than anyone else in the country."

Pa says, "Blood, but what about blue?"

"Blue and blood go together."

She understands Pa's bewilderment. Dr. Fordsworth had to spend a long time explaining to her the role of blood in her coloring, eventually getting out a pen and paper and drawing pictures to represent blood molecules and the enzyme he seemed partial to. Even then, it seemed far-fetched.

"So, he knew about blue before he met you?"

Jubilee nods. "He'd only ever known about it from books, though. Doctors know of six others who've been blue, and three of those were from a tribe in Alaska."

She might as well have said the moon. Pa asks, "Is there a name for it?"

"Methemoglobinemia."

"That's some mouthful." Pa fetches his pencil and has her write it down. After trying three times to pronounce it, he gives up. "And he knew you had this just by looking at you?"

Jubilee tells how the doctor first listened to her chest to rule out problems with her lungs and heart before using a syringe to fill a little glass bottle with her blood for testing. "It looked like oil." Like it had gone off, but when she told the doctor this, he corrected her with a soft tone, using the words "enzyme deficient." "He was back three days later to tell me my blood doesn't have diaphorase, which is an enzyme."

"What's an enzyme?"

Jubilee knows the explanation with all the big words by heart, having studied the papers Dr. Fordsworth gave her, and to help Pa understand now, she fetches them from her suitcase. When she returns, he is pouring himself a glass of Socall's shine. Jubilee lays the papers out on the table, and Pa squints at them. "Why don't you read it to me."

Rather than start at the top, she begins with the sections she has underlined.

"'*The first case of congenital methemoglobinemia was documented in 1845 by French physician Dr. Francois, whose patient presented with cyanosis in the absence of cardiac and pulmonary dysfunction. In 1932, K. Hitzenberger concluded idiopathic cyanosis to be an hereditary ailment.*'"

Pa interrupts. "This is about blue?"

"'Cyanosis' is just a doctor's roundabout way of saying 'blue,' and 'heredi-tary' means your black-sheep theory is not too far off the mark, but I like this part because it says the first blue person showed up almost a hundred years ago in France."

"And here we thought your grandma Opal was the first." Pa runs his fingers over another underlined section. *Giving blood its blue coloration in oxygen-depleted veins is methemoglobin. Methemoglobin is then changed into hemoglobin, which gives blood its red color, and what makes this change happen is diaphorase.* "You can't tell me you know what this means."

She turns to Dr. Fordsworth's sketch of different size bubbles and arrows going left and right to represent how blood molecules are red when they carry oxygen and blue when they don't, and together, she and Pa match each set of bubbles with the items listed in the caption. Pa points to the bubbles on the left. "Methemoglobin." He looks to Jubilee to confirm, before pointing to those on the right. "Hemoglobin?"

"That's right."

"Aha, diaphorase!" Pa pounds a set of ink dots. "What your blood doesn't have." He might as well have discovered the *x* on a treasure map.

"And that's why my blood has too much this." She points to the bubbles labeled METHEMOGLOBIN.

"So this Dr. Fordsworth fella brought you the cure?"

"Not a cure, Pa." She reads her favorite part. *"In 1928, Harrop and Baron demonstrated that the introduction of methylene blue into the bloodstream of a patient with congenital methemoglobinemia caused a complete reversion of met-hemoglobin to hemoglobin."*

Pa stops her. "I want you to tell me this part all in English."

It was only four days ago that Dr. Fordsworth took a tiny glass bottle filled with blue liquid out of his black bag. The antidote, he called it. "Methylene blue is really just blue dye, and one hundred milligrams is all it should take to reverse your symptoms," he'd said.

"He wanted to put more blue in you?" asks Pa.

"It seemed backward logic to me, too." Jubilee had been warned long before she met Dr. Fordsworth that certain doctors would come around every once in a while looking to practice their medicine and perform their experiments on people like her, and suddenly she wasn't so sure she ought to trust the man, not when he was proposing something that made no sense. "All I could think was how the blue dye was going to make me worse, so I told him I wasn't going to go through with it."

Pa's eyes are wide at this point. "But he found a way to convince you."

"By rolling up his own sleeve and giving himself the shot first." That had taken her by surprise, and she watched the doctor a long while until there wasn't any option but to take her turn. She describes how he'd cleaned her arm with alcohol before pricking it and then slowly pushed in the dye, saying the effects would occur after twenty to thirty minutes. "After twenty minutes, I looked at my arm, and it was as blue as ever." Same blue hands, nails as though they'd been polished by coal. If it wasn't the worst idea ever. "Suddenly, there was something not quite right about Dr. Fordsworth," she says, recalling how flushed his cheeks were and that he looked ready to pass out. "I thought I was about to have the same terrible reaction he was having, but it turns out he was startled, is all." She reports how she'd yelled at the doctor to tell her what was wrong with him, and in reply he'd lifted her hand to her face. She supposed it belonged to her, but she didn't know how. Gone from it was any trace of blue. Her arms were the same way, no blue. All at once, she'd gone from twilight to dawn-colored.

Jubilee pushes her chair back from the table, kicks off her boots, and rolls down her nylons to show Pa her dainty feet, the color of dogwood blossoms, and the soles like the smooth bark of a yellowwood tree.

Pa reaches for her toes and gives them a wiggle. "Earthworms!"

She tells Pa that Dr. Fordsworth gave her the dye in pill form, explaining that the effects aren't permanent. "After twenty-four hours or so, my system flushes out the last of the methylene blue, and I have to take another dose."

"So you're still blue?"

"That's why it's not a cure. I'll have to do this every day for the rest of my life."

"What about when the pills run out?"

She tells Pa she has a three-month supply, and a prescription any druggist can fill, even a country one.

"But surely they cost a lot of money." Something along the order of a piece of fertile land, Pa must be thinking.

"A hundred costs about the same as a tube of toothpaste. It's just dye, Pa."

Pa sits down and skims the pages again, and after a while, he says, "If only your brother were alive for this."

And there is the empty place that right-colored skin won't ever cover.

⁂

After washing and putting away the dishes, Pa says for her to put her boots on and go with him on a walk, because he wants to show her what helped him get through, and as soon as they turn off the main path for the lesser trail, she knows they're headed for her aviary. Among all those city people, there had been no defense against the loneliness at night, so to comfort herself, Jubilee would spread out her arms on the cold sheet of her bench-bed and catch a thermal that took her over the tops of the buildings and across the never-ending streets to the timbered hills, where she'd glide through the trees and drop down to her aviary. During those first few visits, her birds would flap around on their perches and wonder why she wasn't setting seed out for them and why she wasn't mending their hurts. In later visits, there were fewer birds, and one night she returned and found only empty cages. This she can't face now, so she asks Pa if it can wait.

"Come on," he insists.

As they near the shed, Pa has to prompt her to go first.

She throws open the door, and instead of finding a place of neglect, she sees cages filled with birds. None of the occupants does she recognize save one.

"Thomas!" she cries, opening the lid, and immediately he climbs onto her hand. "You're fat! How are you ever going to fly with that belly?"

She sinks to the floor, making a nest for him with her skirt, and whistles and coos at the others.

"You've kept it going for me!"

"This was the one place I could feel close to you. I'd come here every day, and we'd talk about you, wouldn't we, boys? This fella here"—he gestures at Thomas—"he even flew a few missions to look for you. He always knew you'd come back."

Pa introduces the others, telling how he found them and what names he's given them. "When word gets out that you're back, the place is going to be overrun. We'll likely have to build on."

Jubilee puts out fresh water and a few bonus scoops of sunflower seeds, and suddenly Havens's presence grows strong. She recalls how he behaved when he was taking pictures of her, like someone who was being told a story and didn't want it to end. If there was harm for her when he took those pictures, there was some kind of harm for him when he quit. And now she is made right, and tomorrow she will be made right again, and every day after that, and what kind of background might he set her against now? When she gets back to the house and Pa is out in the field, she'll look for the black-and-white pictures Havens left behind—the ones of the family, the ones of Thomas and her other birds, and the one she'd taken of him.

HAVENS

⁂

For once, Havens wakes up decisive instead of how he has for the last few months, filled with the same restlessness that used to plague him as a teenager languishing in this very same bed. He cannot spend one more day trying to settle the question of whether or not to return to Chance. He will go to her. He will tell her he took care of the photograph and killed the story. He will tell her other things, that he can't stop thinking about her, the hills, the people he met, the northern flicker, the foxes, even that creepy spider tree, which must be filled now with moths. What he won't tell her is that he lost his job and got evicted from the boarding house for not paying his rent and that he's had to move back to Dayton to live with his parents in his boyhood home. Nor will he mention that he hasn't touched his camera in weeks. He has tried taking photographs since leaving Chance, but he'll no sooner set up his Graflex than the light will be wrong, or if it is a tolerable light, his hand will start to shake, or his interest will be diverted. Each of his landscapes and still-life pictures is underexposed or overexposed or blurred or lacking a focal point, nothing at all compared to the photographs he took of her or the natural world to which she belongs.

He slips his hand under his pillow and pulls out the only picture he has of her, the black-and-white he'd slipped in his shirt pocket while they were in the cellar together. Now he holds it like a card in a winning hand. There is just enough morning light to make out the place on her collarbone where he had put his finger and made her shiver, the crook of her arm where she allowed him to put his hand when they walked back from the aviary, her eyes that draw him in. Her mouth! He turns the image facedown and rests it on his chest. Despite what everyone believes about photographs, they do not preserve memories; they cause them to degrade. With the mind so focused on one split-second image, the hundred moments that led to it as well as the afterglow moments that followed become blurry. Study a photograph too much, and it will obliterate smell, touch, hearts beating double-time.

Havens imagines his hand slipping under her blouse, skimming the pale sky of her belly, rounding her waist to the small of her back, drawing her close to him. Being in her presence was to have a thick callus peeled off his senses, and nothing can compensate for his longing to be with her. Though he has tried to let her go, he can't keep from trying to resuscitate every memory of her and making up fictitious ones, too.

Havens throws aside the covers—why not go today?—but before he is even fully upright, the nagging voice of reason starts chipping away at his resolve. She did not meet him at the shack for a reason. As much as he'd like to believe she'd been detained by her parents, he can't shake free the likelihood that she'd changed her mind and signaled him with her absence that he was to move on as she was preparing to do.

But should he not go to her, even if to be chased away?

After dressing, he heads to the kitchen and stops short in the hallway when he hears his mother complaining to someone, the neighbor next door, he guesses. "He just sits around and mopes all day, and it's been going on for months, ever since he moved back home. He doesn't even try to improve his situation. It was like this when he was a youngster. If you ask me, that business about the photograph has become an excuse not to go out. I never did care for that camera, and I told his father that. I knew he wasn't ever going to make any money off it, for one thing. I told him flat-out, 'What gal's going to go out with you if you're broke all the time?' but did he listen to me? And then, you know, his marriage didn't go well, and after that, he just stuck his head behind that thing day and night, but now he won't touch it."

Why would his mother be telling the neighbor all this?

"I'll say this, though, he sure is lucky to have someone like you care about him, and drive all the way up from Cincinnati."

Betty? The realization has an anesthetizing effect.

"Is that you, Clayton?" his mother calls. "Clayton?"

Glaciers move quicker than he does.

"Well, here he is now. Don't just stand there, Clayton, for heaven's sake."

While Betty stands and makes a presentation of herself, Havens mumbles his greeting and reaches out his hand without knowing quite what to do with it.

Betty doesn't feel good in his arms. She has the feel of utility, like a bureau where you park your loose change. Her kiss misses and lands on his chin. Despite this, she sighs a little.

"Hello, Clayton."

"This is a—I wasn't sure you even—how are you?" The last time he saw Betty was two days after his visit to the offices of *Look* magazine. She'd taken the breakup well, he thought, and hadn't pressed him for details.

"Your mother was just saying you needed some cheering up."

Havens slides his hands into his pockets and assumes what he hopes is an expression of contentment. "I don't know why."

Turning to Betty, his mother asks, "Did you read what they printed about him in the newspaper?"

"Mother, please, it's been months. Can we not bring it up every five minutes?"

Huffing, his mother pretends to make her way to the kitchen, but is likely headed only as far as behind the door.

"It must have been very upsetting for you," Betty commiserates. "For everyone in your family."

Havens wishes she would quit looking at him with such pity. "It could've been worse. The article ran on page eight."

"I read they took back the Pulitzer."

Why would that matter to him? Nor did it matter that Pomeroy had given a lengthy statement to the press about how regrettable the FSA found his actions, which were in no way to be a reflection of the government's dedication to portraying hardworking and honest families across the country. Oddly, the only sympathetic voice had been that of the so-called orphan boy's mother, who was quoted as saying she couldn't see what all the fuss was about. "It's not as if there aren't poor hungry children about." Only the last line of the article mentioned plans to pull off another unspecified hoax for similar gain, and no one has asked him about this until now.

Betty says, "Taking another fake picture was all Ulys's idea, wasn't it?"

He shakes his head. "You mustn't defend me, Betty."

Havens's mother returns with a glass of iced tea for her. "Clayton, where are your manners? Aren't you going to ask your guest to sit?"

"How about we go outside?" he suggests. He is glad the truth about *Orphan Boy* is out, glad that the very lie that had put him at odds with himself is now the ransom by which Jubilee has gone free—would that every wrong yield such a profit.

Betty takes a seat on the bench beneath the wilted wisteria. "Well, I came to tell you Ulys has another harebrained idea, and this one could very well get him killed." She reports that he's sworn off all his old friends who are worried about him and fallen in with a bunch of Marxists obsessed with the Spanish Civil War. "Ulys is leaving next week to go fight in it, and I thought you could try to talk him out of it."

Somehow Massey's enlisting in a foreign war doesn't surprise him. "You know Massey doesn't take advice, and he's certainly not going to listen to me." Never mind that Havens is in no mood for another confrontation with Massey. "Has he spoken to you about Chance?"

"I know he feels bad about what happened to you," she answers. "But you know Ulys—he can't just come out and say that. It's much more like him to show it by doing something heroic." Betty reports that Massey has been writing obituaries for the *Tribune* and freelancing, barely making ends meet. "You two have had your ups and downs, but you've been friends a long time and I know you'll end up hating yourself if something should happen to him over there and things weren't right between you."

"I don't know; maybe some things can't be put right." He tells her he appreciates her coming all this way to put him in the picture, and she insists he give it some thought, handing him a piece of paper with Massey's contact details. She pats the bench for him to join her. "I'm sure everyone will forget about the pictures soon, and you'll be back in the saddle again."

He makes a noncommittal sound.

"I know you needed some time to yourself, but maybe now we can put all this unpleasantness behind us."

Surely Betty cannot be under the impression that their breakup had to do with the scandal. "I don't think I explained properly last time we were together."

She cuts him off. "Everyone at some point regrets something they've done. Nobody's perfect."

"I am so sorry, Betty. I can't do this."

"It was a picture, that's all. It's over now—done—in the past."

She waves her hand to show how fleeting she thinks the past is, how irrelevant, how trifling compared to this interminable future she has in mind, and Havens understands this is why she didn't just telephone him with the news about Massey, but drove here instead.

"I can't be with you anymore, Betty." She waits for him to amend his statement, but he adds, "It wasn't just a picture."

She puts her glass on the ground, smooths her skirt, and says in that no-nonsense way of hers, "There's someone else."

Why deny it? "Yes."

"How long has it been going on?"

"Things between you and me weren't ever going to work out in the long run."

She stands. "Well, she can't care that much for you if she lets you carry on in this condition." Betty waves at his dishevelment.

"Please believe I never meant to hurt you."

"You never mean to hurt anyone, do you? And yet somehow you do." She clutches her purse. "Goodbye, Clay."

Betty's car is backing out of the driveway when Havens's mother comes out with a plate of almond cookies. "You do realize you are going to end up a miserable old man."

A couple of shots ring out from around the side of the house, and a flock of starlings fills the sky. "Oh, go tell your father to quit that before someone calls the police. That's all we need now—a patrol car in our driveway."

Havens finds his father reloading his .22 rifle in the backyard. "Those damn birds aim to roost in my apple tree again."

Havens thinks of Jubilee at her aviary. "You can't shoot birds, Dad."

"Have you seen one bluebird since you've been back? No, because the starlings have put an end to them. Goddamn intruders."

Havens leaves his father to guard his tree and returns to the living room, where he picks up the telephone and asks the operator to connect him to the number Betty's written on the paper.

❧

Havens is part of the great surge of passengers that spills from the train, rushes along the platform and through the tunnel, and eventually empties into the great hall of Cincinnati's Union Station. He'd planned to get here long before the appointed meeting, allowing time to collect his thoughts and establish a position of dominance, but the train was delayed out of Dayton, and he hurries now to the waiting area like a boy late to class. He spots Massey at the hotdog stand, and again second-guesses his decision to come. Massey could not have sounded more indifferent on the telephone, and it was his idea to meet at the station rather than where he is lodging.

"Hello, Massey."

"Jesus, don't you look a sight." Massey orders a second hotdog with a double serving of relish, the way Havens likes it, and refuses to take Havens's money.

Headed for the far corner of the waiting room, Massey asks, "So, you and Betty aren't an item anymore, I hear."

"Not for several months."

"And yet here you are, still doing what she tells you to do." Massey waves his napkin at him. "Hey, I'm kidding." He slides into a leather armchair. "Betty's been recruiting everyone shy of the pope to talk me out of going to Spain, but like I told you on the telephone, nothing's going to stop me."

"When has anyone ever been able to stop you from doing anything?"

Massey cocks an eyebrow and addresses the distracted passersby. "How quickly he forgets." But instead of pursuing the subject of Jubilee's photograph, he speaks of war and how the battle against the Nationalists in Spain has fractured into disputes among the various factions on the Republicans' side. "Orwell was there fighting, you know. They made him a corporal. He'd still be there if the enemy hadn't shot him in the neck."

"Orwell?" The name rings a bell.

"You haven't read *The Road to Wigan Pier*? Required reading for anyone with a political conscience." Massey summarizes the English writer's chronicle of the coal mines in Yorkshire, and describes an epistolary friendship that has sprung up between the two of them. "Hemingway, Neruda, Dos Passos, and a bunch of other writers are already over there fighting, so if I'm crazy, I'll be in excellent company."

"I don't think it's crazy wanting to be a part of something that matters."

Massey seems pleased by this. "Everyone else I know thinks it's baloney, like who the hell am I to think I can take on Franco, but this is the most important battle of the century. If it were a fight over territory or property, who cares, but it's a fight for an Idea, and we've got to fight for it with everything we've got."

Havens recounts what he's read in the papers about prowling gangs of armed men in Barcelona and food lines that go on for more than a mile, and Massey says he's headed for the Aragon front instead.

"The trenches?"

"You know what they say—if your writing isn't good enough, you're not close enough."

"The same is probably true for pictures," Havens offers.

For a moment, neither of them speaks.

Massey fixes his attention on a young couple now sitting across from them. "It wasn't my finest hour," he says.

Havens knows he refers to the Bufords. "Nor mine."

They watch the two neck.

"I was expecting someone to knock on my door asking for comments, but you kept my name out of the papers. You had your chance to get back at me, why didn't you take it?"

"Who says I wasn't waiting for a better opportunity?"

Massey taps his chest as an invitation for Havens to land a blow, and Havens lobs his crumpled napkin at the target instead.

"I don't suppose you've heard anything about them?"

Havens shakes his head. "I'm thinking of going back, though. They deserve to know the story was buried."

"They'd have figured that out by now, don't you suppose?"

Havens recounts the awful events leading up to the last time he saw Jubilee, confiding that she hadn't shown up for the rendezvous. "Do you think it's selfish of me to want to go back? Would I just stir things up again?"

If Massey thought Havens should go, he'd say so. Instead, his expression is sympathetic, as if Havens is in a game where the scoring lead is too great and it's only a matter of running out the clock.

Still, Havens says, "I just think it would be good to have a proper visit and say a proper farewell, maybe even take one on the chin—I don't know, something."

Havens expects Massey to advise against this, but he stands at attention and declares, "Farewells and frontlines—may we both return from them better men."

Havens shakes his outstretched hand. "When are you off?"

"Ship sails day after tomorrow. Shall I tell Betty you did your best to talk me out of it?"

Havens smiles.

"See you around, Havens." Massey salutes.

"So long, Massey."

"Oh, one more thing." Massey reaches into his messenger bag and hands Havens a manila envelope. Inside are all the black-and-whites Havens shot in Chance. "Don't thank me—I wasn't sure if I'd need any of them for the story." Next, Massey slips his hand into the breast pocket of his jacket and pulls out a color photograph of Jubilee caught unawares in Havens's arms. "And you ought to have this one, too." Before Havens looks up again to thank him, Massey has disappeared into the crowd.

On the train ride home, Havens studies the picture. Though the yearning to be with her swells, he can't deny the obvious: he is so out of place and she is exactly where she belongs. His thoughts turn to the birds in his father's apple tree. Whether or not the intruder intends harm, if it goes to a place it has no business going, the resident is threatened. All along, Jubilee knew what he did not want to admit to himself—starlings and bluebirds cannot build nests in the same tree.

JUBILEE

Bolting upright, hands flung to her face, Jubilee wakes up from the dream in which she'd been turned right-colored and returned home. She looks around and sees her room, and checks her hands to make sure about that part, too. Borrowed skin, because the blue has seeped to the surface again. She reaches for the bottle, swallows another pill, and waits. When the change comes, it happens everywhere all at once. Blue one minute, blooming the next. Some of her is the color of a peach, some the color of planed pine, some pale as fresh-churned butter. She peeks down the neck of her nightgown. Those two dark circles are now pale pink. She slips her hands underneath and handles her breasts as though they're china teacups. Her belly is pale as laurel. She looks all the way down, and glances away with a smile. All so ripe-looking now.

Dressing takes twice as long as it used to because she's always getting sidetracked by the mirror, where she gets reacquainted with her twin in sunrise skin, the girl of her dreams: same kinky ginger hair; same flecked green eyes full of what-next worry; nose, cheeks, and chin where they always are except with dainty brown freckles instead of ink blots; and lips no longer the color of death but like some new-born thing. Her double smiles back at her. Pale pink gums, a pink tongue. She might as well have dined on flowers. All of her is brought forth like a new creation.

She feels different, too, this new-skinned version, silky somehow. She shivers a bunch, tickles more easily, and what happens after a pinch is more like an adornment than a bruise. She has no words for this color—"right-colored" doesn't do it justice. "Perfect-colored," perhaps.

From several hand-me-down dresses in her suitcase, she chooses the one patterned with dainty multicolored flowers, then twirls in front of the mirror. Another idea occurs to her. Underneath her mattress, almost out of reach, is the shirt Havens left behind. She takes off the dress, slips into it, and buttons up the front all the way to the collar. The tail falls almost to her knees and the cuffs end well below her fingertips. She wraps his sleeves around herself.

How carefree and beautiful Havens made her feel. Often, she caught him looking at her, and she'd pretended something far away had piqued her interest so he could look all he wanted. She encouraged his looking with gestures—rubbing liniment into her hands, say, or twirling her hair. She did try to bewitch him, just as they accuse Blues of doing. She'd worn her apron low, taken her sweet time coming out of the rainstorm to see if he found wet and shivered blue as pretty as dry blue, lingered in the late afternoon sun making daisy chains for her flaming hair, fluffed her skirt and sang every ballad she knew. How she wanted him to keep his eyes on her. How she wanted something to come of their feelings. All the wrong things she wanted, wants still, now in this color even more.

"Oh my good lord!" a voice exclaims behind her.

She swings around.

Socall fills the doorway, her mouth hanging open. Instead of taking time to form one whole question, Socall asks them all at once in bits and pieces. "But how can—Where—When, exactly?"

Grabbing the dress off the floor, Jubilee rushes behind the closet door and changes in haste. Showing herself again makes Socall act as if she's being paid a visit by the angel Gabriel and is still deciding whether to expect a smiting or a blessing. Jubilee is about to explain about blood molecules when she notices Willow-May peering from behind Socall's skirt. It's their old game, so in a loud voice, Jubilee says, "It's too bad you didn't bring Willow-May with you; she probably won't like the present I brought for her anyhow," and because Willow-May keeps to her post, Jubilee springs around Socall and grabs her sister and pulls her close for a tickle.

Willow-May wrenches away in fright.

"Someone's a little moody this morning." Socall reaches behind her for Willow-May. "Go give your sister a hug."

Jubilee gets on her haunches and holds out her arms. "It's just me—Juby."

Willow-May lets go of Socall and runs off down the breezeway.

"She needs time to get acclimated to—this—you." Socall gets Jubilee by her shoulders and assesses her top to toe, turning her around for a thorough inspection, before closing those massive arms around her. "Never mind a cure, we've got to get some meat on those bones." She asks about Louisville, and out comes the short version—Dr. Fordsworth and the pills, that long word—"methemoglobinemia"—and how it's been little more than a week since she first started treatment. "There's not much more to tell than that."

"Is that polish?"

It's too late to hide her fingernails, even though most of the red varnish has chipped off, so she busies herself straightening the bedcovers, because a person can't hold Socall's gaze and hold down secrets both. "You were right—the big wide world doesn't have much to show for itself." When Socall used to tell her that, Jubilee always took it to mean because Socall had only ever seen the little seaside bit of it where her sister lives in Florida, but Jubilee knows now that a person doesn't have to see much of the world to come to such a conclusion. All you have to do is pay attention to what of the world people drag around with them.

Socall picks up Havens's shirt, folds it, and hands it back to Jubilee. "You don't want your mama to see that."

Jubilee puts it at the back of her closet.

"Does he know about any of this?"

"How would he?"

"Maybe you wrote to him when you were away?"

Wrote? No. "He never gave me his address." Which is not even the impossible part.

"Well, those two were dishing their cards out to about half the town. Your pa got one. I got one. In case you want to—"

"I'm not going to write to him! And say what?" Would Jubilee write about Levi's death, about her mama on some ledge by herself? Seems she'd have to explain those subjects before the subject of skin could even be raised. "What would be the purpose anyhow?"

"If I were him, I'd be glad to hear you are okay."

"If you were him, you would've found a way to answer that question yourself." Jubilee puts an end to the issue by bringing up the matter of Ronny, something which she's been hesitant to raise with Pa.

"It's not going to come as a surprise to you that charges haven't been brought against Ronny." Socall tells of Sheriff Suggins's conducting a lopsided investigation while Pa was searching the hills and hollers, and how Mama was in no condition to answer questions about timelines and motives. "Your pa's challenging Ronny's claim of self-defense. The man he's hired to look into the case is wet behind the ears but persistent as a deer tick."

"How's Pa going to pay him?"

"With what's left of the crop earnings, and several of us are going to pony up when the next bill comes due, but don't you breathe a word of that to him."

"Ronny isn't going to be punished."

"You and I know that, but the case has given your pa hope, and hope's what's been getting him out of bed every morning."

Socall couldn't look more pleased reporting that Urnamy Gault's business is going down the toilet and there's talk of voting for a new mayor come the next election. "On top of that, he has to deny rumors about Estil and Eddie that everyone knows are true." As for Ronny, Socall reports that he doesn't much leave his mother's side anymore. "Estil has stopped going out entirely, though if you ask me, it's vanity if she believes everyone's discussing her and Eddie day and night. Good lord, what more can be said about that bit of nastiness other than Ronny's living proof that two wrongs sure as hell don't make a right."

"What about when Ronny hears I've come back?"

Socall has her sit beside her on the bed, gives her hand a squeeze that about pops her knuckles, and says, "My biggest regret is that I didn't shoot Ronny when I had the chance, but hear this, if he even thinks of getting in your business again, I ain't going to make that mistake a second time." Socall's voice returns to a lighter tone when she speaks of taking Willow-May to Smoke Hole tomorrow to the community fair. "Come with us. It will be good for her to get reacquainted with you someplace other than this house."

The very mention of a fair makes Jubilee stiffen. After what she's gone through, that's the last place she wants to go, but Socall won't hear of her sitting this one out. "What's the use of all this," she says, gesturing at Jubilee's skin, "if you go back to being cooped up?"

After Socall leaves her room, Jubilee consults the mirror once again. She is like a fawn, like a creature who can't cast a shadow. Around her is no hint of darkness. Let her stand in pools of silver and gold.

❧

The field beside the red schoolhouse has been turned into a fairground, with dueling string bands at each corner and booths and tables lined up on all sides displaying all kinds of crafts and eats. Townsfolk, farmers, and miners' families in their Sunday best stroll from display to display, giving their assessments on everything from homemade hatchet handles to quilts to mineral collections while rowdy children play tag, scooting under tables past stockinged legs and ducking out of reach of the grown-ups.

Socall, Willow-May, and Jubilee hitched a ride with Jeremiah Wrightley, who has now gone off with his youngest son to check out the sporting events, leaving Wyatt to tag along after Jubilee. Even though he spent the entire twelve-mile drive staring at her from his side of the pickup, he still can't seem to get his fill.

229

"Don't you have a horseshoe pitching contest to get ready for, Wyatt?" Socall hollers at him and off he trudges, but not after glancing back over his shoulder again.

Willow-May, on the other hand, hasn't spoken a word to Jubilee and keeps her distance by using Socall as a hedge. At the table of preserves, she readily accepts a sample of gooseberry jelly from the woman in the bonnet and apron.

"You like canned peaches?" the woman asks Jubilee. "Because these are made with the best syrup you'll ever taste."

Jubilee doesn't know how to respond. So it goes at every booth: tongue-tied by people being nice. Willow-May makes no secret of how peculiar she finds Jubilee. "What's wrong with her?" she asks Socall. "Why isn't she like she used to be?"

Because Willow-May wants to pet the baby animals, they follow their noses to the farthest corner, where a farmhand offers her a piglet. Being among others comes natural to her sister, and she asks a dozen questions about hatching, breeding, and butchering. Jubilee, on the other hand, can't get the hang of things. She steps back some and notices the same young man they passed a few minutes ago tipping his hat at her a second time.

After Willow-May has coddled every animal in the pen, they scan their programs to decide where next to go, and Socall points to where it says, "Curios & Relics," and just that quick, Jubilee is back again in Louisville smelling sawdust and smoke and roasting peanuts, and hearing Arnold, the barker, outside that tent with a bullhorn at his mouth hollering, *Step right up, ladies and gentlemen.* She'd thought they'd be nice—city people weren't supposed to be narrow like mountain folk, but she'd been asked all manner of questions, things you never imagined a decent person could be capable of asking another. *You blue all the way down?* a man once asked.

"You two go on, I'm just going to find some shade for a few minutes." Jubilee assures Socall she'll catch up before making her way to an unoc-cupied hay bale. How long before her mind will rid itself of former things? She and Levi would sometimes talk about what it might be like to walk where you wanted or do as you pleased, but now she wonders if freedom has more to do with owning what all you've done and are capable of doing, bad parts especially, than just walking and doing as you please. She takes a few deep breaths to still the jitters, fans herself with the program, and considers the color of her hands.

"Are you okay, miss?" The man from before is removing his hat. He's about Levi's age, and has the clothes and manners of an educated man. "I was afraid you were going to faint."

"I'm fine, thank you." She pretends to study her program.

"Would you like me to fetch you a drink of lemonade?"

She shakes her head.

He gestures at the crowd. "This is the biggest turnout the fair's ever had."

Why won't he leave?

"You're not from around here, are you?"

In hopes of ending this inquiry, she says, "I'm from Chance."

"I knew I hadn't seen you here before. I would've remembered if I had." The man is partway through introducing himself when Jubilee takes off through the crowd to the schoolhouse, where she's relieved to see that "Curios" are not "human curiosities" and "oddities of nature" as she feared, but mostly just guns from former wars and old pistols of every sort. At the front of the hall, Willow-May has become enchanted with a display of tiny boxes housing figures the size of grains of rice. DRESSED FLEAS FROM MEXICO, reads the sign.

"They're dead, but they really are fleas!" Willow-May hands Socall the magnifying glass. "Look at these two—they're getting married! Aren't their clothes so fancy?"

"Here's a farmer and his wife."

Willow-May inspects Jubilee's box before nodding in agreement. "Just like Mama and Pa."

Say what you will, those fancy-dressed dead fleas help put things right between sisters.

After lunching on sponge cake and cherry soda, Jubilee has another idea how to put things right and suggests they find the toy store, and the three of them drift down to Main Street, which is double the length of Chance's.

They stroll past the druggist, the hardware store, and the shoe repair place. Socall goes inside the corset shop, leaving Jubilee and Willow-May to browse the toy store two doors down. Inside, Willow-May flits from display to display, exclaiming at everything she sees—Chinese checkers, ring toss, a tiny pastry set, a tea set—and when she comes upon the shelf of baby dolls, she falls silent. Not even a snuffling fat piglet had this effect on her.

Jubilee hands her a doll. "Would you like to have her?"

Willow-May strokes the doll's head and nods, so Jubilee ushers her sister to the counter, where the clerk rings up the purchase and says, "Ah, our best seller; this one cries and wets itself."

Jubilee feels a flash of heat in her face. Surely even Socall wouldn't know how to respond to such a statement.

"Look what Juby bought me!"

If Socall wonders how Jubilee has money to afford such a luxury, she doesn't ask, but after Jubilee's bought Mama a crocheted shawl, Pa a bag of vanilla-scented tobacco, and Grandma a new bonnet, she can't resist commenting. "That purse of yours near empty yet?"

"Oh, Juby's got a lot more money in there."

Socall raises her eyebrows at Jubilee. "In that case, don't you think you ought to get something for yourself?"

Willow-May won't hear of Jubilee settling for a peach cobbler. "You have to get yourself something nice, Juby. A dress!"

Jubilee has only ever worn homemade dresses and hand-me-downs. "But where would I wear it?"

"Come with me." Socall leads them across the street, telling Jubilee the clerk will want to sell her the most expensive dress in stock and then will try to plump her sale by suggesting it needs alterations should she show even the slightest interest. "You tell her you're browsing and act bored, and whatever you do, don't try on anything she suggests."

Inside the store is a lady waving as if they've long been acquainted. Jubilee's never seen so many dresses, enough to clothe all the women in Chance three times over. Right off, a yellow one with a full skirt catches her eye, and the lady rushes over to tell her it comes in six different sizes. Different sizes? For the Bufords, there is only one size dress—if it's too big, you tie a belt around the waist, and if it's too small, you either let out the sides or cut back on the mashed potatoes.

The lady says for Jubilee to call her Margaret. She holds the dress against Jubilee. "You're so lucky, most women can't wear yellow, but I bet you can wear just about any color."

Socall is giving Jubilee a hard look, so she tries making her face flat, but how can she when someone is going on about her perfect complexion?

Margaret says for her to try it on.

"I don't think so."

"Oh, but you must." She pushes Jubilee into a little space about the size of a closet, except it has a curtain where a door should be and a long oval mirror at the back. Jubilee slips off her shoes, shrugs off her dress, and startles herself all over again. Only when she hears Margaret ask about the fit does she remember about the yellow dress she's to try on, which might as well have been made for her.

"Come out so we can see, dear."

Jubilee pushes aside the drape.

Socall puts her hand on a cocked hip and keeps shaking her head as if Jubilee deserves a blue ribbon, and Willow-May springs about on one foot saying, "Get it, get it, get it!"

Margaret's hands are tied like a bow under her chin. "Oh, you are beautiful in that. Don't you just love it?" Turning Jubilee toward the mirror, Margaret handles Jubilee's middle, making Jubilee wonder if she will ever get used to the ways of Right-coloreds. "My, but you are slight around the waist." On right-colored women, a blush always looks pretty, but on Jubilee it looks showy, sliding all the way down her neck, and no amount of willing stops it.

"Our seamstress just has to make a few little tucks here and here, and it'll be just perfect."

Socall clears her throat, so Jubilee says, "I'll take it just as it is."

"Keep it on," Willow-May insists, taking Jubilee's hand as soon as she's done paying, and skipping them back outside.

At the corner, a woman stares disapprovingly at Jubilee's scuffed old shoes. Used to be Jubilee was the woman with the wrong skin; now she's the woman with the wrong shoes. Wrong shoes or not, every step with Willow-May at her side takes her a little farther from Louisville and a little closer to feeling normal. Headed back to meet the Wrightleys for their ride home, something makes Jubilee turn her head. Leaning against a lamppost half a block away is Faro Suggins. From the way he's watching her there's no mistaking it—he's figured out who she is.

JUBILEE

oday the clouds hang low, rumoring rain. The broken corn-
stalks have been turned over and mulched into the soil, the
air smells of rot, and fall's come early, turning the leaves of
the maples orange already. It's as good a day as any for Pa to be taking
Jubilee to see Levi's resting place. They pass the milkwoods and cross
the stream, and Pa makes a beeline for the spruce at the far end, which
always used to be so leafy, but now looks as though it's on its last legs.

She would've walked right over Levi's grave had Pa not taken her arm.
It's a typical grave for a Blue, nothing to mark it save distance. Digging
it, Pa would have counted the exact number of strides from the spruce in
front and the boulders to the left. Instead of flowers, they each place a
stone on the dirt patch.

"Remember that time your brother got stuck in the tree?" Levi was
always one for high places, whether it was a tree or the roof of the barn or
the top of a hill. "He was fearless right from the get-go." Brushing away a
few yellow leaves from the mound, Pa gets on his knees and summons one
memory after another. "I'm glad I was the one to find him and bring him
home, not someone else."

Jubilee nods.

"I wanted to clean him and bandage him before your ma saw him, but there was no stopping her. You'll understand if it takes a while before she comes around to you . . ."

To mourn someone is to be caught up in a flood, which is to say sometimes you are near-drowned and sometimes drifting, and when eventually you will be beached is something over which you have no control. "Mama will get her feet back under her again."

Pa seems relieved. "I just didn't want you to get the idea she isn't pleased to have you back, because she is."

For a while, they each keep their thoughts to themselves, and then Pa says, "Ronny's cried self-defense, but you tell me how two men against one counts as self-defense." Pa addresses the trees in a way that makes her wonder if this isn't a regular talk he has with them. "I tried, Juby. I tried real hard to get Levi to mind me; he always had his own ideas about how to handle things, though. I should've done more. Maybe if I'd gone to see Gault right away . . ."

That she always feared Levi would come to a flat-out halt never stopped her from hoping otherwise, and at the time, that kind of hope had the feel of virtue, but it's hard now not to see it for what it truly was—a failure to act. What good was hope if there wasn't any will behind it, any muscle? Where Pa's regrets trail off hers pick up—she ought to have told Pa the very day she clapped eyes on Levi and Sarah at the creek.

"I miss him so much. My son."

In all her years, she's never seen her pa cry. She steps away to give him time to compose himself, but he just gets worse, making hard gulping noises and about ready to topple over, so she lays her hand on his shoulder, her pa who says some days he doesn't know how to go on.

Jubilee closes her eyes, deciding a prayer's what's called for, but no words come. It's not how they say, that a person quits praying. It's the other way around. The prayer quits the person.

Pa wipes his shirtsleeve across his eyes, then gets out his handkerchief to blow his nose. "Your brother always fought back, which is more than I can say for myself."

They take the long way home, which gives her time to consider how little her altering alters anything. Instead of bearing the burden of blue, the Bufords now bear the burden of grief, but where blue was something they all carried together—all of them accustomed to the shape, weight, and feel of it—grief now has them carrying their own separate burdens, making them all but strangers to one another.

Pa and Jubilee are a ways yet from the house when they see a wagon pass the field and draw up to the porch.

"Eddie." Pa groans. They pick up the pace.

A woman is at the reins with Uncle Eddie slouched against her shoulder. "Who's he got with him?" Jubilee asks.

Under his breath, Pa says, "I'll be." If the mother of God had come to pay a visit it would be no less of a surprise.

Sarah Tuttle. Last time Jubilee saw her, she was not much wider than a broom handle; now she's a barrel. Though Jubilee always took her as being on the vain side, her frizzed hair is only partway pinned into an old sunbonnet, and she has on not one scrap of the makeup she always favored. If Jubilee didn't know better, she'd count the girl twenty years older than what she is. Sarah avoids Pa's eyes when he helps her down from the wagon bench, but she can't hide her shock at seeing Jubilee. Uncle Eddie has to call three times for her to give him a hand. After she's done being his leaning post, she moves to the far side of the horse and takes another peek at Jubilee.

Uncle Eddie's in a bad way from the gout, much worse than the last time he showed himself at Socall's frolic, but he still reeks of shine. "So, it's true; you ain't a coon no more."

With Uncle Eddie, Pa is never confrontational, but now he gets up in his blistered face. "You can take your sorry self someplace else, because I won't tolerate that kind of talk anymore, Eddie." Pa's missing the most important part—that word's getting around about her.

Uncle Eddie mock-surrenders, saying Pa's not to get so het up. "Besides, is this any way to treat a man who's come to introduce his fiancée?"

Pa and Jubilee exchange glances, and Pa tries steering away from the subject by commending him on his fine new horse, and Uncle Eddie says, "Came with Queen of Sheba here."

Sarah's face has gone from splotchy to wan. She says she's in need of the privy, and Jubilee hastens to her side, offering her hand while Uncle Eddie warbles on about his foot having to come off any day.

Supporting her belly with one hand, Sarah comes out of the privy looking no better, so Jubilee leads her to the wash room, where she fills the basin with water, wets a cloth, and hands it to Sarah.

"When are you due?"

"Supposed to be a few weeks yet, but I think sooner than that." Sarah eases herself onto the stool and puts the cloth on the back of her neck. "You could go anywhere you wanted and you came back here? If it were me, I'd be headed to Lexington, or the Big Apple, maybe the Orient, anywhere but this godforsaken place."

"My family's here."

"Well, your brother would've leaped at a chance for a better life, that's for sure."

In Louisville there were days Jubilee didn't want to believe Levi was dead and other days his death was so bitter-real it was easy for her to be who she was paid to be, but there was never a day she didn't wish she could somehow bring him back. "I'd give anything for Levi to have that chance—for both of you to have that chance," Jubilee replies.

There's but the barest softening in Sarah's features. "I know what you're thinking, me taking up with Eddie and all, but who's going to let a preacher serve a church when he's got an unwed daughter at home nursing a baby?" Sarah reports that none of the fellas who used to harass her for a date will go near her, that Eddie's was the only offer. Voice breaking, she adds, "When I think how Levi would feel about this—"

"Don't." Jubilee crouches in front of Sarah and puts her hand on Sarah's knee. "Levi knew better than anyone about having to choose between bad and worse." For Jubilee, she'd had to make a choice between beggar or fair-worker, back alley or that big tent.

"I can help you, if you want," Jubilee pledges.

Sarah gives her a look that says, How, how could you possibly help? "It's not as if I'll be the first woman to cook and clean for a man she can't abide." She catches sight of herself in Pa's shaving mirror. "Levi would run the other way if he saw me now."

"No, he wouldn't." Jubilee picks up the comb and asks permission before removing Sarah's bonnet and gently coaxing her tangles into curls.

"A heart doesn't break clean the way bones do," Sarah says. "If it did, it would knit back together."

"I had someone tell me to let the hurt scab over and not go picking at it, but what about when there's a hole too big for anything to grow over, least of all a scab?" Which was how Jubilee knew it would take a long time to be over Havens, long time as in never.

As soon as they return to the porch, Eddie starts grousing about how lazy Sarah is and how she has to be told over and over what her wifely duties are. "If I wasn't a man of my word, I'd send her back."

Sarah situates herself on a chair, and Jubilee bends down and unlaces her boots to make room for her swollen feet. Going inside to fetch lemonade, Jubilee startles to find Mama hiding behind the door, damp with sweat and shivering as if she's been caught in a rainstorm. How so lopsided a form can stay upright, Jubilee has no idea.

"It's her, isn't it?" Agitated, Mama pulls Jubilee close only to screech in her ear, "I won't have her here!"

It does no good trying to hush Mama.

"You tell that girl we don't want her here! Levi would still be with us if it wasn't for her!"

Jubilee leads Mama back to her room and has Grandma sit with her, then takes the lemonade out to the porch, where Uncle Eddie is in the midst of explaining the real reason for his visit. Gesturing at Sarah's belly, he says, "So if it does come out a Blue like its father, can Jubilee witch it right?"

"This isn't witching," Jubilee argues, but before she can state the facts, the screen door swings open and Mama comes out as if she's wading through a swift-running creek.

"You shut your mouth, Eddie!" Mama roused thus is how they say the near-dead can sometimes spring up from their stupor to impart a long-held secret only to expire a minute later. "You're not half the man Levi was! Be gone with you and don't you ever come back here! Neither of you!"

Mama grabs the broom from against the wall and waves it at them.

Uncle Eddie cusses and protests and says they'll all come to regret this, but Sarah keeps that flat look, as if a beating isn't worth trying to avoid.

As Uncle Eddie is hauling himself onto the wagon, Sarah turns to Jubilee. "Maybe you like being normal now, but wait till you've been normal as long as the rest of us. It's no fairy tale."

Before the wagon has made the turn at the bottom of the field, Mama calls from inside, saying for Pa to wash up because she's fixing chicken fried steak for dinner. Mama putting on her apron has the same effect on Pa as Jubilee coming home in right-colored skin, but ten minutes later, Mama is still standing in front of an empty bowl with a spoon in her hand. Pa takes off her apron, leads her to a chair, and says, "It's good that you spoke his name, Glad. It's a start."

Mama slumps against him and cries, and he tidies her hair. After a while, she pulls herself upright and turns shallow eyes to the window. "Oh, see," she says. "It's going to be one of those pretty sunsets."

The sun is nowhere near setting.

⁂

Long after everyone goes to bed, Jubilee takes a lamp and looks everywhere for the photographs, the one she took of him especially, and can't find them. Frustrated, she returns to her bed, where she lies awake thinking about Sarah's predicament and Levi in his grave and how it is becoming more and more difficult to picture things as they once had been. The full moon rises up over the hills and shines into her room, bullfrogs bellow to each other from across the creek, and a barn owl hoots from the shushing trees, all things she knows Havens would love to photograph. Why can she not forget him? She was raised to make demands of no one, to shear off her needs and desires long before they grew full-sized, and for good reason, because now look—a new skin, and she cannot stop herself from imagining what Havens would make of her.

Her bedroom door squeaks open and a nose sniffles. Propping up on one elbow, Jubilee whispers, "Willow-May?"

A little silhouette takes a step closer.

"What's wrong?" She goes to her sister and strokes her head. It's her sister's first night back at home. "Did you have a bad dream?"

"I'm scared."

"You want to sleep with me?"

Willow-May climbs into Jubilee's bed and stares at Jubilee and says, "You look right, now."

Shadow-colored, her sister means, because the blue has returned.

"Juby?"

"Ssh. Close your eyes now, and go to sleep."

"Can we play a while in the morning before you take your pill?"

"Sure," Jubilee says. "No more talking now."

A few minutes later, Willow-May whispers, "Juby?"

"I'm sleeping."

"I don't want anything bad to happen."

"Nothing bad's going to happen," Jubilee promises.

"You won't leave again, will you?"

"Never."

HAVENS

Sitting in the basement, Havens no longer wonders if he is on the brink of some kind of collapse, but is convinced of it. It's been days since he went outside, maybe more than a week, and he can smell his own body. His mother has given up protesting the beard. Her battles now involve telephone numbers that he is supposed to dial—Dr. Friedman's son, Gerald, has taken over the family practice, his mother tells him, and is more than happy to make a house call. Another number is for Stedman Studios, which is looking for a part-time photo finisher, and the most recent number belongs to Beth-across-the-street's sister's second cousin, who went away to beauty school and has come back to start her own Avon business.

His parents are worried about him, which is why he ought to move out. A couple weeks ago, he gave loose change to a guy who used to pitch for the Reds who's now eking out an existence in Hooverville on the other side of town, which apparently isn't nearly as bad as hopping the freights. Poverty doesn't bother Havens. Nothing bothers him anymore, except his memories of her. Against his better judgment, he'd written to the Bufords by way of the postmaster two months ago in the vain hope that he'd receive a reply. A man can find his footing on a rebuke, but silence is a bottomless cavity through which he keeps falling.

Between his feet is his camera bag. He opens it and takes out his father's .45 Colt. It weighs about as much as his Contax. His grip is firm and the handle warms quickly, and instead of an inanimate thing, the revolver feels like an extension of his arm. His hand does not shake the way it does whenever he tries to raise his camera these days. It is steady, purposeful. He doesn't intend to blow his brains out, but his mind does need to be threatened. It has started to lose his memories of her. Only fragments of her come to him now instead of the whole picture, and this was not part of the deal. His memory is supposed to compensate for the future he cannot have with her, but now not even the photographs can bring her back to him all the way, and every day he loses more of her, which means it is only a matter of time before he wakes up and she is lost to him entirely. Desperate people know their demands have the best chance of being met when they are made with a weapon, and Havens makes his demands now. He directs his hand to the side of his head and it seems that he has made a fist at his temples, not pulled a gun on himself.

Think of her! Think of everything about her.

It seems his mind does clear some. Skin is what first comes to him, but not her skin—his. He remembers how it felt when she first touched him. He remembers exactly how soft her fingers were, how it felt when she buried them in his hair. It was her touch that made him aware for the first time that he needed touching, that he needed tenderness, tending. His chest rises and caves. Gooseflesh runs along his arms.

Remember more!

Thoughts assemble her into something of a fable. She catches lightning in her hand.

Havens jams the muzzle against his temple. Remember straight, damn you!

His mind slips a gear. She is clapping thunderclouds together, relieving heaven of its duties.

No, remember the real Jubilee!

But his mind rewinds back to that awful morning in the clearing, where she lay naked and tied to her brother.

No, not this, don't remember this!

The occasion in which she bloomed and he came to life—why will his mind not relive this? Why will it not bring her back to him as she was that day at her aviary or when he held her during their one and only dance or the way she'd looked at him when she'd pleaded for him to wait at the shack? She'd been happy, but now he can only picture her distress.

He hears footsteps on the stairs and manages to zip the .45 back into the bag just as the light snaps on.

His mother is holding a hamper of clothes. "What on earth, Clayton? You about scared the life out of me!"

He clamors to his feet.

"What are you doing down here in the dark?" She takes stock of the room and eyes the camera bag. "What do you have in there?"

"Nothing." He slings the bag over his shoulder, but she blocks his exit.

"If you are up to funny business."

What if he had pulled the trigger? She would've been the one to find him. For no other reason, he is glad he didn't.

"You're not taking drugs, are you? Because I won't stand for any of that nonsense poor Doris next door has to go through with her son."

He does his best to reassure her. "I'm not on drugs, Mom."

"You've just been acting so strange lately." So unlikely is her embrace that he at first believes his mother is about to beat him. "You're a good boy, Clayton. Come on, son." She pounds his back as though to clear his airways of an obstruction. "When life bucks you out of the saddle, you just have to get back on up."

"I'm fine, Mom, really."

She picks up her hamper and says, "Oh, and there's a letter come for you." From her brittle tone, he can tell she disapproves. "The postmark is that town you went to, the one out in the sticks."

Havens takes the stairs two at a time.

JUBILEE

✦

Fall's shrinking daylight ought to mean the hours pass more quickly, but no, it can take forever to be done with morning, only to have the afternoon follow on millipede legs. Nothing, though, takes as long as night. In the sagging hours between midnight and dawn, the World of Wonders Sideshow will often haunt her. Freak Show is what most called it. Tall canvas banners painted with poor likenesses of her and the others, along with the words ERRORS OF NATURE, THE UNTHINKABLE, and WHAT IS IT drew fairgoers into the tent where she sat. After hiding all her life, she had to show herself. No longer hunted, but caught. Waiting for people to come to her little stall was like hearing a swarm of locusts and hoping they'd find some other field where they could gorge themselves. You can't rightly call it staring, what they did. Eyes can judge, condemn, pity. They can be filled with the kind of menace that made a person glad for that chair and not to be out walking along a dark street. No matter what kind of eyes, though, none of them kept her from feeling like a prediction come to pass.

At daybreak, Jubilee reaches for the bottle and swallows a pill. If she sprouted soft white feathers, it would be no less a miracle, but today she marks the change with less awe and from a distance. Between her and her new skin is a separation she can no longer deny. Maybe it's on account of the distance that returns between her and Willow-May every time blue gives way to right-colored skin, or because a distance persists between her and Grandma, and her and Mama. Some of it could be that Jubilee and this new skin share no memories—they go back together only a few weeks. When she first joined the World of Wonders and the issue of her act was being debated, her friend, the one they called Mr. Lizard, protested the mummy costume Jubilee was to try on, saying, "Just because something fits a person doesn't mean it becomes a person," and now, she wonders if this isn't true of skin, too.

Instead of trying out woman postures in front of the mirror, she throws on an old dress and goes out to the kitchen, where she puts on a pot of coffee and mixes dough for biscuits, which she'll put in the oven once Mama and Grandma are awake, even though Mama can seldom be persuaded to get much more than half a glass of milk down and Grandma will eat only when Jubilee is out of sight.

Outside, Pa is dragging a load of deadfall from the parcel of land he's been clearing, and he turns down her offer to help as though she were in Sunday clothes that weren't for getting dirty. Pa might be wrong about everything turning out fine. Three weeks have passed and few things have gone back to how they used to be, Mama most of all. What Jubilee wouldn't give for Mama to draw closer—even a little closer would comfort her a great deal—but Mama holes up in her room. Jubilee's tried talking to her, but she's as good as stone now. Boil a stone and the heat will run right out of it.

Jubilee is hauling water from the well back to the house when she hears Chappy's honking from down the path. Never does he come this early, and right away she assesses that he is worked up about something and she runs through a list of who might have died in the night.

"Mr. Havens's come!" he blurts, making her drop the pail.

Trying to catch his breath, Chappy repeats himself, and adds, "He came by train last night!"

Holding herself doesn't stop her insides from flip-flopping.

Chappy reports that Havens checked in at Sylvia Fullhart's place. "He said he'd be paying you a visit today."

The ground is trying to buck her off. "He can't come up here, Chappy." Not after everything that happened, especially not after Mama's reaction to Sarah. Pa's also made it ample clear that no one's ever to mention his name, let alone open the door for him. "You have to tell him he can't come."

"He's fixed on seeing you, Juby. Pharaoh's army couldn't stop him."

What if she was to meet him somewhere? She rules out the grave keeper's shed on account of last time, her aviary because it's too close, and Socall's house because Willow-May will be taking her lessons there after breakfast. "Could I meet him at your house? Would your grandma mind?"

Chappy says, "How about you just go to him?"

She considers the idea. If she went now, she could be there before the stores opened and people started milling about. She asks Chappy to wait for her and flies back to the house.

⚜

Maybe he's come about the picture—perhaps it has been printed, after all. Or could he somehow have heard talk of a blue she-devil at the Kentucky State Fair? If he has, how should she answer? What would he make of people lining up to see her? Would it help him to learn how quickly their shock wore off and that they mostly went away disappointed they didn't get more for their money? She could deny it altogether or she could spell out only the good bits—that she'd had a place to sleep, someone to cook her meals and wash her clothes, that she didn't have to lift a finger, just sit all day, and for that alone she earned more money in a week than a factory worker in a month. Maybe he hasn't come for either of these reasons. She permits herself the possibility that he's returned for a visit as he said he would.

She chooses the yellow dress she bought in Smoke Hole, brushes her hair and pins back the sides the way fashionable women wear their hair in the city, and daubs on a little lipstick. She wipes it off. Then puts on some more. The house is still quiet when she tiptoes out the front door. Pa returns her wave when she and Chappy take off for town.

"I told you he was sweet on you," Chappy says.

⚜

Sylvia Fullhart opens the door only halfway and says, "Early for a visitor to be calling, isn't it?"

Jubilee can't stop smiling. This is a new thing—being told off for something other than being blue. Asking for Havens comes out tipsy-sounding, so in a more sober tone, she adds, "Please, it's important."

The matron doesn't hide how peculiar she finds Jubilee. She takes a few steps into the hallway and yells up the stairs, "Havens, a visitor to see you!" and then motions for Jubilee to come inside. "Parlor's through there."

How do Right-coloreds behave when they enter someone's home? Surely not the way she does, expecting people to leap out from behind walls to grab her and throw her out. The front room is not like any she's ever seen, so many chairs, for one thing, each covered in fabric and with its own little pillow, and a carpet patterned with flowers, making it so she doesn't want to tread on them. At the fireplace she studies the clock ticking loudly on the mantle. For the life of her, she can't tell the time. She's remembering the first time she got a close-up look at Havens, standing at Mama's bedroom window that first morning, his hair flopped across his brow, so much goodness in his eyes.

She hears footsteps on the staircase. Should she stay where she is or sit like a lady or meet him at the doorway? Where there used to be one Jubilee, there are now two. One Jubilee would have her run and hide, and the other that she stop acting blue and stand up proud. She instructs her heart to send its taproot way down deep into the earth to keep her from toppling over.

"A young miss is here for you," Jubilee hears Sylvia Fullhart say. "A dippy one, if you ask me." She informs Havens she's about to start cooking breakfast and he's not to get any ideas of having tea or coffee served early.

248

Right-colored blood flows faster than blue. Think straight, speak straight, be straight. Jubilee is still trying to find the best place to light when he enters the parlor.

"Hello?" he says in a sleepy voice.

Her heart is knocking against her chest. She turns to face him. A sprig of hair lands in her eyes, and she pushes it to one side.

There's no way to put it other than the color goes out of him. Spooking someone is not a thing to smile about, but she can't help it. "Hello, Havens."

He looks as if he's been thrown from a horse straight into a fence post. He stands there, mouth agape, eyes the kind they put coins on. She wishes he would say something. Anything. She should've sent Chappy to come alert him first.

"I met a doctor a few weeks back," she begins. She shrugs her shoulders to loosen them. Let him do the talking, she reminds herself.

He takes a step closer, but not in an eager way, more like he expects to stand on a loose floorboard and have it rear up and smack him in the face.

"The doctor figured what was wrong with me and gave me some pills." Events tumble out of order so she's talking about having blue dye put into her veins before the test where the blood was taken out. She leaves too much out of her account to have it make any sense and puts in what hardly matters, and still he doesn't move. This isn't how she imagined it. Flung into his arms was the picture that formed in her mind, him cradling her face. A gift is how she hoped he'd see her, not this, like a grave opened and the dead rose up and called him by name.

His hands are shaking. "It's—You—the change—" He doesn't like it.

A little too loud, she says, "It's still me."

Slowly, his hands leave his sides as if he's trying to get his balance on a narrow log with her on one end and him on the other. His eyes leave her face to take in the rest of her. By what measure is she being tallied? Unblue isn't something you can count in inches and ounces. What they use to figure gravity or the depth of the ocean, maybe.

"Anyway, the doctor says it's not a cure, it's a treatment. I have to take the pills every day." Why must she keep talking about this?

He frowns, squints, blinks. His face makes all the twirl go out of her. A man came to the World of Wonders one day, scoffing and pointing at Jubilee's neck and claiming he could see where the paint ran out. With her saddest face, Jubilee tried to convince him that she was in fact a real-life tragedy, but he complained to the barker that he didn't pay to see a hoax and demanded his dime back. Call her a wrong that can't be made right, a witch, speller, carrion, or curse, but not hoax. Hoax had a skinning feel. And now she feels like the same dirty trick he accused her of being.

"I heard you were going to come up to the house, but my mother is not well. Your visit would be very upsetting."

"Yes, of course. I would've replied to the letter, but I didn't want to wait."

"What letter?"

Stammering, he tells of a letter that was mailed to his old address in Cincinnati and then forwarded to his parents' house, and she can't see what postmarks have to do with anything.

"Who sent it to you?"

"Socall. I thought you knew."

Everything about this is wrong. He came because he was asked to? Because he felt obliged? What all had Socall written?

"She said I'd find you somewhat changed," he continues. "Perhaps she thought this was the kind of news best delivered in person."

"Levi is dead." Isn't that the kind of news that gets delivered in person? She watches one type of shock drain from his face and another type fill it back up. "Ronny killed him."

Havens keeps shaking his head, keeps saying he's sorry, keeps looking at her as if she's to take back the words and go back to being the girl he met last time, but how far she is from that girl, and the sooner he understands this, the better.

"Socall's letter was a mistake."

He extends his hand as if he means to call an injured dog out from under a porch. "Please don't say that. I've been hoping for a letter." He talks of being in two minds about returning, about being afraid she didn't want him to come back and how much he has worried about her, and all she wants is to yell, What about my pretty skin! If you see a butterfly come out of its cocoon, don't you stick out your finger and see if it won't light on it?

"Well, you needn't have come, I'm fine." Words sometimes come with no warning and without your say-so. "I'm due back home," she says.

He reaches for her as she heads for the front door, but this time he looks where his hand touches her skin. "Wait, please don't go yet." He follows her out onto the sidewalk, where she signals Chappy on the other side of the street to go about his business. Havens follows her down the road. "I've upset you. I'm sorry. This isn't how I wanted it to be."

If he's disappointed with what's on the surface, he's going to be appalled by what's underneath.

Where the paved road gives way to gravel, she faces him. "If you really wanted to come back, you wouldn't have waited to be told." Maybe it's her memory at fault, but he seems altered some, too, and not for the better. His coat and trousers hang about him, the beard adds ten years, and he favors his foot as if he's fresh-bitten.

"You didn't meet me at the shack and then you didn't answer my letter—isn't that a pretty clear indication that a man ought to keep his distance?"

"You wrote?"

"Two months ago." He explains that he addressed his letter to Pa though its message was meant for her, and sent it care of Postmaster Combs, who did him the courtesy of writing back to confirm he'd delivered the letter in person. Havens's hand beckons her as though she need only take it to cross the divide, but between him and her is something gouged wide by shame and deep by all the things that can't be undone. "I didn't come here because Socall told me to."

"I need to go."

"I've made a mess of things, which is exactly what I feared I'd do. I have all these things I want to say to you. Give me another chance, that's all I'm asking." He tells her he's paid for two weeks' lodging. "I'll be here every day, so it doesn't have to be today, or tomorrow. It can be a week from now, whenever you want."

"You can't come to my house."

"No, of course. I could meet you anywhere. You could have Chappy tell me where and when."

She considers him a long while, weighing her desire to agree against the fear that he'll regret ever having returned.

"I have to go." She starts for the woods.

"Is that a 'yes'?" he calls after her. "Jubilee? Jubilee!"

⧉

"All right, all right, I'm coming!" Socall yells from inside, but Jubilee keeps pounding on her door until it flies open, and right away, Socall's ill temper is replaced with a guilty look.

"You didn't think to warn me?" Jubilee still can't stop shaking.

"I should've told you, I'm sorry, but I wasn't sure he'd come and I couldn't stand the idea of you being disappointed if he didn't." Socall makes no attempt to hide her enthusiasm. "But he came; that's the main thing!"

"And what did you imagine was going to happen, that we'd go running into each other's arms?"

Socall's face drops. "Oh, honey."

Jubilee retreats from Socall's reach. She doesn't want her to feel sorry for her, doesn't want anyone to feel sorry for her ever again. What if a person can't ever be consoled? "So you knew he wrote me a letter?"

"Levi was gone and you were gone, so when Combs delivered that letter, your Pa took it and all those pictures and fed them to the fireplace. He didn't even read it."

Jubilee slumps down on Socall's freshly painted orange steps, scoots over when Socall gestures to make room, and bats Socall's hand away when she tries to re-pin an errant strand of hair.

"Your skin is nice and all, don't get me wrong, but it's what's going on inside that's been worrying me. And you're not just upset about the letters," Socall guesses. "Would it feel better to get it off your chest?"

Shoring up resolve not to speak of it lasts only so long. "All this color does is hide what's happened." Jubilee tells some about the World of Wonders, about having attracted people like blowflies to a dead cow. "If he knew what's become of me, he'd go away wishing he'd left well enough alone."

Socall grabs Jubilee's hand and gives it a shake. "Each and every one of us has had to do things we're not proud of. What we're not proud of is what makes us all equal. Though in my opinion, you've got to come down a lot lower before you join the rest of us."

"So, you think I should see him?"

"There's unfinished business between you and Snakebite, and you have to see this thing to its conclusion, whatever conclusion that turns out to be."

Together they watch the shadows lengthen, and between them settles the kind of silence that comes after a hard rain breaks a drought.

HAVENS

❦

Ten o'clock, and the sun has yet to burn through the fog. Curtaining off the meadow from the rest of the holler is the hazy suggestion of trees, and a double-veiled hillside reposes at a discreet distance like a seasoned chaperone. Somewhere a woodpecker is drilling against an unyielding trunk. Other than that, nothing but a hush. You can almost hear the blades of grass bending from the strain of heavy dew. Careful not to step in any of the tiny gossamer hammocks, Havens arrived at the aviary two hours earlier than what she'd arranged, and the wait has made him jittery and fearful that this will be a repeat of the last time he waited for her. Twice he has rushed toward a shape thinking it her, only to discover a bush.

Only one other time has Havens felt this way about someone. Over the years it's been easier to attribute his and Virginia's parting of ways to the matter of children rather than admit an attendant issue, for which he was also at fault: using only clues as to Virginia's preferences for a romantic match—what he'd perceived to have been clues, which could just as easily have been red herrings or whims based on her fluctuating moods—Havens had fashioned his nineteen-year-old self into who he believed Virginia's ideal man would be, then spent every moment trying to live up to the construct, which turned out not to suit her in the least. How could she ever have been anything but disappointed? Thirteen years later and scantly more self-assured than his younger self, he now wishes he'd accrued a surplus of attractive features and accomplishments, and the temptation is great to present Jubilee with an intended version of himself in the hope that he'll one day mature into it, but he is resolved to play no part in deceiving her about his deficits, even if it means receiving marching orders sooner rather than later.

He spots her the moment she steps out from between the misty trees. She has Chappy accompany her only as far as the redbud tree, and she comes the rest of the way looking as if she is about to deliver bad news. Instead of a heart, there is a ceiling fan in Havens's chest, and its lopsided wobble at full-speed threatens to loosen the entire fixture. What he plans to say flies right out of his head when she reaches him, and he is struck much as he was when he first saw her at the stream, except this time she doesn't turn away or startle. It seems nothing could startle her anymore. Wearing a pale pink dress and white shawl, she is the color of peeled apples, but there are other changes, too—her auburn hair is shorter, just below her shoulders, and wavy, and she's even more slight around the waist and shoulders. He has to stifle the urge to pick her up.

"Thank you for meeting me." He hands her the posy of lilacs, then takes off his hat and turns the brim around and around as if to steer clear of hazards. He must not come on like gangbusters, not be off-putting.

"I can't stay long." She fiddles with the corner of her shawl.

"It's just so wonderful to see you, to be here, in your company. It doesn't feel real, does it?" He apologizes for how he conducted himself at the boarding house the day before, and confesses that he didn't sleep a wink.

Her eyes are gray in this light, washed almost entirely of green, and still her gaze makes him feel numb. She has a guarded way about her, different from the wariness of strangers she had when they first met.

"Shall we sit?" He beckons to the nearby log, but she stays where she is, and an awkward silence gathers between them. None of the easy way from when last they were together exists, and how could it? How can she feel about him now as she did before?

"Your foot's not all the way healed."

Foot? "Oh, right. I overdo it sometimes, and it lets me know. The doctor says the limp will go away in time." Why ramble on about this?

"They didn't print my picture, did they?" she asks.

He gives a brief account of chasing down the photograph and making sure the story got buried.

"You lost your job?"

"My loss is nothing compared to what you've gone through." Last night Sylvia Fullhart filled him in on Ronny's assertions of killing Levi in self-defense, adding that few people took it to be chapter-and-verse.

"I tell myself I ought to take comfort that Levi found love before he died." She tips her head back and turns cloudy eyes heavenward. After a long pause, she continues, "Everyone says time heals, but I don't think so. I think time just keeps robbing a person." She explains that it's getting harder to remember the sound of his voice, that she's having trouble remembering some of his songs. "Some days I can't even picture his face. I lost him, and somehow I still keep losing him, and the crazy thing is I wish you still had that picture of him so I could see him again."

Havens knows exactly the moment he'd have photographed Levi—on the porch that humid midsummer evening, flat-picking those guitar strings, bouncing the heel of his boot on the floor boards and singing in a bold voice full of plaintive arcs and drops. "I'd give anything to turn back the clock."

"Turn it back to where? Because if it's to a time before anyone gets hurt, you'd have to turn it to way before I was born."

He reaches for her trembling hand and feels his chest swell when she permits him to hold it. Or maybe he'd stop the clock right now.

"Do you still take pictures?"

Havens evades the question. "I haven't been myself, not since I left you."

"Who I was is not who I am now."

"I couldn't expect you to be exactly the same. I'm not the same, either." For the sake of transparency, he describes the morose, indecisive, self-pitying bum he's allowed himself to be the past few months. Still, she does not give him the boot. He moves his thumb across the back of her hand, aware at once of everything about her—the tendons in her neck pulled taught, how rigid she stands, how shallow she breathes. "I've missed you so much, Jubilee." So much he could crush her. Inching closer to her, he says, "There hasn't been a day go by that I haven't thought of you."

"I expected you to go on with your life. I didn't think you'd come back."

Havens shows her the color picture Massey gave him. Even though he is barely in the frame, Havens's posture and expression are a giveaway. "You tell me that's a man who's going to forget the woman in his arms and go on with his life." He tells her she'd visit him in his dreams. "You'd be as real to me as you are now." Sometimes, he'd wake up and look out the window, and he'd see her walking toward him, a trick doubly cruel for being so fleeting. "Everything reminded me of you," he adds. "I couldn't even see a pigeon and not think of you tending your birds." He shows her the handkerchief she'd embroidered for him. "I don't go anywhere without this. It's my way of taking you with me."

Briefly, she smiles, and he feels he could run a victory lap around the meadow.

She juts her chin in the direction. "Thomas is still here."

"Of course he is. Only a fool would take off."

"Do you want to say hello?"

As soon as they enter, the northern flicker flies off his perch and lands on her arm, fluffing his wings in a display of pride. Havens's greeting he returns with indifference. Together, he and Jubilee clean the cages and put out fresh seed for the convalescing birds, and he answers her questions about his daily routine in Dayton and the people he encounters along the way—the bus driver who always gives him money advice, the shoe shiner who sings Cab Calloway tunes, and the old beauty queen at the soda fountain who is the neighborhood matchmaker. "She knows all about you."

"She does?"

"I imagine I'll be back in her good graces when she hears I came to see you."

"I know what a city is like now," Jubilee volunteers, her tone changing and her eyes becoming hooded again. "I can't say I care much for it."

She stands in the doorway with her back to him. He watches her shoulders rise and drop. Though he's anxious to know this part of her story, whether she'd been admitted to a hospital in Louisville or whether she'd met a doctor some other way, he senses her qualms and knows to let her go at her own pace.

"Ronny's the reason I ended up in Louisville." Facing him, she describes being ambushed on her way to the shack and finding out about Levi on the back of a pickup and being thrown on the four-twenty train, and Havens clenches and unclenches his fists.

"I was on that train! I should've found you!"

He follows her outside to the log, afraid to hear what comes next, and yet he says, "There isn't anything you could tell me that will change my mind about you."

As though having come to a crevasse, she hesitates. Eventually, with now-or-never resolve, she takes a deep breath and tells him she found employment at the World of Wonders Sideshow. "I was the Blue She-Devil. People paid to see me sit on a chair and shout curses."

Havens is winded. He has difficulty tracking what she says. All manner of ghastly images are flooding his mind. To keep the shock from showing, he tries imitating a tree stump, but he has to put his hands on his knees. "How long?" Let it have been only one day, he prays.

She folds her hands in her lap. "Four months."

His head swings side to side. He balls his hand into a fist and presses his knuckles against his mouth as if to knock out his own front teeth. He paces two strides to the right and two strides to the left, while she describes traveling with the cast to a couple of small towns before spending almost six weeks at the state fair. Something is said about a nearsighted showgirl who sewed a costume for Jubilee and taught her about makeup.

"You had to wear a costume?"

"A person can hide in a costume," she replies.

Havens slumps onto the log beside her, clasps his hands together, and searches her face for some alternative ending.

"It wasn't so terrible. I made friends." She speaks of a man named Mr. Lizard, who had his own skin troubles and who took her under his wing and taught her that everyone has unfixable parts. With fondness, she speaks of the Cannibal Man, who only ever ate vegetables, a woman of ample proportions named Lotta, and the bearded lady, who was really a man. That she's been so grievously wronged is the only thing Havens can fully comprehend. That and how he'd like to kill Ronny. Anyone who's ever hurt her ought to pay for what they've done, and that goes for the man who put her in that tent and any man who shelled out a coin to see her.

She touches his shoulder and waits for him to compose himself before telling him about the doctor.

By the time Chappy returns, the sunlight roosts above them on the last of the fog, the airwaves belong to the finches, and Jubilee and Havens have each tilted away from their respective darkness, their heads together.

"Can't you stay a little longer?" Havens asks, reluctant to let go of her hand when she rises.

"I can come tomorrow. If I haven't scared you off."

"The only thing that scares me is being apart from you." He suddenly remembers the new birdcall he whittled for her. "An improved version."

She blows softly, and a warbler on a nearby branch trills in reply. Before she turns to go, his lips graze her cheek. "Hurry back." He watches her disappear between the trees, and watches the space long after she has passed through it—his eyes do not deceive him: it glimmers. She is a good distance away when he hears her whistle to him.

JUBILEE

❧

The last three days, she's met Havens at the aviary, and each time she's returned home at a later hour, each time lighter from having told him a little more about the World of Wonders. All night she tosses and turns. She forgets to eat. Nothing she does will hurry time along. If Pa notices her long absences, he doesn't mention it, and Mama and Grandma are lost in their own worlds. What she's overlooked, though, is her sister's nose for sniffing out secrets. All morning Willow-May's been tailing Jubilee, from the coop to the barn and now back to the bedroom, where she watches Jubilee style her hair.

"Do you have a boyfriend?"

Jubilee puts down her hairbrush. "Why would you say a thing like that?"

"This." Willow-May's hand dives into Jubilee's apron pocket and pulls out the lipstick.

"Give me that."

Willow-May dashes over to the bed, lifts Jubilee's pillow, and holds up the birdcall. "And this."

"Who said you could snoop in my things?"

Willow-May puts her hands on her hips. "Also, you've been acting funny."

"No, I haven't."

"You hum all the time."

"No, I don't."

"You were sad all the time, and now you're happy all the time."

"Aren't you supposed to be at Socall's for your lesson?"

"I'm feeling a bit poorly today." Willow-May forces a cough. "Is your boyfriend handsome?"

"Willow-May, I do not have a boyfriend, now cut it out." Jubilee makes a go for Willow-May's ribs.

"It's not Wyatt Wrightley, is it?"

"No!"

Her sister heaves a sigh of relief. "If he's nice, you should marry him."

"That does it. Shoo!" She pushes her sister out of her room. Instead of changing into a pretty dress and raising her sister's suspicions even more, she pretends she has all day to mend clothes and clean the house and play hide-and-seek with Willow-May, and by the time Jubilee shakes free and gets to her aviary, it is midafternoon. Havens, who has been waiting for hours, waves away her apology, puts his arm around her shoulder, and steers her into the shed, where he's set up two wooden crates and a barrel to serve as their dining area. He strikes a match and lights a candle on the middle crate. "You have to imagine this is a five-star joint now." He motions to her birds. "Don't mind the other diners; they're just jealous because you're my date and not theirs."

She remarks about the blanket on the shelf, and he confesses to having spent the night in the aviary. "I wanted to be close to you."

Though it's clear he's been getting little sleep, in three days his shoulders have less of a stoop to them and the lines across his forehead have smoothed out. His presence, the way he disturbs the air around her, is still the same as before, and his eyes have that knowing way of seeing her again.

"Are you cold?"

"A little, maybe."

He takes off his jacket, threads her arms through the sleeves, and reaches for her hand as though she might disappear in his garment altogether. He leans into her hair. "You are lovely this afternoon." He holds a crate for her to sit.

"Are you hungry?" From a sack, he unpacks two Cokes, a couple of sandwiches, an apple, a banana, an orange, and a candy bar. "I didn't know what you might be in the mood for."

She eyes the orange, and he starts peeling it for her, handing her one segment after another. Is this how a queen feels?

"Willow-May knows I have a boyfriend."

"Smart cookie, that one." He says he wishes he could see her again.

"If Mama wasn't so poorly, I could test the subject of you visiting—"

He stops her. "I don't want you to feel any pressure about this."

"But I don't want you to leave."

He strokes her cheek. "Who said anything about leaving?"

"You can't stay here forever."

"Why not?" He turns to the cages. "I'm not the worst roommate who's ever lived, am I, fellas?"

The flicker's head pops out from under his wing, making her laugh.

She leans toward Havens, breathing in his smell, resting her head against his neck. He strokes her hair. She nuzzles closer. She places her hand against his chest, slides the tip of her finger between his shirt buttons, and touches his skin, and his hand follows the curve from the nape of her neck to the little notch at the base of her throat, as though her neck's never been yanked or throttled or used to drive her to a place she didn't want to go. His fingers trail down to the neckline of her dress.

Never has she wanted to be loved as much as she does now. She undoes her top button. With his thumbs, he pries apart her collar, and the breath he lets out is the one she holds in. His hand glides beneath her slip and hovers over her brassiere. She presses herself against his hand, which cups and closes around her breast. From some secret place, boldness springs up in her, and what used to be a timid creature is a woman who wants.

As soon as the fairgoers' jeering faces jump into her head, she squeezes her eyes shut. *You blue all the way down?* that voice asks again. More faces crowd around, all of them greedy and flushed and beaded with sweat, so she opens her eyes to see if a hard stare will chase them away. As soon as she closes her eyes again, they are back. Doesn't she know how to be anything other than someone who sits and endures someone else's looking?

Havens raises his head from her bosom, sensing her distress. "I'm so sorry."

"I can't."

Havens touches her cheek. "It's my fault." He buttons her dress, grabs the blanket, and wraps it around her shoulders. "I'm a damn fool."

"It's me. It's my head. It gets muddled sometimes."

"I love this head." He plants the softest kiss on her temple. "The other parts aren't bad, either."

The frightful faces fall back again. She opens the blanket for him to scoot in.

"This is perfect, just like this," he says. Wrapped together, they trade sips of Coke. They talk, and before long, the afternoon is spent.

She looks at his watch.

"That thing lies," he says.

Neither of them lets go of the other.

"I don't want to leave."

"Don't." He kisses the side of her head. "Leaving doesn't suit you at all."

He stands only because she does, and still neither breaks free from their blanket cocoon. Together, they shuffle to the door.

"Are you dancing with me?"

"Smooth, aren't I?" he boasts. They squeeze through the doorway, knocking knees and poking each other with elbows, but still keeping the blanket in place, and she doesn't know why it strikes her as funny, maybe because she wonders what the birds must make of this, but here she is, in a fit of giggles. Imagine.

"We'd be champions at sack-racing," Havens says as they shuffle past the shed.

She laughs.

"We could start a new division—long-distance blanket-racing." They shuffle all the way out into the meadow. "Cross-country blanket-racing."

And while she's laughing, she's making note that nothing's ever felt as good as his body pressed against hers. They make it to the trees without falling. He kisses each of her eyelids, and then her lips, and she tilts her chin up at him, and he kisses her again, this time slow and firm.

"I'll come early tomorrow morning," she promises. "Pa's going hunting, so we'll have the whole day."

After letting her out, he wraps her end of the blanket over his shoulder. "I'll be here." His gaze is warm on her back, and when she looks over her shoulder before passing through the trees, he waves, but worry has shadowed his face again, as if it might be the last time he sees her.

⚬

She decides to take the long way home, going through the ravine and along the old rock quarry to check Pa's traps, and while she's still savoring the feel of her skin, tingling where Havens's hand stroked it, she is startled by the scream of a vixen. Worrying that it's got itself snared in a trap, she rushes toward the sound, and still she cannot see it. The small clearing is surrounded by spindly sugar maples and, on the far end, one gnarled wolf tree, and it's from there that the cries come.

She's wrong—it's not a fox; not a coyote, either. She takes a few steps closer to the tree, and the thing falls silent. She looks around to see if this is some kind of trick. No one jumps down from the rock pile or steps out from behind a tree, so she takes two steps closer. Just barely can she make out a shape inside the burrowed-out trunk. One step closer, and she sees the bundle rustle a little. Not a sack of kittens.

"Hello?" she calls out to the surrounding cliff.

The echo takes its time coming back as if it, too, would prefer to be any place but here.

"Anyone there?"

She strains for signs of an ambush, but there are none, so she crouches down, reaches inside the hollow, and retrieves the bundle, peeling back the burlap and revealing what makes no sense. Scarcely bigger than a pigeon is a baby. A baby boy. He's wearing only a white cotton vest, and his lips are frozen into a pout, his eyes are glassy with tears, and he's turned blue from the—

Not the cold.

In an ages-long moment, she realizes what she's got here is another Blue, Sarah and Levi's baby. She covers him, shelters him in the warmth of her bosom, and rocks him. "You're okay, little one, I've got you."

What is he doing here? Who brought him? Are they coming back?

"Hello?" her call rings out.

He's a good little boy, so content to nestle against her chest.

She doesn't know what to make of this. Has Sarah put down her child so she can forage, and if so, why hasn't she come running? Maybe she got herself hurt. Jubilee walks in wider and wider circles, searching and calling for Sarah. "I've found your baby."

Even the birds are afraid to answer.

She waits a long time for his claiming, but it doesn't come. Somebody ought to have come by now. They say to put baby birds back in the nest.

"I'm not taking this baby, you hear? I'm putting him back where I found him."

From leaves and burlap she makes up a soft bed and wraps him in her sweater. He protests as soon as she lays him down, but rather than pacify him, she tells him to scream as loud as he can. She finds a nearby bush to hide behind, and waits for his mother to come, for anyone to come. Federal agents come through these woods every so often looking for stills, once a census-taker and once a map-maker, and what seems like forever ago, two men on assignment for President Roosevelt. Someone please come and take this crying child.

Can't they hear his distress? Why won't they come?

Both she and the child have had their fill of waiting. She picks him up again, cradles him against her chest, and offers him the tip of her little finger to suckle, peeking again at his legs and arms. His color is a shade much paler than hers and Levi's, but he has the Buford nose and Levi's short chin. She strokes and teases the ginger fuzz on the crown of his head.

"You're a little rooster, aren't you?" She peels open his tiny fist. He is perfect and beautiful, and she is breathless with love for him. It's as though some of Levi is brought back.

"You're going to be okay, little rooster."

The baby is asleep by the time she opens the front door.

Mama turns from her post at the kitchen window, and it's as if a fraction of her former self returns when she shakes her head and says, "You cannot bring a critter in this house, how many times do you have to be told?"

"It's not a critter, Mama."

What Mama sees in Jubilee's face makes her take slow, careful steps forward. "What you got there?"

Bringing a falling star into this house ought to come with a warning first, some way to prepare Mama for the impact, but what is there to do but unwrap the sweater so she can also be dazzled?

Mama spins the other way. As though to set her seeing straight, she turns around for another look, and stops her mouth with her hand. She doesn't need to be told this is Levi's boy. She makes a scoop of her hands and says, "Give."

Passing him feels like passing trouble and salvation both. How Jubilee came to find him and in what location are of no interest to Mama.

"You're the spitting image of your daddy," Mama whispers to him, lifting the sweater to count toes. Easing herself into the rocking chair, she tells Jubilee where to find the box with Willow-May's old baby bottle and says to warm some milk, but first Jubilee goes to where Pa's pumping out the privy, and tells him Levi's baby's in the house. "Mama's got him," she adds so he'll make haste.

In front of Mama and the baby, Pa becomes fixed as granite.

"Isn't he beautiful, Del?" It's as though Mama's come out from under a bad spell.

Pa's voice is high. "That's a newborn."

"He's little, but he's strong." She shows how he grips her finger. "Aren't you, little fella? Just like your daddy."

White with worry, Pa instructs Jubilee to saddle up Lass. "I'll ride down to Eddie's and get him back to his mother."

Mama's head whips up. "You're not taking this child anywhere, least of all that swamp. Didn't you hear what Jubilee just said? He was left in the woods. They don't want him."

"Gladden, he's to be returned to Sarah right away."

"There's no pardon for what she's done and there won't be for you, either, putting him back in harm's way."

"We don't know what the circumstances are."

"What do you mean, we don't know? He was left there to perish. Because he's a Blue." Mama tells Jubilee to quit standing around and get his bottle.

On his haunches, Pa speaks to Mama the way he speaks to the cow when it's time to calve. "Glad, we have to return this child to his rightful family, and that's all there is to it."

"This is your grandson, Delbert. We are his rightful family. And don't you talk to me like I've never lived through a baby being born blue. Those people pushed us out on account of our blue young'uns and now they've pushed out this one and we are going to take care of him."

Pa hangs his head and the baby starts to cry.

"Do you have the milk ready or do I have to do it myself?" Mama snaps at Jubilee.

She prepares the bottle and cools it in a basin of water, and when she hands it to Mama, she may as well be making a terrible pact with her.

Mama flicks a few drops onto her wrist before offering the bottle to the baby, who is straightaway pacified while the statue that resembles Pa says, "As soon as he's finished eating, okay, Gladden?"

Mama makes it clear she doesn't want to hear any more, and Pa and Jubilee drift to the far corner like soot from a sudden wildfire. Instead of bringing the baby here, Jubilee should've taken him to Socall's. She would've known what to do.

"I'm sorry, Pa," she whispers. "I didn't think it through."

Pa's too busy watching Mama to mind her.

When the baby finishes his bottle, Mama gets up and puts him against her shoulder and walks him around the front room, patting his back and congratulating burps, and once he's asleep, she nestles with him in the rocking chair again. After a while, Pa approaches her.

"Glad, I don't want to risk going down the holler with him in the dark."

Mama glares at him. "One boy was taken from me, and what happened? He was left to die out there on his own. I won't have that happen again."

Pa starts to crumble. After a long pause, he tries again to reason with Mama, but she cuts him off. "Have you even looked at this child? Look at him."

Pa's eyes go watery.

To lend Pa support, Jubilee says, "We can't keep him, Mama. This will get us into a lot of trouble, especially if someone gets the notion we kidnapped him."

"What makes you think you have any say in this? You changed your color and now you aim to behave like them, is that it?"

"Gladden."

On the subject of Jubilee's new skin color, Mama's had nothing to say—she's barely looked at Jubilee—but now it's blue-this and blue-that. "Blue wasn't ever something Levi was ashamed of, but it's not good enough for you."

Pa sends Jubilee on a made-up errand, and appeals to Mama to mind her words, but before Jubilee steps out the back door, Mama hollers at her, "Why don't you go live with them if you like being right-colored so well?"

"Gladden!"

Jubilee returns to where Mama now bestows on this child the affection she has craved since her return. "I thought my color would make you happy."

"Happy?" Mama snorts and nods at Pa like she's being asked to reason with a turnip. "When did happiness ever have anything to do with color?"

"You can't say because you've never been blue."

"Birthing you counts for nothing, does it? Loving blue and fearing for blue and mourning blue? Don't you dare tell me I don't know about blue!"

"You don't have to worry about blue anymore, that's all I'm trying to say."

"You walk around pretending to be someone else, and I'm not supposed to worry?" She clicks her tongue. "Do whatever the hell you want, just don't tell me changing yourself is on my account."

Only after the evening star comes out can Jubilee bring herself to go back indoors. Sitting at the table with his head propped up by his hand, Pa has brought the law into it and Mama is talking like a gunslinger, saying Sheriff Suggins, the judge, the whole damn town is no match for her. "This baby is making up for what they stole from us. This baby is our justice. Why are you crying, Delbert? For goodness sake, this is a happy day. A happy day, don't you see? This is our second chance."

This is another kind of madness than the one to which Jubilee came home, but Mama shines. Oh, how she shines.

JUBILEE

What her new skin hasn't done for the Bufords, the baby does overnight. Grandma forgets all about her suitcase and no longer eyes Jubilee as if she's about to make off with the valuables, Willow-May is handing out musical instruments and telling everyone babies love singalongs, and Mama appears to have taken up living again, except now as if with all the company of heaven. This morning the house is filled with the smell of warm milk and fresh bread, the sound of women cooing like turtledoves, and the glow of stolen treasure.

Bringing home Levi's child felt like a rescue yesterday, but today it's just plain stealing.

Pa and Jubilee meet at the table, each of them ill at ease while Mama bustles around the kitchen with the baby in the crook of her arm. As a way to win her affection and make amends for their quarrel yesterday, Jubilee's forgone taking her pill today, and is surprised to feel more like her regular self. Back to blue is like putting on favorite old clothes only to realize the ball gown never did fit quite right in the first place and was nowhere near as comfortable.

Willow-May skips up to Jubilee. "Mouth harp or spoons?"

Mama's face gives nothing away regarding Jubilee's color, but she does hand Jubilee the baby and asks her to change him, gesturing to the pile of diapers she's cut from an old cotton sheet. Jubilee fetches one and lays the baby on the table. He is an alert little boy, too afraid he'll miss something, and he behaves as though he understands every word Jubilee speaks.

"I think we ought to name him Lenny," Mama says, "After your father, Del."

"It's not our business to name him," Pa replies, doused-looking.

"Well, whose business do you think it ought to be? Are we to wait until he's old enough to tell us himself what he'd like to be called?"

"We said we'd keep him just one night, Glad."

"No, you said just one night." Mama was never one for letting her emotions out, but her anger pops off now as easy as a drunk's pistol. "If I have to, I'll raise this child myself, Delbert, so help me God, I will!"

Jubilee keeps her head down and unwraps his swaddling, and is taken aback by his fading color. The skin behind his knees and in the crease of his elbows even has a hint of pink. Has Mama not noticed this? She tries to catch Pa's attention, but Mama snatches up the baby and sends Jubilee outside with the pail of soiled diapers.

While she is doing the washing, Pa trudges toward her.

"What are we going to do, Pa? She's not going to give him up."

Mama eyes them from the back door, ignoring Pa's signals for her to go back inside.

"I'd planned to ride down to Eddie's already and get the lay of the land, but your ma's glued to me."

"I could go."

Pa won't hear of it. "I don't want you anywhere near Eddie. Besides, if you take the baby it'll only put more of a strain between you and your ma." Pa says he'll try for Eddie's before lunch, but in the meantime, he will continue to press Mama. "She'll come around to it by then."

If Pa's so sure nobody's going to get wind of them keeping a baby who doesn't belong to them and that everything's going to be settled by noon, why does he go out to the shed and collect his box of ammunition?

With this turn of events, Jubilee can't go to Havens, and she knows he'll grow worried before long. As soon as Pa leaves with the baby, she'll run down to her aviary.

When she goes back into the house, Mama's roped Willow-May into her fantasy, listing all the functions of a big sister. "Most important, you've got to watch him all the time—you can't ever let him out of your sight."

Willow-May makes a note of this on her chalkboard.

Jubilee fetches a sheet of paper and the tin of buttons and corn kernels, and challenges her sister to a game of Fox & Hens, but she cannot be coaxed away from Mama. Each of Pa's bids to get Mama to part with the baby fails the same way. For the first time since Jubilee's return, though, everyone comes together at the table for a meal.

By late afternoon, Jubilee corners Pa again, and he whispers something about working on a new plan, which, as far as she can tell, entails circling the outskirts of Mama's willpower. To give herself something to do other than stand and chew on her nails, Jubilee goes out to the wash line. A weak sun today means everything is still damp and will need to be draped over the furniture. She unpins the diapers, pausing to take in how suddenly life can change, right down to a wash line, and her attention is pulled to a lone figure some distance down the path. At first, she fears it's someone come about the baby, but that stoop, that foot-scuffing gait as though sandbags are tied to his calves, can only belong to one man. Havens. Her heart is a bell with a clapper that's too big. She tries waving at him to come no closer, but he quickens his pace. She lifts her skirt and rushes to meet him.

He removes his hat. He is sweating and flushed and in a state. In a raspy voice, he says, "Thank goodness you're here! I've been so worried! Are you okay? Is everything all right?"

Jubilee glances back at the house.

"I know I shouldn't be here. I'm sorry. I would've sent Chappy, but I couldn't find him, and I couldn't wait any longer. You have no idea what's been going on in my head." He takes a big breath and lets out a sigh. "I'm just so relieved to find you here. I don't know what I would've done—"

She wants to hold him, but she can't chance it. "I'm okay, but you should go now. I'll explain everything tomorrow."

"What's happened? Has someone upset you?"

"Nothing like that. It's just something with Mama."

It takes a good deal more assuring for him to agree. He is about to put on his hat, but stops and smiles. "You look—"

"Blue again, yes." What is he to make of her—blue, not blue, then blue again?

"I was about to say beautiful. You take a man's breath away."

His expression changes, and Jubilee turns to see the cause—Mama is coming at them as though to drive off a flock of crows from a cornfield.

"She's not well" is Jubilee's hasty warning.

Havens tucks his shirt tight into his trousers and smooths down his hair. "It had to happen sometime." He gives Jubilee a look of reassurance.

Mama sets herself between Jubilee and Havens.

"Mrs. Buford, good afternoon."

She narrows her eyes. "You think you can come back here, given all that's happened?"

Havens is in the midst of offering his condolences, when she says, "Come to gawk at her again, is that it? Once wasn't enough? You leave us be and go find someone else to abase with your picture-taking." It doesn't even sound like Mama's voice. It sounds like it belongs to a woodcutter, someone accustomed to stubborn timber.

"Mama, please."

Steady-tempered, Havens says, "I can't abase what I believe to be perfect."

"Perfect, is she? With a dead brother, that's what you call perfect?"

Pa joins them now, brow wrinkled the way it is when he's made a stack of coins and realizes there isn't enough to solve his money problems. "Why are you here?"

"I've returned to Chance to court your daughter, sir."

Mama brings color into it, one moment charging he's only interested in blue, and the next that it's only because of her curing, and this time, Havens is the one doing the objecting. "Blue or not blue is for Jubilee to choose. To me, it doesn't matter at all." Havens doesn't rush his words. "The truth is I love her and if she'll permit me, I'm ready to prove myself a candidate for her affection."

Pa looks as if his land has just been sold out from under him. Turning to Jubilee, he says, "You don't want him. Tell the man."

"Please don't make me choose, Pa."

"It's an impossible notion!" declares Mama. "We won't permit it!"

"You need to leave," Pa orders.

"I certainly understand your misgiving. In your shoes, I would feel the same." Havens puts on his hat. "Nevertheless, Jubilee is the one to decide." Turning to her, he pats where his heart lies. "You know where to find me."

"What does he know about being in our shoes?" Mama says, watching Havens head off.

He loves her. The wind could pick her up and carry her away.

&

Back inside the house, it's no use trying to lie to Mama and Pa, so she tells them straight-out where she's spent the last few days and that she intends to see him again and promise herself to him. They could not appear more unnatural than if they were pillars of salt.

"Have you forgotten your brother made this mistake?" Pa asks, which provokes Mama into insisting that Levi didn't make any mistake and that Sarah Tuttle's solely to blame. Jubilee wonders why her parents cannot see their daughter full, whole, for the first time believing she deserves the love of a kind man and deserving, too, of being allowed to make her own choice about loving him back.

"Love isn't ever a mistake," she insists.

Mama plucks up the baby, clicking her tongue.

"You're bound for hurt," Pa says. Why isn't he minding Mama and the hurt she's bound for with that baby still in her possession? Why hasn't he seen about returning him yet, instead of standing here and telling Jubilee about hurt?

"Is that why you didn't tell me about his letter?"

"You mind your pa; he knows better than you what's best," Mama scolds.

"What would you have me do with the rest of my life, Pa? Hide? Because hiding didn't solve anything—it just made things worse. We've hidden ourselves for so long we've become lost."

"I know exactly where I am," snaps Mama.

"No one's saying you should hide," Pa says. "You've got your pills now, so there's no need to hide. We're saying, he's not right for you. There's bound to be another man who's more suited."

"You don't think those pills are a way of hiding?" Jubilee challenges. "I take those pills and go to Smoke Hole and all anyone sees is pretty skin. And another man? What man wants to go to sleep with a Right-colored and wake up in the morning and find a Blue in his bed?"

"I've never heard such nonsense," says Mama.

"You said yourself I've been trying to act like someone else, Mama, and it's true. I thought if I could just look like everyone else, everything would be okay, but I took those pills and ended up feeling lost in my own self. I'm formed around blue, and there's no pill for that. But that man you're so set against is the one person who loves what's inside, and if I don't let myself love him back, then I'm destined for a coward's life, just like Levi said."

"What about children?"

Telling Pa why he doesn't have to worry about any more blue offspring doesn't much console him. "Two makes a family," Jubilee says. She goes to the front door. "Now I'm going to give him my answer."

At Levi's grave, Pa had said the deceased don't stay in their graves, but Jubilee doesn't believe this. As long as she's given her heart to someone who still walks the earth, she might just thank the Lord kindly when it comes time for her soul to make its final journey, and consent instead to stay in her grave until his body is put to rest, and should he be an unbeliever and what they say is true about there being no heavenly welcome for heathen folk, then she will wait with him till the earth crumbles and the dust of them mixes together and a great wind carries them away in a cloud.

＊

Dusk wafts in on an expectant breeze and when she reaches the meadow, Havens is sitting with his back against the shed facing her direction. As soon as he sees her, he leaps to his feet. This time he doesn't wave and he doesn't move toward her. He waits for her to make up all the distance on her own, giving her the freedom to change her mind at every step. He wants her sure.

To love someone is to keep them safe, that's what Jubilee used to believe, that's how she loved Levi, how she thought Sarah ought to love her brother, too, but what if love and safe-keeping have little to do with each other? What if love calls a person out from her shelter, way out?

She reaches Havens sure as she'll ever be. He takes her wrist as though it were the oar of a canoe run ashore and leads her into the aviary, closing the door with his foot.

He kisses her.

"I've never—you know—"

He nuzzles her neck in reply. He runs his lips up her neck to her ear and tastes the tip. His breath makes every seam in her tighten, then go slack, and what was stitched up all these years by fear and shame is no match for his fingers at the loosening thread. She pulls the clips from her bun, and he fills his hands with her hair and buries his face. He pushes a sleeve off one shoulder and kisses her skin, and she pushes aside the other sleeve, letting her dress fall away like a shadow.

"You are so lovely, Jubilee, so beautiful." For a long time, he just admires what he sees. "You have no idea, do you?"

She shivers.

"Can I show you?"

"Yes."

Gently and unhurried, he outlines her shape, feeling his way around a curve, sliding the edge of his hand into a soft corner. She believes in his love. His touch makes her proud, and for the first time, she feels fully at home in herself.

He makes a bed for them with the blanket and his clothes, rolling up his jacket for a pillow for her, before laying her down.

This is how the forest grows when nobody is looking. Thick roots curl over one another, vines make loops and latch onto tree branches, bark shivers when moss scuttles over it, and leaves unravel all at once, making a tree quiver—all this while the ground softens and arcs, and the river, once dammed at the bend, surges ahead into the ready creek bed.

Outside, the dark woods stand guard, the stars start sprinkling themselves in the tree branches like tinsel, and the moon glints like a coin tossed into a wishing well.

JUBILEE

＊

t first light, she is still awake, still thinking of Havens, still imagining his hand running across her body, which feels so different now after his loving. Her whole being feels strummed. She can't stop humming. As soon as she hears the baby crying, she gets up and dresses with haste. Why has Pa still not done something about this?

Mama is bending over the squalling child. "You've done this!" she accuses Jubilee, lifting Lenny from Grandma's suitcase, which serves as a crib to show Jubilee her crime. Gone from him is any trace of blue. "You've given him your pills!"

"No, I didn't." Reassuring doesn't work.

Hair matted and eyes narrowed, Mama is one part Gladden, three parts witch. She screams, "Get out!"

Jubilee finds Pa in the barn saddling Lass. To get a read on Pa's mood, a person need only check how he's positioned his hat. Sitting far back on his crown and exposing his face all the way to his hairline means he's in good spirits and will gladly converse, squared and yanked down so his ears bend means his task is not to be interrupted, and positioned at an angle means you can expect a song or a joke, but if it's the way it is now, front brim pulled low to hide his eyes, it's best to rectify your ways or keep your distance. Jubilee broaches the subject of the baby's color, and he says he already knows. He admits Mama's reasoning has worsened, too.

"She plans never to be parted from the child," Jubilee says.

"That's why I'm going to force the matter." Pa says the minute she sets Lenny down, he's going to take him. Pa tugs the brim of his hat even lower when she offers to help.

Jubilee is bringing a bundle of wood inside when she sees that Pa has somehow blown his cover. Milk is boiling over on the stove, Pa is trying to strike some sort of deal, Mama is pounding her fists against Pa's chest, yelling that he will take Lenny away over her dead body, and Lenny is lying in the suitcase-crib wondering if someone's ever going to feed him. There's but one way out of this. Jubilee snatches up Lenny, runs out of the house and down the steps, and unties Lass from the porch railing.

Mama blasts after her, screaming, "Give me back Levi!"

"This isn't Levi, Mama, this is Sarah's baby." With a firm hold on the baby, Jubilee flicks the reins and tucks in her heels and sets off, Mama screeching at her to stop and Pa running after her. How few times does the right way make itself so plain, and still there's a part of Jubilee that wants to turn back and give Mama what she most wants.

Uncle Eddie lives where the holler flattens and widens. At a gallop, Lass could have them there in twenty minutes, but there's the baby to consider, so she takes it slow, especially along the steeper parts of the trail. The air is cold and damp, and they make foggy breaths, Lenny's just a tiny little puff. He's wide awake, taking in everything.

Uncle Eddie's cabin is set in a hard field that is nothing but dirt and scrubby bushes. A rusty old manure spreader sits in the middle of his land from the one time he thought he might make something of it. His livestock have long since succumbed to starvation, even the last of his goats are gone, and now only Reverend Tuttle's pony is in the coral. The poor thing looks far gone. Uncle Eddie's cabin is dug partway into the ground, so when Jubilee walks up to the front door she can see the weeds growing up from the dirt roof.

She knocks several times. "Sarah?"

She walks around to the back. The outdoor kitchen has a piece of corrugated iron for a roof, a couple of tarps for sides, and a coatrack from which pots hang, but Sarah's not here or in the outhouse either. Hearing moaning inside the cabin, she steps over a tub of rotting potatoes and enters through the back door. There's barely any light to see by. "Sarah?" The walls are papered with flattened cereal boxes, a new dartboard hangs above the fireplace, and the table is a mess of playing cards and darts and beer bottles. The only womanly touch is the dainty white lace curtain that hangs in the window above the iron bed, where Uncle Eddie is slouched among army blankets. The smell is strongest at the foot of the bed, where a five-gallon drum serves as a latrine.

"Foot's gone." Uncle Eddie pulls at the covers, disturbing a colony of flies, and exposes a bandaged stump soaked through with blood. She has to cover her nose to keep from gagging. Uncle Eddie watches the flies settle on his stump. "So, you blue again. Couldn't cut it as one of us, that it?"

"Where's Sarah?" she asks.

A heavy swing of his head brings muddy eyes to hers. "Where's my foot, is what I'd like to know." He reaches for the bottle beside his pillow and takes a swig. "Do they bury a foot? Or do they grind it up and feed it to the hogs?" Uncle Eddie seems to be enjoying himself until he spies what Jubilee is holding. "Is that a baby?"

Taking a step backward, she answers, "This is Sarah's child. I need to give him to her."

Uncle Eddie sneers. "You can't trick me. Her baby's long gone."

She goes cold at the words. "Did you leave this child to die in the woods?"

"Does it look like I can go anywhere on this leg?"

Uncle Eddie slumps to one side, instantly nodding off.

She prods him.

His eyes clack open. "They wanted to take my leg all the way up to my nuts."

"Who took Sarah's baby? Did she agree to it?"

"You always were a meddlesome little coon." Agitated, Uncle Eddie tries to sit up, slinging his good leg over the side of the bed and reaching for his stump. "Scoot that bucket over." Uncle Eddie starts fussing with his pants. "Quick!"

She pushes the pail with her foot and turns away as Uncle Eddie leans forward and takes aim.

"Who left this child out there in the woods?"

"Why are you pestering me?"

"Who was it?"

"Why should I tell you anything? You've never helped me. Your father never helped me. He just stole my inheritance. But I've got my own boy now. He'll help me turn this place around, and next summer you won't be able to see anything out there except tobacco, then your pa will be the one coming to me with his hand out."

"Ronny took Sarah's baby?"

"Oh, he'll be along presently, and he's not going to be too pleased." Uncle Eddie starts coughing and then retching. The only reason she doesn't let him suffocate on his own vomit is so he can tell her of Sarah's whereabouts. Could she be lying out there somewhere?

"What did you do to Sarah? Where is she?"

"I'm glad she's gone. Let her father put up with all her blubbering."

Jubilee has no time to lose. With Uncle Eddie yelling that there are ways to make it so a witness can't talk, she tears out of the cabin, mounts Lass, and gallops off. A Blue going into town is asking for trouble, but skin can't be worth much if it isn't worth risking to save someone else. "Come on, little one; let's go find your mama."

Once they cross the wash, there is no turning back. They follow it to the road, where the sheltering trees fall back and Beaver Creek rushes to their left, and Lass becomes skittish, as if she knows blue skin is no condition for coming to town, especially with someone else's ill-got baby.

"Just a little farther," she tells Lenny as they pass Rudy's filling station, which would be a pile of rubble were it not for the Regal beer signs holding it together. On the swaybacked porch sit four of Chappy's kin. They tip their hats.

As they reach the first of the electric poles at the four-way, with town but a mile ahead, she hears horses behind her, and she turns in the saddle to see Ronny and Faro racing toward her. She considers bolting for town, but Lass is no match for Ronny's stallion, so she tucks Lenny under her blouse, doubles her coat around her, and trots on, waiting for them to catch up. "Not a sound now, okay, Lenny?"

Ronny's face is sanded smooth with spite. He steers his horse in a circle around Lass. "You must have some kind of death wish."

She nudges for Lass to keep going, but Ronny brings his horse to a halt in front of her, blocking their passage. She reminds herself she has a man who loves her and a little one who has given her a purpose much bigger than Ronny's wickedness. Town's in view now, so she fixes her sights dead ahead, keeps a firm grip on Lenny, and steers Lass around the stallion.

She hears Ronny ask Faro, "Was I not clear when I made a deal with her?"

"Oh, you were clear, all right."

"Was it not a fair deal?"

"I'd say more than fair."

Again, Ronny blocks her way. She ought to know better, but the words are out before she can stop them. "You killed my brother, Ronny, and there wasn't ever any deal."

His voice has a rusty edge to it. "He got himself killed! What kind of fool takes on two guys bigger than himself with an itty-bitty pocketknife?"

She won't listen to this. She flicks the reins, but Ronny blocks Lass going to the right, and she veers to the left, and he blocks that side, too.

"Poor Mrs. Gault's gonna die any day because of your brother!"

Ronny rebukes Faro, who argues that since Levi's not around, it's only right that Jubilee take responsibility for the fact nobody will talk to Mrs. Gault, not even her friends or even her own husband, and that she didn't even ask for Eddie's baby or any babies for that matter. "It's not fair Eddie makes you do all his dirty work, neither. Just so he won't blab more details about your mama."

"Shut the fuck up, Faro!" Ronny shouts.

Jubilee understands that she is not just dealing with malice anymore. Avenging is Ronny's aim.

Ronny leans in close to her. He smells like lard gone off. "You don't feel bad about what you've done to my mama, do you? And now you've come to town so you can rub her nose in it."

If the World of Wonders taught Jubilee anything it's how to make as though your adversary is gone.

"Jesus, she's something, isn't she?"

Suddenly Lenny whimpers.

"Is that a baby?"

"What man would be stupid enough to breed with a Blue?" asks Faro.

Jubilee shoots the gap between the horses, flicking the reins for Lass to give it her all. She clicks her tongue for Lass to go faster, but she's no match for the two horses, which close rank and put an end to the chase.

A viper's eyes have more feeling than Ronny's. "It's not yours, is it?"

There are people in the street up ahead now; if Ronny does something, he's going to have to do it in full view of an audience.

"I know what you did, Ronny."

"Hand it over!"

"No one's going to excuse you of that much hate, not even those who can't stand Blues."

Ronny tries reaching for Lenny, but Jubilee slaps the reins and Lass lunges ahead as though a wolf's snapped at her heels.

Instead of chasing, Ronny and Faro peel off the road and head for the path that runs along the railway tracks.

Lass slows when they reach Main Street, flicking her tail and twitching her ears. She stops a hundred yards from the nearest cabin, locks her knees, and sets her head in that stubborn position as if someone's just thrown a sack over it.

"Come on now, Lass."

She flares her nostrils as though she's caught the scent of trouble and won't budge.

"Lass, move." Jubilee digs in her heels, and Lass obliges with two steps before stopping again. At this rate, they'll reach Sarah's front door by

Christmas. Keeping Lenny tight in her arm, Jubilee dismounts and leads Lass by the reins, and still the horse keeps yanking her head back. "None of us likes being here, okay?" Dragging a stubborn horse is not how she wanted to come to town. She wanted everyone to see her as resolved, proud to do the right thing, proud, too, of blue.

The Tuttles live on the south side of town, up the dirt road that leads to the church. If she goes through the middle of town, there's no telling what kind of crowd she'll draw, so she leads Lass along the gravel road to her right and goes by way of Anderson's mill.

Lenny squirms and whimpers.

"Nearly there." She hums, even though you can't call it a tune.

A man in his front yard eyes her as she goes by, and falls in behind them, along with two other men and a boy on his bicycle. Two women pass her, each swiveling to join the men. Sweat sticks Jubilee's dress to her legs. Just keep going. People are marching behind her, others streaming toward her from every which way, faces bearing down on her, eyes boring into the back of her head. Three houses from her destination Verily Suggins dashes into the road from nowhere, yelling about this being private property and grabbing Jubilee's jacket, revealing what Jubilee intended to keep private. Lenny starts bellowing.

A person can go her whole life running and hiding and believing she's put on this earth only to be sorry for being blue, but Jubilee is not sorry anymore. "This is Sarah Tuttle's boy and I aim to return him to her, so best you get out of my way."

As though she's had her head held underwater, Verily gasps and tells the crowd, "She's dug up the grave! She's robbed the grave! Fetch Sheriff Suggins!"

Jubilee prepares to run bull-hard against anyone who dares step in front of her, but the crowd suddenly allows her passage, and she can't be sure what has subdued them more, Lenny's presence or a Blue standing up for herself.

Jubilee ties Lass to the hitching post in the Tuttle's front yard and rushes up to the door. No one answers her knock, so she yells at the window.

"Sarah, I've brought back your baby!" Jubilee raps on another window. "Sarah, your baby is out here and he needs you!"

A gaunt face appears from behind the lace curtain.

"See for yourself." Jubilee lifts Lenny.

The front door opens a crack, and Sarah pushes past her father. She's so frail. There's hardly any woman left to her. All it takes for the life to go filling up in her is a look at Lenny's face. "My baby!"

Jubilee lays him in the cradle Sarah makes of her arms. He fits so perfectly. It's this she'll tell Mama when she's ready to hear.

Mrs. Tuttle comes to her daughter's side with a baby blanket, and Reverend Tuttle introduces himself to his grandson while Jubilee gives an account of where she found him and how she took him home because she didn't know what else to do and that she is sorry she didn't come right away. Instead of telling about Mama, she explains how they've all come to love him in just two days and what a good boy he is and that they've been calling him Lenny in the meantime, but of course he's hers to name.

"You did a very brave thing today." Reverend Tuttle thanks her, but she would rather he save his respect for Levi. "My brother wanted to marry Sarah. He would've done everything to make her happy and he would've raised this boy not to hate anyone."

Sarah tells Lenny, "Your daddy would've been so proud of you for being so brave out there in the woods all by yourself." Never has there been a Buford so content. "He favors Levi, don't you think?" Sarah asks Jubilee. But her face clouds over. "He came out blue, and Eddie just went crazy. He hurt me pretty bad, and when I came to, he said my baby had died and been buried, and I was to go along with him being stillborn and forget it." Her eyes flicker as she describes searching everywhere for her baby in the hope that Eddie was lying, and having to give up eventually. "I told myself it was better that he was with his daddy in heaven than in this wicked world."

So she won't cry, Jubilee touches Lenny's little face and brings her back to what matters now.

She recounts her run-in with Ronny. "It was Eddie's plan, but Ronny carried it out, though I expect they'll find a way to try pin this on me."

"I will have a word with Sheriff Suggins," promises Reverend Tuttle.

"Who's done exactly nothing about Levi's murder!"

Mrs. Tuttle rests a hand on Sarah's shoulder, but Sarah won't be placated. "We let Ronny get away with killing an innocent man; are we going to let him get away with trying to kill an innocent child? When's he going to be stopped?"

Reverend Tuttle looks like a man at the bottom of a well with a rope that's too short. "We've got a town council meeting coming up this week. I can raise the issue of having Sheriff Suggins replaced."

"And what makes you so sure they won't replace you, Pa?" argues Sarah.

"I think I'll be on my way." Jubilee teases Lenny's cockscomb and passes her finger over his cheek. "Goodbye, little rooster." This little boy, beautiful and perfect and purpose-giving. "You being in the world makes it less wicked."

Sarah follows Jubilee to the steps. "Why isn't he blue anymore?"

"I don't know, but you'll see when he cries that some of it comes back in his lips and fingernails." There will be time later for explaining all Jubilee's learned about blue, but for now she tells her about Dr. Fordsworth, who will welcome a letter from Sarah on the matter, and will surely write back with an answer as to why his color faded and if it's likely to come back.

"I'll never be able to repay you." There's something different about how Sarah holds her head now. "Maybe I can bring him by for a visit sometime, if your ma will allow it?"

"We would all like that very much."

Reverend Tuttle follows Jubilee to her horse, thanking her and saying again how sorry he is about Levi. "I can only promise his child will want for nothing, and I will make sure he grows up surrounded by music."

"Not just church music," Jubilee barters from her saddle. "Sarah's and Levi's kind of music, too."

Reverend Tuttle leads Lass to the front gate where he pauses and looks up at Jubilee and says in earshot of the crowd gathered around, "The Lord looks with favor on those who walk in the paths of righteousness."

She feels she's contradicting God when she says, "Favor's good, but justice is better."

The crowd parts for her as soon as Verily starts yelling for people to mind they don't get touched or cursed, but Reverend Tuttle's reprimand is stern and loud. "No one wants to hear that kind of talk, Verily!"

Not everything can be put right by what Jubilee's done, Mama's heart for sure, but has not one stolen item now been returned to its rightful owner, one prisoner gone free? All this time Jubilee supposed the Year of the Lord's Favor would be a rush of captives going free all at once, every debt forgiven, every sin pardoned in one fell swoop, but perhaps the Jubilee Year begins small, with one true deed followed by another true deed.

JUBILEE

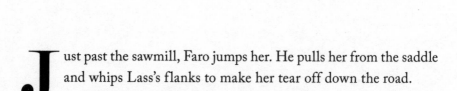

Just past the sawmill, Faro jumps her. He pulls her from the saddle and whips Lass's flanks to make her tear off down the road.

"Time someone taught a witch a lesson."

Ronny is waiting behind the mill shed. Faro's eyes slide around like loose marbles on a cracked saucer, but Ronny's are wide and fixed. "We were down to no Blues, but now there are two again. Pretty soon, there'll be three, then four, then the whole goddamn town will be crawling with them."

"We are people, Ronny. We have names."

They drag her to the weedy clearing on the other side of the greenbrier, where a car tire is propped against a barrel. As soon as she sees that it's to be fitted over her, she fights and struggles against Ronny, and when that gets her nowhere, she drops into a crouch, which only makes it easier for Faro to throw it over her head. Ronny pulls her to her feet so Faro can tug the tire down past her shoulders, pinning her arms to her sides.

She makes a dash for the road, but the weight of the tire makes her lose her balance. She screams for help.

"Get her up." Her panic has only made Ronny more patient.

Faro pulls her off her knees, turns the tire, spinning her around and around before letting go. She lurches left then right, trying to find her balance and eating dirt instead. Faro's laughing sounds like buzzards bickering over a fresh carcass.

Fighting the urge to throw up, she struggles to her feet again. "You won't get away with this, Ronny. The truth is going to come out about what you did, and everyone will know if you do anything to me."

"People will thank me."

"No, they won't."

"Shut her up." He orders Faro to shove a rag in her mouth.

She shakes her head wildly, pleading with them to stop, when Faro fetches a gasoline can.

Faro mimics her, "Blahrahrahamama," as he dribbles gasoline on her shoes. Please, not this.

Fumes burn her nose and eyes, and she tears off, but lopsided running doesn't take her far. She topples over again, a beetle upended.

Faro drags her back to the puddle of gasoline, and she kicks at him and works the rag out of her mouth and screams again for help. Why doesn't anyone come? Can't anybody hear? She keeps screaming until Faro strikes the side of her head. Black and white spots appear. He shoves the rag back in her mouth. It takes every effort to make her eyes look in the same direction. Ten feet away, Ronny takes out a box of matches. He makes a big show of twirling a match between his fingers before lighting a cigarette.

"Last words?" Faro suggests to Ronny, who blows out the match, and gestures for the rag to be pulled out of her mouth.

"Help! Someone, help me! Help—"

Faro plugs her mouth again.

Ronny takes out another match. Nothing in all creation is as loud as the sound of a match striking tinder, not a tree toppling over or a mine collapsing. The earth could crack in two and it would not be nearly as loud as the roar of that one small flame.

"Do it!" Faro says.

"See you in hell, witch." Ronny flicks the match.

The ground seems to shrink away, but the tumbling match gains on it, and one small flare becomes a row of fiery fence rails headed her way.

Stumbling backward, she tries stamping out the flames, and her shoes light up. The hem of her dress snags on a splinter of heat, and she reaches down to flick away the flames, then cover what the fire exposes.

To her right, someone else is yelling, "Stop! Stop!"

She turns. How could she have forgotten about this man even for a minute? Havens is sprinting toward her, bad foot and all, his face wrung with horror, and she wishes he didn't have to see her like this. Better that he remember her after their loving, remember her leaning over his sprawled body and using her hair as a paint brush to draw hearts across his bare chest. Remember her in a state of being free.

HAVENS

❧

Sweaty from fright and startled upright, Havens wakes again in
Sylvia Fullhart's guestroom to the smell of gasoline and singed
hair and burned flesh, his ears ringing from gunshot. Two days
have passed since he saw the flames engulf Jubilee's boots, saw her hands
pinned against her sides, saw her turn to him with that awful resignation,
a look that broke him then and breaks him still. It must have been only
seconds before he reached her, wrestled the tire off her head, and fell over
her with his coat to smother the flames. Start to finish, the fiery ordeal
must have lasted no more than a couple of minutes, but it might as well
have gone on forever because one thing a fire burns away is all notion of
time. In the smoldering replays, he flinches at the sound of gunfire, and
watches as Faro catches a load of buckshot in the chest and crumples like
a shabby load of laundry. A madwoman in a dirty nightgown advances,
reloads, and aims her shotgun at the retreating shape of Ronny Gault,
who drops to his knees. It's only when the woman runs toward Havens
and Jubilee that he recognizes her as Gladden Buford.

Havens throws aside the covers, sits on the edge of the bed, and waits
for his breathing to become more even and the room to settle back into

its dimensions even as the loom of his memory keeps spinning those final moments.

It was with a calm voice that he spoke to Jubilee, though he couldn't be sure she heard or understood him. "You're going to be okay, I'm here." He lifted her, angry that there wasn't even a scorch mark on the ground. In his arms, she seemed to be drifting far away. "Stay with me," he insisted, noticing that Ronny was back on his feet again and staggering toward the bushes. It shames him, but just for a split second Havens considered putting Jubilee down and chasing after him. With Gladden Buford by Havens's side, he carried Jubilee to the doctor's office, terrified that if her attention was pulled away from him for even a fraction, he would lose her. Only once did he glance at her legs, but she didn't ask him how bad and he didn't have to lie. He paid no attention to the people clustered outside the clinic, their sympathy swinging too late in her favor, or the sheriff's questions, or even the doctor tending her burns and requesting Havens wait behind the screen. He calculated how far Ronny might have gone with his injuries, concluding that if he raced back, he'd be able to catch him. "I'll be right back," Havens whispered in her ear. Closing her eyes, she said, "Please don't leave me." And what could he do but pledge to stay with her? He wanted so desperately to touch her, but he couldn't think of anywhere his hand might light without hurting her, so he rested his forehead against hers.

It takes this entire replay before Havens can put aside bitter thoughts of vengeance and anger, shake the lameness from his muscles, and set about fulfilling his promise, and still he gets up from the bed a divided man. One part of him would like to rush into offices and pound desks and insist on a better search party, and part of him would like to comb the woods himself for Ronny, but his most urgent desire is to be with her.

Havens has never much given consideration to his appearance before, and though he could cut short his grooming in order to hasten to her side, he takes care so as to present his best possible self. For her, he shaves meticulously, trims his fingernails, and combs his hair. He uses Sylvia Fullhart's polish to shine his shoes, and he puts on the clean damp shirt he laundered last night. He sets out for the holler a purposeful man.

In the saddle, Buford is about to ride off his property when Havens arrives. Though he's consented to it, Buford can't find it easy to put up with these daily visits from Havens. He pulls up beside Havens, who dismounts and ties the horse to the porch rail.

"That Tuttle's mare?"

"Yes, sir."

"You're not wore out yet, trekking up and down this holler?"

"No, sir." Though he is grateful for the use of the horse, he'd crawl on his hands and knees if it came to it.

"Word is Combs is taking you on at the post office."

Havens confirms his employment, adding that it will only be part-time initially. "I'll still be able to come up here every day."

"So, you aim to stay."

"I love Jubilee. I understand that you can't trust that, but I'm going to see to it that Jubilee never doubts it."

Buford repositions his hat. "You didn't strike me as a man who could set his mind to something and see it through, but maybe I was wrong."

"You and I both know that if we subtract all my faults, I still won't add up to the man Jubilee deserves."

Either Buford is sucking on that sore molar again or he's stifling a smile. "Sheriff was up here yesterday after you left."

"Did Jubilee talk to him?" As far as Havens knows, Jubilee has yet to talk to anyone, even him.

"Wouldn't say a word. Socall thinks it's shock and Gladden thinks it's the syrup that the doctor's given her for the pain, but I think it's because Ronny's still out there somewhere and she's afraid her words will somehow get back to him."

Havens asks if Jubilee's doing any better.

"About the same as yesterday. Shaking's not as bad, maybe."

Though he is anxious to go inside and see her, Havens asks whether it's true that charges won't be brought against Gladden, and Buford nods.

"But I don't expect she'll ever be the old Gladden again. I tell myself just to enjoy those times she's clear-headed."

Despite their differences, both men have come to understand that love does not insist on its own way. Love goes at the pace of the one most wounded.

In a voice almost too low to be heard, Buford says, "I should've been the one to return the baby. I don't know what I'll do if Jubilee—"

"Jubilee's going to pull through this, you'll see."

Sending a trail of tiny yellow leaves through the air is a frigid westerly, and on its heels a light drizzle. Havens offers to pick up supplies from Chance and spare Buford a trip, but the farmer says he's not going to town.

"If Ronny's still alive, he better pray someone finds him before I do."

⚕

Before entering her room, Havens watches her from the doorway. What seems like years ago he was the one ailing in bed. Buford has taken his advice and moved her bed beside the window so she can enjoy the view, as she is doing now with such longing, it seems, that it could shatter the pane. Havens marvels at the beauty before him, marks how the sunlight drapes over her shoulder. The buckled floor, the dilapidated walls, the cracked ceiling, all serve to highlight the perfection of one who can soften shadows and make corners curl in on themselves. Even the light cannot hold still around her. Her hair has fallen from its knot and obscures part of her face and neck.

Aware of him now, she turns her face to the doorway and rewards him with a soft gaze.

How he longs to touch even the scarred places. "Good morning, my lovely."

He hurries to her side, putting his copy of Audubon's *Birds of America* on her lap. She runs her fingers across the cover, then leafs through the pages.

"I marked which birds to watch for this time of year." He points out the winter wren. "Tomorrow I'm going to hang a feeder out there so you'll have a lot of company, and I've thought of bringing Thomas up for a visit." He, Buford, and Socall take turns caring for her birds.

Silently, she reads several entries before closing her eyes.

He watches her sleep.

A couple of times Gladden lingers in the doorway, once with plates for him and Jubilee, though he does little more than rearrange his food, and now with Willow-May, who has second thoughts about presenting Jubilee with her drawing of a rooster. Havens follows her outside and entices her into a game of tag, and while she is chasing him past the vegetable patch, Reverend Tuttle and Sarah pull up in the horse-drawn wagon. By the time Havens reaches the porch, the exchange between Gladden, the preacher, and his daughter has resulted in Sarah letting Gladden hold her baby before slipping into the house.

"He's gotten so heavy," Gladden remarks.

"All he does is eat," says Reverend Tuttle. Neither of them takes their eyes off the child.

Sarah is sitting on the bed beside Jubilee, and Havens explains about Jubilee's silence.

"When she's ready, she'll talk," Sarah says.

Everything Sarah describes about Lenny has Jubilee's full attention, but as soon as the frightful ordeal is referenced, she turns her head. At the mention of her assailant's name, the tremors start up again.

"Let's leave that subject for another time," Havens suggests.

"No, that's why I've come." Leaning close to Jubilee, she moves aside her hair. What she whispers makes Jubilee grow still and her eyes widen. She pulls the covers up over her mouth.

Sarah, meanwhile, with heavy-lidded eyes, appears imperturbable. "Do you understand?"

In reply, Jubilee places her bandaged hand on Sarah's lap.

Sarah promises Jubilee she'll visit again in a few days, adding, "You've got yourself a good man here; let him take care of you."

Havens stops Sarah in the breezeway. "What was that about Ronny?"

"I told her she doesn't have to worry about him anymore, that's all."

"How do you know? Has he been caught?" Havens thinks immediately of Buford, who has yet to return.

Sarah sees her father beckon her to come, and without another word, she hurries to his side and waits for him to deliver the baby from Gladden's arms to hers.

⁂

Today, when Havens arrives at the Bufords', Jubilee is sitting on a chair beside the chestnut tree, her bandaged feet propped up on a stool. She is facing east, her head tipped to the weak morning sun, her hair loose and gleaming. Havens dismounts, ties up the horse, and keeps himself from breaking into a run. She turns her pale green eyes to him, and he is a book falling open to the savored verse.

He holds out the canvas sack. "I brought you something."

"What is it?"

In a gush of optimism, he wants to say, My darling, my beloved, how much I've missed hearing your voice, how lovely you are, how afraid I've been that you'd changed your mind about me, but he knows he must go slow. "See for yourself."

Her fingers graze his as she takes her gift. She peeks inside. "Bulbs."

"Hyacinth bulbs," he specifies. "And they're ready for planting."

She thanks him and sets the bag on her lap. "I'm afraid I'm not very good company."

Grateful, light-headed, every hope renewed, he says, "We needn't talk. I could just sit beside you for a while."

Because she does not object, he hurries to retrieve a chair from the porch, where Buford is restringing Levi's guitar.

"Tuttle's asked if we'd consider passing this on to the boy. Poor kid's going to have lessons whether he likes it or not." Nothing of yesterday's vigilante mood is present today. Havens asks what he makes of the fact that Ronny is still at large, despite what Sarah implied, and all Buford will say on the matter is, "I expect he'll turn up soon enough."

Havens returns to Jubilee's side. In the quiet they sit. Where she looks, he looks. Twice she turns to him and he is quick to match her gaze, looking away only after she does. When the shadows begin to shorten, she finally speaks. "Willow-May started school today."

"That is such wonderful news. Was she nervous?"

"The rest of us were, but she was raring to go before the sun even came up. Pa told her there was no need to show up at the schoolhouse an hour before the teacher, but he ended up taking her anyway."

He loves the sound of her voice. She could read him the *Farmer's Almanac* and he would be rapt.

She takes up with her own thoughts, and after a while, she asks, "Would you help me inside?"

She is so light in his arms.

"Your hand," she says, referring to his burns.

"Nothing about you brings me pain," he replies.

When he lays her on her bed, she says, "Goodbye, Havens."

He says, "See you tomorrow, Jubilee."

※

So it goes for the rest of the week. Each day he comes to the house and they sit beside the tree, which donates the last of its leaves for a carpet for her feet. You can no more measure what exchanges between them in these long loose morning silences than you can weigh the notes of a symphony to determine its heft. To an outsider, the only observable difference is the distance between their chairs—each visit he places his a little closer to hers, until the day when their chairs touch. On that day, he reached out and took her hand, and she didn't pull it away.

She tells him about her bird sightings and Willow-May's adventures in school, and he tells her about learning the ropes of the postal service. Not once does she revisit that fateful day and Havens never mentions Ronny or the investigation. But he is of two minds today. Before leaving the boarding house this morning, Havens had been summoned into the parlor to face another round of questions from Sheriff Suggins, even though he'd twice gone to the station, once to give a detailed statement of what he'd witnessed, and a second time to inquire about any developments in the case. Today, the sheriff had asked for an account of Havens's whereabouts, from the time he'd last seen Ronny to the present time, which is how Havens knew something had changed.

"Have I done something wrong?" he asked the sheriff.

"That's what I'd like you to tell me." Sheriff Suggins explained that Ronny's body had been found at dawn. "You knew the location of his hideout, I'm told."

Havens had to be reminded that Ronny's hideout was where he and Chappy had found Jubilee and Levi tied up nearly five months ago. "You're assuming I could find my way back there." Surely others in town knew of its location, and as soon as he raised this point, the sheriff rebutted by saying, "Others in town don't have the motive you did."

"To do what exactly?"

"Track Ronny down and put a bullet in his neck."

Coming to Havens's defense, Sylvia Fullhart said everyone in Chance had a gun and she could think of a number of people who could've pulled the trigger. "It's just a shame that Gladden's buckshot didn't do the job in the first place."

What flashed through Havens's mind were Sarah's cryptic words of assurance, the strange expression on Reverend Tuttle's face when she returned to his side, and Buford with a rifle tucked behind his saddle. And hadn't Socall also led a search party of tenant farmers all eager to claim the bounty she'd put on Ronny's head?

"I don't even own a gun," Havens told the sheriff. Having no alibi for large chunks of his time was more damning, however, than having no weapon.

If this were Dayton or Cincinnati or any other big city, a murder charge would have to be built on facts, evidence, eyewitnesses. Rewind policing and legal practices back a hundred or two hundred years, and what you have is a police force comprising one man with a tarnished badge who has a professed reliance on his hunches and a deep distrust of outsiders, what he termed as "men with no standing."

Were Havens to tell Jubilee he is the prime suspect in the murder of Ronny Gault, it would only cause her distress, so Havens instead asks if she's ever given consideration to living somewhere else. As long as they are together, Havens could move out to where there's nothing but saguaros, igloos, even.

"Levi and I would sometimes lie under the trees and dream up places where we'd like to live. His places always had castles or buildings that touched the clouds or cities that floated out in the middle of the ocean, and my places always looked more or less like here. He'd get mad at me and tell me to think of something grand, so I'd think my hardest and come up with a stable for a hundred horses or a great big pond and no winter so the geese wouldn't have to leave."

Havens follows her gaze. The pale light has flattened the land into a pastel tableau and the hills no longer seem harnessed to a miserly land. What once seemed too remote and foreign is now familiar, inviting even.

"My roots are here," she says. "My family is here. Levi is buried here, and now his little boy is here. This is my home."

"Well, that settles it, then." The sheriff will surely match the bullet to someone's gun. But what if that bullet gets traced back to one of Buford's weapons?

"You're troubled," Jubilee says. "I'm worried this way of life is going to be too solitary for you. Aren't you going to miss your family and city life?"

He can't stand to see her concerned. "Here's what we're going to do: we're going to see about getting a piece of land and have one of those barn-raisings I keep hearing about, and move in all the horses that get old or go lame, and then I'm going to dredge out a pond the size of Lake Michigan, and I don't know what I'm going to do about winter, but you just sprung that on me so you're going to have to give me a little time to figure that one out."

"And you're going to start taking pictures again."

"We'll take pictures together."

Now she smiles.

"We'll make our fresh start here," he says.

JUBILEE

I f it's a Jubilee Year upon them, you can't tell by some calendar, only by how things take a different course. Instead of running along that worn-smooth easy-hating way, the flow is along the way of amend-making. Peace is on everyone's mind, it seems, everyone except Socall, who offered to shoot Verily Suggins for sowing lies in Sheriff Suggins's ear as well as anyone who cast a ballot in favor of Urnamy Gault, even though he was soundly defeated in his bid for mayor, and when Pa announced he was going to host a molasses stir-off, she carried on as though he'd tipped a wheelbarrow of manure on her boots. But Pa's right—starting up what used to be an annual event when the Prices and Ellises all lived here sends a message, even if Pa's late harvest of sorghum has yielded less than a modest crop. Mama said she has no feelings on the issue either way, just as long as she's not expected to stand over a boiling pot all day, and Jubilee agreed it might lift spirits and mend fences, though she made it clear she wouldn't be taking the pills, so whoever wanted to participate had to go along with blue or stay home.

And so they come, the same people who hunted Blues or sent their sons to hunt them or turned the other way when hunting was on, these same people who could not abide them come to the Buford homestead.

300

Pa swears he explained properly, but somehow her having been right-colored for a little while and Sarah's baby being a lusty, rosy-cheeked baby instead of one who lies in a grave have been credited to Jubilee's so-called special powers by some folk, which means a few who come are the afflicted hoping for curing. Whatever their intent, they arrive on horses or carts, sometimes by foot, bringing with them fruit pies and squawking chickens and heirlooms, even.

Everyone leaves their horses to graze in the pasture and gathers in the back, where the autumn air is chilly, filled with smoke, and smelling of candy. Pa's set up a makeshift overhang beside the shed, beneath which two steel drums of green broth bubble on open fires. Socall and Chappy's grandmother preside over one pot, taking turns stirring, skimming foam from the surface and telling tales about the old days, and Reverend Tuttle has two tenant farmers help him at the second pot. Come evening, that cane juice turning into molasses will rival the miracle in Cana, when water was turned into wine.

Jeremiah Wrightley supervises at the small mill, herding Lass in circles while his two sons feed sorghum stalks between the mill stones, and Willow-May and two pigtailed friends from school are squealing and clapping as juice pours down the chute into a pot.

Jubilee has asked Pa to seat her in the sun beside Sarah. Though she's not the same girl Levi fell in love with, Sarah has a resilience about her that wasn't there before. She helps prop Jubilee's bandaged legs on the milking stool and hands her the baby.

"When do the bandages come off?"

"Before too long," Jubilee answers.

"You must be tired of sitting all the time."

This kind of sitting is helping her make peace with the former kind of sitting in that tent.

Sarah pulls out an envelope. "Dr. Fordsworth wrote back." Aloud, she reads that his greetings be passed to Jubilee and that Sarah and her family are welcome to visit his office at any time for consulting or testing. Lenny's fading color, he writes, is on account of him having only one blue-making gene and not two, and that Sarah's not to worry about it returning. While Sarah reads Dr. Fordsworth's complicated explanation, Jubilee's only task is to get Lenny to smile at her.

A shadow falls across them both. Havens has finally come! With glistening eyes, she looks up at him. "Isn't he the sweetest boy?"

Havens crouches in front of her and takes a tiny fist and inspects the fingertips. "No calluses yet."

"Don't let that fool you," Sarah says. "Music lessons have already begun."

Exiting the kitchen, Mrs. Tuttle adds a basket of steaming biscuits to the serving table, where yellow jackets zigzag above the covered dishes. "Can I fix you a plate, Mr. Havens?" she offers.

"He's got to work up an appetite first." Jeremiah Wrightley removes his cap to wipe the sweat from his brow, pops a biscuit in his mouth, and tugs on Havens's shirt, mumbling, "No time for cootering around when there's work to be done."

Havens winks at Jubilee and follows his tour guide to the first pot, where Socall offers him the long-handled paddle. A minute later he has sweated up his shirt and returned the instrument with a comment that makes everyone laugh. He greets Chappy, who is rearranging the empty mason jars that later will be filled with molasses, and settles on the task of hauling sorghum stalks to the mill. He rolls up his sleeves and whistles a tune he knows is Jubilee's favorite, and once he's sure he has her attention, he motions for Jeremiah to pile the load of cane even higher.

Throughout the day the visitors cluster in different configurations. Some stay only a little while, some will ride home after dark. Nobody ever apologizes for the past. Maybe they don't apologize because they know summoning and granting forgiveness can take a toll on a person. The visitors never make any mention of Jubilee's burning, Levi's slaying, or Mama's rampage, but they don't mention Faro's funeral or Ronny's recovered body, either. Mostly, they lament about the weather and grouse over how much Willard is charging for feed and speculate on what crops ought to be planted and how much they'll fetch come market-time. Peace-making is not how they say, waving a white kerchief or shaking hands. If only it was that easy. Rather, it's having to sit in the company of those known before only as foes, and then growing comfortable with how much is held in common. By midday, Jubilee's become certain of one thing—the Bufords are not the only people to have prayed thy-kingdom-come only to be waiting still. Maybe the kingdom doesn't come on those hard words that about loosen a person's teeth on the way out. Maybe it comes in small talk, the kind of talk that fills the quiet, that packs the cracks so the bitter truth doesn't always have to blow through. Maybe the kingdom's no more grand than Them and Us under one roof, hardship making each indistinguishable from the other.

Eventually testing time comes, and everyone grabs a piece of cane and gathers around the pots and scoops up servings of molasses. Never been a sweeter batch is the consensus. All this toil has resulted in sweetness that'll find its way down the holler and into kitchens all through town, and isn't that some kind of peace-making, too? Bringing Jubilee a sample, Havens is halfway across the yard when Sheriff Suggins rounds the house and apprehends him. Before Pa or anyone can reason with the man, he has snapped a pair of handcuffs around Havens's wrists and is leading him away. Jubilee rises to her feet, only to fall to her knees in pain. Havens hears her cry out and turns to give Jubilee a smile as if to say, Nothing to worry about, be back in a moment.

❧

Pa returns from town a couple hours later with news of Verily Suggins being the so-called eyewitness claiming to have seen Havens take off into the woods with a pistol in his hand. Almost as terrifying is the news of Havens in a cell by himself and being denied visitors. Desperate as Jubilee is, Pa point-blank refuses to ride her down to the station.

Reverend Tuttle has gone in to see the sheriff, Pa reports. If his attempts fail, Pa will put his lawman on the case. "Suggins doesn't have anything to bring a case against Havens, and he knows it," Pa tries to reassure her. "This is just so everyone will credit him with doing his job."

Jubilee sleeps hardly at all, and she is at her post beside the window before sunrise. She watches the first snow of the season powder the hills. All day she waits, and just when she is ready to threaten Pa with what she knows and demand that things be put right, Havens comes galloping up the path. Before the mare has even come to a halt, he's kicked free of the stirrups and slid from the saddle. How this old house loves to receive him, its wood creaking sweetly from his weight. In one wide stride, he is beside her, twigs and leaves in his hair, his shirt soaked through and his pants ripped at the knee. "Took a bit of a tumble," he says, grinning. He stands beside her bed with his arms crossed, breathing hard, one shoulder higher than the other, looking at her as if she's some prize, and why shouldn't he look his fill? His looking never was like anyone else's looking. His looking makes her feel found. His arms go around her and he lifts her off the bed and twirls her around, and she clings to his shoulders, buries her face in his neck, and fills herself with his woody smell. Those charred places in her green up a little more.

"I've been so worried!" she cries.

"Don't ever let go of me," he says.

With care, he eventually sets her back on the bed and has to tell her ten times over that Sheriff Suggins is not going to press charges, just as Pa predicted.

"But it's not going to clear your name," Jubilee fears. "And I don't want there to be any doubt in anyone's mind that it wasn't you."

As though he doesn't like to correct her, he uses a soft voice to tell her, "No, let people think I did it." This is how Jubilee understands that Havens has figured out who killed Ronny. "Besides, I only care about what you think of me."

His fingers burrow under her sleeve and trace a path along the inside of her arm.

"Are you trying to change the subject?" she asks.

"Most definitely." He kisses her once, kisses her again, then looks out the window at a curdled sky, heavy now with snow. Pulling blankets from the bed, he hurries out. When he returns, he helps her into her coat, lifts her in his arms, and carries her through the front room, where Mama and Socall are quilting.

"You're not taking her out in this cold," Socall says.

"We won't be long."

Havens carries her down the porch steps to where the wheelbarrow is loaded with her blankets. "Your carriage awaits, my lady." He sets her in it and covers her and says for her to quit snickering because this is a mission most serious. It doesn't help to keep asking where he's taking her because he won't do anything but whistle a waltz. Every time they go over a bump, she tries not to wince. By the time they reach the grove of trees Havens is sweating and panting and out of steam, but he pushes her to the tallest evergreen before lifting her from the wheelbarrow and setting her on a boulder as though it were a throne.

"I was going to wait until we took our first walk together so you could walk away from me if you needed to," he begins.

"I wouldn't walk away from you." Because of this man she has found her way back to herself. His love has made her proud and brave, and it's surely not possible to love him any more than she does now.

The air becomes so still that the first tiny snowflakes cease their falling and hover about their heads. Nothing moves. Even hearts hold still.

Havens gets on one knee. Between his fingers is a dainty ring with a blue stone. "Jubilee Buford, will you complete my joy and be my wife?"

If she loved him one degree less, her reply would be an immediate yes, but every day she loves him one degree more, which means she wants his welfare more than her own. "What if you end up having to take care of me?" She considers her feet. She hasn't told anyone what she fears, that there is the start of an infection. "What if it turns out that things aren't level between us?"

He wastes no time in replying. "Why does it matter if things are level? What if I want to take care of you and protect you more than anything else? If that makes the ground between us uneven, so what?"

She folds her arms around Havens's neck.

"Is that a 'yes'?"

"Yes." She presents her marrying finger, and he about busts out of his shirt fitting the ring. He cups her head and kisses her, and she slides her fingers into his hair and kisses him back.

Once upon a time, being unblue was the only happy ending she ever wished for, but the love of a colorblind man has changed that. Being blue, she is someone who returned a stolen child, who looked her adversary in the eye, and did not submit to hate, who is allowing the World of Wonders to own only so much space in her. And here now: a bride-to-be.

It's dark when she wakes from her nap to find him sitting beside the bed. His arms are folded on the backrest of the chair, his chin propped up on one fist.

"How long have I been sleeping?"

"A couple of hours, maybe."

"You haven't been watching me the whole time, have you?"

He shrugs. "You were having a nice dream."

"I was dreaming about you."

"Were we naked?" He reaches for her hand and singles out her ring finger for special treatment.

She rolls her eyes at him. "You were taking pictures again. They were beautiful."

"They must've been pictures of you."

"I asked you once what kind of setting would suit me, and you wouldn't answer. Do you remember?"

He nods and gestures to the window. "Stars would suit you."

"So all I have to do is climb a ladder into the night sky, and you'll start taking pictures again?"

He leans back to peer at her through a frame he makes with his fingers, and she tilts her chin at him.

"When are you going back for your camera?" she presses.

"Soon." He nuzzles beside her.

"You keep saying that. I want you to do it. This week."

"You're going to be stubborn about this, aren't you?"

"I made you a promise, and now you've got to make me a promise."

Still Havens barters. He'll go this week as long as he can visit the mercantile for fabric samples so she can choose what she wants for a wedding dress, and as long as she'll agree to look through all the shoe catalogs he'll bring back so she can order the perfect pair. "And as long as you set a date."

"I want to enjoy being your intended for a while first."

"You mean you want me to woo you some more?"

"Since you're so good at it."

Havens rises, holds out his hand, and says, "In that case, how about a dance?" He gathers her in his arms and starts to whistle, and it is not unlike their first dance at Socall's frolic, their hearts finding the same rhythm. She holds on to his neck as he waltzes her to the window, where the night sky is a velvet cloth with bright notes flung against it.

⚘

Sarah comes the day after the snowstorm clears, when the sky is a vivid blue, crystals sparkle in the breeze, and cardinals chime across the holler. Pa picks up Jubilee from her bed and carries her to the front room, where he eases her into a chair. Sarah wears a smart coat and a modest dress that fits her figure well, a little white belt cinching her waist and turning her into a Christmas parcel. Looking at her, you wouldn't think it was only a month ago that she gave birth. Mama puts out her arms for Lenny, and doesn't stay for the conversation but whisks him off to the hearth and indicates for Pa to put on another log.

Sarah asks after Jubilee's health, and Jubilee says nothing of the worsening pain in her right foot or why she's in bed again, or that the doctor also now fears an infection, but cannot find the source on account of scar tissue. "Just a week or two before I'm allowed to walk," she says.

In that direct manner of hers, Sarah wastes no time apologizing for Havens's arrest. "My pa was going to turn himself in if it came to it." She keeps her gaze only on Lenny, as if every act from now on will be done for his benefit alone.

Pa says what a good man Reverend Tuttle is and that the Lord would never forsake one of his own, and Mama gives him a sideways glance to remind him forsaking happens too many times to the favored for it to be some kind of heavenly oversight.

"There's something else," Sarah adds, and Jubilee sees clouds start to form. "My pa's been reassigned to a new church."

Jubilee monitors Mama, who's got her shoulders hunched now as though against an icy draft. "Where?" A short train ride, Jubilee prays.

"Knoxville, Tennessee."

"I see," Jubilee says. So far away!

"They need preachers for all the churches they keep building out there," Pa's tone is unnaturally bright for Mama's sake, who hands Lenny back to Sarah as though she knew this was coming, as though all a mother is every really required to do in life is give up those she loves most. With Pa in close pursuit, Mama goes around the house with a sack, filling it with things that Lenny can remember his kin by, while Sarah and Jubilee do nothing but regard each other.

Passing the time at the World of Wonders, Jubilee learned how to look through people's staring eyes to their own drab lives. One woman she could see lying rigid in bed next to her husband, pretend-sleeping so he wouldn't touch the last of her alive parts, and another woman in her kitchen deaf to her children's cries, and sometimes Jubilee could even see all the way through to their dimly lit futures. When she looks into Sarah's eyes, she pictures everything Sarah confessed that day—sneaking off just hours after her son had been returned to her and stealing the pistol from behind her father's pulpit, the one with the snake carved into the handle, and tracking Ronny to where he'd once lured her. She sees Sarah aim for the spot between his eyes and miss only by a few inches. But beyond Sarah's vengeance, what Jubilee sees are hopes and dreams for this child, and doesn't that count for something? Doesn't it count as the fiercest kind of mothering?

When it comes time to say farewell, Mama hands Sarah the sack, and in taking it, Sarah seems to be accepting Mama's blessing, too. In exchange, she promises, "Lenny won't grow up ignorant or hateful of people who are different."

Grace isn't always handed down from heaven. Sometimes it springs up like a dandelion through the floorboards of an old worn porch, and there's nothing to do but lean toward the tuft and let out that great big breath you've been holding so long and see the seeds fly off where they may. And won't some of those seeds carry far?

With his arm around Mama, Pa makes a speech about everyone in Knoxville going around in an automobile these days and that perhaps Sarah can learn how to drive and bring Lenny back for a visit.

"I'll write," she promises. "I'll send you a picture."

Jubilee gives Sarah's hand a squeeze. "Levi would be so proud of you."

Sarah bends down to whisper in Jubilee's ear when Pa and Mama step out onto the porch. "If it should ever come up again that Havens's innocence needs to be proved or your Pa's innocence or anyone's for that matter, you go out to that old wolf tree where you found my baby, and dig up that pistol."

"But what's to say they won't come after you?"

Sarah straightens up. "They won't find me. I'm already someone else."

HAVENS

⬦

After eight days away, Havens is back again in Spooklight Holler. In his absence, the days have grown shorter and colder, but mercifully, the first heavy snow of winter has thawed enough to allow his passage through the holler without mishap. Though being separated from Jubilee has made him irritable and impatient, he has to admit she was right—making his way up the holler, the Contax feels good around his neck again, like he's put on a treasured talisman, and it is taking him twice as long as it should to get to her house because he has to keep stopping to photograph things for her—the eastern bluebird on a tree branch right above his head, the place where the overnight freeze has turned the edges of the creek into lace, and the fingers of light parting the trees at the turn-off to her aviary. Every picture is a winner and he can't wait to develop the film and show her. How does she always know what's good for him?

According to the poll his mother conducted up and down the telephone wires and around the cul-de-sac, no one thinks moving to a backwater town in the Appalachian Mountains makes any sense, and Havens telling his mother that sense never led him anywhere in life expanded her understanding by zero degrees.

"Who would be foolish enough to give up everything and take such a risk?" she fretted.

"Has living a sensible life made you happy, Mom?"

She clucked at that and made Havens's father look up the number for the Lutheran minister. "He had a very good talk to Doris's son when he was having problems settling down."

"Mom, Jeffrey robbed a bank after that talk and went to prison for ten years."

"I just don't know why you have to be so rash."

In his youth, Havens was penned in by illness, and in his adulthood by convention, but now his heart beckons from over the guardrails to a wild borderless land, and he couldn't wait to get away from the stunted future once intended for him. He pacified his longing for Jubilee by writing her long love letters that will likely only reach her next week, but he has also written her poems, clumsy and wordy, which he'll deliver in person.

As soon as Buford opens the front door, Havens knows it was a mistake to have left her.

"What's wrong?" he asks, but Buford takes too long to form an answer, and Havens tears through the breezeway to her room to see for himself. He can barely make her out for the heap of blankets. The room is thick with the smell of pine resin.

"Jubilee?"

Calling her name again when he is right beside her elicits no response. He eases back the covers and is shocked by how gray her skin is. Havens runs his hand across her brow.

"Hello, my darling, hello, my lovely."

Jubilee's eyes flicker open.

"Hey, there you are." Havens holds up his camera. "Look what I've got." He thinks this is what it must feel like to be an apprentice magician whose sole trick fails.

She struggles to raise herself, and the effort does nothing except trigger a spluttering cough that turns quickly into a rib-rearranging hack. While she labors to clear her airways, he holds her upright and rubs small circles on her back.

Havens turns to her parents. "What does the doctor say?"

Because Buford has his fist against his mouth as though to stifle his own cough, Gladden Buford is the one to explain. "He says it can happen when someone's in bed too long and the lungs don't clear like they're supposed to." She offers Havens a mug of hot cider, which he waves away.

"Pneumonia?" Havens asks. "I shouldn't have taken her out in the cold that day."

"Not your fault." Jubilee's voice is croupy.

Havens asks about treatment, and is told rest and fluids are the only remedies. Gladden adds that she's giving Jubilee holly for her cough, pokeweed for when the fever spikes, and boiled hog's hoof, which Chappy's grandmother swears by.

Hog's hoof? "We must get her to a hospital right away so she can be treated properly," Havens insists.

Jubilee puts her hand on his arm, but he won't be calm, he'll take her now, he'll carry her if he has to.

"The doctor said a hospital can't do anything for her that we can't do better."

"I don't buy that. They'll have medicine for her—"

"I can't go anywhere." Jubilee sinks back into her pillows and closes her eyes. "Please."

"Okay, my sweet, you rest." Havens strokes her hair and, in an instant, she is asleep.

Though she doesn't wake until noon the next day, her eyes seem clearer and she's strong enough to sit up without assistance.

"I must have given you a scare," she says.

Havens could cry. He bends forward and rests his head in her lap, and she runs her fingers through his hair. "I'm better now you're awake."

She wants to know about his trip, and he supplies a few mundane details.

"Does your mother think you're crazy?" she asks.

"My mother believes I'm marrying into the Hatfield family and am going to make moonshine for a living, so she's thrilled. Couldn't be happier, really." The one thing he enjoyed about his trip was shopping for Jubilee. From his rucksack, he pulls out three packages and places them in her lap.

"This is too much."

"There's going to be a lot more where that came from," he says.

She unwraps the first gift and presses the silk pillowslip against her cheek. "So soft."

When she notices the monogram, he suddenly worries that she'll disapprove of his decision to have the initial of her last name match his, thinking it premature. "You could put it away till the wedding, if you want."

She hands him her pillow to make the switch, and opens the next gift, a bar of lavender soap. Beaming, she unties the black pouch and lifts out the silver locket. "Oh, Havens." He shows the miniature portrait of him and her tucked inside, and she has him clasp it around her neck, where her engagement ring hangs from a ribbon.

"My finger got too skinny."

"Well, we're going to see about fattening it up again."

When he returns with a bowl of food, she is coughing again.

"You mustn't worry. The doctor said it's running its course," she says in the cough's wake. In an attempt to cheer him, she adds, "Look, he took the bandages off." She rolls down her socks partway to shows Havens her calves and ankles, where her skin is shiny and puckered, and she demonstrates her ability to bear her own weight by getting out of bed and relocating to the chair. She holds out her hand for the bowl, also, he suspects, for his benefit. Gamely, she finishes it, smiling between mouthfuls.

꙳

Though the cough does not abate and Jubilee sleeps too much during the day, she does grow restless, which Havens takes to be a good sign. Until she is strong enough to go outside, he has decided to bring the outdoors to her, shooting roll after roll that he immediately develops in Buford's cellar. He has her write captions for each image and lets her say where on the wall each should be pinned. Because her preferred subjects are animals, Havens has taken dozens of bird shots, and befriended just about everyone in Chance just to photograph their cats, dogs, and horses. Jeremiah Wrightley let him photograph the mice he feeds his timber rattler, and Chappy took him to a cousin who keeps a porcupine as a pet. Jubilee's latest request, though, has been for people pictures, and Havens has shot portraits of Willow-May, Socall, Chappy, and any child who will sit still long enough. This latest batch he is developing in the cellar when he figures out what Jubilee's up to. She's been giving him assignments. She's having him go out and participate in life without her.

She lowers her book as he enters her bedroom. In an instant, her expression becomes grave. "What's wrong?"

"I'm not taking any more pictures."

"But I love your pictures." She gestures around her room, where his images cover much of the walls. "They make me happy. They make me feel like I'm still part of the world."

He waits for her to finish coughing. "They take me away from you."

"You can't spend all your time in this room."

"Why not?"

She consults the ceiling for a long time before turning to him with an expression of surrender that he has never seen in her face before.

He starts yanking pictures from the wall. "This was a mistake. If you want to be part of the world, you're going to get out of that bed and come with me and be in it!"

"Havens, please."

"I don't want to take pictures anymore!"

She begs him to stop. She gets out of bed and stumbles over to him, pulling at his shirt. "Don't take them down. Please."

His shoulders start to shake. He doesn't want to turn around and have her see him like this.

Arms as thin as a child's wind around him as he weeps, and she rests her head against his back.

Eventually, he manages to speak. "You've got to get well."

"I will."

"I need you to promise me."

"I promise," she whispers, doing her best to suppress her cough.

❧

Three days go well. Jubilee eats more, sleeps less, and spends time each day sitting in her chair, but on the fourth day, her body gives up all the gains. She coughs even when she sleeps. Dr. Eckles is summoned, and his verdict is for the Bufords and Havens to prepare themselves. In a fit, Havens sends him away and insists another doctor be consulted, one from Smoke Hole. Havens is defiant. She made a promise, he keeps reiterating, and Buford feels it necessary to take him out of earshot and speak of accepting things.

"You accept what you want," he tells Buford, "but I am marrying Jubilee, just as we promised each other."

In the early hours the following morning Jubilee begins burning up with a fever and Havens races out to the wash shed for the basin and fresh water, but Gladden insists on taking it from him at the doorway to her bedroom, asking him to wait. He watches from the doorway. So much has been taken from her, but at the bedside she calmly undresses Jubilee and bathes her, soothing her daughter in a temperate tone, describing some memory of when Jubilee was a little girl.

It's while she's sponging Jubilee's feet that Gladden grows quiet and especially focused. "Oh dear God," she exclaims. "Clayton!"

Havens rushes to her side. "Get Del to bring Dr. Eckles," she orders. "It just burst open," Gladden says of the large open wound between Jubilee's toes, its inflammation having been camouflaged all this time by blue skin and scarring.

❧

Jubilee sleeps through the entire day. Seldom does Havens leave her side. Between bargaining with the God on whom he has seldom called and never relied, he reads her entries from the Audubon book and the poems he wrote, and tells her silly stories from his youth. Their future, too, he describes. For her part, she labors to breathe. It's just as dawn is breaking the next morning that she finally awakes, gasping for water.

Havens helps her sip from the glass.

"Cold," she croaks, even as sweat beads along her brow.

Havens gets into bed beside her, eases her onto his lap, and cradles her in his arms. He's frightened by how emaciated she is. When he was fourteen, he had whooping cough so bad that he stopped breathing, and the pressure that built up in his chest made him feel like he was drowning—that's nothing compared to how he feels now.

Though weak, Jubilee stays awake. "Pictures," she requests.

He reaches for the latest photographs and shows her the cottontail at the edge of the field, Willow-May coming out of the schoolhouse with a gaggle of friends, the cardinals jockeying for position at the birdfeeder, and, for the first time, a picture of himself. It's this one Jubilee clasps, comparing the likeness to the real version.

"Your sister's got serious talent to make me look that good."

"Handsome," Jubilee rasps.

"She's volunteered to be the photographer at our wedding." He searches Jubilee's wet eyes. "It's time we set a date."

She moistens her cracked, lead-colored lips and tries to speak, but presses her hand against her chest and rides out another punishing offensive. In the lull, she reaches for his hand, and he is surprised by how much strength is still in her grasp. He has to put his ear right against her lips to hear her say, "I'll marry you in the spring."

He wants to plead, why not tomorrow, why not today, now, but he lays his cheek against her fingers. "In the spring, then, my darling. It won't be long."

SEPTEMBER
1972

It's with fingers arthritic with age that Havens accepts the glass of water this stranger, Rory Ashe, has poured for him, the very stranger Havens spent the better part of the morning chasing off his property and accosting in the cemetery and who has made friends with Lord Byron and now has just waltzed himself into Havens's kitchen and helped himself to a good old look around the place. On the coffee table beside Havens is the portrait Rory has come about, the one Havens took of the Buford family on their porch thirty-five years ago. Long gone are Buford and Gladden and the old grandmother with her suitcase. Little Willow-May, so perky in this picture, is a middle-aged woman now, still teaching grade school in Frankfort and taking care of her husband, Paul, who did not go off to war on account of his asthma but made a fine contribution to the nation by fathering five sons. Willow-May and her family used to visit Chance fairly often when their boys were young, but they are grown now and have lives of their own, and Willow-May writes letters telling Havens that roads run both ways.

"This is your book?" Rory has wandered over to the cluttered bookshelf and spotted Havens's first published work, *Edge of Splendor*, which received critical praise though most of the copies that were printed are boxed up in the shed. "Do you mind if I take a look?" Rory reads the back cover. "It says you've helped identify and document three hundred species in Central Appalachia. You are famous!"

"Fame is something I plan to enjoy posthumously."

"These are amazing." Rory is particularly enthusiastic about the close-up of a bobcat. He returns it to the shelf and notices the three old portraits of Jubilee in a pewter frame: one of her in the doorway of her aviary, one of her hanging the wash, and another sitting on a rock.

Havens takes up beside Rory. Jubilee doesn't inhabit a space, she commands it. The ground rises up to meet her step, the doorway widens for her entrance, the wash line lowers itself to accommodate her reach.

"She's beautiful," Rory says.

"Jubilee, never 'she,' okay, Rory?"

"Yes, sir."

Her face, more familiar to him perhaps than his own, is full of that serenity that undid him then and undoes him a little now. "Jubilee was twenty-three when I met her and even at that age, she was astute, which took a person by surprise because she had grown up so isolated, but she knew a lot more about human nature than I did, that's for sure. And when it came to animals, she just had this sense about them." Havens is surprised by how much he wants to talk about her. All he's ever wanted is to talk about her, to have every conversation start and end with her.

"It must have been a hard life looking different from everyone else."

"What showed was her heart." Never one ounce of bitterness.

Rory points to the picture where she's sitting on a rock and looking back over her shoulder at the camera, her dimple like a comma, that half-smile, which had the ability to strip away a man's motives. "I think Jubilee was taken with you."

Havens could kiss Rory for saying so.

"And you loved her."

"From the minute I saw her."

"Did the two of you become a pair?"

Pairing is what happens between two of a kind; what happened between him and Jubilee had more to do with belonging. In each other, they found their home. "You got a lady?" Havens asks.

"Yes, sort of."

"What kind of answer is that?"

"Well, she's studying for the bar exam so she doesn't have a lot of time."

"Let me give you a piece of advice." Havens straightens the frame and tidies the pile of books around it. "If you love her, go after her and win her over, and don't let anyone talk you out of it, especially not her."

Rory comments that Jubilee appears to be the same age in these pictures as in the one he brought. "I'm guessing this was sometime in the twenties?"

"Geez, kid, how old do you think I am?" Havens quips. "That was 1937."

"What a coincidence—that's the year I was born. Theoretically, that is."

"What do you mean, 'theoretically'?" And what is it about a coincidence that always makes the needle of a person's internal pressure gauge start bouncing around?

Rory explains that in going through his mother's documents, he couldn't find his birth certificate, and that according to the state, his birth was never registered, and all the while Havens is registering that the needle inside his chest is deep in the red zone. "All I have is a baptismal certificate."

A few winters back, Havens got caught in a whiteout. Within hollering distance from the house, as it would later turn out, he had completely lost his bearings, which is the exact same feeling he's having again. "But surely your father must know."

Rory shakes his head. "And he's not my real father. I told you my whole life changed when my mother died." He snaps his fingers. "Just like that, you think you know who you are, and then you don't." Havens has to force himself to concentrate on what Rory is saying, that the man who raised him told him after the funeral that Rory had been fathered by someone else. "He doesn't know the man's name or anything about him, and it doesn't really matter to him because I am in every sense his son. He said he's always believed I had the right to know and if he'd had his way, it would've been out in the open years ago, but he respected my mother's wishes. You don't know who your mother really is, then a day later you don't know who your father is!"

"She changed her name," Havens says to himself, dashing inside. "Of course she changed her name," he mutters to himself. Why wouldn't she? He heads for the studio at the far end of the house, rushing down the hallway—a gallery of wildlife photographs. To get to his old pictures, he has to move aside the setup for his macro work, get on all fours, and reach all the way to the back of the photo cabinet for the shoebox. It takes no small effort to get back up. When he returns to the sunroom, he takes the commissioned black-and-white photographs from the box and deals them out in front of Rory as though they were tarot cards. Mixed in with the scenics of the town are the portraits of its residents.

Viewing them now, a person would think it was a grind, sunup till sack time for these folk. Romance is not in any one of these pictures. It was easier to depict people showing affection to their mules than to one another. The men look like beasts, fit only for picking coal out of caves or hoeing dirt or socking one another in the jaw, and the women, scabbed with grease and worry, peer right past their children into the future, as though it can't come quickly enough. If all you had to go by were these photographs, you wouldn't be able to imagine anything but misery coming out of that time, anything but the taste of dirt and the smell of sweat and the loss of dreams stacked on top of one another like broken plates. Weight is what a person thinks looking at them. How could they have carried anything but weight?

Photographs are tumbling from his trembling hands. Why has he been so stupid, so slow? Why hadn't he seen the resemblance until now? He sifts through the portraits, scattering some to the floor, until finally he singles one out—the portrait of Revered Tuttle at the altar, and in the background, his daughter trimming candlewicks.

"That's your—"

In unison with Havens, Rory exclaims, "Mother!"

"She was known around here as Sarah Tuttle."

Rory holds the photograph close to his face. "She's so young in this picture. And poor." He has taken on both a stiffness and a hollowness, like clothing washed in cheap soap and baked on a line.

Havens ought to take one of those pills the doctor gave him a couple years back for when his heart starts clocking it. He excuses himself and, forgetting he is a seasoned outdoorsman, gets lost in his own kitchen. He cannot find the damn pills. "You drink whiskey, Rory?" he yells. Getting no reply, he reaches for the dusty bottle on the top shelf, pours two fingers in each glass, and returns to the sunroom, where Rory is slumped in the rocking chair with the photograph in his lap. "You knew my mother."

"Not well. She left Chance soon after I moved here." He can't stop staring at the kid. "That's your grandfather, Reverend Tuttle."

"I knew him only as Pop. He died when I was four, and my grandmother about a year later. I vaguely remember going to my grandfather's church, but my mother said that's not my memory, only what she told me."

Havens takes a big swig of whiskey, makes a face, and breathes out the fumes through his teeth. "Lenny."

Over the top of the photograph, Rory regards Havens.

"That's what your name used to be." Havens takes another sip.

"My mother sometimes used to call me that."

"The first time I met you, you were just a few weeks old."

"I was born here?" Rory pores over the other pictures.

Havens nods. Running through his head is only one refrain: How can it be?

"Do you have any other photos of my mother? Do you have any of my father? Do you know him?"

How is Havens expected to tell about this man's roots, about his father? Which question is he supposed to answer first, and what of the things Rory hasn't yet thought to ask?

Shuffling through the pictures as if to rustle up the figure who will explain everything, Rory stops to examine another picture, one of Willow-May sitting on the porch steps with her doll.

"That's my guitar! I have that guitar! See where the black finish has worn off? That's my guitar!"

Havens puts on his reading glasses, and Rory taps the area on the porch just to the right of the front door, where Levi's guitar is propped against the wall.

"My mom told me a very important person wanted me to have that guitar," Rory continues. "She said more songs were caught in those guitar strings than trout on a fisherman's rod, but I always wondered what kind of important person would give a kid a banged-up cheap guitar. She insisted I learn how to play it. Sometimes she would have me play something she could sing, but then she'd usually start crying, and that's why I took up the keyboard instead. I never liked that guitar."

"That was your father's guitar. His name was Levi Buford. He was the son of Gladden and Del Buford, the brother of Jubilee and Willow-May."

For a while, Rory doesn't speak. "He's dead, too, isn't he?"

Havens downs the rest of his drink. "Levi was a decent man and a hell of a musician, and he died before his time."

"How old was I when he died?"

"You hadn't been born yet. He knew about you, though. He was happy about it, too, and wanted to make a go of it with your mother."

"So what stopped him?"

Havens takes the roundabout way, explaining about Levi's rare blood condition that made his skin appear blue, and Rory stops him partway through the story.

"My mother used to sing a song called "The Lark and the Boy So Blue." All this time, I thought 'blue' meant sad."

"He and your mother made each other very happy, and you're the product of that happiness."

Havens checks his watch. He's lost track of time. Hurrying into the kitchen, he gathers up his camera and fills a couple of canteens with water.

Rory follows him. "So he died from his condition?"

"In a way, you could say yes." Thirty-five years and it still pains Havens to talk of Levi's death. "Prejudice got him in the end." Havens can't think how to stall Rory except to hold up his hand. "Not all at once, kid. Please."

He inspects Rory's shoes. "What size do you wear?"

"Ten. Why?"

"I'll be right back." When Havens returns from the shed, he hands Rory hiking boots and a pair of snake chaps. "Put those on over your trousers, just to be on the safe side." He packs the rucksack, grabs his hat, and flings open the screen door. "Are you always this slow?" Havens hands him the large paper sack that's been propped up against the porch rail, and Rory peeks inside.

"Is this a wreath?" he asks.

Setting a brisk pace, Havens cuts through the back of the property, showing Rory where to watch out for stands of poison ivy, in places neck-high, and in no time they have reached the path that runs alongside the creek. They cross where it bottlenecks, and then pick up the path as it veers to the left and begins its steep incline, flowering jewelweed and poke growing thick on both sides. Havens leads him along the same route he and Massey explored all those years ago, the only difference now is Havens could walk it blindfolded. Several times along the way, he checks on his companion, who has stopped asking about bears and snakes and sinking sand. When they arrive at the overlook, Havens pauses for a drink, and surveys the vale where the house stands—the house he built—and the stables and the pond that took forever to dredge, which has yet to be visited by a single goose. "Say what's on your mind, son."

"When you said prejudice got my father in the end, do you mean someone killed him?"

No flies on this one. "As far as I'm concerned, the man who killed your father doesn't have a name. If there's an entry for him in the Book of Life, it's just a smudge."

"The old woman in the cemetery, the one who called you a murderer, was that the smudge's mother?"

Faro's aunt, Verily Suggins, is who that is. "Let's save that story for the walk back."

Havens points out a pileated woodpecker drilling into a dead tree, and a bit farther, the little family of grouse scurrying into the undergrowth. Just before they come to the place, Havens tells Rory, "This is where your father's buried."

"Why all the way out here? Why not in the cemetery?"

Picking a sprig of foxglove, Havens explains that this is where many of his relatives are buried, beginning with his great-grandmother Opal. "Back then, the people in town wouldn't allow her to be buried in the church graveyard because she was blue." Sentiments have changed over the years, but who wouldn't prefer to be buried here? One day, Havens will be buried here.

Just beyond the carpet of wild ginseng is Del Buford's grave, a small stony plot in the shadow of a regal maple tree. None of the graves up here used to be marked, but Havens has had engraved headstones placed at every one, and Buford's grave has already been cleared of weeds and its pattern of pebbles around the edge tidied.

Rory nods in the direction of the area shaded by birch trees on the far side of the clearing. "Who's that?"

Havens beams. "Wait here a minute." He takes the paper sack from Rory, and, rushing ahead, whistles to the beautiful gray-haired woman kneeling beside Levi's grave.

"You're late. I was starting to get worried."

"I got held up."

"I left the hyacinth bulbs for you to plant." She has him notice the violets she's planted at the foot of the grave. "I have enough left over for Socall, but I'm going to have to trim back the laurel around her grave because it's gone crazy." From the sack, she pulls the wreath and the colorful paper flowers that the two of them spent a week making. "See how pretty it's going to look on Levi's headstone? Why are you looking at me like that?"

Havens sweeps her hair from her face and tucks the foxglove above her ear. He doesn't like to think how close she came to dying in the fall of 1937. Gladden once told him she'd bathed Jubilee so thoroughly that day, sponging every inch of skin, because it was the only way she knew how to say goodbye, that she would never have imagined it would lead her to the site of the infection that the doctor hadn't before been able to source and therefore treat. Jubilee used to complain at times, especially in the early years of their marriage, that Havens worried too much about her, that he had to let her roam the hills by herself when she needed to, and he can't say he ever worried less, only that he got better about keeping it to himself. When Jubilee consented to marry him all those years ago, she raised the question of whether love is ever on the level, and what marriage has taught them both is that love's incline changes depending on who needs the flow of affection most. In truth, it has favored him more, though she is the one most deserving. Now there is another young man who is about to be favored by her love. Havens caresses her cheek. "Oh, my darling."

"What's wrong?"

"Nothing's wrong. There's someone I'd like you to meet."

"Who?" She glances past him. "Who've you brought, Clay?"

What he has to say to her is part fairy tale, part Gospel by-and-by, and there is no suitable introduction. "It's Lenny. Levi's boy has come."

Believing and knowing aren't the same thing. Believing is the little fort you build in your head, while knowing is what you feel first in your knees. It's what makes a body go slack. He holds her around her waist and shores her up, and she puts her hand on his chest while he beckons for Rory to come forward.

"Hello?" Rory's eyes are wide with wonder as he makes his approach.

A lifetime ago, Jubilee would've been inclined to hide, but she has spent many years doing as she pleases—mostly putting out hay for the horses and nursing their neighbors' livestock back to health and giving Havens a run for his money photographing little creatures—and has therefore come to trust the blessing of an unremarkable life. Of the two of them, Havens prefers privacy, whereas Jubilee has long been reconciled with those who used to keep their distance, and welcomes company. She eases from Havens's embrace. Making a little steeple of her fingers against her mouth, she keeps shaking her head. He can't hear what she is whispering to herself. She seems to falter, but only for a moment, and then unsteady steps become wide strides and graceful arms stretch out to welcome what was long ago given up.

With the proceeds from the sale of their books, Havens and Jubilee bought all this land, in part to secure an undisturbed peace for these unmarked graves, but now that they are old, they've discussed what might happen to the land when they're gone, who might they bequeath it to so that both the land and the story of the Blues will be forever intertwined and preserved. What could be more fitting than entrusting this legacy to the member of the next generation? Married all these years to Jubilee, Havens has discovered that life is a string of beginnings. Sometimes, a beginning has worn away a bit more of that old regret of having once brought her harm. Sometimes, a beginning has made him feel proud, and sometimes like he'll never be good enough for her. Now Lenny's return is another beginning, and who knows what all it might call forth.

Havens opens his rucksack and pulls out the Nikon F Jubilee gave him a few years ago to celebrate the third book they collaborated on, which was funded by the U.S. Fish and Wildlife Service and published under a pseudonym. He slips the strap over his head, pops off the lens cap, and squints through the viewfinder. Jubilee is introducing herself to her nephew. He is bending a little and she is reaching up to touch his cheek. Havens catches just a fragment—she's telling him how little he used to be. Little rooster, she calls him. Maybe she'll want to show him that old wolf tree where she found him all those years ago, but now she takes his hand and starts to introduce him to those who lie in repose, telling him the tale that's only ever been hers to tell.

ACKNOWLEDGMENTS

I wish to thank my agent, Emma Sweeney, who with every draft of each novel taught me how to be a better writer, dispensing sage advice along the way. "Just keep writing" was her exhortation when I fretted about the publishing business and my prospects, and because she is right about everything, I did/do. I will miss her and be in her debt always. Margaret Sutherland Brown read this book when I was convinced it was done, but with one eye a telescope and the other a microscope, she gave the story direction that turned out to be transformative. In gratitude, I hereby pledge to do it her way from now on.

That this book found such an enthusiastic reception from Jessica Case is something for which I am deeply grateful. I couldn't ask for a better editor or publisher. Nor could I ask for a better cover design, thanks to Derek Thornton. Also deserving of praise are Maria Fernandez, Rita Madrigal and Barbara Greenberg for making each page sparkle. I further wish to acknowledge Carol Trost whose article, "The Blue People of Troublesome Creek," served as an inspiration for this book; Walker Evans and James Agee whose work for the WPA provided a portal to a bygone era; and the Library of Congress for its painstaking preservation of Depression-era photographs and audio recordings, which allowed me access to such rich culture.

It is impossible to convey my gratitude to Carol Saggese for her unwavering support, whether demonstrated by reading and proofing drafts, or praying God's ears off, or suggesting voodoo dolls. Similarly, I have benefitted from the encouragement of Helena Ogle and George Tagg. Emily Morley is the bright lamp in my life that keeps me steering toward beauty and truth, and if I write accurately about love at all, it is because I have encountered so pure a form in her. She is also to be credited for the title. Robert Morley has been an indefatigable champion of my peculiar calling, and I have come to rely heavily on his input. As is the case with my life, the book is better because of him.